SHABONO

SHABONO

Florinda Donner

THE BODLEY HEAD
LONDON SYDNEY
TORONTO

British Library Cataloguing
in Publication Data
Donner, Florinda
Shabono
1. Yanoama Indians – Social life and customs
I. Title
987′.6   F2520.1.Y3
ISBN 0-370-30494-2

© Florinda Donner 1982
Printed in Great Britain for
The Bodley Head Ltd
9 Bow Street, London WC2E 7AL
by Redwood Burn Ltd, Trowbridge
First published in Great Britain in 1982

For the five-legged spider
that carries me on its back

SHABONO

AUTHOR'S NOTE

The *Yanomama* Indians, also known in anthropological literature as the Waika, Shamatari, Barafiri, Shirishana, and Guaharibo, inhabit the most isolated portion of the border between southern Venezuela and northern Brazil. It has been roughly estimated that there are between ten and twenty thousand of them, occupying an area of approximately seven thousand square miles. This territory encompasses the headwaters of the Orinoco, Mavaca, Siapo, Ocamo, Padamo, and Ventuari rivers in Venezuela, and the Uraricoera, Catrimani, Dimini, and Araça rivers in Brazil.

The *Yanomama* live in hamlets of palm-thatched dwellings called *shabonos*, which are scattered throughout the forest. The number of individuals residing in each of these widely dispersed hamlets varies between sixty and a hundred people. Some of the *shabonos* are located close to Catholic or Protestant missions or in other areas accessible to the white man; others have withdrawn deeper into the jungle. Hamlets still exist in remote parts of the forest that have not been contacted by outsiders.

My experience with the Iticoteri, the inhabitants of one of these unknown *shabonos*, is what this book is about. It is a subjective account of the surplus data, so to speak, of anthropological field research I conducted on curing practices in Venezuela.

The most important part of my training as an anthropologist emphasized the fact that objectivity is what gives validity to anthropological work. It happened that throughout my stay with this *Yanomama* group I did not keep the distance and detachment required of objective research. Special links of gratitude and friendship with them made it impossible for me to interpret facts or draw conclusions from what I witnessed and learned. Because I am a woman and because of my physical appearance and a certain bent of character, I posed no threat to the Indians. They accepted me as an amenable oddity and I was able to fit, if only for a moment in time, into the peculiar rhythm of their lives.

In my account I have made two alterations of my original notes. The first has to do with names—the name Iticoteri as well as the names of the persons portrayed are imaginary. The second has to do with style. For dramatic effect I have altered the sequence of events and for narrative purposes I have rendered conversations in the proper English syntax and grammatic structure. Had I literally translated their language, I could not have done justice to its complexity, flexibility, its highly poetic and metaphoric expressions. The versatility of suffixes and prefixes gives the *Yanomama* language delicate shades of meaning that have no real equivalent in English.

Even though I was patiently drilled until I could differentiate and reproduce most of their words, I never became a fluent speaker. However, my inability to command their language was no obstacle in communicating with them. I learned to "talk" with them long before I had an adequate vocabulary. Talking was more of a bodily sensation than an actual interchange of words. How accurate our interchange was is another matter. For them and for me it was effective. They made allowances when I could not explain myself or when I could not understand the information they were conveying about their world; after all, they did not expect me to cope with the subtleties and intricacies of their language. The *Yanomama*, just like ourselves, have their own biases; they believe whites are infantile and thus less intelligent.

PRINCIPAL ITICOTERI
(*EETEE CO TEH REE*)
CHARACTERS

ANGELICA (*An geh lee ca*) — An old Indian woman at the Catholic mission who sets up the journey to the Iticoteri country

MILAGROS (*Mee la gros*) — Angelica's son, a man who belongs to both worlds, the Indian's and the white man's

PURIWARIWE (*Puh ree wah ree weh*) — Angelica's brother, an old shaman at the Iticoteri settlement

KAMOSIWE (*Kah moh see weh*) — Angelica's father

ARASUWE (*Arah suh weh*) — Milagros's brother-in-law, headman of the Iticoteri

HAYAMA (*Hah yah muh*) — Angelica's oldest living sister, mother-in-law of Arasuwe, grandmother of Ritimi

ETEWA (*Eh teh wuh*) — Arasuwe's son-in-law

RITIMI (*Ree tee mee*) — Arasuwe's daughter, first wife of Etewa

TUTEMI (*Tuh teh mee*) Etewa's young second wife

TEXOMA (*Teh'sho muh*) Ritimi's and Etewa's four-year-old daughter

SISIWE (*See see weh*) Ritimi's and Etewa's six-year-old son

HOAXIWE
  (*How ba shee weh*) Tutemi's and Etewa's newborn son

IRAMAMOWE
  (*Eerah mah moh weh*) Arasuwe's brother, a shaman at the Iticoteri settlement

XOROWE (*Shoh roh weh*) Iramamowe's son

MATUWE (*Mah tuh weh*) Hayama's youngest son

XOTOMI (*Shoh toh mee*) Arasuwe's daughter, Ritimi's half-sister

MOCOTOTERI
  (*Moh coh toh teh ree*) The inhabitants of a nearby *shabono*

PART ONE

1

I was half asleep. Yet I could sense people moving around me. As if from a great distance, I heard the soft rustle of bare feet over the packed dirt of the hut, the coughing and clearing of throats, and the faint voices of women. Leisurely I opened my eyes. It was not quite dawn. In the semidarkness I could see Ritimi and Tutemi, their naked bodies bent over the hearths where the embers of the night's fires still glowed. Tobacco leaves, water-filled gourds, quivers with poisoned arrowheads, animal skulls, and bundles of green plantains hung from the palm-frond ceiling, appearing to be suspended in the air below the rising smoke.

Yawning, Tutemi stood up. She stretched, then bent over the hammock to lift Hoaxiwe into her arms. Giggling softly, she nuzzled her face against the baby's stomach. She mumbled something unintelligible as she pushed her nipple into the boy's mouth. Sighing, she eased herself back into her hammock.

Ritimi pulled down some dried tobacco leaves, soaked them in a calabash bowl filled with water, then took one wet leaf and, before rolling it into a wad, sprinkled it with ashes. Placing the quid between her gum and lower lip, she sucked at it noisily while preparing two more. She gave one to Tutemi, then approached me. I closed my eyes, hoping to give the impression that I was asleep. Squatting at the head of my hammock, Ritimi ran her tobacco-soaked finger, wet with her saliva, between my gum and lower lip, but did not leave a quid in my mouth. Chuckling, she edged toward Etewa, who had been watching from his hammock. She spat her wad into her palm and handed it to him. A soft moan escaped her lips as she placed the third quid in her mouth and lowered herself on top of him.

The fire filled the hut with smoke, gradually warming the chilly damp air. Burning day and night, the hearth fires were the center of each dwelling. The smoke stains they left on the thatch ceiling set one household apart from the next, for there were no dividing walls between the huts. They stood so close together that adjacent roofs overlapped each other, giving the impression of one enormous circular dwelling. There was a large main entrance to the entire compound with a few narrow openings between some huts. Each hut was supported by two long and two shorter poles. The higher side of the hut was open and faced a clearing in the middle of the circular structure, while the lower, exterior side of the hut was closed with a wall of short poles wedged against the roof.

A heavy mist shrouded the surrounding trees. The palm fronds, hanging over the interior edge of the hut, were silhouetted against the grayness of the sky. Etewa's hunting dog lifted its head from under its curled-up body and, without quite waking, opened its mouth in a wide yawn. I closed my eyes, dozing off to the smell of green plantains roasting in the fires. My back was stiff and my legs ached from having squatted for hours the day before, digging weeds in the nearby gardens.

I opened my eyes abruptly as my hammock was vigorously rocked back and forth and gasped as a small knee pressed into my stomach. Instinctively I pulled the ham-

mock's sides over me to protect myself from the cock-
roaches and spiders that invariably fell from the thick
palm-thatched roof whenever the poles holding up the
huts were shaken.

Giggling, the children crawled on top and around me.
Their brown naked bodies were soft and warm against my
skin. As they had done almost every morning since I had
first arrived, the children ran their chubby hands over my
face, breasts, stomach, and legs, coaxing me to identify
each part of my anatomy. I pretended to sleep, snoring
loudly. Two little boys snuggled against my sides and the
little girl on top of me pressed her dark head under my
chin. They smelled of smoke and dirt.

I had not known a word of their language when I first
arrived at their settlement deep in the jungle between
Venezuela and Brazil. Yet that had not been an obstacle
to the eighty or so people occupying the *shabono* in accepting me. For the Indians, not to understand their language
was tantamount to being *aka boreki*—dumb. As such, I was
fed, loved, and indulged; my mistakes were excused or
overlooked as if I were a child. Mostly my blunders were
acknowledged by boisterous outbursts of laughter that
shook their bodies until they rolled on the ground, tears
brimming in their eyes.

The pressure of a tiny hand against my cheek stopped
my reveries. Texoma, Ritimi's and Etewa's four-year-old
daughter, lying on top of me, opened her eyes and, moving
her face closer, began to flutter her stubby eyelashes
against mine. "Don't you want to get up?" the little girl
asked, running her fingers through my hair. "The plantains are ready."

I had no desire to abandon my warm hammock. "I
wonder—how many months have I been here?" I asked.

"Many," three voices answered in unison.

I could not help smiling. Anything beyond three was

expressed as many, or more than three. "Yes, many months," I said softly.

"Tutemi's baby was still sleeping inside her belly when you first arrived," Texoma murmured, snuggling against me.

It was not that I had ceased being aware of time, but the days, weeks, and months had lost their precise boundaries. Here only the present mattered. For these people only what happened each day amidst the immense green shadows of the forest counted. Yesterday and tomorrow, they said, were as undetermined as a vague dream, as fragile as a spider's web, which was visible only when a streak of sunlight sears through the leaves.

Measuring time had been my obsession during the first few weeks. I wore my self-winding watch day and night and recorded each sunrise in a diary as if my very existence depended on it. I cannot pinpoint when I realized that a fundamental change had taken place within me. I believe it all started even before I arrived at the Iticoteri settlement, in a small town in eastern Venezuela where I had been doing research on healing practices.

After transcribing, translating, and analyzing the numerous tapes and hundreds of pages of notes gathered during months of field work among three curers in the Barlovento area, I had seriously begun doubting the validity and purpose of my research. My endeavor to organize the data into a meaningful theoretical framework proved to be futile, in that the material was ridden with inconsistencies and contradictions.

The emphasis of my work had been directed toward discovering the meaning that curing practices have for the healers and for their patients in the context of their everyday life activities. My concern had been in discerning how social reality, in terms of health and illness, was created

out of their interlocked activity. I reasoned that I needed
to master the manner in which practitioners regard each
other and their knowledge, for only then would I be able
to operate in their social setting and within their own system of interpretation. And thus the analysis of my data
would come from the system in which I had been operating and would not be superimposed from my own cultural
milieu.

While in the field I lived in the home of doña Mercedes, one of the three curers I was working with. Not only
did I record, observe, and interview the curers and their
numerous patients, but I also participated in the curing
sessions, immersing myself totally in the new situation.

Yet I was faced day to day with blatant inconsistencies in
their curing practices and their explanations of them.
Doña Mercedes laughed at my bewilderment and what she
considered my lack of fluidity in accepting changes and
innovations.

"Are you sure I said that?" she asked upon listening to
one of the tapes I insisted on playing for her.

"It's not me speaking," I said tartly, and began reading
from my typed notes, hoping she would become aware of
the contradictory information she had given me.

"That sounds wonderful," doña Mercedes said, interrupting my reading. "Is that really me you are talking
about? You have converted me into a real genius. Read me
your notes on your sessions with Rafael and Serafino."

These were the other two curers I was working with.

I did as she asked, then turned on the tape recorder once
more, hoping she would help me with the conflicting information. However, doña Mercedes was not interested at
all in what she had said months earlier. To her that was
something in the past and thus had no validity. Boldly she
gave me to understand that the tape recorder was at fault
for having recorded something she had no memory of hav-

ing said. "If I really said these things, it's your doing.
Every time you ask me about curing I start talking without
really knowing what I am saying. You always put words
into my mouth. If you knew how to cure, you wouldn't
bother writing or talking about it. You would just do it."

I was not willing to believe that my work was useless. I
went to see the other two curers. To my great chagrin they
were not much help either. They acknowledged the inconsistencies and explained them much as doña Mercedes had.

In retrospect my despair over this failure seems comical.
In a fit of rage, I dared doña Mercedes to burn my notes.
She willingly complied, burning sheet after sheet over the
flame of one of the candles illuminating the statue of the
Virgin Mary on the altar in her curing room. "I really
can't understand why you get so upset about what your
machine says and what I say," doña Mercedes observed,
lighting another candle on the altar. "What difference
does it make about what I do now and what I did a few
months ago? All that matters is that the patients get well.
Years ago, a psychologist and a sociologist came here and
recorded everything I said on a machine like yours. I believe it was a better machine; it was much larger. They
were only here for a week. With the information they got,
they wrote a book about curing."

"I know the book," I snapped. "I don't think it's an
accurate study. It's simplistic, superficial, and lacks a true
understanding."

Doña Mercedes peered at me quizzically, her glance half
pitying, half deprecatory. In silence I watched the last page
turn to ashes. I was not bothered by what she had done; I
still had the English translation of the tapes and notes. She
got up from her chair and sat next to me on the wooden
bench. "Very soon you'll feel that a heavy load has been
lifted off your back," she consoled me.

I was compelled to go into a lengthy explanation concerning the importance of studying non-Western healing practices. Doña Mercedes listened attentively, a mocking smile on her face.

"If I were you," she suggested, "I would accept your friend's offer to go hunting up the Orinoco River. It would be a good change for you."

Although I had intended to return to Los Angeles as soon as possible in order to conclude my work, I had seriously considered accepting a friend's invitation for a two-week trip into the jungle. I had no interest in hunting but believed I might have the opportunity of meeting a shaman, or witnessing a curing ceremony, through one of the Indian guides he planned to hire upon arriving at the Catholic mission, which was the last outpost of civilization.

"I think I should do that," I said to doña Mercedes. "Maybe I'll meet a great Indian curer who will tell me things about healing that not even you know."

"I'm sure you'll hear all kinds of interesting things," doña Mercedes laughed. "But don't bother to write them down—you won't do any kind of research."

"Oh, really. And how do you know that?"

"Remember I'm a *bruja*," she said, patting my cheek. There was an expression of ineffable gentleness in her dark eyes. "And don't worry about your English notes safely tucked away in your desk. By the time you return, you won't have any use for your notes."

2

A week later I was on my way in a small plane to one of the Catholic missions on the upper Orinoco with my friend. There we were to meet the other members of the party, who had set out by boat a few days earlier with the hunting gear and the necessary provisions to last us two weeks in the jungle.

My friend was eager to show me the wonders of the muddy, turbulent Orinoco River. He maneuvered the small aircraft with daring and skill. At one moment we were so close to the water's surface that we scared the alligators sunning themselves on the sandy bank. The next instant we were up in the air, above the seemingly endless, impenetrable forest. No sooner had I relaxed than he would dive once again—so low that we would see the turtles basking on logs at the edge of the river.

I was shaking with dizziness and nausea when we finally landed on the small clearing near the cultivated fields of the mission. We were welcomed by Father Coriolano, the priest in charge of the mission, the rest of our party, who had arrived the day before, and a group of Indians, who cried excitedly as they scrambled into the small plane.

Father Coriolano led us through the plots of maize, manioc, plantains, and sugar cane. He was a thin man with long arms and short legs. Heavy eyebrows almost hid his deep-set eyes and a mass of unruly beard covered the rest of his face. At odds with his black cassock was his torn straw hat, which he kept pushing back so that the breeze could dry his sweat-covered forehead.

My clothes clung damply to my body as we walked past a makeshift pier of piles driven into the mud at the bank of the river where the boat was tied. We stopped and Father Coriolano began discussing our departure the next day. I was encircled by a group of Indian women, who did not say a word but only smiled shyly at me. Their ill-fitting dresses came up in front and dipped in back, giving the impression that they were all pregnant. Among them was an old woman so small and wrinkled she reminded me of an ancient child. She did not smile like the others. There was a silent plea in the old woman's eyes as she held her hand out to me. My feelings were strange as I watched her eyes fill with tears; I did not want to see them roll down her clay-colored cheeks. I placed my hand in hers. Smiling contentedly, she led me toward the fruit trees surrounding the long, one-story mission.

In the shade, underneath the wide overhang of the building's asbestos roof, squatted a group of old men holding enameled tin cups in their trembling hands. They were dressed in khaki clothes, their faces partly covered by sweat-stained straw hats. They laughed and talked in high-pitched voices, smacking their lips over their rum-laced coffee. A noisy pair of macaws, their brightly colored wings clipped, perched on one of the men's shoulders.

I could not see the men's features, nor the color of their skin. They seemed to be speaking in Spanish, yet their words sounded unintelligible to me. "Are those men Indians?" I asked the old woman as she led me into a small room at the back of one of the houses fringing the mission.

The old woman laughed. Her eyes, scarcely visible between the slits of her lids, came to rest on my face. "They are *racionales*. Those who are not Indians are called *racionales*," she repeated. "Those old men have been here for too long. They came to look for gold and diamonds."

"Did they find any?"

"Many of them did."

"Why are they still here?"

"They are the ones who cannot return to where they came from," she said, resting her bony hands on my shoulders. I was not surprised by her gesture. There was something cordial and affectionate in her touch. I just thought she was a bit crazy. "They have lost their souls in the forest." The old woman's eyes had grown wide; they were the color of dried tobacco leaves.

Not knowing what to say, I averted my eyes from her penetrating gaze and looked around the room. The blue-painted walls were faded from the sun and peeling from the dampness. Next to a narrow window stood a crudely constructed wooden bed. It looked like an oversized crib on which mosquito wire had been nailed all around. The more I looked at it, the more it reminded me of a cage that could be entered only by lifting the heavy mosquito-screened top.

"I am Angelica," the old woman said, peering at me. "Is this all you have brought with you?" she asked, removing the orange knapsack from my back.

Speechless and with a look of complete astonishment, I watched her take out my underwear, a pair of jeans, and a long T-shirt. "That's all I need for two weeks," I said, pointing to my camera and the toilet kit at the bottom of the knapsack.

Carefully, she removed the camera and unzipped the plastic toilet kit and promptly emptied its contents on the floor. It contained a comb, nail clipper, toothpaste and brush, a bottle of shampoo, and a bar of soap. Shaking her head in disbelief, she turned the knapsack inside out. Absentmindedly, she brushed away the dark hair sticking to her forehead. There was a vague air of dreamy recollection in her eyes as her face wrinkled into a smile. She put everything back into the knapsack and without a word led me back to my friends.

Long after the mission was dark and silent I was still awake, listening to the unfamiliar sounds of the night coming through the opened window. I don't know whether it was because of my fatigue or the relaxed atmosphere at the mission, but before retiring that evening I had decided not to accompany my friends on their hunting expedition. Instead I was going to stay the two weeks in the mission. Happily, no one minded. In fact, everybody seemed relieved. Although they had not voiced it, some of my friends believed that a person who did not know how to use a gun had no business going on a hunt.

Spellbound, I watched the blue transparency of the air dissolve the shadows of the night. A softness spread over the sky, revealing the contours of the branches and leaves waving with the breeze outside my window. The solitary cry of a howler monkey was the last thing I heard before falling into a deep sleep.

"So you are an anthropologist," Father Coriolano said at lunch the next day. "The anthropologists I have met were all loaded with recording and filming equipment and who knows what other gadgets." He offered me another serving of baked fish and corn on the cob. "Are you interested in the Indians?"

I explained to him what I had been doing in Barlovento, touching upon the difficulties I had encountered with the data. "I would like to see some curing sessions while I'm here."

"I'm afraid you won't see much of that around here,"

Father Coriolano said, picking out crumbs of cassava bread lodged in his beard. "We have a well-equipped dispensary. Indians come from far away to bring their sick. But perhaps I can arrange for you to visit one of the nearby settlements, where you could meet a shaman."

"I would be very grateful if that were possible," I said. "Not that I came to do field work, but it would be interesting to see a shaman."

"You don't look like an anthropologist." Father Coriolano's heavy eyebrows arched and met. "Of course most of the ones I have met were men; but there've been a few women." He scratched his head. "Somehow you don't match my description of a woman anthropologist."

"You can't expect us to all look alike," I said lightly, wondering whom he had met.

"I suppose not," he said sheepishly. "What I mean is that you don't look fully grown. This morning, after your friends left, I was asked by various people why the child was left with me."

His eyes were lively as he joked about how the Indians expected a fully grown white adult to tower over them. "Especially if they are blond and blue eyed," he said. "Those are supposed to be veritable giants."

That night I had the most terrifying nightmare in my mosquito-netted crib. I dreamt that the top had been nailed shut. All my efforts to extricate myself proved futile against the pressure of the lid. Panic overtook me. I screamed and shook the frame until the whole contraption tumbled over. I was still half asleep as I lay on the floor, my head resting against the small bulge of the old woman's hanging breasts. For a moment I could not remember where I was. A childish fear made me press closer to the old Indian, knowing that I was safe.

The old woman rubbed the top of my head and whispered incomprehensible words into my ear until I was fully awake. I felt reassured by her touch and the alien, nasal sound of her voice. I was not able to rationalize this feeling, but there was something that made me cling to her. She led me to her room, back of the kitchen. I lay next to her in a heavy hammock fastened to two poles. Protected by the presence of the strange old woman, I closed my eyes without fear. The faint beat of her heart and the drip of water filtering through an earthen water jar put me to sleep.

"It will be much better if you sleep here," the old woman said the following morning as she hung a cotton hammock next to hers.

From that day on Angelica hardly ever left my side. Most of the time we stayed by the river, talking and bathing by its bank, where the gray-red sand was the color of ashes mixed with blood. Completely at peace, I would sit for hours watching the Indian women wash their garments and listen to Angelica's tales of her past. Like clouds wandering about the sky, her words intermingled with the images of women rinsing their clothes in the water and spreading them out on the stones to dry.

Angelica was not a Maquiritare like most of the Indians at the mission. She had been given to a Maquiritare man when she was very young. He had treated her well, she was fond of saying. Quickly she had learned their way of life, which had not been so different from the ways of her own people. She had also been to the city. She never told me which city. Neither did she tell me her Indian name, which according to the customs of her tribe was not to be said aloud.

Whenever she talked about her past, her voice sounded foreign to my ears. It became very nasal and often she would switch from Spanish into her own language, mixing up time and place. Frequently she stopped in the middle of a sentence; hours later, or even the following day, she would resume the conversation at the exact spot where she had left off, as if it were the most natural thing in the world to converse in that fashion.

"I will take you to my people," Angelica said one afternoon. She looked at me, a flickering smile on her lips. I had the feeling she had been about to say something else and I wondered if she knew about Father Coriolano's arrangement with Mr. Barth to take me to the nearby Maquiritare settlement.

Mr. Barth was an American miner who had been in the Venezuelan jungle for over twenty years. He lived down-river with an Indian woman, and many an evening he invited himself to the mission for dinner. Although he had no desire to return to the States, he greatly enjoyed hearing about them.

"I will take you to my people," Angelica said again. "It will take many days to get there. Milagros will guide us through the jungle."

"Who is Milagros?"

"He's an Indian like me. He speaks Spanish well." Angelica rubbed her hands with glee. "He was supposed to accompany your friends, but he decided to stay behind. Now I know why."

Angelica spoke with an odd intensity; her eyes sparkled and I had the same feeling I had had when I first arrived, that she was a bit crazy. "He knew all along that I would need him to accompany us," the old woman said. Her lids closed as if she no longer had the strength to lift them. Abruptly, as if fearing to fall asleep, she opened her eyes wide. "It doesn't matter what you say to me now. I know that you will come with me."

That night I lay awake in my hammock. By the sound of Angelica's breathing I knew that she was asleep. I prayed that she would not forget her offer to take me into the jungle. Doña Mercedes's words ran through my head. "By the time you return you won't have any use for your notes." Perhaps I would do some field work among the Indians. The thought amused me. I had not brought a tape recorder; neither did I have paper and pencils—only a small diary and a ball-point pen. I had brought my camera but only three rolls of film.

Restlessly I turned in my hammock. No, I had no intention of going into the jungle with an old woman, whom I believed to be a bit mad, and an Indian whom I had never seen. Yet there was something so tempting about a trip through the jungle. I could easily take some time off. I had no deadlines to meet; there was no one waiting for me. I could leave a letter for my friends explaining my sudden decision. They would not think much of it. The more I thought about it, the more intrigued I became. Father Coriolano, no doubt, would be able to supply me with enough paper and pencils. And yes, perhaps doña Mercedes had been right. I would have no use for my old notes on curing when—and if, the thought intruded ominously— I returned from such a journey.

I got out of my hammock and looked at the frail old woman while she slept. As if she were sensing my presence, her lids fluttered, her lips began to move. "I will not die here but among my own people. My body will be burned and my ashes will remain with them." Her eyes slowly opened; they were dull, befogged by sleep, and they expressed nothing, but I sensed a deep sadness in her voice. I touched her hollowed cheeks. She smiled at me, but her mind was clearly elsewhere.

I awoke with the feeling I was being watched. Angelica told me that she had been waiting for me to wake up. She motioned me to look at a box, the size of a vanity case, made out of tree bark, standing next to her. She opened the tightly fitting lid and with great relish proceeded to show me each item, breaking into loud exclamations of joy and surprise, as if it were the first time she had seen each article. There was a mirror, a comb, a necklace made out of plastic pearls, a few empty Pond's cold cream jars, a lipstick, a pair of rusted scissors, a faded blouse and skirt.

"And what do you think this is?" she asked, holding something behind her back.

I confessed my ignorance and she laughed. "This is my writing book." She opened her notebook, its pages yellow with age. On each page were rows of crooked letters. "Watch me." Taking out a chewed-up pencil from the box, she began to print her name. "I learned to do this at another mission. A much larger one than this one. It also had a school. That was many years ago, but I haven't forgotten what I learned." Again and again she printed her name on the faded pages. "Do you like it?"

"Very much." I was bewildered by the sight of the old woman squatting on the floor with her body bent forward, her head almost touching the notebook on the ground. Yet she was perfectly balanced as she painstakingly traced the letters of her name.

Suddenly she straightened up, closing her notebook. "I have been to the city," she said, her eyes fixed on a spot beyond the window. "A city full of people that looked all the same. At first I liked it, but I grew tired of it very fast. There was too much for me to watch. And it was so noisy. Not only people talked, but things talked as well." She paused, scowling in a tremendous effort to concentrate, all the lines in her face deepened. Finally she said, "I didn't like the city at all."

I asked her which city she had been to and at which mission she had learned to write her name. She looked at me as if she had not heard what I asked, then continued with her tale. As she had done before, she began to mix up time and place, relapsing into her own language. At times she laughed, repeating over and over, "I will not go to Father Coriolano's heaven."

"Are you really serious about going to see your people?" I asked. "Don't you think it's dangerous for two women to go into the forest? Do you actually know the way?"

"Of course I know the way," she said, snapping out of her almost trancelike state. "An old woman is always safe."

"I'm not old."

She stroked my hair. "You aren't old, but your hair is the color of palm fibers and your eyes the color of the sky. You'll be safe too."

"I'm sure we'll get lost," I said softly. "You can't even remember how long ago it was you last saw your people. You told me they always move farther into the forest."

"Milagros is going with us," Angelica said convincingly. "He knows the forest well. He knows about all the people living in the jungle." Angelica began putting her belongings into the bark box. "I better find him so we can leave as soon as possible. You'll have to give him something."

"I haven't got anything he'd want," I said. "Maybe I can arrange for my friends to leave the machetes they brought with them at the mission for Milagros."

"Give him your camera," Angelica suggested. "I know he wants a camera as much as he wants another machete."

"Does he know how to use a camera?"

"I don't know." She giggled, holding her hand over her mouth. "He told me once that he wants to take pictures of the white people who come to the mission to look at the Indians."

I was not keen on parting with my camera. It was a good one and very expensive. I wished I had brought a cheaper one with me. "I'll give him my camera," I said, hoping that once I explained to Milagros how complicated it was to operate, he would prefer a machete.

"The less you have to carry, the better," Angelica said, closing the lid on her box with a bang. "I'm going to give all this to one of the women here. I won't need it anymore. If you go empty-handed, no one will expect a thing from you."

"I'd like to take the hammock you gave me," I said in jest.

"That might be a good idea." Angelica looked at me, nodding her head. "You're a fussy sleeper and probably won't be able to rest in the fiber hammocks my people use." She picked up her box and walked out of the room. "I'll be back when I find Milagros."

As Father Coriolano drank his coffee, he looked at me as though I were a stranger. With great effort he got up, steadying himself against a chair. Seemingly disoriented, he gazed at me without saying a word. It was the silence of an old man. As he ran his stiff, gnarled fingers across his face, I realized for the first time how frail he was.

"You're crazy to go into the jungle with Angelica," he finally said. "She is very old; she won't get very far. Walking through the forest is no excursion."

"Milagros will accompany us."

Father Coriolano turned toward the window, deep in thought. He kept pushing his beard back and forth with his hand. "Milagros refused to go with your friends. I'm sure he will not accompany Angelica into the jungle."

"He will." My certainty was incomprehensible. It was a feeling completely foreign to my everyday reason.

"Although he is a trustworthy man, he is strange," Father Coriolano said thoughtfully. "He has acted as a guide to various expeditions. Yet . . ." Father Coriolano returned to his chair and, leaning toward me, continued. "You aren't prepared to go into the jungle. You cannot begin to imagine the hardships and dangers entailed in such an adventure. You haven't even got the proper shoes."

"I have been told by various people who have been in the jungle that tennis shoes are the best thing to wear. They dry fast on your feet without getting tight and they don't cause blisters."

Father Coriolano ignored my comment. "Why do you want to go?" he asked in an exasperated tone. "Mr. Barth will take you to meet a Maquiritare shaman; you will get to see a curing ceremony without having to go very far."

"I don't really know why I want to go." I looked at him helplessly. "Maybe I want to see more than a curing ceremony. In fact, I wanted to ask you to let me have some writing paper and pencils."

"What about your friends? What am I supposed to tell them? That you just disappeared with a senile old woman?" he asked as he poured himself another cup of coffee. "I've been here for over thirty years and never have I heard of such a preposterous plan."

It was past siesta time, yet the mission was still quiet as I stretched in my hammock hanging under the shade of the twisted branches and jagged leaves of two poma-rosa trees. In the distance I saw the tall figure of Mr. Barth approaching the mission clearing. Strange, I thought, for he usually came in the evening. Then I guessed why he was here.

Stopping by the steps leading up to the veranda, close to where I lay, he squatted on the ground and lit one of the cigarettes my friends had brought him.

Mr. Barth seemed uneasy. He stood up and walked back and forth as if he were a sentry guarding the building. I was about to call out to him when he began talking to himself, his words pouring out with the smoke. He rubbed the white stubble on his chin and scraped one boot against the other in an effort to get rid of the mud. Squatting once more, he began to shake his head as if in that way he could rid himself of what was going through his mind.

"You have come to tell me about the diamonds you have found in the Gran Sabana," I said as a way of greeting, hoping to dispel the melancholy expression in his gentle brown eyes.

He drew on the cigarette and blew the smoke out through his nose in short bursts. After spitting out a few particles of tobacco that had stuck to the tip of his tongue, he asked, "Why do you want to go with Angelica into the forest?"

"I already told Father Coriolano, I don't really know."

Mr. Barth softly repeated my words, making a question out of them. Lighting another cigarette, he exhaled slowly, gazing at the spiral of tobacco smoke melting into the transparent air. "Let's go for a walk," he suggested.

We strolled along the river's bank where vast, inter-woven roots emerged from the earth like sculptures of wood and mud. Quickly the warm, sticky dampness per-meated my skin. From under a layer of branches and leaves, Mr. Barth pulled out a canoe, pushed it into the water, then motioned me to climb in. He steered the craft right across the river, making for the shelter of the left-hand bank, which offered some protection from the full strength of the current. With precise, strong movements, he guided the canoe upstream until we reached a narrow tributary. The bamboo thicket yielded to a dark heavy growth, an endless wall of trees standing trunk to trunk at the very edge of the river. Roots and branches overhung the water; vines climbed down the trees, winding them-selves around their trunks like snakes crushing them in a tight embrace.

"Oh, there it is," Mr. Barth said, pointing to an opening in that seemingly impenetrable wall.

We pulled the boat across the marshy bank and tied it securely around a tree trunk. The sun hardly penetrated through the dense foliage; the light faded to a tenuous green as I followed Mr. Barth through the thicket. Vines and branches brushed against me like things alive. The heat was not so intense anymore, but the sticky dampness made my clothes cling to me like slime. Soon my face was covered with grimy vegetable dust and spiderwebs that smelled of decay.

"Is this a path?" I asked incredulously, almost stumbling into a greenish puddle of water. Its surface quivered with hundreds of insects that were hardly more than pulsating dots in the turbid liquid. Birds flew away and amidst the greenness I could not discern their color or size but only heard their furious screeches, protesting our intrusion. I understood Mr. Barth was trying to frighten me. The thought that he might be taking me to another Catholic mission also crossed my mind. "Is this a path?" I asked again.

Abruptly Mr. Barth stopped in front of a tree, so tall its upper branches seemed to reach into the sky. Climbing plants twisted and turned upward around the trunk and branches. "I intended to give you a lecture and scare the devil out of you," Mr. Barth said with a sulky expression. "But whatever I rehearsed to say seems foolish now. Let's rest for a moment and then we'll go back."

Mr. Barth let the boat drift with the current, paddling only whenever we got too close to the bank. "The jungle is a world you cannot possibly imagine," he said. "I can't describe it to you even though I have experienced it so often. It's a personal affair—each person's experience is different and unique."

Instead of returning to the mission, Mr. Barth invited me to his house. It was a large round hut with a conical roof of palm leaves. It was quite dark inside, the only light coming from a small entrance and the rectangular window in the palm-thatched roof, operated by means of a rawhide pulley. Two hammocks hung in the middle of the hut. Baskets filled with books and magazines stood against the whitewashed walls; above them hung calabashes, ladles, machetes, and a gun.

A naked young woman got up from one of the hammocks. She was tall, with large breasts and broad hips, but her face was that of a child, round and smooth, with slanted dark eyes. Smiling, she reached for her dress, hanging next to a woven fire fan. "Coffee?" she asked in Spanish as she sat on the ground in front of the hearth next to the aluminum pots and pans.

"Do you know Milagros well?" I asked Mr. Barth after he had introduced me to his wife and we were all seated in the hammocks, the young woman and I sharing one.

"That's hard to say," he said, reaching for his coffee mug on the ground. "He comes and goes; he's like the river. He never stops, never seems to rest. How far Milagros goes, how long he stays anywhere, no one knows. All I've heard is that when he was young he was taken from his people by white men. He is never consistent with his story. At one time he says they were rubber collectors, at another time they were missionaries, the next time he says they were miners, scientists. Regardless of who they were, he traveled with them for many years."

"To which tribe does he belong? Where does he live?"

"He is a Maquiritare," Mr. Barth said. "But no one knows where he lives. Periodically he returns to his people. To which settlement he belongs, I don't know."

"Angelica went to look for him. I wonder if she knows where to find him."

"I'm sure she does," Mr. Barth said. "They are very close. I wonder if they are related." He deposited the mug on the ground and got up from his hammock, momentarily disappearing in the thick bush outside the hut. Mr. Barth reappeared seconds later with a small metal box. "Open it," he said, handing me the box.

Inside was a brown leather pouch. "Diamonds?" I asked, feeling its contents.

Smiling, Mr. Barth nodded, then motioned me to sit down beside him on the dirt floor. He took off his shirt, spread it on the ground, then asked me to empty the pouch on the cloth surface. I could barely hide my disappointment. The stones did not sparkle; they rather looked like opaque quartz.

"Are you sure these are diamonds?" I asked.

"Absolutely sure," Mr. Barth said, placing a stone the size of a cherry tomato in my palm. "If it's cut properly, it'll make a most handsome ring."

"Did you find these diamonds here?"

"No," Mr. Barth laughed. "Near the Sierra Parima, years ago." Half closing his eyes, he rocked back and forth. His cheeks were ruddy with little veins and the stubble on his chin was damp. "A long time ago my only interest in life was to find diamonds in order to return home a wealthy man." Mr. Barth sighed heavily, his gaze lost on some place beyond the hut. "Then one day I realized that my dream to become rich had dried out, so to speak; it no longer obsessed me, and neither did I want to return to the world I had once known. I remained here." Mr. Barth's eyes shone with unshed tears as he gestured to the diamonds. "With them." He blinked repeatedly, then looked at me and smiled. "I like them as I like this land."

I wanted to ask him so many questions but was afraid to distress him. We remained silent, listening to the steady, deep murmur of the river.

Mr. Barth spoke again. "You know, anthropologists and missionaries have a lot in common. Both are bad for this land. Anthropologists are more hypocritical; they cheat and lie in order to get the information they want. I suppose they believe that in the name of science all is fair. No, no, don't interrupt me," Mr. Barth admonished, shaking his hand in front of my face.

"Anthropologists," he continued in the same harsh tone, "have complained to me about the arrogance of the missionaries, about their high-handedness and paternalistic attitude toward the Indians. And look at them, the most arrogant of them all, prying into other people's lives as if they had every right to do so." Mr. Barth sighed loudly as if exhausted by his outburst.

I decided not to defend anthropologists, for I feared another outburst, so I contented myself with examining the diamond in my hand. "It's very beautiful," I said, handing him the stone.

"Keep it," he said, then picked up the remaining stones. One by one he dropped them into the leather pouch.

"I'm afraid I can't keep such a valuable gift." I began to giggle and added as an excuse, "I never wear jewelry."

"Don't think of it as a valuable gift. Regard it as a talisman. Only people in the cities regard it as a jewel," he said casually, closing my fingers over the stone. "It will bring you luck." He got up, brushing the dampness off the seat of his pants with his hands, then stretched in his hammock.

The young woman refilled our mugs. Sipping the heavily sweetened black coffee, we watched the whitewashed walls turn purple with twilight. Shadows had no time to grow, for in an instant it was dark.

I was awakened by Angelica whispering into my ear. "We're going in the morning."

"What?" I jumped out of my hammock fully awake. "I thought it would take you a couple of days to find Milagros. I better get packed."

Angelica laughed. "Packed? You haven't got anything to

pack. I gave your extra pair of pants and a top to an Indian boy. You won't need two pairs. You better go back to sleep. It will be a long day tomorrow. Milagros is a fast walker."

"I can't sleep," I said excitedly. "It'll be dawn soon. I'll write a note to my friends. I hope the hammock and the thin blanket will fit in my knapsack. What about food?"

"Father Coriolano put sardines and cassava bread aside for us to pack in the morning. I will carry it in a basket."

"Did you talk to him tonight? What did he say?"

"He said it's in the hands of God."

I was all packed when the chapel bell began to chime. For the first time since I had arrived at the mission, I went to mass. Indians and *racionales* filled the wooden benches. They laughed and talked as if they were at a social gathering. It took Father Coriolano a long time to silence them before he could say mass.

The woman sitting next to me complained that Father Coriolano always managed to wake her baby with his loud voice. The infant indeed began to cry, but before his first great shriek was heard, the woman uncovered her breast and pressed it against the baby's mouth.

Kneeling down, I raised my eyes to the Virgin above the altar. She wore a blue cloak embroidered in gold. Her face was tilted heavenward, her eyes were blue, her cheeks pale, and her mouth a deep red. In one arm she held the infant Jesus; the other arm was extended, its hand white and delicate, reaching out to the strange heathens at her feet.

3

Machete in hand, Milagros led the way on the narrow path bordering the river. His muscular back showed through his torn red shirt. The khaki pants, rolled halfway up his calves and fastened above his waist with a cotton string, made him look shorter than his medium height. He walked at a fast pace, supporting his weight on the outer edge of his feet, which were narrow at the heel and spread like an open fan at the toes. His short-trimmed hair and the wide tonsure on the crown of his head reminded me of a monk.

I stopped and turned around before following on the trail leading into the forest. Across the river, almost hidden around a bend, lay the mission. Shrouded in the early morning sunlight, it seemed like something already out of touch. I felt oddly removed, not only from the place and the people I had been with for the past week, but from all familiar things. I sensed some change within me, as if crossing the river marked the end of a phase, a turning point. Something of this must have shown in my face for when I looked to my side and caught Angelica's gaze there was understanding in it.

"Already far away," Milagros said, stopping next to us. Folding his arms across his chest, he let his gaze wander along the river. The morning light dazzling over the water reflected in his face, tinting it with a golden sheen. It was an angular, bony face in which the small nose and full lower lip added an unexpected vulnerability that contrasted sharply with the deep circles and wrinkles around his slanted brown eyes. They were uncannily similar to Angelica's eyes, with that same timeless expression in them.

In absolute silence we walked beneath the towering trees, along trails hidden by massive bushes entangled with vines, branches and leaves, creepers and roots. Spiderwebs clung to my face like an invisible veil. Greenness was all I could see and dampness all I could smell. We went over and around logs, across streams and swamps shaded by immense bamboo growths. Sometimes Milagros was in front of me; at other times Angelica was, with her U-shaped basket on her back, held in place by a tumpline of bark that went around her head. It was filled with gourds, cassava bread, and cans of sardines.

I had no sense of which direction we were going. I could not see the sun—only its light, filtering through the dense foliage. Soon my neck was stiff from looking up at the incredible height of the motionless trees. Only the straight palms, undefeated in their vertical thrust toward the light, seemed to sweep the few visible patches of sky with their silver-shaded fronds.

"I've got to rest," I said, sitting down heavily on a fallen tree trunk. By my watch it was already after three in the afternoon. We had walked nonstop for over six hours. "I'm famished."

Handing me a calabash from her basket, Angelica sat next to me. "Fill it," she said, motioning with her chin to the nearby shallow stream.

Squatting in the river, with his legs apart, palms resting on his thighs, Milagros bent forward until his lips touched the water. He drank without getting his nose wet. "Drink," he said, straightening up. He must be nearly fifty, I

thought. Yet the unexpected grace of his flowing movements made him seem much younger. He smiled briefly,
then waded downstream.

"Watch out or you'll be taking a bath!" Angelica exclaimed, smiling mockingly.

Startled by her voice, I lost my balance and toppled over
headfirst into the water. "I'm no good at drinking water
the way Milagros does," I said casually, handing her the
filled gourd. "I think I'll just stick to the calabash." Sitting next to her, I took off my soaked tennis shoes. "Whoever said that sneakers were the best thing for the jungle
never walked for six hours in them." My feet were red and
blistered, my ankles scratched and bleeding.

"It's not too bad," Angelica said, examining my feet.
She ran her fingers gently over my soles and the blistered
toes. "You have pretty good calluses. Why don't you walk
barefoot? Wet shoes will only soften your feet more."

I looked at the bottoms of my feet; they were covered by
thick calloused skin that I had acquired from practicing
karate for years. "What if I step on a snake?" I asked. "Or
on a thorn?" Although I had not yet seen a single reptile, I
had watched Milagros and Angelica stop at various times
to pull thorns out of their feet.

"One has to be pretty stupid to step on a snake," she
said, pushing my feet off her lap. "Compared to mosquitoes, thorns are not too bad. You are lucky the little
devils don't bite you the way they do the *racionales*." She
rubbed my arms and hands as if expecting to find a clue
there. "I wonder why?"

Angelica had already marveled at the mission that I
slept like the Indians, without mosquito netting. "I've got
evil blood," I said, grinning. Seeing her puzzled look, I
explained that as a child I had often gone with my father
to the jungle to look for orchids. Invariably, he would be

stung by mosquitoes, flies, and whatever biting insects were around. Somehow they never bothered me. Once my father had even been bitten by a snake.

"Did he die?" Angelica asked.

"No. It was a most curious incident. The same snake bit me too. I cried out right after my father did. He thought I was making fun of him until I showed him the tiny red spots on my foot. Only it didn't swell and turn purple the way his did. We were driven by friends to the closest town, where my father was given antivenin serum. He was ill for days."

"And you?"

"Nothing happened to me," I said, and told her it was his friends who said half jokingly that I had evil blood. They did not believe, as the doctor did, that the snake had exhausted its supply of poison on the first bite and whatever it had left had been insufficient to have any effect on me. I told Angelica that on one occasion I was bitten by seven wasps, the ones they call *mata caballo*—horse killer. The doctor thought I was going to die. I only developed a fever and in a few days I was fine.

I had never seen Angelica so attentive, listening with her head slightly bent as if afraid to miss a single word. "I was also bitten by a snake once," she said. "People believed I was going to die." She was quiet for a moment, deep in thought, then a timid smile creased her face. "Do you think it spent its poison on someone else first?"

"I'm sure it did," I said, touching her withered hands.

"Maybe I have evil blood too," she said, smiling. She looked so frail and old. For an instant I had the feeling she might disappear amidst the shadows.

"I'm ancient," Angelica said, looking at me as though I had expressed my thoughts out loud. "I should have died a long time ago. I've kept death waiting." She turned to watch a row of ants demolish a bush as they cut away squares of leaves and carried them off in their mouths. "I knew it was you who would take me to my people—I knew it the moment I saw you." There was a long pause. She either did not want to say anything else or was trying to find the appropriate words. She was watching me, a vague smile on her lips. "You also knew it—otherwise you wouldn't be here," she finally said with utter conviction.

I giggled nervously; she always succeeded in making me uneasy with that intense glint in her eyes. "I'm not sure what I'm doing here," I said. "I don't know why I'm going with you."

"You knew you were meant to come here," Angelica insisted.

There was something about Angelica's sureness that made me feel argumentative. It would have been so easy to agree with her, especially since I did not know myself why I was in the jungle on my way to God knows where. "To tell you the truth, I had no intention of going anyplace," I said. "Remember, I didn't even accompany my friends up-river to hunt alligators as I had planned."

"But that's exactly what I'm saying," she assured me as if she were speaking to a stupid child. "You found an excuse to cancel your trip so you could come with me." She laid her bony hands on my head. "Believe me, I didn't have to think much about it. Neither did you. The decision was made the moment I laid eyes on you."

I buried my head in the old woman's lap to hide my laughter. There was no way to argue with her. Besides, she might be right, I thought. I had no explanation myself.

"I waited a long time," Angelica went on. "I had almost forgotten that you were supposed to come to me. But when I saw you I knew that the man had been right. Not that I ever doubted him, but he had told me so long ago that I believed I had missed my chance."

"What man?" I asked, lifting my head from her lap. "Who told you I was coming?"

"I'll tell you another time." Angelica pulled the basket closer and picked out a large piece of cassava bread. "We better eat," she added, and opened a can of sardines.

There was no point in insisting. Once Angelica had decided not to talk, there was no way to make her change her mind. My curiosity unsatisfied, I contented myself in examining the neat row of fat sardines lying in the thick tomato sauce. I had seen that kind in the supermarket in Los Angeles; a friend of mine used to buy them for her cat. I took one out with my finger and spread it on the piece of flat white bread.

"I wonder where Milagros is," I said, biting into the sardine sandwich. It tasted quite good.

Angelica did not answer; neither did she eat. From time to time she sipped water from the gourd. A faint smile lingered at the corners of her mouth and I wondered what it was that the old woman was thinking about that created such a look of longing in her eyes. All of a sudden she stared at me as if awakening from a dream. "Look," she said, nudging my arm.

In front of us stood a man, naked except for the red cotton strands around his upper arms and a string around his waist that circled his foreskin, tying his penis against his abdomen. His whole body was covered with brownish-red designs. In one hand he held a long bow and arrows, in the other a machete.

"Milagros?" I finally managed to mumble, recovering from my initial shock. Still, I barely recognized him. It was not only that he was naked; he seemed taller, more muscular. The red zigzag lines running from his forehead down to his cheeks, across his nose, and around his mouth sharpened the contours of his face, erasing its vulnerability. There was something else besides the physical change, something I could not pinpoint. It was as though by discarding the clothes of a *racional*, he had shed some invisible weight.

Milagros began to laugh in a loud, uproarious manner. A laughter that sprang from deep inside him, it shook his whole body. Echoing and booming through the forest, it mingled with the startled cries of a flock of parrots that had taken flight. Squatting before me, he stopped abruptly and said, "You almost didn't recognize me." He thrust his face so close to mine that our noses touched, then asked, "Do you want me to paint your face?"

"Yes," I said, taking the camera from my knapsack. "But can I take a picture of you first?"

"That's my camera," he said emphatically, reaching for it. "I thought you had left it at the mission for me."

"I would like to use it while we're at the Indian settlement." I began demonstrating to him how the camera worked by first putting in a roll of film. He was very attentive to my explanation, nodding his head every time I asked if he understood. I hoped to confuse him by pointing out all the intricacies of the gadget. "Now let me take a picture of you, so you can see how the camera should be held."

"No, no." He was quick to stop me, taking the camera from my hands. Without any difficulty he opened the back cover and lifted out the film, exposing it to the light. "It's mine, you promised. Only I can take pictures with it."

Speechless, I watched him hang the camera over his chest. It looked so incongruous against his nakedness I was unable to repress my laughter. With exaggerated gestures he began to focus, adjust, and point the camera all around him, talking to imaginary subjects, telling them to smile, to stand closer or to move farther apart. I had the strong urge to pull at the cotton string around his neck that held the arrow-point quiver and the fire drill swinging from his back.

"You won't get any pictures without film," I said, handing him the third and last roll.

"I never said I wanted to take pictures." Gleefully he exposed the film to the light, then very deliberately put the camera in its leather case. "Indians don't like to be photographed," he said seriously, then turned toward Angelica's basket on the ground and searched through its contents until he found a small gourd sealed with a piece of animal skin. "This is *onoto*," he said, showing me a red paste. It was greasy and had a faint aromatic odor I was unable to define. "This is the color of life and joy," he said.

"Where did you leave your clothes?" I asked him as he cut a piece of vine, the length of a pencil, with his teeth. "Do you live nearby?"

Busying himself with chewing one end of the vine until it resembled a makeshift brush, Milagros did not bother to answer. He spat on the *onoto*, then stirred the red paste with the brush until it was soft. With a precise, even hand he drew wavy lines across my forehead, down my cheeks, chin, and neck, circled my eyes, and decorated my arms with round spots.

"Is there an Indian settlement around here?"

"No."

"Do you live by yourself?"

"Why do you ask so many questions?" The expression of annoyance, heightened by the sharp lines of his painted face, matched the irritated tone of his voice.

I opened my mouth, uttered a sound, then hesitated to say that it was important for me to know about him and Angelica—that the more I knew, the better I would feel. "I was trained to be curious," I said after a while, sensing he would not understand the fleeting anxiety that I tried to alleviate by asking questions. Knowing about them, I thought, would give me some sense of control.

Smiling, totally oblivious to what I had said, Milagros looked at me askance, examined my painted face, then burst into loud guffaws. It was a cheerful, hilarious laugh, like that of a child. "A blond Indian," he said, wiping tears from his eyes.

I laughed with him, all my momentary apprehension dispelled. Stopping abruptly, Milagros leaned toward me and whispered an incomprehensible word into my ear. "That's your new name," he said seriously, putting his hand over my lips to prevent me from repeating it out loud. Turning toward Angelica, he whispered the name into her ear.

As soon as Milagros had eaten, he motioned us to follow him. Disregarding my blisters I quickly put on my shoes. I could discern nothing but green as we climbed up hills and down plains—an unending green of vines, branches, leaves, and prickly thorns, where all the hours were hours of twilight. I no longer lifted my head to catch glimpses of the sky through patches of leaves but was content to see its reflection in puddles and streams.

Mr. Barth had been right when he told me that the jungle was a world impossible to imagine. I could not believe it was I walking through this unending greenness on my way to an unknown destination. My mind ran wild with anthropologists' descriptions of fierce and belligerent Indians belonging to unacculturated tribes.

My parents had been acquainted with some German explorers and scientists who had been in the Amazon jungle. As a child I had been bewildered by their tales of headhunters and cannibals; all of them told of incidents where they had escaped a sure death by saving the life of a sick Indian, usually a tribal chief or one of his relatives. A

German couple and their small daughter, who had returned from a two-year journey through the South American jungle, made the deepest impression on me. I was seven when I saw the cultural artifacts and life-size photographs they had collected during their travels.

Totally captivated by their eight-year-old daughter, I followed her through the palm-decorated room in the foyer of the Sears building in Caracas. I hardly had a chance to look at the assortment of bows and arrows, baskets, quivers, feathers, and masks hanging on the walls as she hurried me into a darkened alcove. Squatting on the floor, she pulled out a red-dyed wooden box from under a pile of palm fronds and opened it with a key hanging from her neck. "This was given to me by one of my Indian friends," she said, taking out a small wrinkled head. "It's a *tsantsa*, a shrunken enemy head," she added, caressing the long dark hair as if it were a doll.

I was awed as she told me that she had not been frightened to be in the jungle and that it had not been at all the way her parents described it. "The Indians weren't horrifying or fierce," she had said very earnestly. Not for an instant did I doubt her words as she looked at me with her large serious eyes. "They were gentle and full of laughter—they were my friends."

I could not remember the girl's name, who having lived through the same events as her parents had not experienced them with the same prejudices and fears. I chuckled to myself, almost falling over a gnarled root covered by slippery moss.

"Are you talking to yourself?" Angelica's voice cut into my reveries. "Or to the spirits of the forest?"

"Are there any?"

"Yes. Spirits dwell in the midst of all this," she said softly, gesturing around her. "In the thick of the creeping lianas, in company with the monkeys, snakes, spiders, and jaguars."

"No rain tonight," Milagros asserted, sniffing the air as we stopped by some boulders bordering a shallow river. Its calm, clear waters were strewn with pink flowers from the trees standing like sentries on the opposite bank. I took off my shoes, letting my sore feet dangle in the soothing coolness, and watched the sky, a golden crimson, turn gradually to orange, to vermilion, and finally into a deep purple. The dampness of the evening filled my nose with the scent of the forest, a smell of earth, of life, of decay.

Before the shadows closed in around us completely, Milagros had made two hammocks from strips of bark, knotted on either end to a suspension rope of vines. I could not disguise my delight when he hung my cotton hammock between the two uncomfortable-looking bark cradles.

Full of anticipation, I followed Milagros's movements as he loosened the quiver and fire drill from his back. My disappointment was immense when, upon removing the piece of monkey fur sealing the quiver, he took out a box of matches and lit the wood Angelica had gathered.

"Cat food," I said peevishly as Milagros handed me an open can of sardines. I had envisioned my first dinner in the jungle consisting of freshly hunted tapir or armadillo meat roasted to perfection over a crackling fire. All the smoldering twigs did was to send a thin line of smoke into the air, its low flames barely illuminating our surroundings.

The scant light of the fire dramatized Angelica's and Milagros's features, filling hollows with shadows, adding a shine to their temples, above their protruding eyebrows, along their short noses and their high cheekbones. I wondered why the fire made them look so much alike.

"Are you related?" I finally asked, puzzled by the resemblance.

"Yes," Milagros said. "I'm her son."

"Her son!" I repeated in disbelief. I had expected him to be a younger brother or a cousin; he looked as if he was in his fifties. "Then you are only half Maquiritare?"

They both began to giggle, as if enjoying a secret joke. "No, he isn't half Maquiritare," Angelica said in between fits of laughter. "He was born when I was still with my people." She did not say another word but moved her face close to mine with an expression at once challenging and bemused.

I shifted nervously under her piercing gaze, wondering if my question had offended her. Curiosity must be a learned trait, I decided. I was anxious to know everything about them, yet they never asked me anything about myself. All that seemed to matter to them was that we were together in the forest. At the mission Angelica had shown no interest in my background. Neither was she willing to let me know about hers, except for the few stories regarding her life at the mission.

Our hunger satisfied, we stretched in our hammocks; Angelica's and mine hung close to the fire. She was soon asleep, her legs tucked under her dress. The air felt chilly and I offered the thin blanket I had brought with me to Milagros, which he gladly accepted.

Glowworms, like dots of fire, lit up the dense darkness. The night pulsated with the cries of crickets and the croaking of frogs. I could not sleep; exhaustion and nervousness prevented me from relaxing. I watched the hours move by on my illuminated wristwatch and listened to the sounds in the jungle that I could no longer identify. There were creatures that growled, whistled, creaked, and howled. Shadows slithered beneath my hammock, moving soundlessly as time itself.

In an effort to see through the darkness I sat up, blinking, not sure if I was asleep or awake. Monkeys with phosphorescent eyes darted from behind ferns. Beasts with snarling mouths gaped at me from the branches overhead, and giant spiders crawling on legs as fine as hair spun silver webs over my eyes.

The more I watched, the more frightened I became. A cold sweat trickled from my neck to the base of my spine as I beheld a naked figure with bow drawn, aiming at the black sky. When I clearly heard the hissing sound of the arrow I put my hand over my mouth to stifle a scream.

"Don't be afraid of the night," Milagros said, laying his hand on my face. It was a fleshy, calloused hand; it smelled of earth and roots. He fastened his hammock above mine, so close I could feel the warmth of his body through the strips of bark. Softly he began to talk in his own language, a procession of rhythmical, monotonous words that shut off all the other sounds of the forest. A feeling of peace crept into me and my eyes began to close.

Milagros's hammock no longer hung above mine when I awoke. The sounds of night, now very faint, still lingered between the misty palms, the bamboo, the nameless vines, and parasitic growths. There was no color in the sky yet—only a vague clarity, forecasting a rainless day.

Crouching over the fire, Angelica stoked and blew on the embers, bringing them to life again. Smiling, she motioned me to join her. "I heard you in my sleep," she said. "Were you afraid?"

"The forest is so different at night," I said, a little embarrassed. "I must have been overly tired."

Nodding her head, she said, "Watch the light—see how it reflects from leaf to leaf until it descends to the ground, to the sleeping shadows. That's the way dawn puts to sleep the spirits of the night." Angelica began to caress the leaves on the ground. "During the day the shadows sleep. At night they dance in the darkness."

I smiled sheepishly, not quite knowing what to say. "Where did Milagros go?" I asked after a while.

Angelica did not answer; she rose, looking around her. "Don't be afraid of the jungle," she said. Lifting her arms above her head, she began to dance with little jerky steps and to chant in a low monotonous tone that abruptly changed to a very high pitch. "Dance with the night shadows and go to sleep lighthearted. If you let the shadows frighten you, they will destroy you." Her voice faded to a murmur. She turned her back to me and slowly walked toward the river.

The water was cold as I squatted naked in the middle of the stream; its placid pools held the first morning light. I watched Angelica collect wood, placing each branch in the crook of her arm as if she were holding a child. She must be stronger then she looks, I thought, rinsing the shampoo out of my hair. But then she might not be as old as she appeared either. Father Coriolano had told me that by the time an Indian woman is thirty she is often a grandmother. If they reach forty they have attained old age.

I washed the clothes I had worn, impaled them on a stick close to the fire, then put on a long T-shirt that reached almost to my knees. It was much more comfortable than my tight jeans.

"You smell good," Angelica said, running her fingers through my wet hair. "Does it come from the bottle?"

I nodded. "Do you want me to wash your hair?"

She hesitated for a moment, then rapidly took off her dress. She was so wrinkled that not an inch of smooth skin was left on her. She reminded me of one of the frail trees bordering the path, with their thin gray trunks, almost withered, yet supporting branches with green leaves. I had never seen Angelica naked before, for she wore her cotton dress day and night. I was certain then that she was more than forty years old—ancient, in fact, as she had told me.

Sitting in the water, Angelica shrieked and laughed with delight as she splashed around, spreading the suds from her head all over her body. With a broken gourd I rinsed off the soap, and after drying her with the thin blanket, I combed her dark short hair, shaping the bangs at an angle. "Too bad we don't have a mirror," I said. "Do I still have the red paint on?"

"Just a little bit," Angelica said, moving close to the fire. "Milagros will have to paint your face again."

"In a moment we'll be smelling like smoke," I said, turning toward Angelica's bark hammock. Easing myself inside, I wondered how she could have slept there without falling out. It was barely long enough for me and so narrow that I could not turn to the side. Yet, in spite of the itchy bark against my back and head, I found myself dozing off as I watched the old woman break the gathered wood into even-sized twigs.

An odd heaviness kept me between that crack of consciousness that is neither wakefulness nor sleep. I could feel the red of the sun through my closed lids. I was aware of Angelica to my left, mumbling to herself as she fed the fire, and of the forest around me, pulling me deeper and deeper into its green caverns. I called the old woman's name, but no sound escaped my lips. I called again and again, but only soundless forms glided out of me, rising and falling with the breeze like dead butterflies. The words began to speak without lips, mocking my desire to know, asking a thousand questions. They exploded in my ears, their echoes reverberating around me like a flock of parrots crossing the sky.

I opened my eyes, aware of the smell of singed hair. On a crudely built roasting platform, about a foot above the fire, lay a monkey, complete with tail, hands, and feet. Wistfully, I eyed Angelica's basket, still replete with cans of sardines and cassava bread.

Milagros lay in my hammock asleep, his bow leaning against a tree trunk, his quiver and machete on the ground, within reach.

"Is this all he killed?" I asked Angelica, getting out of the hammock. Hoping it would never be ready, I added, "How long will it take until it's done?"

Angelica looked at me with a rapt smile of unmistakable glee. "A bit longer," she said. "You'll like it better than sardines."

Milagros dismembered the monkey by hand, serving me the choicest part, the head, considered a delicacy. Unable to bring myself to suck out the brain from the cracked skull, I opted for a piece of the well-done thigh. It was stringy and tough and tasted like an old gamy bird, slightly bitter. Finishing the monkey's brain with rather exaggerated relish, Milagros and Angelica proceeded to eat the inner organs, which had been cooking in the embers, each individually wrapped in strong, fan-shaped leaves. They dipped each morsel in the ashes before they put them in their mouths. I did likewise with the pieces of thigh and was surprised to notice the added saltiness of the meat. What we did not finish was wrapped in leaves, tied securely with vines, and placed in Angelica's basket for our next meal.

4

The next four days and nights seemed to melt into each other as we walked, bathed, and slept. They had a dream-like quality, in which oddly shaped trees and vines repeated themselves like images endlessly reflected in invisible mirrors—images that vanished upon emerging into a clearing of the forest or by a river beach where the sun shone fully on us.

By the fifth day my feet were no longer blistered. Milagros had cut up my sneakers, attaching softened pieces of vegetable fiber to the soles. Each morning he tied the makeshift sandals anew, and my feet, as if obeying an impulse of their own, would follow Milagros and the old woman.

We walked always in silence, along trails bordered by leaves and ferns the size of a man. We crawled beneath the underbrush or cut our way through the walls of creepers and branches that left our faces dirty and scratched. There were times when I lost sight of my companions, but easily followed the twigs Milagros was in the habit of breaking as he walked. We crossed rivers and streams spanned by suspension bridges made out of vines fastened to trees on either bank. They were so fragile-looking that each time we crossed one I feared it would not support our weight.

Milagros laughed, assuring me that his people, although weak navigators, knew the art of building bridges.

On some trails we discovered footprints in the mud, which according to Milagros indicated we were in the vicinity of an Indian settlement. We never got close to one for he wanted us to reach our destination without delay. "If I were on my own I would have arrived long ago," Milagros said every time I inquired as to when we would reach Angelica's village. Then, looking at us, he would shake his head and add in a resigned tone, "Women slow you down."

But Milagros did not mind our relaxed pace. Often he made camp in the early afternoon, at some wide river beach, where we bathed in the sun-warmed pools and dried ourselves on enormous smooth rocks jutting out of the water. Drowsily we watched the motionless clouds, so slow to change their formations that it would be dusk before they disintegrated into different configurations.

It was during these lazy afternoons that I pondered over my motives in joining this bewildering venture. Was it to fulfill a fantasy of mine? Was I running away from some responsibility I could no longer handle? I even considered the possibility that Angelica might have cast a spell on me.

As the days passed my eyes became accustomed to the ever present greenness. Soon I began to distinguish red and blue macaws, rare toucans with black and yellow beaks. Once I even saw a tapir crashing through the undergrowth in search of water. It ended up as our next meal.

Monkeys with reddish fur followed us from above only to disappear as we continued through stretches of river, between cascades, and by quiet channels reflecting the sky. Buried deep in the underbrush, on moss-covered logs, red and yellow mushrooms grew, so delicate that upon my touch they disintegrated as if made of colored dust.

I tried to orient myself by the large rivers we encountered, thinking they would correspond to those I remembered in geography books. But each time I asked for their names, they never coincided with mine, for Milagros only referred to them by their Indian designations.

At night under the light of the faint fire, when a white fog seemed to emanate from the ground and I felt the dampness of the night dew on my face, Milagros would begin talking in his low nasal voice about the myths of his people.

Angelica, with her eyes wide open, as if she were trying to keep awake rather than to pay attention, would sit up straight for about ten minutes before she was fast asleep. Milagros talked long into the night, bringing alive the time when beings who were part spirit, part animal, part human, inhabited the forest—creatures who caused floods and disease, replenished the forest with game and fruits, and taught mankind about hunting and planting.

Milagros's favorite myth was about Iwrame, an alligator, who before becoming an animal of the river walked and talked like a man. Iwrame was the keeper of fire, which he hid in his mouth, refusing to share it with others. The creatures of the forest decided to entertain the alligator with a sumptuous feast, for they knew that only by making Iwrame laugh could they steal the fire. Joke upon joke was told until finally, unable to contain himself any longer, Iwrame burst into laughter. A small bird flew into the opened jaw, snatched the fire, and flew high into a sacred tree.

Without changing the basic structure of the various myths he chose to tell, Milagros modified and embellished them according to his mood. He added details that he had not thought of before, interjecting personal views that seemed to come at the spur of the moment.

"Dream, dream," Milagros said each night upon finishing his tales. "A person who dreams lives long."

* * *

Was it real, was it a dream? Was I awake or asleep when I heard Angelica stirring? She mumbled something unintelligible and sat up. Still befuddled, she pulled away the hair sticking to her face, looked around, then approached my hammock. She gazed at me with a strange intensity; her eyes were enormous in her thin, wrinkled face.

She opened her mouth; strange sounds came from her throat and her whole body began to shake. I reached out my hand, but there was nothing—only a vague shadow receding into the bushes. "Old woman, where are you going?" I heard myself ask. There was no reply—only the sound of dripping mist from the leaves. For an instant I saw her once more, the way I had seen her that same afternoon bathing in the river; then she vanished in the thick night fog.

Without being able to stop her, I saw how she disappeared into an invisible crevice of the earth. No matter how much I searched I could not even find her dress. It's only a dream, I repeated to myself, yet I continued looking for her among the shadows, amidst the leaves shrouded in mist. But there was no vestige of her.

I awoke with a profound anxiety. I noticed the heavy palpitations of my heart. The sun was already high above the treetops. I had never slept so late since starting our journey—not because I had not wanted to, but because Milagros insisted we rise at dawn. Angelica was not there; neither were her hammock or basket. Leaning against a tree trunk were Milagros's bow and arrows. Strange, I thought. He had never left without them before. He must have gone with the old woman to gather the fruits or nuts he discovered yesterday afternoon, I kept repeating to myself, trying to appease my mounting distress.

I walked to the water's edge, not knowing what to do. They had never gone together before, leaving me behind.

A tree, infinitely lonely, stood at the other bank of the river, its branches bowed over the water, their weight supporting a network of creepers on which delicate red flowers bloomed. They clung like trapped butterflies in a gigantic spider's web.

A flock of parrots noisily settled on some vines that appeared to be growing out of the water without any visible support, for I could not distinguish the trees to which they belonged. I began to imitate the parrot's shrieks, but they remained completely unaware of my existence. Only when I walked into the water did they take flight, spanning a green arch across the sky.

I waited until the sun disappeared beyond the trees and the blood red sky tainted the river with its fire. Listlessly I walked back to my hammock, poked the fire, and tried to revive the ashes. I became numb with terror as a green snake with amber-colored eyes stared into my face. With its head poised in midair, it seemed as startled as I. Afraid to breathe, I listened to the rustling of leaves as it slowly disappeared among the gnarled roots.

With absolute certainty I knew that never again would I see Angelica. I did not want to weep but could not control my tears as I buried my face in the dead leaves on the ground. "Old woman, where have you gone?" I whispered, as I had done in my dream. I called her name across the immense green sea of growth. There was no answer from the ancient trees. Mutely, they witnessed my sorrow.

I barely made out Milagros's figure in the thickening shadows. Rigid, he stood before me, his face and body blackened by ashes. For an instant he held my gaze, then his eyes closed, his legs bent beneath him, and, exhausted, he sank to the earth.

"Did you bury her?" I asked, draping his arm over my shoulders in order to drag him toward my hammock. With great difficulty I lifted him inside—first his torso, then his legs.

He opened his eyes, stretching his hand toward the sky as if the distant clouds were within his reach. "Her soul ascended to heaven, to the house of thunder," he said with great effort. "The fire released her soul from her bones," he added, then fell into a deep sleep.

As I watched over his restless dreams, I saw the shadowy bulk of phantom trees grow before my tired eyes. In the darkness of the night, these chimerical trees seemed more real and taller than the palms. I was no longer sad. Angelica had disappeared in my dream; she was part of the real and the fictitious trees. Forever she would roam among the spirits of vanished animals and mythical beings.

It was almost dawn when Milagros reached for his machete and his bow and arrows lying on the ground. Absentmindedly he hung his quiver on his back and without saying a word he walked into the thicket. I followed, afraid to lose him among the shadows.

In silence we walked for about two hours, then Milagros abruptly stopped by the edge of a cleared area in the forest. "The smoke of the dead is harmful to women and children," he said, pointing to a log pyre. It had partly collapsed and in the midst of the ashes I could see darkened bones.

I sat on the ground and watched Milagros dry over a small fire a log mortar that he had made from a tree trunk. Something between horror and fascination kept my eyes glued on Milagros as he began sifting through the ashes for Angelica's bones. He crushed them with a slender pole until they were reduced to a gray-black powder.

"Through the smoke of the fire, her soul reached the house of thunder," Milagros said. It was already night when he filled our gourds with the powdered bones. He sealed them with a sticky resin.

"If she could only have kept death waiting a little longer," I said wistfully.

"It makes no difference," Milagros said, looking up from the mortar. His face was without expression yet his black eyes were bright with unshed tears. His lower lip trembled then set in a half smile. "All she wanted was for her life essence to be once again part of her people."

"It's not the same," I said, without really understanding what Milagros was saying.

"Her life essence is in her bones," he said, as if excusing my ignorance. "Her ashes will be among her people in the forest."

"She isn't alive," I insisted. "What good are her ashes when she had wanted to see her people?" An uncontrollable sadness overcame me at the thought that never again would I see the old woman's smile or hear her voice and laughter. "She never got to tell me why she was so certain I would come with her."

Milagros began to cry, and picking up pieces of coal from the pyre, he rubbed them against his tear-stained face. "One of our shamans told Angelica that although she would leave her settlement, she would die among her own people and her soul would remain a part of her tribe." Milagros looked at me sharply as I was about to interrupt him. "The shaman assured her that a girl with the color of your hair and eyes would make sure that she did."

"But I thought her people had no contact with whites," I said.

Tears still flowed from Milagros's eyes as he explained that there had been a time when his people had lived closer to the big river. "Nowadays there are only some old people left who still remember those days," he said softly. "For a long time we have been moving farther and farther into the forest."

I see no reason to continue the journey, I thought despondently. What would I do without the old woman among her people. She had been my reason for being here. "What shall I do now? Are you going to take me back to the mission?" I asked, then seeing Milagros's puzzled expression, added, "It's not the same to take her ashes."

"It is the same," he murmured. "For her it was the most important part," he added, tying one of the ash-filled gourds around my waist.

My body stiffened for an instant, then relaxed as I looked into Milagros's eyes. His blackened face was awesome and sad at the same time. He pressed his tear-stained cheeks against mine, then blackened them with coals. Timidly I touched the gourd around my waist; it was light, like the old woman's laughter.

5

For two days, at an ever accelerating pace, we walked up and down hills without rest. Apprehensively, I watched Milagros's silent figure slip in and out of the shadows. The urgency of his movements only intensified my feelings of uncertainty; there were moments when I felt like screaming at him to take me back to the mission.

The afternoon closed over the forest as the clouds turned from white to gray to black. Heavy and oppressive, they hovered over the treetops. A deafening roar of thunder broke the stillness; water came down in sheets, tearing at branches and leaves with relentless fury.

Motioning me to take cover under the gigantic leaves he had cut, Milagros squatted on the ground. Instead of joining him, I took off my knapsack, untied the gourd filled with Angelica's powdered bones from around my waist, and pulled off my T-shirt. Warm and soothing, the water beat against my aching body. Lathering first my head, then my body with shampoo, I washed away the ashes, the smell of death from my skin. I turned to look at Milagros; his blackened face was drawn with fatigue, his eyes held such sadness that I regretted having cleaned myself in such haste. Nervously I began to wash my T-shirt and without looking at him asked, "Are we almost to the settlement?" I was certain we had walked well over a hundred miles since leaving the mission.

"We will be there tomorrow," Milagros said, unwrapping a small bundle of roasted meat held together with lianas and leaves. A peculiar smile lifted the corners of his mouth and deepened the wrinkles around his slanted eyes. "That is, if we walk at my pace."

The rain thinned. The clouds dispersed. I breathed deeply, filling my lungs with the clear, fresh air. Drops continued to trickle from the leaves long after the rain abated. As they caught the reflection of the sun they glittered with the dazzling intensity of bits of broken glass.

"I hear someone coming," Milagros whispered. "Stay still."

I heard nothing—not even the call of a bird or the rustling of leaves. I was about to say so when a branch cracked and a naked man appeared on the path in front of us. He was not much taller than myself—perhaps five feet four. I wondered if it was his muscular chest or his nakedness that made him seem so much bigger than me. He carried a long bow and several arrows. His face and body were covered with red serpentine lines that extended all the way down the sides of his legs, ending in dots around his ankles.

A short distance behind him, two naked young women stared at me. A frozen expression of surprise held their dark eyes wide open. Tufts of fibers seemed to grow from their ears. Matchlike sticks stuck out from the corners of their mouths and lower lips. Fastened about their waists, upper arms, wrists, and below their knees were bands of red cotton string. Their dark hair was cut short, and like the man, they had a clean, wide-shaven tonsure on the crown.

No one said a word and out of sheer nervousness I shouted, *"Shori noje, shori noje!"* Angelica had advised me that if I ever happened to meet Indians in the forest, I should greet them by shouting: Good friend, good friend!

"*Aia, aia, shori,*" the man answered, moving closer. Red feathers adorned his ears; they were sticking out of two pieces of short cane, the size of my little finger, which were inserted through each lobe. He began to speak to Milagros, gesticulating a great deal, motioning with his hand or a nod of his head toward the path leading into the thicket. Repeatedly he raised one of his arms straight above his head, his fingers extended as if reaching for a ray of sunlight.

I beckoned the women to come closer. Giggling, they hid behind bushes. When I saw the bananas in the baskets fastened to their backs I opened my mouth wide and gestured with my hands that I wanted to eat one of them. Cautiously the older of the two women approached, and without looking at me she unfastened her basket, then broke the softest, yellowest banana from the bunch. In one swift motion she removed the slender sticks from around her mouth, sank her teeth in the peel, bit along it, broke it open, then held the naked fruit in front of my face. It had an oddly triangular shape and was certainly the thickest banana I had ever seen.

"Delicious," I said in Spanish, rubbing my stomach. It tasted very much like an ordinary banana but left a heavy coating in my mouth.

She gave me two more. As she was peeling the fourth I tried to make her understand that I could not eat another. Grinning, she dropped the remaining fruit on the ground, then placed her hands on my stomach. They were calloused hands, yet the delicate, slender fingers were gentle as she hesitantly touched my breasts, shoulders, and face, as if she wanted to verify that I was real. She began to talk in a high-pitched nasal tone that reminded me of Angelica's voice. She pulled the elastic on my panties and called her companion to take a look. It was only then that I felt embarrassed; I tried to pull away. Laughing and squealing with delight, they embraced me, stroking the back and front of my body. Then they took my hand and guided it over their own faces and bodies. They were slightly shorter than I, yet they were massive; with their full breasts, protruding stomachs, and wide hips, they seemed to dwarf me.

"They are from the Iticoteri village," Milagros said in Spanish, turning toward me. "Etewa and his two wives, Ritimi and Tutemi, as well as other people from the settlement, have made camp for a few days at an old abandoned garden nearby." He reached for his bow and arrows, which he had left leaning against a tree trunk, and added, "We will travel with them."

Meanwhile the women had discovered my wet T-shirt. Enthralled, they rubbed it against their painted faces and bodies before I had a chance to slip it over my head. Stretched and streaked with red *onoto* paste, it hung on me like a dirty oversized rice sack.

I put the ash-filled gourd in my knapsack and as I lifted it on my back the women began to giggle uncontrollably. Etewa came to stand next to me; he stared at me with his brown eyes, then a wide grin lit his face as he ran his fingers through my hair. His finely chiseled nose and the gentle curve of his lips gave his round face an almost girlish appearance.

"I will go with Etewa to track down a tapir he spotted a while ago," Milagros said. "You walk with the women."

For an instant I could only stare at him in disbelief. "But . . ." I finally managed to utter, not knowing what else to say. I must have looked comical for Milagros began to laugh; his slanted eyes all but disappeared between his forehead and his high cheekbones. He put one hand on my shoulder. He tried to look serious but a flickering smile remained on his lips.

"These are Angelica's and my people," he said, turning toward Etewa and his two wives. "Ritimi is her grandniece. Angelica never saw her."

I smiled at the two women; they nodded their heads as if they had understood Milagros's words.

Milagros's and Etewa's laughter echoed through the lianas, then died away as they reached the bamboo thicket bordering the path along the river. Ritimi took my hand and led me into the thicket.

I walked between Ritimi and Tutemi. We moved silently in single file toward the abandoned gardens of the Iticoteri. I wondered whether it was because of the heavy load on their backs or whether it gave their feet a better grip on the ground that they walked with their knees and toes pointing inward. Our shadows grew and diminished with the faint rays of sunlight filtering through the treetops. My ankles were weak from exhaustion. I moved clumsily, stumbling over branches and roots. Ritimi put her arm around my waist, but it made walking on the narrow path even more awkward. She pulled the knapsack from my back and stuffed it in Tutemi's basket.

I was seized by an odd apprehension. I wanted to retrieve my knapsack, pull out the ash-filled gourd, and tie it around my waist. I had the vague notion of having severed some kind of a bond. Had I been asked to put my feelings into words I would not have been able to do so. Yet I sensed that from that moment on some of the magic and enchantment Angelica had transfused into me had vanished.

The sun was already below the horizon of trees as we reached a clearing in the forest. Amidst all the other shades of green I clearly distinguished the lighter, almost translucent green of the plantain fronds. Strung out on the edge of what once must have been a large garden were low triangular-shaped huts arranged in a semicircle with their backs to the forest. The dwellings were open on all sides except for the roofs, which were covered with several layers of broad banana leaves.

As if someone had given a signal, we were instantly surrounded by open-mouthed, wide-eyed women and men. I held on to Ritimi's arm; her having walked with me through the forest made her different from these gaping figures. Encircling me by the waist, she drew me close to her. The rapid, excited tone of her voice kept the crowd at bay for a moment longer. Suddenly their faces were only inches away from mine. Saliva dribbled down their chins and their features were disfigured by the tobacco wads stuck between their gums and lower lips. I forgot all about the objectivity with which an anthropologist is to regard another culture. At the moment these Indians were nothing more than a group of ugly, dirty people. I closed my eyes only to open them the next instant as an unsteady bony hand touched my cheeks. It was an old man. Grinning, he began to shout: *"Aia, aia, aiiia shori!"*

Echoing his shouts, everyone at once tried to embrace me, almost crushing me with joy. They managed to pull my T-shirt over my head. I felt their hands, lips, and tongues on my face and body. They smelled of smoke and earth; their saliva, which clung to my skin, smelled of rotten tobacco leaves. Appalled, I burst into tears.

With apprehensive expressions on their faces, they pulled away. Although I could not understand their words, their tone clearly revealed their bewilderment.

Later that night I learned from Milagros that Ritimi had explained to the group that she had found me in the forest. At first she had believed I was a spirit and had been afraid to come near me. Only after she had seen me devour the bananas was she convinced I was human, for only humans eat that greedily.

Between my hammock and Milagros's burned a fire; smoking and sputtering, it threw a faint light over the open hut, leaving the trees outside in one solid mass of darkness. It was a reddish light that combined with the smoke made my eyes water. People sat around the fire, so close to each other their shoulders touched. Their shadowed faces looked all the same to me; the red and black designs on their bodies seemed to have a life of their own as they moved and twisted with each gesture.

Ritimi sat on the ground, her legs fully extended, her left arm resting against my hammock. Her skin was a soft deep yellow in the wavering light; the painted lines on her face ran toward her temples, accentuating her Asiatic features. Clearly I could see the small holes, free of the sticks, at the corners of her mouth, lower lip, and the septum of her wide nostrils. Aware of my stare, she looked at me directly, her round face creasing into a smile. She had square short teeth; they were strong and very white.

I began to doze off to the gentle murmur of their voices, yet slept fitfully, wondering what Milagros was telling them as I kept waking to the sound of laughter.

PART TWO

6

"When do you think you'll be back?" I asked Milagros six months later, handing him the letter I had written to Father Coriolano at the mission. In it I briefly notified him that I intended to stay for at least two more months with the Iticoteri. I asked him to inform my friends in Caracas; and most important of all, I begged him to send with Milagros as many writing pads and pencils as he could spare. "When will you be back?" I asked again.

"In two weeks or so," Milagros said casually, fitting the letter into his bamboo quiver. He must have detected the anxiousness in my face for he added, "There is no way to tell, but I'll be back."

I watched as he started down the path leading to the river. He adjusted the quiver on his back, then turned to me briefly, his movements momentarily arrested as though there were something he wished to say. Instead he lifted his hand to wave good-bye.

Slowly I headed back to the *shabono*, passing several men felling trees next to the gardens. Carefully I stepped around the logs cluttered all over the cleared patch, making sure not to cut my feet on the pieces of bark, chips, and slivers of wood buried amidst the dead leaves on the ground.

"He'll be back as soon as the plantains are ripe," Etewa shouted, waving his hand the way Milagros had just done. "He won't miss the feast."

Smiling, I waved back, wanting to ask when the feast would take place. I did not need to; he had already given me the answer: When the plantains were ripe.

The brush and logs that were scattered each night in front of the main entrance of the *shabono* to keep out intruders had already been moved aside. It was still early, yet the huts facing the round, open clearing were mostly empty. Women and men were working in the nearby gardens or had gone into the forest to gather wild fruits, honey, and firewood.

Armed with miniature bows and arrows, a group of little boys gathered around me. "See the lizard I killed," Sisiwe said, holding the dead animal by the tail.

"That's all he can do—shoot lizards," a boy in the group said mockingly, scratching his ankle with the toes of his other foot. "And most of the time he misses."

"I don't," Sisiwe shouted, his face turning red with rage.

I caressed the stubbles on the crown of his head. In the sunlight his hair was not black but a reddish brown. Searching for the right words from my limited vocabulary, I hoped to assure him that one day he would be the best hunter in the settlement.

Sisiwe, Ritimi's and Etewa's son, was six, at the most seven, years old for he did not yet wear a pubic waist string. Ritimi, believing that the sooner a boy tied his penis against his abdomen the faster he would grow, had repeatedly forced the child to do so. But Sisiwe had refused, arguing that it hurt. Etewa had not insisted. His son was growing healthy and strong. Soon, the father had argued, Sisiwe would realize that it was improper for a man to be seen without a waist string. Like most children, Sisiwe wore a piece of fragrant root tied around his neck, a charm against disease, and as soon as the designs on his body faded, he was painted anew with *onoto*.

Smiling, his anger forgotten, Sisiwe held on to my hand and in one swift motion climbed up on me as if I were a tree. He wrapped his legs around my waist. He swung backward and, stretching his arms toward the sky, shouted, "Look how blue it is—the color of your eyes."

From the middle of the clearing the sky seemed immense. There were no trees, lianas, or leaves to mar its splendor. The dense vegetation loomed outside the *shabono*, beyond the palisades of logs protecting the settlement. The trees appeared to bide their time, as if they knew they were only provisionally held in check.

Tugging at my arm, the children pulled me together with Sisiwe to the ground. At first I had not been able to associate them with any particular parent for they wandered in and out of the huts, eating and sleeping wherever it was convenient. I only knew where the babies belonged, for they were perennially hanging around their mother's bodies. Whether it was day or night, the infants never seemed disturbed, regardless of what activity their mothers were engaged in.

I wondered how I would do without Milagros. Each day he had spent several hours teaching me the language, customs, and beliefs of his people, which I eagerly recorded in my notepads.

Learning who was who among the Iticoteri proved to be most confusing. They never called each other by name, except when someone was to be insulted. Ritimi and Etewa were known as Mother and Father of Sisiwe and Texoma. (It was permissible to use children's names, but as soon as they reached puberty everyone refrained from it.) Matters were further complicated in that males and females from a given lineage called each other brother and sister; males and females from another lineage were referred to as brother-in-law and sister-in-law. A male who married a woman from an eligible lineage called all the women of that lineage wives, but did not have sexual contact with them.

Milagros often pointed out that it was not only I who had to adapt. The Iticoteri were just as baffled by my odd behavior; to them I was neither woman, man, or child, and as such they did not quite know what to think of me or where they could fit me in.

Old Hayama emerged from her hut. In a high-pitched voice she told the children to leave me alone. "Her stomach is still empty," she said. Putting her arm around my waist, she led me to the hearth in her hut.

Making sure not to step on or collide with any of the aluminum and enamel cooking pots (acquired through trade with other settlements), the tortoise shells, gourds, and baskets scattered on the ground, I sat across from Hayama. I extended my legs fully, in the way of the Iticoteri women, and scratching the head of her pet parrot, I waited for the food.

"Eat," she said, handing me a baked plantain on a broken calabash. Attentively the old woman watched as I chewed with my mouth open, smacking my lips repeatedly. She smiled, content that I was fully appreciating the soft sweet plantain.

Hayama had been introduced to me by Milagros as Angelica's sister. Every time I looked at her I tried to find some resemblance to the frail old woman I had lost in the forest. About five feet four, Hayama was tall for an Iticoteri woman. Not only was she physically different from Angelica, but she did not have her sister's lightness of spirit. There was a harshness to Hayama's voice and manner that often made me feel uncomfortable. And her heavy, drooping eyelids gave her face a peculiarly sinister expression.

"You stay here with me until Milagros returns," the old woman said, serving me another baked plantain.

I stuffed the hot fruit in my mouth so I would not have to answer. Milagros had introduced me to his brother-in-law Arasuwe, who was the headman of the Iticoteri, as well as to the other members of the settlement. However, it was Ritimi who, by hanging my hammock in the hut she shared with Etewa and their two children, had made it known that I belonged to her. "The white girl sleeps here," she had said to Milagros, explaining that little Texoma and Sisiwe would have their hammocks hung around Tutemi's hearth in the adjoining hut.

No one had interfered with Ritimi's scheme. Silently, a smile of gentle mockery on his face, Etewa had watched as Ritimi rushed between their hut and Tutemi's, rearranging the hammocks in the customary triangle around the fire. On a small loft built between the back poles supporting the dwelling, she placed my knapsack, amidst bark boxes, an assortment of baskets, an ax, and gourds with *onoto,* seeds, and roots.

Ritimi's self-assuredness stemmed not only from the fact that she was the headman Arasuwe's oldest daughter—by his first wife, a daughter of old Hayama, now dead—and that she was Etewa's first and favorite wife, but also because Ritimi knew that in spite of her quick temper everyone in the *shabono* respected and liked her.

"No more," I pleaded with Hayama as she took another plantain from the fire. "My belly is full." Pulling up my T-shirt, I pushed out my stomach so she could see how filled it looked.

"You need to grow fat around your bones," the old woman said, mashing up the banana with her fingers. "Your breasts are as small as a child's." Giggling, she pulled my T-shirt up further. "No man will ever want you—he'll be afraid to hurt himself on the bones."

Opening my eyes wide in mock horror, I pretended to gobble down the mush. "I'll surely get fat and beautiful eating your food," I said with my mouth full.

Still wet from her river bath, Ritimi came into the hut combing her hair with a densely thistled pod. Sitting next to me, she put her arms around my neck and planted resounding kisses on my face. I had to restrain myself from laughing. The Iticoteri's kisses tickled me. They kissed differently; each time they put their mouth against my cheek and neck they vibrated their lips while sonorously ejecting air.

"You are not moving the white girl's hammock in here," Ritimi said, looking at her grandmother. The certainty of her tone was not matched by the inquiring softness of her dark eyes.

Not wanting to be the cause of an argument, I made it clear that it did not make much difference where my hammock hung. Since there were no walls between the huts, we practically lived together. Hayama's hut stood on Tutemi's left, and on our right was Arasuwe the headman's, which he shared with his oldest wife and three of his smallest children. His other two wives and their respective offspring occupied adjacent huts.

Ritimi fixed her gaze on me, a pleading expression in her eyes. "Milagros asked me to take care of you," she said, running the thistled pod through my hair, softly, so as not to scratch my scalp.

After what seemed an interminable silence, Hayama finally said, "You can leave your hammock where it is, but you will eat here with me."

It was a good arrangement, I thought. Etewa already had four mouths to feed. Hayama, on the other hand, was taken good care of by her youngest son. Judging by the amount of animal skulls and plantains hanging from the thatched palm roof, her son was a good hunter and cultivator. Other than the baked plantains eaten in the morning, there was only one meal, in the late afternoon, when families gathered together to eat. People snacked throughout the day on whatever was available—fruit, nuts, or such delicacies as roasted ants and grubs.

Ritimi also seemed pleased with the eating arrangement. Smiling, she walked over to our hut, pulled down the basket she had given me, which was hanging above my hammock, then took out my notepad and pencil. "Now let us work," she said in a commanding tone.

In the days that followed Ritimi taught me about her people as Milagros had done for the past six months. He had set up a few hours each day for what I referred to as formal instruction.

At first I had great difficulty in learning the language. Not only did I find it to be heavily nasal, but it was extremely difficult to understand people when they talked with wads of tobacco in their mouths. I tried to devise some sort of a comparative grammar but gave it up when I realized that not only did I not have the proper linguistic training, but the more I tried to be rational about learning their language, the less I could speak.

My best teachers were the children. Although they pointed things out to me and greatly enjoyed giving me words to repeat, they made no conscious effort to explain anything. With them I was able to rattle on, totally uninhibited about making mistakes. After Milagros's departure, there was still much I did not comprehend, yet I was astonished by how well I managed to communicate with others, reading correctly the inflection of their voices, the expression on their faces, and the eloquent movements of their hands and bodies.

During those hours of formal instruction, Ritimi took me to visit the women in the different huts and I was allowed to ask questions to my heart's content. Baffled by my curiosity, the women talked freely, as if they were playing a game. They patiently explained again and again whatever I did not understand.

I was grateful Milagros had set that precedent. Not only was curiosity regarded as bad manners, but it went against their will to be questioned. Yet Milagros had lavishly indulged me in what he called my eccentric whim, stating that the more I knew about the language and customs of the Iticoteri, the quicker I would feel at home with them.

It soon became apparent that I did not need to ask too many direct questions. Often the most casual remark on my part was reciprocated by a flow of information I would not have dreamed of eliciting.

Each day, just before nightfall, aided by Ritimi and Tutemi, I would go over the data gathered during the day and try to order it under some kind of classificatory scheme such as social structure, cultural values, subsistence techniques, and other universal categories of human social behavior.

However, to my great disappointment, there was one subject Milagros had not touched upon: shamanism. I had observed from my hammock two curing sessions, of which I had written detailed accounts.

"Arasuwe is a great *shapori*," Milagros had said to me as I watched my first curing ritual.

"Does he invoke the help of the spirits when he chants?" I asked as I watched Milagros's brother-in-law massage, suck, and rub the prostrate body of a child.

Milagros had given me an outraged look. "There are things one doesn't talk about." He had gotten up abruptly and before walking out of the hut had added, "Don't ask about these things. If you do, you will run into serious trouble."

I had not been surprised by his response, but I had been

unprepared for his outright anger. I wondered if his refusal to talk about the subject was because I was a woman or rather that shamanism was a taboo topic. I did not dare to find out at the time. Being a woman, white, and alone was precarious enough.

I was aware that in most societies knowledge regarding shamanistic and curing practices are never revealed except to the initiates. During Milagros's absence I did not mention the word shamanism once but spent hours deliberating over what would be the best way to learn about it without arousing any anger and suspicion.

From my notes on the two sessions it became evident that the Iticoteri believed the *shapori*'s body underwent a change when under the influence of the hallucinogenic snuff *epena*. That is, the shaman acted under the assumption that his human body transformed itself into a supernatural body. Thus he made contact with the spirits in the forest. My obvious approach would be to arrive at an understanding of shamanism via the body—not as an object determined by psychochemical laws, holistic forces in nature, the environment, or the psyche itself, but through an understanding of the body as lived experience, the body as an expressive unity known through performance.

Most studies on shamanism, including mine, have focused on the psychotherapeutic and social aspects of healing. I thought that my approach would not only provide a novel explanation but would furnish me with a way of learning about curing without becoming suspect. Questions concerning the body need not necessarily be associated with shamanism. I had no doubt that little by little I would retrieve the necessary data without the Iticoteri ever being aware of what I was really after.

Any pangs of conscience I felt regarding the dishonesty of my task were quickly stilled by repeating to myself that my work was important for the understanding of non-

Western healing practices. The strange, often bizarre customs of shamanism would become understandable in the light of a different interpretational context, thus furthering anthropological knowledge in general.

"You haven't worked for two days," Ritimi said to me one afternoon. "You haven't asked about last night's songs and dances. Don't you know they are important? If we don't sing and dance the hunters will return without meat for the feast." Scowling, she threw the notepad into my lap. "You haven't even painted in your book."

"I'm resting for a few days," I said, clutching the notepad against my breast as if it were the dearest thing I possessed. I had no intention of letting her know that every precious page was to be filled exclusively with data on shamanism.

Ritimi took my hands in hers, examined them intently, then, assuming a very serious expression, commented, "They look very tired—they need rest."

We burst out laughing. Ritimi had always been baffled that I considered decorating my book to be work. To her work meant digging weeds in the garden, collecting firewood, and repairing the roof of the *shabono*.

"I liked the dances and songs very much," I said. "I recognized your voice—it was beautiful."

Ritimi beamed at me. "I sing very well." There was a charming candor and assurance in her statement; she was not boasting but only stating a fact. "I'm sure the hunters will return with plenty of game to feed the guests at the feast."

Nodding in agreement, I looked for a twig, then began to sketch a human figure on the soft dirt. "This is the body of a white person," I said as I sketched the main organs and bones. "I wonder how the body of an Iticoteri looks?"

"You must be very tired to ask such a stupid question,"

Ritimi said, staring at me as if I were dim-witted. She stood up and began to dance, chanting in a loud melodious voice: "This is my head, this is my arm, this is my breast, this is my stomach, this is my . . ."

In no time at all, attracted by Ritimi's antics, a group of women and men gathered around us. Squealing and laughing, they made obscene remarks about each other's bodies. Some of the adolescent boys were laughing so hard, they rolled on the ground, holding their penises.

"Can anyone draw a body the way I drew mine?" I asked.

Several responded to this challenge. Grabbing a piece of wood, a twig, or a broken bow, they began to draw on the dirt. Their drawings differed markedly from each other's, not only because of the obvious sexual differences, which they made sure to emphasize, but because all the men's bodies were depicted with tiny figures inside the chest.

I could hardly hide my delight. I thought these must be the spirits I had heard Arasuwe summon with his chant before he began the curing session. "What are these?" I asked casually.

"The *hekuras* of the forest who live in a man's chest," one of the men said.

"Are all men *shapori*?"

"All men have *hekuras* in their chests," the man said. "But only a real *shapori* can make use of them. Only a great *shapori* can command his *hekuras* to aid the sick and counteract the spells of enemy *shapori*." Studying my sketch, he asked, "Why does your picture have *hekuras*, even in the legs? Women don't have *hekuras*."

I explained that these were not spirits, but organs and bones, and they promptly added them to their own drawings. Content with what I had learned, I willingly accompanied Ritimi to gather firewood in the forest—the women's most arduous and unwelcome task. They could never get enough wood, for the fires were never allowed to die.

That evening, as she had done every night since I arrived at the settlement, Ritimi examined my feet for thorns and splinters. Satisfied that there were none, she rubbed them clean with her hands.

"I wonder if the bodies of the *shapori* go through some kind of transformation when they are under the influence of *epena*," I said. It was important to have it confirmed in their own words, since the original premise of my theoretical scheme was that the shaman operated under certain assumptions concerning the body. I needed to know if these assumptions were shared by the group and if they were of a conscious or unconscious nature.

"Did you see Iramamowe yesterday?" Ritimi asked. "Did you see him walk? His feet didn't touch the ground. He is a powerful *shapori*. He became the great jaguar."

"He didn't cure anyone," I said glumly. It disappointed me that Arasuwe's brother was considered a great shaman. I had seen him beat his wife on two occasions.

No longer interested in pursuing the conversation, Ritimi turned away from me and began to get ready for our evening ritual. Lifting the basket that held my belongings from the small loft at the back of the hut, she placed it on the ground. One by one she took out each item and held it above her head, waiting for me to identify it. As soon as I did she repeated the name in Spanish, then in English, starting a nocturnal chorus as the headman's wives and several other women who each night gathered in our hut echoed the foreign words.

I relaxed in my hammock as Tutemi's fingers parted my hair searching for imaginary lice; I was certain I did not have any—not yet. Tutemi appeared to be five or six years younger than Ritimi, whom I believed to be twenty. She was taller and heavier, her stomach round with her first pregnancy. She was shy and retiring. Often I had discovered a sad, faraway look in her dark eyes, and at times she talked to herself as if she were thinking aloud.

"Lice! Lice!" Tutemi shouted, interrupting the women's Spanish-English chant.

"Let me see," I said, convinced that she was joking. "Are lice white?" I asked, examining the tiny white bugs on her finger. I had always believed they were dark.

"White girl, white lice," Tutemi said mischievously. With gleeful delight she crunched them one by one between her teeth and swallowed them. "All lice are white."

7

It was the day of the feast. Since noon I had been under the
ministrations of Ritimi and Tutemi, who took great
trouble to beautify me. With a sharpened piece of bamboo
Tutemi cut my hair in the customary style, and with a
knife-sharp grass blade she shaved the crown of my head.
The hair on my legs she removed with an abrasive paste
made from ashes, vegetable resin, and dirt.

Ritimi painted wavy lines across my face and intricate
geometric patterns over my entire body with a piece of
chewed-up twig. My legs, red and swollen from the depila-
tion, were left unpainted. On my looped earrings, which I
claimed could not be removed, she tied a pink flower together with tufts of white feathers. Around my upper
arms, wrists, and ankles she fastened red cotton strands.

"Oh no. You're not going to do that," I said, jumping
out of Ritimi's reach.

"It won't hurt," she assured me, then asked in an exasperated manner, "Do you want to look like an old
woman? It won't hurt," Ritimi insisted, coming after me.

"Leave her alone," Etewa said, reaching for a bark box
on the loft. He looked at me, then burst into laughter. His
big white teeth, his squinting eyes seemed to mock my
embarrassment. "She doesn't have much pubic hair."

Gratefully I tied the red cotton belt Ritimi had given me around my hips and laughed with him. Making sure I fastened the wide flat belt in such a manner that the fringed ends covered the offending hair, I said to Ritimi, "Now you can't see a thing."

Ritimi was not impressed but gave an indifferent shrug and continued examining her pubis for any hair.

Dark circles and arabesques decorated Etewa's brown face and body. Over his waistband he tied a thick round belt made of red cotton yarn; around his upper arms he fastened narrow bands of monkey fur, to which Ritimi attached the black and white feathers Etewa had selected from the bark box.

Dipping her fingers in the sticky resin paste one of Arasuwe's wives had prepared in the morning, Ritimi wiped them over Etewa's hair. Immediately Tutemi took a handful of white down feathers from another box and plastered them on his head until he looked as if he were wearing a white fur cap.

"When will the feast start?" I asked, watching a group of men haul away enormous piles of plantain skins from the already cleaned, weed-free clearing.

"When the plantain soup and all the meat is ready," Etewa said, strutting about, making sure we could see him from every angle. His lips were twisted in a smile and his humorous eyes still squinted. He looked at me, then removed the wad of tobacco from his mouth. Placing it on a piece of broken calabash on the ground, he spat over his hammock in a sharp, strong arc. With the assurance of someone who feels pleased and delighted with his own looks, he turned toward us once more, then walked out of the hut.

Little Texoma picked up the slimy quid. Stuffing it into her mouth she began to suck on it with the same gratification I would have felt biting into a piece of chocolate. Her small face, disfigured with half of the wad protruding from her mouth, looked grotesque. Grinning, she climbed into my hammock and promptly fell asleep.

In the next hut I could see the headman Arasuwe lying in his hammock. From there he supervised the cooking of plantains and the roasting of the meat, brought by the hunters who had left a few days before. Like workers on an assembly line, several men had in record time disposed of the numerous bundles of plantains. One sank his sharp teeth into the peel, cutting it open; another pried the hard skin away, then threw the fruit into the bark trough Etewa had built early that morning; a third watched over the three small fires he had lit underneath.

"How come only men are cooking?" I asked Tutemi. I knew women never cooked large game, but I was baffled that none of them had even gotten close to the plantains.

"Women are too careless," Arasuwe answered for Tutemi as he stepped into the hut. His eyes seemed to challenge me to contradict his statement. Smiling, he added, "They get distracted too easily and let the fire burn through the bark."

Before I had a chance to say anything, he was back in his hammock. "Did he only come in to say that?"

"No," Ritimi said. "He came to look you over."

I was reluctant to ask if I had passed Arasuwe's inspection lest I remind her of my unplucked pubic hair. "Look," I said, "visitors are arriving."

"That's Puriwariwe, Angelica's oldest brother," Ritimi said, pointing to an old man among the group of men. "He is a feared *shapori*. He was killed once but didn't die."

"Killed once but didn't die." I repeated this slowly, wondering if I was supposed to take it literally or if it was a figure of speech.

"Killed in a raid," Etewa said, walking into the hut. "Dead, dead, dead, but didn't die." He spoke distinctly, moving his lips in an exaggerated manner as if he could thus make me understand the true meaning of his words.

"Are there still raids taking place?"

No one answered my question. Etewa reached for a long hollow cane and a small gourd hidden behind one of the rafters, then left us to greet the visitors who stood in the middle of the clearing facing Arasuwe's hut.

More men walked into the compound and I wondered aloud if any women had been invited to the feast.

"They are outside," Ritimi said. "With the rest of the guests, decorating themselves while the men take *epena*."

The headman Arasuwe, his brother Iramamowe, Etewa, and six other Iticoteri men—all decorated with feathers, fur, and red *onoto* paste—squatted face to face with the visitors, who were already on their haunches. They talked for a while, avoiding one another's eyes.

Arasuwe unfastened the small gourd hanging around his neck, poured some of the brownish-green powder into one end of his hollow cane, then faced Angelica's brother. Placing the end of the cane against the shaman's nose, Arasuwe blew the hallucinogenic powder with great force into one of the old man's nostrils. The shaman did not flinch, groan, or stagger off, as I had seen other men do. But his eyes did become bleary and soon green slime dripped from his nose and mouth, which he flicked away with a twig. Slowly he began to chant. I did not catch his words; they were spoken too softly, and the groans of the others drowned them out.

Glassy-eyed, with mucus and saliva dripping down his chin and chest, Arasuwe jumped into the air. The red macaw feathers hanging from his ears and arms fluttered around him. He jumped repeatedly, touching the ground with a lightness that seemed incredible in someone so stockily built. His face seemed to be carved in stone. Straight bangs hung over a jutting brow. The wide, flaring nose, the snarling mouth reminded me of one of the four guardian kings I had once seen in a temple in Japan.

A few of the men had staggered away from the rest of the group, holding their heads as they vomited. The old man's chant became louder; one by one the men gathered once more around him. Quietly, they squatted, their folded arms over their knees, their eyes lost on some invisible spot only they could see, until the *shapori* finished his song.

Each of the Iticoteri men returned to his hut accompanied by a guest. Arasuwe had invited Puriwariwe; Etewa walked into his hut with one of the young men who had vomited. Without glancing at us, the guest stretched in Etewa's hammock as if it were his own; he did not look older than sixteen.

"Why didn't all the Iticoteri men take *epena* or decorate themselves?" I whispered to Ritimi, who was busy cleaning and repainting Etewa's face with *onoto*.

"Tomorrow they will all be decorated. More guests will come in the next few days," she said. "Today is for Angelica's relatives."

"But Milagros isn't here."

"He came this morning."

"This morning!" I repeated in disbelief. The young man lying in Etewa's hammock opened his eyes wide, looked at me, then shut them again. Texoma awoke and began to wail. I tried to calm her by pushing the tobacco quid, which had fallen to the ground, back into her mouth. Refusing it, she began to cry even louder. I handed her to Tutemi, who rocked the child back and forth until she was still. Why had Milagros not let me know he was back? I wondered, feeling angry and hurt. Tears of self-pity welled up in my eyes.

"Look, he's coming," Tutemi said, pointing toward the *shabono*'s entrance.

Followed by a group of men, women, and children, Milagros walked directly toward Arasuwe's hut. Red and black lines circled his eyes and mouth. Spellbound, I gaped at the black monkey tail wrapped around his head, from which multicolored macaw feathers dangled, matching the ones that hung from his fur armbands. Instead of the festive cotton belt, he wore a bright red loincloth.

An inexplicable uneasiness overtook me as he approached my hammock. I felt my heart pound with fear as I gazed up into his tense, strained face.

"Bring your gourd," he said in Spanish, then turned around and walked toward the trough filled with plantain soup.

Without paying the slightest attention to me everyone followed Milagros into the clearing. Speechless, I reached for my basket, set it on the ground before me, and took out all my possessions. At the bottom, wrapped in my knapsack, was the smooth, ochre-colored calabash with Angelica's ashes. I had often wondered what I was supposed to do with it. Ritimi had never touched the knapsack when she went through my belongings.

The gourd felt heavy in my stiff, cold hands. It had been so light when I had carried it tied around my waist in the forest.

"Empty it into the trough," Milagros said. Again he spoke in Spanish.

"It's filled with soup," I said stupidly. I felt my voice quiver and my hands were so unsteady I thought I would not be able to pull the resin plug from the calabash.

"Empty it," Milagros repeated, tilting my arm gently.

I squatted awkwardly and slowly poured the burnt, finely powdered bones into the soup. I stared hypnotically at the dark heap they formed on the thick yellow surface. The smell made me nauseous. The ashes did not submerge. Milagros poured the contents of his own gourd on top of them. The women began to wail and cry. Was I supposed to join them? I wondered. I felt certain no matter how hard I tried not a single tear would come to my eyes.

Startled by sharp cracking sounds, I straightened up. With the handle of his machete, Milagros had split the two gourds into perfect halves. Next he mixed the powder into the soup, blending it so well that the yellow pap turned into a dirty gray.

I watched him bring the soup-filled gourd to his mouth, then empty it in one long gulp. Wiping his chin with the back of his hand, he filled it once more and handed the ladle to me.

Horrified, I looked at the faces around me; intently they watched every movement and gesture I made, with eyes that no longer seemed human. The women had stopped wailing. I could hear the accelerated beats of my heart. Swallowing repeatedly in an effort to overcome the dryness in my mouth, I held out a shaking hand. Then I shut my eyes tightly and gulped down the heavy liquid. To my surprise the sweet, slightly salty soup glided smoothly down my throat. A faint smile relaxed Milagros's tense face as he took the empty gourd from me. I turned around and slowly walked away as ripples of nausea tightened my stomach.

High-pitched chatter and squeals of laughter issued from the hut. Sisiwe, surrounded by his friends, sat on the ground, showing them each one of my personal belongings, which I had left scattered around. My nausea dissolved into rage as I saw my notepads smoldering on the hearth.

Startled, the children laughed at me as I burned my fingers trying to retrieve what was left of the pads. Slowly the bemused expressions on their faces changed to amazement when they realized I was crying.

I ran out of the *shabono* down the path toward the river, clutching the burnt pages to my breast. "I'll ask Milagros to take me back to the mission," I mumbled, wiping the tears from my face. The idea struck me as so absurd that I burst out laughing. How could I face Father Coriolano with a shaven tonsure.

Squatting at the edge of the water, I stuck my finger in my throat and tried to vomit. It was no use. Exhausted, I lay face up on a flat boulder jutting over the water and examined what was left of my notes. A cool breeze blew my hair. I turned on my stomach. The warmth of the stone filled me with a soft laziness that melted all my anger and weariness away.

I looked for my face in the clear water but the wind ruffled away all reflection from the surface. The river gave back nothing. Trapped in the dark pools along the bank, the brilliant green of the vegetation was a cloudy mass.

"Let your notes drift with the river," Milagros said, sitting beside me on the rock. His sudden presence did not startle me. I had been expecting him.

With a slight movement of my head I silently assented and let my hand dangle over the rock. My fingers unclasped. I heard a faint splash as the scorched pad fell into the water. I felt as if a burden had been lifted off my back as I watched my notes drift downriver. "You didn't go to the mission," I said. "Why didn't you tell me you had to bring Angelica's relatives?"

Milagros did not answer but stared out across the river.

"Did you tell the children to burn my notes?" I asked.

He turned his face toward me but remained silent. The contraction of his mouth revealed a vague disillusionment I failed to comprehend. When he spoke at last it was in a soft tone that seemed forced from him against his will. "The Iticoteri as well as other settlements have moved over the years deeper and deeper into the forest, away from the mission and the big rivers where the white man passes by." He turned to look at a lizard crawling uneasily over the stone. For an instant it stared at us with lidless eyes, then slithered off. "Other settlements have chosen to do the opposite," Milagros continued. "They seek the goods the *racionales* offer. They have failed to understand that only the forest can give them security. Too late, they will discover that to the white man the Indian is no better than a dog."

He knew, he said, having lived all his life between the two worlds, that the Indians did not have a chance in the world of the white man, no matter what a few individuals of either race did or believed to the contrary.

I talked about anthropologists and their work, the importance of recording customs and beliefs, which as he had mentioned on a previous occasion were doomed to be forgotten.

The hint of a mocking smile twisted his lips. "I know about anthropologists; I once worked for one of them as an informant," he said, and began to laugh; it was a high-pitched laughter, but there was no emotion in his face. His eyes were not laughing but shone with animosity.

I was taken aback because his anger seemed directed at me. "You knew I was an anthropologist," I said hesitantly. "You yourself helped me fill part of my notebook with information about the Iticoteri. It was you who took me from hut to hut, who encouraged others to talk to me, to teach me your language and your customs."

Impassively Milagros sat there, his painted face an expressionless mask. I felt like shaking him. It was as if he had not heard my words. Milagros stared at the trees, already black against the fading sky; I looked up into his face. His head was silhouetted against the sky. I saw the flaming macaw feathers and purple manes of monkey fur as if the sky were streaked with them.

Milagros shook his head sadly. "You know you didn't come here to do your work. You could've done that much better at one of the settlements close to the mission." Tears formed at the edge of his eyelids; they clung to his stubby lashes, shining, trembling. "Knowledge of our ways and beliefs was given to you so you would move with the rhythm of our lives; so you would feel secure and protected. It was a gift, not to be used or to be given to others."

I could not shift my gaze away from his bright moist eyes; there was no resentment in them. I saw my face mirrored in his black pupils. Angelica's and Milagros's gift. I finally understood. I had been guided through the forest, not to see their people with the eyes of an anthropologist—sifting, judging, analyzing all I saw and heard—but to see them as Angelica would have seen them, for one last time. She too had known that her time and the time of her people was coming to an end.

I shifted my gaze to the water. I had not felt my watch falling in the river, but there it was lying amidst the pebbles, an unstable vision of tiny illuminated spots coming together and moving apart in the water. One of the metal links on the watchband must have broken, I thought, but made no effort to retrieve the watch, my last link with the world beyond the forest.

Milagros's voice broke into my reveries. "A long time ago at a settlement close to the big river, I worked for an anthropologist. He didn't live with us in the *shabono,* but built himself a hut outside the log palisade. It had walls and a door that locked from the inside and the outside." Milagros paused for a moment, wiping the tears that had dried around his wrinkled eyes, then asked me, "Do you want to know what I did to him?"

"Yes," I said hesitantly.

"I gave him *epena.*" Milagros paused for a moment and

smiled as if he were enjoying my apprehension. "This anthropologist acted like everyone else who inhaled the sacred powder. He said he had the same visions as the shaman."

"There is nothing strange about that," I said, a little piqued by Milagros's smug tone.

"Yes, there is," he said, and laughed. "Because all I blew up his nostrils were ashes. All ashes do is make your nose bleed."

"Is that what you are going to give me?" I asked, and flushed at the obvious self-pity that permeated my voice.

"I gave you part of Angelica's soul," he said softly, helping me to my feet.

The *shabono*'s boundaries seemed to dissolve against the darkness. I could see well in the faint light. The people gathered around the trough reminded me of forest creatures, their shining eyes smeared with the light from the fires.

I sat next to Hayama and accepted the piece of meat she offered me. Ritimi rubbed her head against my arm. Little Texoma sat in my lap. I felt content, protected by the familiar odors and sounds. Intently I watched the faces around me, wondering how many of them were related to Angelica. There was not a single face resembling hers. Even Milagros's features, which had once seemed so much like Angelica's, looked different. Perhaps I had already forgotten what she looked like, I thought sadly. Then on a beam of light extending from the fire I saw her smiling face. I shook my head, trying to erase the vision, and found myself staring at the old shaman Puriwariwe, squatting a bit apart from the group.

He was a small, thin, dried-up man with a brownish-yellow skin; the muscles of his arms and legs were already shrunken. But his hair was still dark, curling slightly around his head. He was not adorned; all he wore was a bowstring around his waist. Sparse hairs hung from his chin and the vestiges of a mustache shadowed the edges of his upper lip. Under heavy wrinkled lids his eyes were like tiny lights, reflecting the gleam of the fire.

Yawning, he opened a cavernous mouth where yellowed teeth hung like stalagmites. Laughter and conversation ceased as he began to chant in a voice that gave the impression of belonging to another time and place. He possessed two voices: the one coming from his throat was high-pitched and wrathful; the other, coming from his belly, was deep and soothing.

Long after everyone had retired to their hammocks and the fires had burned down, Puriwariwe remained crouched in front of a small fire in the middle of the clearing. He sang in a low-keyed voice.

I got up from my hammock and squatted next to him, trying to bring my buttocks to touch the earth. According to the Iticoteri it was the only way one could squat for hours and be totally relaxed. Puriwariwe looked at me, acknowledging my gaze, then stared into space as though I had disturbed his train of thought. He did not move and I had the odd sensation he had fallen asleep. Then he shifted his buttocks on the ground without relaxing his legs and gradually began to chant once more in a voice that was but a faint murmur. I was not able to understand a single word.

It began to rain and I returned to my hammock. The drops pattered softly onto the thatched palm roof, creating a strange, trancelike rhythm. When I looked again toward the center of the clearing the old man had disappeared. And as dawn lit up the forest I felt myself slip into a timeless sleep.

8

The red sunset tinted the air with a fiery glow. The sky was aflame for a few minutes before it dissolved rapidly into darkness. It was the third day of the feast. From my hammock, together with Etewa's and Arasuwe's children, I watched the sixty or so men, Iticoteri as well as their guests, who without food or rest had been dancing since noon in the middle of the clearing. To the rhythm of their own shrill shouts, to the clacking of their bows and arrows, they turned one way, then another, stepping backward and forward, a throbbing, never-ending beat of sound and motion, an undulating array of feathers and bodies, a blur of crimson and black designs.

A full moon rose above the treetops, casting a radiant light over the clearing. For a moment there was a lull in the unceasing noise and movement. Then the dancers broke out in savage, strangled cries that filled the air with an ear-piercing sound as they flung aside their bows and arrows.

Running inside the huts, the dancers grabbed burning logs from the hearths and with a frenzied violence banged them against the poles holding up the *shabono*. All sorts of crawling insects scurried for safety in the palm-thatch roof before they fell like a cascade to the ground.

Terrified that the huts might come crashing down, or that the flying embers might set the roofs on fire, I ran outside with the children. The earth trembled under the men's stomping feet as they trampled out all the hearths in the huts. Brandishing the lighted logs high above their heads, they ran out into the center of the clearing and resumed their dance with mounting frenzy. They circled the plaza, their heads wagging back and forth like marionettes whose strings had broken. The soft white feathers in their hair fluttered onto their sweat-glistening shoulders.

The moon moved behind a black cloud; only the sparks of the fiery logs illuminated the clearing. The men's shrill cries rose to a higher pitch; wielding their clubs overhead, they invited the women to join in the dance.

Shouting and laughing, the women darted back and forth, expertly dodging the swinging logs. The frenzy of the dancers mounted to a compelling intensity, converging toward a final climax as young girls, holding clusters of yellow palm fruit in their upraised arms, joined the crowd, their bodies swaying with sensual abandon.

I was not sure if it was Ritimi who grabbed my hand and pulled me into the dance, for in the next instant I stood alone among the ecstatic faces whirling around me. Caught between shadows and bodies, I tried to reach old Hayama standing in the safety of a hut but did not know in which direction to move. I did not recognize the man who, brandishing a log above his head, pushed me back amidst the dancers.

I cried out. Terror-stricken, I realized it was as if my cries were mute, exhausted in countless echoes reverberating inside me. I felt a sharp pain on the side of my head, right behind my ear, as I fell face down on the ground. I opened my eyes, trying to see through the shadows thickening about me, and wondered if those frenzied feet whirling and leaping in the air realized I had fallen amidst them. Then there was darkness, punctuated by pinpoints of light darting in and out of my head like glowworms in the night.

I was vaguely aware of someone dragging me away from the trampling dancers to a hammock. I forced my eyes open, but the figure hovering above me remained blurred. I felt a pair of gentle, slightly shaky hands touch my face, the back of my head. For an instant I thought it was Angelica. But upon hearing that unmistakable voice coming from the depths of his stomach, I knew it was the old shaman Puriwariwe, chanting. I tried to focus my eyes, but his face remained distorted, as if I were seeing it through layers of water. I wanted to ask him where he had been, for I had not seen him since the first day of the feast, but the words were nothing but visions in my head.

I don't know whether I had been unconscious or whether I had slept, but when I awoke Puriwariwe was no longer there. Instead I saw Etewa's face bending over mine, so close I could have touched the red circles on his cheeks, between his brows, and at the corners of each eye. I stretched out my arm, but there was no one there. I shut my eyes; the circles danced inside my head like a red veil in a dark void. I shut them tighter until the image broke into a thousand fragments. The fire had been relit; it filled the hut with a cozy warmth that made me feel as if I were wrapped in an opaque cocoon of smoke. Dancing shadows silhouetted against the darkness were reflected on the golden patina of gourds hanging from the rafters.

Laughing happily, old Hayama came into the hut and sat on the ground beside me. "I thought you would sleep till morning." Raising both hands to my head, her fingers probed until she found the swollen lump behind my ear. "It's big," she said. Her weathered features expressed a distant sorrow; her eyes held a soft gentle light.

I sat up in the fiber hammock. Only then did I realize I was not in Etewa's hut.

"Iramamowe's," Hayama said before I had a chance to ask where I was. "His hut was the closest for Puriwariwe to bring you in after you were pushed against one of the men's clubs."

The moon had traveled high in the sky. Its pale shimmer spilled into the clearing. The dancing had ceased, yet an inaudible vibration still hung in the air.

Shouting, clacking their bows and arrows, a group of men positioned themselves in a semicircle in front of the hut. Iramamowe and one of the visitors stepped into the center of the gesticulating men. I could not tell which settlement the guest was from; I had been unable to distinguish the various groups who had come and gone since the beginning of the feast.

Iramamowe spread his legs in a firm stance, raised his left arm over his head, exposing his chest fully. *"Ha, ha, ahaha, aita, aita,"* he shouted, tapping his foot on the ground, a fearless cry that was meant to dare his opponent to strike him.

The young visitor adjusted his distance by measuring his arm length to Iramamowe's body; he took several dry runs, then with his closed fist delivered one powerful blow on the left side of Iramamowe's chest.

My body recoiled in shock. I felt nauseous as though the pain had swept through my own chest. "Why are they fighting?" I asked Hayama.

"They aren't fighting," she said, laughing. "They want to hear how their *hekuras,* the life essence that dwells inside their chests, resound. They want to hear how the *hekuras* vibrate with each blow."

The crowd cheered enthusiastically. The young visitor stood back, his chest heaving with excitement, and punched Iramamowe once more. Chin arrogantly raised, eyes perfectly steady, body stiff in defiance, Iramamowe acknowledged the cheers of the men. It was only after the third blow that he broke his stance. For an instant his lips parted in an appreciative grin, then set once more in a snarl of indifference and contempt. The persistent tapping of his foot, Hayama assured me, revealed nothing other than annoyance; his adversary had not yet struck him hard enough.

With a morbid, righteous kind of satisfaction I hoped Iramamowe felt the pain of each blow. He deserved it, I thought. Ever since I had seen him strike his wife, I had built up a resentment against him. Yet as I watched I could not help but admire the gallant way he stood in the middle of the crowd. There was something childishly defiant in the ramrod straightness of his back, the manner in which his bruised chest was thrust forward. His round, flat face, with its narrow forehead and flared upper lip appeared so vulnerable as he stared at the young man in front of him. I wondered if the slight flicker of his brown eyes betrayed that he was shaken.

With a shattering force the fourth blow landed on Iramamowe's chest. It reverberated like the rocks that tumbled down the river during a storm.

"I believe I heard his *hekuras*," I said, certain Iramamowe's rib had been broken.

"He's *waiteri*," the Iticoteri and their guests shouted in unison. With rapt expressions on their faces they bounced up and down on their haunches, clacking their bows and arrows over their heads.

"Yes. He is a brave one," Hayama repeated, her eyes fixed on Iramamowe, who, satisfied that his *hekuras* had resounded potently, stood erect amidst the cheering men, his bruised chest puffed up with pride.

Silencing the onlookers, the headman Arasuwe stepped toward his brother. "Now you take Iramamowe's blow," he said to the young man who had delivered the four punches.

The visitor positioned himself in the same defiant stance in front of Iramamowe. Blood spilled from the young man's mouth as he collapsed to the ground after receiving Iramamowe's third blow.

Iramamowe jumped in the air, then began to dance around the fallen man. Sweat glistened on his face, on the strained muscles of his neck and shoulders. But his voice sounded clear, vibrant with joy, as he shouted, *"Ai ai aiaiaiai, aiai!"*

Two of the visiting women carried the injured man into the empty hammock next to where Hayama and I sat. One of them cried; the other bent over the man and began to suck blood and saliva from his mouth until his breath came in slow, measured gasps.

Iramamowe challenged another of the guests to strike him. After receiving the first punch he knelt on the ground, from where he dared his opponent to hit him once more. He spat blood after the next blow. The guest got down on his haunches facing Iramamowe. Wrapping their arms around each other, they embraced.

"You hit well," Iramamowe said, his voice a barely audible whisper. "My *hekuras* are full of life, potent and happy. Our blood has flown. This is good. Our sons will be strong. Our gardens and the fruits in the forest will ripen to sweetness."

The guest voiced similar thoughts. Vowing eternal friendship, he promised Iramamowe a machete he had acquired from a group of Indians who had settled near the big river.

"I have to watch this one more closely," Hayama said,

walking out of the hut. Her youngest son was one of the men who had stepped into the circle for the next round of ritual blows.

I did not want to remain with the injured visitor in Ira-mamowe's hut. The two women who had brought him in had left to ask the shaman from their own group to prepare some medicine that would ease the pain in the man's chest.

My head began to spin as I stood up. Slowly I walked through the empty huts until I reached Etewa's. I stretched in my cotton hammock; an eerie silence closed in on me as if I were falling into a light faint.

I was awakened by angry shouts. Someone said, "Etewa, you have slept with my woman without my permission." The voice was so close it was as if he had spoken into my ear. Startled, I sat up. A group of men and giggling women had gathered in front of the hut. Etewa, standing perfectly still in the middle of the crowd, his face an unreadable mask, did not deny the charge. Suddenly he shouted, "You and your family have eaten like hungry dogs for the last three days." It was a deplorable accusation; visitors were given whatever they asked, for during a feast the hosts' gardens and hunting territory were at their guests' disposal. To be insulted in such a manner implied that the man had taken advantage of his privileged status. "Ritimi, get me my *nabrushi,*" Etewa shouted, scowling at the angry young man in front of him.

Sobbing, Ritimi ran into the hut, picked up the club, and without looking at her husband handed the four-foot-long stick to him. "I can't watch," she said, throwing herself into my hammock. I put my arms around her, trying to comfort her. Had it not been that she was so distressed I would have laughed. Not in the least concerned with Etewa's infidelity, Ritimi was afraid the night might end with a serious fight. Watching the two angry men shout at each other and the crowd's excited reaction, I could not help but be alarmed in turn.

"Hit me on the head," the enraged visitor demanded. "Hit me, if you are a man. Let's see if we can laugh together again. Let's see if my anger passes."

"We are both angry," Etewa shouted with insolent vigor, hefting the *nabrushi* in his hand. "We must appease our wrath." Then, without further ado, he delivered a solid whack on the man's shaven tonsure.

Blood gushed from the wound. Slowly it spread over the man's face until it was covered like some grotesque red mask. His legs shook, almost buckling under him. But he did not fall.

"Hit me and we'll be friends again," Etewa shouted belligerently, silencing the aroused crowd. He leaned on his club, lowered his head, and waited. When the man struck him, Etewa was momentarily dazed; blood flowed down his brow and lashes, forcing him to close his eyes. The explosive yells of the men broke the silence, a chorus of approving shouts demanding they hit each other again.

With a mixture of fascination and disgust I watched the two men facing each other. Their muscles were drawn tightly, the veins in their necks distended, their eyes bright, as if rejuvenated by the raging flow of blood. Their faces, set in contemptuous red masks, betrayed no pain as they stepped around one another like two injured cocks.

With the back of his hand Etewa wiped the blood obstructing his vision, then spat. Lifting his club, he let it fall on his opponent's head, who without uttering a sound collapsed on the ground.

Clicking their tongues, their eyes a bit out of focus, the spectators emitted fearsome cries. I was certain a fight would break out as the whole *shabono* filled with their earpiercing yells. I held on to Ritimi's arm and was surprised that her tear-stained face was set in a complacent, almost cheerful expression. She explained that she could tell by the tone of the men's shouts that they were no longer concerned with the initial insults. All they were interested in was to witness the power of each man's *hekuras*. There were no winners or losers. If a warrior fell, all it meant was that his *hekuras* were not strong enough at the moment.

One of the onlookers emptied a water-filled calabash on the prostrate guest, pulled his ears, wiped the blood from his face. Then, helping him up, he handed the half-dazed man his club and urged him to hit Etewa once more on the head. The man had barely enough strength to lift the heavy stick; instead of landing on Etewa's skull, it struck him in the middle of the chest.

Etewa fell to his knees; blood spilled from his mouth, over his lips, chin, and throat, down his chest and thighs, a red trail seeping into the earth. "How well you hit," Etewa said in a strangled voice. "Our blood has flown. We are no longer troubled. We have calmed our wrath."

Ritimi went to Etewa. Sighing loudly, I lay back in my hammock and closed my eyes. I had seen enough blood for the night. I probed the swollen area on my head, wondering if I had a slight concussion.

I almost fell from my hammock as someone held on to the liana rope tying it to one of the poles in the hut. Startled, I looked up into Etewa's bloodied face. Either he did not see me or was beyond caring where he rested, for he just slumped on top of me. The odor of blood, warm and pungent, mingled with the acrid smell of his skin. Repelled and fascinated, I could not help but stare at the open gash on his skull, still bleeding, and his swollen purple chest.

I was wondering how I could extricate my legs from under his weight when Ritimi stepped into the hut carrying a water-filled gourd, which she heated over the fire.

Expertly she lifted Etewa halfway up and motioned me to slip behind him in the hammock so that she could prop him against my raised knees. Gently, she washed his face and chest clean.

Etewa was perhaps twenty-five; yet with his hair clinging damply to his forehead, his lips slightly parted, he looked as helpless as a child in sleep. It occurred to me that he might die of internal injuries.

"He will be well tomorrow," Ritimi said as if she had guessed my thoughts. Softly she began to laugh; her laughter had a ring of childishly secret delight. "It's good for blood to flow. His *hekuras* are strong. He is *waiteri*."

Etewa opened his eyes, pleased to hear Ritimi's praise. He mumbled something unintelligible as he gazed into my face.

"Yes. He is *waiteri*," I agreed with Ritimi.

Tutemi arrived shortly with a dark hot brew.

"What is that?" I asked.

"Medicine," Tutemi said, smiling. She stuck her finger in the concoction, then put it against my lips. "Puriwariwe made it from roots and magical plants." A gleam of contentment shone in Tutemi's eyes as she forced Etewa to drink the bitter-tasting brew. Blood had flown; she was convinced she would bear a strong, healthy son.

Ritimi examined my legs, which were cut and bruised from being dragged across the clearing by Puriwariwe, and washed them with the remaining warm water. I lay down in Etewa's uncomfortable fiber hammock.

The moon, circled by a yellow haze, had moved until it was almost over the horizon of trees. A few men were still dancing and singing in the clearing; then a cloud hid the moon, obscuring everything in sight. Only the sound of voices, no longer shrill but a gentle murmur, told that the men were still there. The moon revealed itself once more, a pale light illuminating the tops of the trees, and the brown-skinned figures materialized against the darkness, shadows of long bodies giving substance to the soft clacking of bows and arrows.

Some of the men sang until a rim of light began to appear over the trees to the east. Dark purple clouds the color of Etewa's bruised chest covered the sky. Dew shone on the leaves, on the fringe of the palm fronds hanging around the huts. The voices began to fade, drifting away on the chilly breeze of dawn.

PART THREE

9

Planting and sowing was primarily a man's task, yet most women accompanied their husbands, fathers, and brothers whenever they went to work in the gardens in the mornings. Besides keeping them company, the women helped weed or took the opportunity to collect firewood if new trees had been felled.

For several weeks I had gone with Etewa, Ritimi, and Tutemi to their plots. The long, arduous hours spent weeding seemed to be wasted, for there never was any improvement to be seen. The sun and rain favored the growth of all species impartially, without recognizing human preferences.

Every household had their own area of land separated by the trunks of felled trees. Etewa's garden was next to Arasuwe's, who cultivated the largest area among the Iticoteri, for it was from the headman's plot that guests were fed at a feast.

At first I had recognized nothing but plantains, several kinds of bananas, and various palm trees scattered throughout the gardens. The palms were also purposely cultivated for their fruit, each tree belonging to the individual who planted it. I had been surprised to discover among the tangle of weeds an assortment of edible roots, such as manioc and sweet potatoes, and a variety of gourd-bearing vines, cotton, tobacco, and magical plants. Also growing in the gardens as well as around the *shabono* were the pink-flowered and red-podded trees from which the *onoto* paste was made.

Clusters of the red spiny pods were cut down, shelled, and the bright crimson seeds together with the pulpy flesh surrounding them were placed in a large water-filled calabash. As it was stirred and crushed, the *onoto* was boiled for a whole afternoon. After it had cooled during the night, the semisolid mass was wrapped in perforated layers of plantain leaves, then tied to one of the rafters in the hut to dry. A few days later the red paste was transferred to small gourds, ready for use.

Ritimi, Tutemi, and Etewa each had their own patches of tobacco and magical plants in Etewa's garden. Like everyone else's tobacco plots, they were fenced off with sticks and sharpened bones to discourage intruders. Tobacco was never taken without permission; quarrels ensued whenever it was. Ritimi had pointed out several of her magical plants to me. Some were used as aphrodisiacs and protective agents; others were employed for malevolent purposes. Etewa never talked about his magical plants and Ritimi and Tutemi pretended they did not know anything about them.

Once I watched Etewa dig up a bulbous root. The following day, before leaving to hunt, he rubbed his feet and legs with the mashed-up root. For our evening meal that day we had armadillo meat. "What a powerful plant," I had commented. Puzzled, he had regarded me for a long time, then, grinning, said, "*Adoma* roots protect one from snake bites."

On another occasion, as I was sitting in the garden with little Sisiwe, listening to his detailed explanation concerning the variety of edible ants, we saw his father dig up another of his roots. Etewa crushed the root, mixed its sap with *onoto*, then rubbed the substance over his entire body. "A peccary will cross my father's path," Sisiwe whispered. "I know by the kind of root he used. For every animal there is a magical plant."

"Even for monkeys?" I asked.

"Monkeys are frightened by terrifying yells," Sisiwe said knowingly. "Paralyzed, the monkeys can no longer run away and the men can shoot them."

One morning, almost hidden behind the tangled mass of calabash vines and weeds, I caught sight of Ritimi. I could only see her head rising behind the woody stems, pointed leaves, and clusters of white, bell-shaped flowers of the manioc plants. She seemed to be talking to herself; I could not hear what she was saying, but her lips moved incessantly, as if she were reciting some incantation. I wondered if she was charming her tobacco plants to grow faster or whether she was actually intending to help herself to some from Etewa's patch, which was next to hers.

Surreptitiously, Ritimi edged her way toward the middle of her own tobacco plot. Her air of urgency was unmistakable as she snapped branches and leaves. Looking around, she stuffed them into her basket, then covered them with banana fronds. Smiling, she rose, hesitated for an instant, then walked toward me.

I looked up in feigned surprise as I felt her shadow above me.

Ritimi placed her basket on the ground and sat next to me. I was bursting with curiosity, yet I knew it would be futile to ask what she had been doing.

"Don't touch the bundle in my basket," she said after a moment, unable to suppress her laughter. "I know you were watching me."

I felt myself blushing and smiled. "Did you snatch some of Etewa's tobacco?"

"No," she said in mock horror. "He knows his leaves so well he would notice if one were missing."

"I thought I saw you in his plot," I said casually.

Lifting the banana fronds from the basket Ritimi said, "I was in my own patch. Look, I took some branches of *oko-shiki,* a magical plant," she whispered. "I will make a powerful concoction."

"Are you going to cure someone?"

"Cure! Don't you know that only the *shapori* cures?" Tilting her head slightly to one side, she deliberated before she continued. "I'm going to bewitch that woman who had intercourse with Etewa at the feast," she said, smiling broadly.

"Maybe you should also prepare a potion for Etewa," I said, looking into her face. Her change of expression took me by surprise. Her mouth was set in a straight line; her eyes were narrowly focused on me. "After all, he was as guilty as the woman," I mumbled apologetically, feeling uneasy under her hard scrutiny.

"Didn't you see how shamelessly that woman taunted him?" Ritimi said reproachfully. "Didn't you see how vulgarly all those visiting women behaved?" Ritimi sighed, almost comically, then added with unconcealed disappointment, "Sometimes you are quite stupid."

I didn't know what to say. I was convinced that Etewa was as guilty as the woman. For want of anything better, I smiled. The first time I discovered Etewa in a compromising situation had been quite accidental. As everyone else did, I left the hut at dawn every day to relieve myself. I always strayed a bit farther into the forest, beyond the area set aside for human evacuation. One morning I was startled by a soft moan. Believing it was a wounded animal, I crawled, as quietly as I could, toward the noise. Totally surprised, I could only stare as I saw Etewa on top of Iramamowe's youngest wife. He looked into my face, smiling sheepishly, but did not stop moving on top of the woman.

Later that day Etewa offered me some of the honey he had found in the forest. Honey was a rare delicacy and was hardly ever shared with the same willingness as other foods were. In fact, most of the time honey was consumed at the spot where it was found. I thanked Etewa for the treat, assuming I was being bribed.

Sugars were something I constantly craved. I was no longer squeamish about consuming the honey together with wax combs, bees, maggots, pupae, and pollen the way the Iticoteri did. Whenever Etewa brought honey to the settlement, I would sit next to him and stare longingly at the runny paste studded with bees in varying stages of the metamorphic process until he offered me some. It never occured to me that he believed I had finally learned that to eye something one desired, or to ask for it outright, was considered proper behavior. Once, hoping to remind him that I knew of his philandering, I had asked him if he was not afraid to get hit on the head again by some enraged husband.

Etewa had looked at me in absolute astonishment. "It's because you don't know better—otherwise you wouldn't say such things." His tone was distant, the look in his eyes haughty as he turned toward a group of young boys engaged in sharpening pieces of bamboo that were to be used as arrowheads.

There were other occasions, not always accidental, when I encountered Etewa in similar circumstances. It soon became obvious that dawn was not only a time for attending to the baser bodily functions but provided the safest opportunity for extramarital activity. I became greatly interested in who was cuckolding whom. Cueing themselves the evening before, the involved parties would disappear at dawn in the thicket. A few hours later, very casually, they returned by different routes, often carrying nuts, fruits, honey, sometimes even firewood. Some husbands reacted more violently than others upon finding out about their women's doings—they beat them, as I had seen Iramamowe do. Others, besides beating their wives, demanded a club duel with the male culprit, which sometimes ended in a larger fight that others joined.

Ritimi's words cut into my reveries. "Why are you laughing?"

"Because you are right," I said. "Sometimes I'm quite stupid." It suddenly dawned on me that Ritimi knew of Etewa's activities—probably everyone in the *shabono* was aware of what was going on. No doubt it had been a coincidence when Etewa had offered me the honey that first time. Only I had examined the event with suspicion, believing all the time I was his accomplice.

Ritimi put her arms around my neck and planted smacking kisses on my cheek, assuring me that I was not stupid—only very ignorant. She explained that as long as she knew with whom Etewa was involved she was not greatly concerned about his amorous pursuits. She was by no means pleased by it, but believed she had some kind of control if it was with someone from the *shabono*. What distressed her was the possibility Etewa might take a third wife from some other settlement.

"How are you going to bewitch that woman?" I asked. "Are you going to make the concoction yourself?"

Standing up, Ritimi smiled with obvious satisfaction. "If I tell you now, the magic won't work." She paused, a quizzical expression in her eyes. "I'll tell you about it when I have bewitched the woman. Maybe someday you too will need to know how to bewitch someone."

"Are you going to kill her?"

"No. I'm not that courageous," she said. "The woman will have pains in her back until she has a miscarriage."

Ritimi slung the basket over her shoulders, then headed toward one of the few trees left standing near her tobacco patch. "Come, I need to rest before bathing in the river."

I stood for a moment to ease my cramped muscles, then followed her. Ritimi sat on the ground, resting her back against the massive tree trunk. Its leaves were like open hands between us and the sun, providing a cool shade. The earth, padded with leaves, was soft. I lay my head on Ritimi's thigh and watched the sky—so blue, so pale, it seemed transparent. The breeze rustled through the cane brush that grew behind us, gently, as if reluctant to impose itself on the midmorning stillness.

"The bump is gone," Ritimi said, running her fingers through my hair. "And there are no scars left on your legs," she added mockingly.

I agreed drowsily. Ritimi had laughed at my fear of getting sick from what she considered an insignificant injury. Having been pulled to safety by Puriwariwe was insurance enough that I would be well, she had assured me. However, I had been afraid that the cuts on my legs would become infected and I had insisted she wash them with boiled water every day. Old Hayama, as an added precaution, had rubbed the powder of burnt ants' nest on the wounds, claiming that it was a natural disinfectant. I had no ill effects from the stinging powder; the cuts healed quickly.

Through half-closed lids I gazed at the airy spaciousness of the gardens in front of me. Startled by shouts coming from the far end of the gardens, I opened my eyes. Iramamowe seemed to have materialized from beneath the banana fronds on his way toward the sky. Spellbound, I followed his movements as he worked his way up the spiny trunk of a *rasha* palm. So as not to hurt himself with the thorns, he worked with two pairs of crossed poles tied together, which he placed on the trunk one at a time. Relaxed, one motion leading to the next without a noticeable break, he alternated between standing on a pair of crossed poles and lifting the other set to place it higher on the trunk, until he reached the yellow clusters of *rasha,* at least sixty feet above the ground. For a moment he disappeared under the palm fronds that made a silvery arc against the sky. Iramamowe cut the drupes, tied the heavy clumps on a long vine, then eased them to the ground. Slowly, he worked his way down, vanishing in the greenness of banana leaves.

"I like the boiled drupes; they taste like . . ." I said, then realized I did not know the word for potato. I sat up. With her head to the side, her mouth slightly open, Ritimi was sound asleep. "Let's go bathe," I said, tickling her nose with a grass blade.

Ritimi stared at me; she had the disoriented look of someone just awakened from a dream. Leisurely she rose to her feet, yawning and stretching like a cat. "Yes, let's go," she said, fastening the basket on her back. "The water will wash my dream away."

"Did you have a bad one?"

She looked at me gravely, then brushed the hair off her forehead. "You were alone on a mountain," she said vaguely, as if she were trying to recollect her dream. "You weren't frightened, yet you were crying." Ritimi gazed at me intently, then added, "Then you woke me."

As we turned into the path leading to the river, Etewa came running after us. "Get some *pishaansi* leaves," he said to Ritimi. He turned to me. "You come with me."

I followed him through the newly cleared area of forest where fresh plantain suckers had already been planted between the rubble of felled trees, the trimmed leaf sheaths exposed above the ground. They were spaced from ten to twelve feet apart, allowing for the future full-grown plants to overlap leaves, but not to shade one another. Only a few days ago, Etewa, Iramamowe, and other close kin of the headman Arasuwe had helped him separate the suckers from the large basal corm of the plantains. On a contraption made with vines and thick leaves, fitted with a tumpline, they transported the heavy suckers to the new site.

"Did you find any honey?" I asked expectantly.

"No honey," Etewa said, "but something just as delicious." He pointed to where Arasuwe and his two oldest sons stood. They were taking turns at kicking an old banana tree. Hundreds of whitish, fat larvae fell out from between the multilayered green trunk.

As soon as Ritimi returned with the *pishaansi* leaves from the forest, the boys picked up the wriggling worms and put them on the sturdy wide leaves. Arasuwe lit a small fire. One of his sons held an elliptically-shaped piece of wood with his feet firmly planted on the ground while Arasuwe twirled the drill between his palms with an astounding speed. The ignited wood dust set fire to the termites' nest over which dry twigs and sticks were added.

Ritimi cooked the larvae for only a moment until the *pishaansi* leaves were black and brittle. Opening one of the bundles, Etewa wet his forefinger with saliva, rolled it in the roasted grub, then offered it to me. "It tastes good," he insisted as I turned my face away. Shrugging, he sucked his own finger clean.

Mumbling between mouthfuls, Ritimi urged me to give them a try. "How can you say you don't like them if you haven't even tasted them?"

With thumb and forefinger I placed one of the grayish, still soft grubs into my mouth. They are no different from escargot, I told myself, or cooked oysters. But when I tried to swallow the grub, it remained stuck to my tongue. I took it out again, waited till I had enough saliva, then swallowed the worm as if it were a pill. "In the morning, all I can eat is plantain," I said as Etewa pushed a bundle in front of me.

"You have worked in the garden," he said. "You have to eat. When there is no meat it is good to eat these." He reminded me that I had liked the ants and centipedes he had offered me on various occasions.

Looking into his expectant face, I could not bring myself to say that I had not liked them one bit, even though the centipedes had tasted like deep-fried vegetable tidbits. Reluctantly I forced myself to swallow a few more of the roasted grubs.

Ritimi and I followed behind the men on our way to the river. Children splashing in the water sang about a fat tapir that had fallen into a deep pool and drowned. Men and women were rubbing themselves with leaves; their bodies glistened in the sun, golden and smooth. Sparkling droplets on the tips of their straight hair reflected the light like diamond beads.

Old Hayama beckoned me to sit next to her on a large boulder at the edge of the water. I believe I had become Ritimi's grandmother's special charge, and she had taken it as a personal challenge to fatten me up. Like the children in the *shabono,* who were well fed so they would grow healthy and strong, old Hayama made sure I had plenty to snack on at all hours of the day. She indulged my insatiable appetite for sugars. Whenever someone found the sweet, thick, light-colored honey produced by nonstinging bees—the only kind given to the children—old Hayama made sure I was given at least a taste. If honey of the stinging black bees was brought to the *shabono,* Hayama also secured me some. Only adults partook of this kind, for the Iticoteri believed it caused nausea and even death to children. The Iticoteri were certain no harm would result if I ate both kinds, for they were unable to decide whether I was an adult or a child.

"Eat these," old Hayama said, offering me a few *sopaa* fruit. Greenish yellow, they were the size of lemons. I cracked them open with a stone (I had already broken a tooth trying to open nuts and fruits as the Iticoteri did) and sucked the sweet white pulp; the small brown seeds I spat out. The sticky juice gummed up my fingers and mouth.

Little Texoma climbed on my back, perching the small capuchin monkey she carried with her day and night on my head. The pet wrapped its long tail around my neck, so tightly I almost choked. One furry hand held on to my hair while the other swung in front of my face, striving to snatch away my fruit. Afraid to swallow monkey hair and lice, I tried to shake myself free. But Texoma and her pet shrieked with delight, believing I was playing a game. Lowering my feet in the water, I tried to slip my T-shirt over my head. Caught unawares, child and monkey jumped away.

The children pulled me down to the sand, tumbling beside me. Giggling, they began to walk, one by one, on my back, and I gave myself up to the pleasure of their small, cool feet on my aching muscles. In vain I had tried to convince the women to massage my shoulders, neck, and back after I had weeded for hours in the gardens. Whenever I had tried to show them how good it felt, they gave me to understand that although they liked being touched, massaging was something only the *shapori* did when a person was ill or bewitched. Fortunately they had no objections to letting the children walk on my back. To the Iticoteri it was quite inconceivable that someone could actually derive pleasure from such a barbaric act.

Tutemi sat next to me in the sand and began to unwrap

the *pishaansi* bundle Ritimi had given her. Her pregnant belly and swollen breasts seemed to be held in place by the taut stretched skin. She never complained of aches or nausea; neither did she have any cravings. In fact, there were so many food taboos a pregnant woman had to obey that I often wondered how they bore healthy babies. They were not allowed to eat large game. Their only source of protein were insects, nuts, larvae, fish, and certain kinds of small birds.

"When will you have the baby?" I asked, caressing the side of her stomach.

Knitting her brows in concentration, Tutemi deliberated for a while. "This moon comes and goes; another comes and goes, then one more comes and before it disappears, I will bear a healthy son."

I wondered if she was right. By her calculations that meant in three months. To me she looked as though she were about to give birth any day now.

"There are fish upriver—the kind you like," Tutemi said, smiling at me.

"I will take a quick swim, then I'll go with you to catch them."

"Take me swimming with you," little Texoma pleaded.

"You have to leave your monkey behind," Tutemi said.

Texoma perched the capuchin on Tutemi's head and came running after me. Shrieking with pleasure, she lay on my back in the water, her hands holding on to my shoulders. I stretched my legs and arms slowly and fully with each stroke until we reached a pool at the opposite bank.

"Do you want to dive to the bottom?" I asked her.

"I do, I do," she cried, nuzzling her small wet nose against my cheek. "I'll keep my eyes open, I'll not breathe, I'll hold on tight without choking you."

The water was not very deep. The blurred grayish, vermilion, and white pebbles resting in the amber sand shimmered brightly in spite of the trees shading the pool. I felt Texoma's hands tugging at my neck; quickly I swam to the surface.

"Come out," Tutemi shouted as soon as she saw our heads. "We're waiting for you." She pointed to the women next to her.

"I'll go back to the *shabono* now," Ritimi said. "If you see Kamosiwe give this to him." She handed me the last of the larvae bundles.

I followed the women and several men on the well-trodden trail. Shortly we encountered Kamosiwe, standing in the middle of the path. Reclining against his bow, he appeared to be fast asleep. I placed the bundle at his feet. The old man opened his one good eye; the bright sun made him squint, grotesquely disfiguring his scarred face. He picked up the larvae; slowly he began to eat, shifting from one foot to the other.

Following Kamosiwe as we climbed a small hill thick with growth, I marveled at the uncanny agility with which he moved. He never looked where he walked, yet always avoided the roots and thorns on the trail.

Slight, shrunken with age, he was the oldest-looking man I had ever seen. His hair was neither black, gray, or white, but an indistinctly colored woolly mop that apparently had not been combed for years. Yet it was short, as if cut periodically. It probably had stopped growing, I decided, like the stubbles on his chin that were always the same length. The scars on his wrinkled face were caused by a blow from a club that had taken out one of his eyes. When he spoke his voice was but a murmur, the meaning of which I had to guess.

At night he would often stand in the middle of the clearing, speaking for hours on end. Children crouched at his feet, feeding the fire that had been lit for him. His spent voice carried a strength, a tenderness that seemed at odds with his looks. There was always a feeling of urgent necessity in his words, a sense of warning, of enchantment as they scattered into the night. "There are words of knowledge, of tradition, preserved in the memory of this old man," Milagros had explained. It was only after the feast that he mentioned that Kamosiwe was Angelica's father.

"You mean he is your grandfather?" I had asked in disbelief.

Nodding, Milagros had added, "When I was born, Kamosiwe was the headman of the Iticoteri."

Kamosiwe lived by himself in one of the huts close to the entrance of the *shabono*. He neither hunted nor worked in the gardens any longer; yet he was never without food or firewood. He accompanied the women to the gardens or into the forest when they went to collect nuts, berries, and wood. While the women worked, Kamosiwe stood watch, leaning against his bow, a banana leaf stuck on the tip of his arrow to shade his face from the sun.

Sometimes he waved his hand in the air—perhaps at a bird, perhaps at a cloud, which he believed was the soul of an Iticoteri. Sometimes he laughed to himself. But mostly he stood still, either dreaming or listening to the sound of the wind rustling through the leaves.

Although he had never acknowledged my presence among his people, I often caught his one eye on me. Sometimes I had the distinct feeling he purposely sought my presence, for he always accompanied the group of women I was with. And at dusk, when I would seek the solitude of the river, he would be there, squatting not too far from me.

We stopped at a point where the river widened between the banks. The dark rocks scattered on the yellow sand appeared as if someone had purposely arranged them in a symmetrical order. The shadowed still water was like a dark mirror reflecting the aerial roots of the giant *matapalos*. Coming down from a height of ninety feet, they choked and constricted the tree. It was on one of its branches, as a tiny seed dropped by a bird, that the deadly roots had first germinated. I could not tell what kind of a tree it had been—perhaps a ceiba, for the branches bending in tragic grandeur were full of thorns.

Equipped with branches from the *arapuri* tree growing nearby, some of the women waded into the shallow river. Their piercing, shrill cries shattered the stillness as they beat the water. The frightened fish took refuge under the rotten leaves on the opposite bank, where the other women caught them with their bare hands. Biting off their heads, they flung the still wriggling fish into the flat baskets on the sand.

"Come with me," one of the headman's wives said. Taking me by the hand, she led me further upriver. "Let's try our luck with the men's arrows."

The men and young boys who had accompanied us were circled by a group of shrieking women demanding they lend them their weapons. Fishing was considered a woman's activity; men only went to laugh and jeer. It was the only time they allowed the women to use their bows and arrows. Some men handed their weapons to the women, then quickly ran to the safety of the bank, afraid of getting hit accidentally. They were delighted that none of them made a kill.

"Try," Arasuwe said, handing me his bow.

I had taken archery lessons at school and felt certain of my skill. However, as soon as I held his bow I knew this was impossible. I could barely draw the bow; my arm shook uncontrollably as I released the short arrow. I tried repeatedly, but not once did I hit a fish.

"What a bold way to shoot," old Kamosiwe said, handing me a smaller bow belonging to one of Iramamowe's sons. The boy did not complain but glowered at me sullenly. At his age no man would willingly hand his weapon to a woman.

"Try again," Kamosiwe urged. His one eye shone with a strange intensity.

Without the slightest hesitation I drew the bow once more, aiming the arrow at the shimmering silvery body that for an instant seemed motionless under the surface. I felt the tension of the drawn bow suddenly relax; the arrow released effortlessly. I distinctly heard the sharp sound of the arrow hitting the water and then saw a trail of blood. Cheering, the women retrieved the arrow-pierced fish. It was no' bigger than a medium-sized trout. I returned the weapon to the boy, who stared at me with astonished admiration.

I looked for old Kamosiwe, but he was gone.

"I will make you a small bow," Arasuwe said, "and slender arrows—the kind used for shooting fish."

The men and women had gathered around me. "Did you really shoot the fish?" one of the men asked. "Try it again. I didn't see it."

"She did, she did," Arasuwe's wife assured him, showing him the trophy.

"*Ahahahaha*," the men exclaimed.

"Where did you learn to shoot with a bow and arrow?" Arasuwe asked.

As best as I could, I attempted to explain what a school was. Watching Arasuwe's puzzled eyes, I wished I had said that my father had taught me. Explaining something that required more than a few sentences at a time could be a frustrating experience, not only for me, but for my listeners as well. It was not always a matter of knowing the right words; rather the difficulty stemmed from the fact that certain words did not exist in their language. The more I talked, the more troubled Arasuwe's expression became. Frowning with disappointment, he insisted I explain why I knew how to use the bow and arrow. I wished Milagros had not gone to visit another settlement.

"I know of whites who are good marksmen with a gun," Arasuwe said. "But I have never seen a white use the bow and arrow skillfully."

I felt a need to belittle the fact that I had actually hit a fish, alleging that it was sheer luck, which it was. However, Arasuwe kept insisting that I knew how to use the Indians' weapons. Even Kamosiwe had noticed the way I held the bow, he said loudly.

I believe that somehow I got the idea of school across, for they insisted I tell them what else I had been taught. The men laughed outrageously upon hearing that the way I had decorated my notebook was something I had learned at school. "You haven't been taught properly," Arasuwe said with conviction. "Your designs were very poor."

"Do you know how to make machetes?" one of the men asked.

"You need hundreds of people for that," I said. "Machetes are made in a factory." The harder I tried to make them understand, the more tongue-tied I became. "Only men make machetes," I finally said, pleased to have found an explanation that satisfied them.

"What else did you learn?" Arasuwe asked.

I wished I had some gadget with me, such as a tape recorder, a flashlight, or some such thing, to impress them with. Then I remembered the gymnastics I had practiced for several years. "I can jump through the air," I said off-hand. Clearing off a square area of the sandy beach, I placed four of the fish-filled baskets in each of its corners. "No one can step into this space." Standing in the middle of my arena, I gazed at the curious faces around me. They broke into hilarious guffaws as they watched me do a series of stretch exercises. Although the sand did not have the

springiness of a floor exercise mat, I was at least comforted
by the thought that I would not hurt myself if I missed my
footing. I did a couple of handstands, cartwheels, front and
back walkovers, then a forward and backward somersault. I
did not land with the grace of an accomplished gymnast,
but I was pleased by the admiring faces around me.

"What strange things you were taught," Arasuwe said.
"Do it again."

"One can only do it once." I sat on the sand to catch my
breath. Even if I had wanted to I could not repeat my
performance.

The men and women came closer, their intent eyes fixed
on me. "What else can you do?" one of them asked.

For an instant I was at a loss; I thought I had done
plenty. After a moment's consideration, I said, "I can sit
on my head."

Laughter shook their bodies until tears rolled down
their cheeks. "Sit on the head," they repeated, each time
bursting into new peals of laughter.

I flattened my forearms on the ground, placed my forehead on my intertwined palms, and slowly lifted my body
upward. Sure of my balance, I crossed my upraised legs.
The laughter stopped. Arasuwe lay flat on the ground,
his face close to mine. He smiled, crinkling the corners of
his eyes. "White girl, I don't know what to think of you,
but I know if I walk with you through the forest, the
monkeys will stop to see you. Enchanted, they will sit still
to watch you, and I will shoot them." He touched my face
with his large calloused hand. "Sit on your buttocks again.
Your face is red, as if it were painted with *onoto*. I'm
afraid your eyes will fall out of your head."

Back in the *shabono*, Tutemi placed one of the bundles of
fish, cooked in *pishaansi* leaves, in front of me on the
ground. Fish was my favorite food. To everyone's surprise,

I preferred it to armadillo, peccary, or monkey meat. The *pishaansi* leaves and the salty solution derived from the ashes of the *kurori* tree added a spiciness that greatly enhanced its natural flavor.

"Did your father want you to learn to use the bow and arrow?" Arasuwe asked, squatting next to me. Before I had a chance to answer, he continued, "Had he wanted a boy when you were born?"

"I don't think so. He was very pleased when I was born. He already had two sons."

Arasuwe opened the bundle in front of him. Silently he shifted the fish toward the middle of the leaves, as if he were pondering a mystery for which he had no adequate words. He motioned me to take some of his food. With two fingers and a thumb, I lifted a large portion of fish into my mouth. As was proper, I licked the juice dribbling down my arm and when I ran into a spine I spat it on the ground, without spitting out any of the flaky meat.

"Why did you learn to shoot arrows?" Arasuwe asked in a compelling tone.

Without thinking I answered, "Maybe something in me knew I was to come here someday."

"You should have known that girls don't use the bow and arrow." He smiled at me briefly, then began to eat.

10

The soft patter of rain and the voices of men singing outside the hut woke me from my afternoon nap. Shadows
began to lengthen and the wind played with the palm
fronds hanging over the roofs. Sounds and presences filled
the huts all at once. Fires were stoked. Soon everything
smelled of smoke, of dampness, of food and wet dogs.
There were men chanting outside, oblivious to the drops
pecking at their backs, at their masklike faces. Their eyes,
watery from the *epena*, were fixed on the distant clouds,
open wide to the spirits of the forest.

I walked out into the rain to the river. The heavy drops
drumming on the ceiba leaves awakened the tiny frogs
hiding under the tall grass blades that grew along the
bank. I sat down at the edge of the water. Unaware of time
passing, I watched the concentric circles of rain spreading
over the river, pink flowers drifting by like forsaken
dreams of another place. The sky darkened; the outline of
the clouds began to blur as they merged into each other.
The trees turned into a single mass. Leaves lost their dis-
tinctive shapes, becoming indistinguishable from the evening sky.

I heard a whimpering sound behind me; I turned
around but saw only the faintest gleam of rain on the

leaves. Seized by an inexplicable apprehension, I ascended the trail leading to the *shabono*. At night I was never sure of anything; the river, the forest were like presences I could only feel but never understand. I slipped on the muddy path, stubbing my toe on a gnarled root. Once more I heard a soft whimpering sound. It reminded me of the mournful cries of Iramamowe's hunting dog, which he had shot in a fit of rage with a poisoned arrow during a hunt when the animal had barked inopportunely. The injured dog had returned to the settlement and hid outside the wooden palisade, where it had whined for hours until Arasuwe put an end to its suffering with another arrow.

I called softly. The cries stopped and then I distinctly heard an agonized moan. Maybe it's true that there are forest spirits, I thought, straightening up. The Iticoteri claimed that there were beings who cross a tenuous boundary that separates animal from man. These creatures call the Indians at night, luring them to their deaths. I stifled a cry; it seemed as if a shape loomed from the dark— some concealed figure that moved among the trees only a pace from where I stood. I sat down again in an effort to conceal myself. I heard a faint breathing; it was more like a sighing, accompanied by a rattling, choking sound. Through my head rushed the stories of revenge, of bloody raids the men were so fond of talking about at night. In particular I remembered the story about Angelica's brother, the old shaman Puriwariwe, who supposedly had been killed in a raid, yet had not died.

"He was shot in the stomach, where death hides," Arasuwe had said one evening. "He didn't lie down in his hammock, but remained standing in the middle of the clearing, leaning on his bow and arrow. He swayed but didn't fall.

"The raiders remained rooted on the spot, unable to shoot another arrow as the old man chanted to the spirits.

With the arrow still stuck in the spot where death lies, he disappeared into the forest. He was gone for many days and nights. He lived in the darkness of the forest without food or drink. He chanted to the *hekuras* of animals and trees, creatures that are harmless in the clear light of the day, but in the shadows of the night they cause terror to the one who cannot command them. From his hiding place, the old *shapori* lured his enemies; he killed them one by one, with magical arrows."

Again I heard the whimpering sound, then a choking noise. I crawled, carefully feeling for thorns in the undergrowth. I gasped in terror as I touched a hand; its fingers were curled around a broken bow. I did not recognize the sprawled-out body until I touched Kamosiwe's scarred face. "Old man," I called, afraid that he was dead.

He turned on his side, pulled his legs up with the ease of a child that seeks warmth and comfort. He tried to focus with his single, deeply set eye as he looked at me helplessly. It was as though he were returning from a great distance, from another world. Steadying himself against the broken bow, he tried to get on his feet. He clutched my arm, then let out an eerie sound as he sank to the ground. I could not hold him up. I shook him, but he lay still.

I felt for his heartbeat to see if he was dead. Kamosiwe opened his one eye; his gaze seemed to hold a silent plea. The dilated pupil reflected no light; like a deep, dark tunnel, it seemed to draw the strength out of my body. Afraid I would make a mistake, I talked to him in Spanish, softly, as if he were a child. I hoped he would close that awesome eye and fall asleep.

Lifting him by the armpits, I dragged him toward the *shabono*. Although he was only skin and bones, his body seemed to weigh a ton. After a few minutes I had to sit and rest, wondering if he was still alive. His lips trembled; he spat out his tobacco quid. The dark saliva dribbled over my leg. His eye filled with tears. I put the wad back into his mouth, but he refused it. I took his hands, rubbed them against my body so as to imbue them with some warmth. He started to say something, but I heard only an unintelligible mutter.

One of the young boys who slept close to the entrance, next to the old man's hut, helped me lift Kamosiwe into his hammock. "Put logs on the fire," I said to one of the gaping boys. "And call Arasuwe, Etewa, or someone who can help the old man."

Kamosiwe opened his mouth to ease his breathing. The wavering light of the small fire accentuated his ghostlike paleness. His face twisted into an odd smile, a grimace that reassured me I had done the right thing.

The hut filled with people. Their eyes shone with tears; their sorrowful wails spread throughout the *shabono*.

"Death is not like the darkness of night," Kamosiwe said in a barely audible whisper. His words fell into silence as the people, gathered around his hammock, momentarily stopped their laments.

"Do not leave us alone," the men moaned as they burst into loud weeping. They began to talk about the old man's courage, about the enemies he had killed, about his children, about the days he was headman of the Iticoteri and the prosperity and glory he had brought to the settlement.

"I will not die yet." The old man's words silenced them once again. "Your weeping makes me too sad." He opened his eye and scanned the faces around him. "The *hekuras* are still in my chest. Chant to them, for they are the ones who keep me alive."

Arasuwe, Iramamowe, and four other men blew *epena* into each other's nostrils. With blurred eyes they began to sing to the spirits dwelling below and above the earth.

"What ails you?" Arasuwe asked after a while, bending over the old man. His strong hands massaged the weak, withered chest; his lips blew warmth into the immobile form.

"I'm only sad," Kamosiwe whispered. "The *hekuras* will soon abandon my chest. It's my sadness that makes me weak."

I returned with Ritimi to our hut. "He will not die," she said, wiping the tears from her face. "I don't know why he wants to live so long. He is so old, he is no longer a man."

"What is he?"

"His face," she said, "has become so small, so thin . . ." Ritimi looked at me as if at a loss for words to express her thoughts. She made a vague gesture with her hand, as if grasping for something she did not know how to voice. Shrugging, she smiled. "The men will chant throughout the night, and the *hekuras* will keep the old man alive."

A monotonous rain, warm and persistent, mingled with the men's songs. Whenever I sat up in my hammock I could see them across the clearing in Kamosiwe's hut, crouched in front of the fire. They chanted with a compelling force, convinced that their invocations could preserve life, as the rest of the Iticoteri slept.

The voices faded with the rosy melancholy of dawn. I got up and walked across the clearing. The air was chilly, the ground damp from the rain. The fire had died down, yet the hut was warm from the misty smoke. The men huddled together still crouched around Kamosiwe. Their faces were drawn; their eyes were hollowed by deep circles.

I returned to my hammock as Ritimi was getting up to rekindle the fire. "Kamosiwe seems well," I said, lying down to sleep.

As I stood up from behind a bush I saw Arasuwe's youngest wife and her mother slowly pushing their way through the thicket in the direction of the river. Quietly I followed the two women. They had no baskets with them—only a piece of sharpened bamboo. The pregnant woman held her hands to her belly as if supporting its heavy weight. They stopped under an *arapuri* tree, where the undergrowth had been cleared and broad *platanillo* leaves had been scattered on the ground. The pregnant woman knelt on the leaves, pressing her abdomen with both hands. A soft moan escaped her lips and she gave birth.

I held my hand over my mouth to stifle a giggle. I could not conceive that giving birth could be so effortless, so fast. The two women talked in whispers, but neither one of them looked at, or picked up, the shiny wet infant on the leaves.

With the bamboo knife, the old woman cut the umbilical cord, then looked around until she found a straight branch. I watched her place the stick across the baby's neck, then step with both feet at either end. There was a faint snapping sound. I was not sure if it was the baby's neck or if it was the branch that had cracked.

The afterbirth they wrapped in one bundle of *platanillo* leaves, the small lifeless body into another. They tied the bundles with vines and placed them under the tree.

I tried to hide behind the bushes as the women got up to leave, but my legs would not obey me. I felt drained of all emotion, as if the scene in front of me were some bizarre nightmare. The women looked at me. A faint flicker of surprise registered on their faces, but I saw no pain or regret in their eyes.

As soon as they were gone I untied the vines. The lifeless body of a baby girl lay on the leaves as if in sleep. Long black hair, like silk strands, stuck to her slippery head. The lashless lids were swollen, covering the closed eyes. The trickle of blood running from nose and mouth had dried,

like some macabre *onoto* design on the faint purplish skin.
I pried open the small fists. I checked the toes to see if they
were complete; I found no visible deformity.

The late afternoon had spent itself. The dried leaves
made no rustling sound under my bare feet; they were
damp with the night. The wind parted the leafy branches
of the ceibas. Thousands of eyes seemed to be staring at
me; indifferent eyes, veiled in green shadows. I walked
down the river and sat on a fallen log that had not yet
died. I touched the clusters of new shoots that desperately
wanted to see the light. The cricket's call seemed to mock
my tears.

I could smell the smoke from the huts and I resented
those fires that burned day and night, swallowing time and
events. Black clouds hid the moon, cloaking the river in a
veil of mourning. I listened to the animals—those that
wake from their day's sleep and roam the forest at night. I
was not afraid. A silence, like a soft dust from the stars, fell
around me. I wanted to fall asleep and wake up knowing it
had all been a dream.

Through a patch of clear sky I saw a shooting star. I
could not help smiling. I had always been fast to make a
wish, but I could not think of any.

I felt Ritimi's arm around my neck. Like some forest
spirit she had sat down noiselessly beside me. The pale
sticks at the corners of her mouth shone in the dark as if
they were made of gold. I was grateful she was near me,
that she did not say a word.

The wind brushed away the clouds that obscured the
moon; its light covered us in a faint blue. Only then did I
notice old Kamosiwe squatting beside the log, his eye
fixed on me. He began to talk, slowly, enunciating each
word. But I was not listening. Leaning heavily on his bow,
he motioned us to follow him to the *shabono*. He stopped
by his hut; Ritimi and I walked on to ours.

"Only a week ago, women and men cried," I said, sitting in my hammock. "They cried believing Kamosiwe was going to die. Today I saw Arasuwe's wife kill her newborn child."

Ritimi handed me some water. "How could the woman feed a new baby at her breast when she has a child that still suckles?" she said briskly. "A child who has lived this long."

Intellectually I grasped Ritimi's words. I was aware that infanticide was a common practice among Amazonian Indians. Children were spaced approximately two to three years apart. The mother lactated during this time and refrained from bearing another child in order to sustain an ample supply of milk. If a deformed or female child were born during this time, it was killed, so as to give the nursing child a better chance of survival.

Emotionally, however, I was unable to accept it. Ritimi held my face, forcing me to look at her. Her eyes shone, her lips trembled with feeling. "The one who has not yet glimpsed at the sky has to return from where it came." She stretched her arm toward the immense black shadows that began at our feet and ended in the sky. "To the house of thunder."

11

Instead of the women's soft chattering, I was awakened one morning by Iramamowe's shouts announcing that he would prepare curare that day.

I sat up in my hammock. Iramamowe stood in the middle of the clearing. Legs apart, arms folded over his chest, he scrutinized the young men who had gathered around him. At the top of his voice he warned them that if they planned to help him prepare the poison, they were not to sleep with a woman that day. Iramamowe went on ranting as if the men had already misbehaved, reminding them that he would know if they disobeyed him for he would test the poison on a monkey. Should the animal survive he would never again ask the men to assist him. He told them that if they wished to accompany him into the forest to collect the various vines needed to make the *mamucori*, they had to refrain from eating and drinking until the poison had been smeared on their arrowheads.

Calm returned to the *shabono* as soon as the men left. Tutemi, after stoking the fires, rolled the tobacco quids for herself, Ritimi, and Etewa, then returned to her hammock. I thought there was time to snatch a bit more sleep before the plantains buried under the embers were done. I turned over in my hammock; the smoke warmed the chilly air. As they did every morning after relieving themselves, little Texoma and Sisiwe, as well as Arasuwe's two youngest children, climbed into my hammock and snuggled up to me.

Ritimi had been oblivious to the morning events. She was still sound asleep on the ground. Sleep did not interfere with Ritimi's vanity. Her head, resting on her arm, was propped in such a manner that it allowed her to wear her full beauty regalia; slender polished rods were stuck through the septum of her nose and the corners of her mouth. Her exposed cheek revealed two brown lines, a sign recognizable by everyone in the *shabono* that she was menstruating. For the last two nights Ritimi had not slept in her hammock, had not eaten meat, had not cooked any of the meals, and had not touched Etewa or any of his belongings.

Men feared menstruating women. Ritimi had told me that women were known not to have *hekuras* in their chest but were linked to the life essence of the otter, the ancestor of the first woman on earth. During their menses, women were thought to be imbued with the supernatural powers of the otter. She did not seem to know what these powers were, but she said that if a man saw an otter in the river he never killed it for fear that a woman in the settlement would die that same instant.

The Iticoteri women had at first been puzzled as to why I had not menstruated since my arrival. My explanation— loss of weight, change of diet, new surroundings—was not thought to be the reason. Instead they believed that as a non-Indian, I was not fully human. I had no link to the life essence of any animal, plant, or spirit.

It was only Ritimi who wanted to believe and prove to the other women that I was human. "You have to tell me immediately when you are *roo,* as if I were your mother," Ritimi would say to me every time she herself menstruated. "And I will make the proper preparations so you will not be turned into a stone by the tiny creatures that live underground."

Ritimi's insistence was probably another reason my body did not follow its normal cycles. Since I have a tendency to suffer from claustrophobia, I had periodic attacks of anxiety triggered by the possibility of having to endure the same restrictions that an Iticoteri girl going through her first menses does.

Only a week before, Xotomi, one of the headman's daughters, had emerged from a three-week confinement. Her mother, upon learning that Xotomi had begun her first period, built an enclosure made out of sticks, palm fronds, and vines in a corner of their hut. A narrow space had been left open. It was barely large enough for her mother to slip in and out of twice a day to feed the meager fire inside (which was never allowed to die) and remove the soiled *platanillo* leaves covering the ground. The men, afraid of dying young or of becoming ill, did not so much as glance toward that area in the hut.

For the first three days of her menstrual period Xotomi was only given water and had to sleep on the ground. Thereafter she was given three small plantains a day and was permitted to rest in the small bark hammock that was hung inside. She was not allowed to speak or weep during her confinement. All I heard from behind the tied palm fronds was the faint sound of Xotomi scratching herself with a stick, for she was not supposed to touch her body.

By the end of the third week, Xotomi's mother dismantled the enclosure, tied the palm leaves into a tight bundle, then asked some of her daughter's playmates to hide them in the forest. Xotomi did not move, as if the palm fronds were still around her. She remained crouched on the ground with downcast eyes. Her slightly hunched shoulders seemed so frail that I was sure if someone grasped them the bones would give way with a hollow crack. More than ever she looked like a frightened child, thin and dirty.

"Keep your eyes on the ground," her mother said, helping the twelve-, perhaps thirteen-year-old girl to her feet. With her arms around her waist, she led Xotomi to the hearth. "Don't rest your eyes on any of the men in the clearing," she admonished the girl, "lest you want their legs to tremble when they have to climb trees."

Water had been heated. Lovingly, Ritimi washed her half-sister from head to foot, then rubbed her body with *onoto* until it glowed uniformly red. Fresh banana leaves were placed on the fire as Ritimi guided the girl around the hearth. Only after Xotomi's skin smelled of nothing but burnt leaves was she allowed to look at us and speak.

She bit her lower lip as she slowly lifted her head. "Mother, I don't want to move out of my father's hut," she finally said, then burst into tears.

"Ohoo, you silly child," the mother exclaimed, taking Xotomi's face into her hands. Brushing aside the tears, the woman reminded the girl how lucky she was to become the wife of Hayama's youngest son Matuwe, that she was fortunate to be so close to her brothers, who would protect her should he mistreat her. The mother's dark eyes glittered, blurred with tears. "I had reasons to be heavy-hearted when I first came to this *shabono*. I had left my mother and brothers behind. I had no one to protect me."

Tutemi embraced the young girl. "Look at me. I also came from far away, but now I'm happy. I will soon have a child."

"But I don't want a child," Xotomi sobbed. "I only want to hold my pet monkey."

In a swift impulse I reached for the monkey perched on a cluster of bananas and handed it to Xotomi. The women burst into giggles. "If you treat your husband right, he'll be like your pet monkey," one of them said in between fits of laughter.

"Don't say such things to the girl," old Hayama said reprovingly. Smiling, she faced Xotomi. "My son is a good man," she said soothingly. "You'll have nothing to fear." Hayama went on praising her son, stressing Matuwe's prowess as a hunter and provider.

The day of the wedding Xotomi sobbed quietly. Hayama came to her side. "Don't cry anymore. We will adorn you. You'll be so beautiful today, everyone will gasp in wonder." She took Xotomi's hand, then motioned the women to follow them through a side exit into the forest.

Sitting on a tree stump, Xotomi wiped her tears with the back of her hand. A whimsical smile appeared on her lips as she gazed into old Hayama's face, then she readily submitted to the women's ministrations. Her hair was cut short, her tonsure shaven. Tufts of soft white feathers were pushed through her perforated earlobes; they contrasted sharply with her black hair, adding an ethereal beauty to her thin face. The holes at the corners of her mouth and lower lip were decorated with red macaw feathers. Through the perforated septum in her nose Ritimi inserted an almost white, very slender polished stick.

"How lovely you look," we exclaimed as Xotomi stood in front of us.

"Mother, I'm ready to go," she said solemnly. Her dark slanted eyes shone, her skin looked flushed with the *onoto*. She smiled briefly, revealing strong, even white teeth, then led the way back to the *shabono*. Only for an instant—just before entering the clearing—was there a silent plea in her eyes as she turned to look at her mother.

Her head held high, her gaze focused on no one in particular, Xotomi slowly circled the clearing, seemingly unperturbed by the admiring words and glances of the men. She entered her father's hut and sat in front of the trough

filled with plantain pap. First she offered some of the soup
to Arasuwe, then to her uncles, her brothers, and finally to
each man in the *shabono*. After she had served the women,
she walked toward Hayama's hut, sat down in one of the
hammocks, and began to eat the game prepared by her
husband, to whom she had been promised before she had
been born.

Tutemi's words cut into my reveries. "Are you going to eat
your plantain here or at Hayama's?"

"I'd better eat there," I said, grinning at Ritimi's grandmother, who was already waiting for me in the hut next to
Tutemi's.

Xotomi smiled at me as I came over. She had changed a
great deal. It had nothing to do with the weight she had
gained back since emerging from her confinement. Rather
it was her mature behavior, the way she looked at me, the
way she urged me to eat the plantain. I wondered if it was
because girls, as opposed to boys, who were able to prolong
their childhood into their teens, were encouraged by the
time they were six or eight to help their mothers with the
domestic chores—gathering wood, weeding in the gardens,
taking care of their younger siblings. By the time a boy was
considered an adult, a girl of the same age was married and
often the mother of a child or two.

After eating, Tutemi, Xotomi, and I worked for several
hours in the gardens, then walked into the *shabono*, re-
freshed from our bath in the river. A group of men, their
faces and bodies painted black, sat together in the clearing.
Some were scraping the bark off thick pieces of branches.

"Who are these people?" I asked.

"Don't you recognize them?" Tutemi laughed at me.
"It's Iramamowe and the men who went with him yesterday into the forest."

"Why are they painted black?"

"Iramamowe!" Tutemi shouted. "The white girl wants to know—why are your faces all black?" she asked, then ran into her hut.

"It's good you are running," Iramamowe said, standing up. "The baby in your womb might weaken the *mamucori* by adding water." Frowning, he turned to Xotomi and me; before he had a chance to say anything else, Xotomi pulled me by the hand into Etewa's hut.

In between fits of laughter Xotomi explained that anyone who had been in the water that day was not supposed to come close to the men preparing curare. Water was believed to weaken the poison. "If the *mamucori* doesn't work right, he will blame you."

"I would have liked to watch them prepare the *mamucori*," I said disappointedly.

"Who would want to watch anything like that?" Ritimi said, sitting up. "I can tell you what they are going to do." She yawned and stretched, then folded the *platanillo* leaves she had been sleeping on and covered the ground with fresh ones. "The men are painted black because *mamucori* is not only useful for hunting but also for making war," Ritimi said, motioning me to sit next to her. She peeled a banana, then with a full mouth explained how the men were boiling the *mamucori* vine until it turned into a dark liquid. Later the dried *ashukamaki* vine would be added to thicken the poison. Once the mixture had been boiled down, it would be ready to be brushed on the men's arrowheads.

Resignedly I helped Tutemi prepare the tobacco leaves for drying. Following her precise instructions, I split each leaf along the nervation, pulling upward so they bundled up, then tied them in bunches on the rafters. From where I sat I was unable to see what was going on outside Iramamowe's hut. Children surrounded the working men, hoping to be asked to help. No wonder I had not seen a single child that morning bathing in the river.

"Get some water from the stream," Iramamowe said to little Sisiwe. "But don't get your feet wet. Step on trunks, roots, or stones. If you get wet, I'll have to send someone else."

It was late afternoon when Iramamowe was almost finished mixing and boiling the curare. "Now the *mamucori* is becoming strong. I can feel my hands going to sleep." In a slow, monotonous voice he began to chant to the spirits of the poison as he stirred the curare.

Around midmorning the following day Iramamowe came running into the *shabono*. "The *mamucori* is useless. I shot a monkey but it didn't die. It walked away with the useless arrow stuck in its leg." Iramamowe ran from hut to hut, insulting the men who had helped him prepare the curare. "Didn't I warn you not to sleep with women. Now the *mamucori* is worthless. If an enemy should attack us, you won't even be able to defend your women. You think you are brave warriors. But you are as useless as your arrows. You should be carrying baskets instead of weapons."

For a moment I thought Iramamowe was going to cry as he sat on the ground in the middle of the clearing. "I'll make the poison by myself. You are all incompetent," he muttered over and over until his anger was spent, until he was thoroughly exhausted.

A few days later at dawn, shortly before the monkey Iramamowe had shot with his newly poisoned arrow was fully cooked, a stranger walked into the *shabono* carrying a large bundle. His hair was still wet from a river bath; his face and body were extravagantly painted with *onoto*. Placing his bundle, as well as his bow and arrows, on the ground, he stood silently in the middle of the clearing for a few minutes before he approached Arasuwe's hut.

"I've come to invite you to my people's feast," the man said in a loud singsong voice. "The headman of the Mocototeri has sent me to tell you that we have many ripe plantains."

Arasuwe, without getting up from his hammock, told the man that he could not attend the feast. "I cannot leave my gardens now. I've planted new banana saplings; they need my care." Arasuwe made a sweeping gesture with his hand. "Look at all the fruit hanging from the rafters; I don't want them to spoil."

The visitor walked over to our hut and addressed Etewa. "Your father-in-law doesn't wish to come. I hope you will be able to visit my people who have sent me to invite you."

Etewa slapped his thighs with pleasure. "Yes. I'll come. I don't mind leaving my plantains behind. I'll give others permission to eat them."

The visitor's dark lively eyes shone with delight as he went from hut to hut inviting the Iticoteri to his settlement. The man was invited to rest in old Kamosiwe's hut. He was offered plantain soup and monkey meat. Later in the evening he untied his bundle in the middle of the clearing. "A hammock," the men who had gathered around him murmured disappointedly. Even though the Iticoteri acknowledged the comfort and warmth of cotton hammocks, only a few women owned one. The men preferred the bark or vine ones, replacing them periodically. The visitor was eager to trade the cotton hammock for poisoned arrowheads and *epena* powder made from seeds. Talking and exchanging news, some Iticoteri men stayed up all night with the visitor.

Arasuwe was adamant that I should not be part of the group going to the Mocototeri feast. "Milagros has entrusted you to me," the headman reminded me. "How can I protect you if you are at another place?"

"What do I need to be protected for?" I asked. "Are the Mocototeri dangerous people?"

"The Mocototeri are not to be trusted," Arasuwe said after a long silence. "I can feel it in my legs that it is not right for you to go."

"When I first met Angelica she told me that it was not dangerous for a woman to walk through the forest."

Arasuwe did not bother to answer or comment on my statement but looked at me as if I had become invisible. Obviously he considered the matter settled and did not intend to demean himself by any further bantering with an ignorant girl.

"Maybe Milagros will be there," I said.

Arasuwe smiled. "Milagros will not be there. If he were I would have no reason to worry."

"Why are the Mocototeri not to be trusted?" I persisted.

"You ask too many questions," Arasuwe said. "We are not on friendly terms with them," he added grudgingly.

I looked at him in disbelief. "Why then do they invite you to a feast?"

"You are ignorant," Arasuwe said, walking out of the hut.

It was not only I who was disillusioned by Arasuwe's decision. Ritimi was so disappointed she could not show me off to the Mocototeri that she enlisted Etewa and Iramamowe, as well as old Kamosiwe, to help convince her father to let me accompany them. Although old people's advice was valued and respected, it was Iramamowe, known for his bravery, who finally persuaded and assured his brother that no harm would befall me at the Mocototeri settlement.

"You should take the bow and arrows I made for you,"

Arasuwe said to me later that evening. He began to laugh uproariously. "That would certainly astonish the Mocototeri. It would almost be worth it for me to go and witness their surprise." Seeing that I was checking my arrows, Arasuwe added soberly, "You cannot take them. It's not proper for a woman to walk through the forest carrying a man's weapon."

"I will take care of her," Ritimi promised her father. "I'll make sure she never leaves my side—not even when she has to go into the bush."

"I'm sure Milagros would have wanted me to go," I said, hoping to make Arasuwe feel more at ease.

Eyeing me gloomily, he shrugged his shoulders. "I trust you will return safely."

Anticipation and apprehension kept me awake that night. The familiar noises of the collapsing logs in the fire filled me with misgivings. Etewa stirred the embers with a stick before lying down. Through the smoke and mist the distant crowns of trees looked like ghosts. The space between the leaves were like hollow eyes accusing me of something I did not understand. I was almost tempted to follow Arasuwe's advice, but the light of day dispelled my apprehension.

12

The sun had barely taken the chill off the morning air when we set out with baskets stocked with plantains, calabashes, hammocks, the paraphernalia for decorating ourselves, and the items for trade: thick bundles of undyed cotton yarn, newly fashioned arrowheads, bamboo containers filled with *epena* and *onoto*. With their own hammocks slung around their necks, the older children walked close behind their mothers. The men, closing up the rear of each family unit, carried nothing but their bows and arrows.

There were twenty-three of us. For four days we walked silently through the forest at a relaxed pace set by the old people and children. Whenever they became aware of the slightest movement or sound in the thicket, the women stood still, pointing with their chins in the direction of the disturbance. Swiftly the men disappeared in the specified direction. More often than not, they returned with an agouti—a rabbitlike rodent—or a peccary, or a bird, which was cooked as soon as we made camp in the afternoon. The children were forever on the lookout for wild fruit. Their keen eyes would follow the flight of bees until they reached their hives in a hollow tree trunk. While the insects were still in flight, they were able to accurately identify whether they belonged to the stinging or nonstinging variety.

Hayama, Kamosiwe, and several of the old people wrapped strips of the fibrous bast of a tree around their thorax and abdomen. They claimed it restored their energy and made walking easier. I tried it too, but the tightly wrapped bast only gave me a rash.

As we climbed up and down hills, I wondered if it was a different route from the one I had been on with Milagros. There was not a tree, rock, or stretch of river I could recall. Neither did I remember having encountered mosquitoes and other insects hovering above the marshes. Attracted by our sweaty bodies, they buzzed around us with a maddening persistence. I, who had never been bothered by them, could not decide which part of my body to scratch first. My torn T-shirt offered no protection. Even Iramamowe, who initially had been oblivious to their unrelenting bites, occasionally acknowledged the inconvenience by slapping his neck, his arm, or by lifting his leg to scratch his ankle.

Around noon of the fifth day we made camp at the edge of the Mocototeri's gardens. The cleared-out undergrowth made the giant ceibas appear even more monumental than in the forest. Shafts of sunlight filtered through the leaves, illuminating and shadowing the dark ground.

We bathed in the nearby river, where red flowers, suspended from lianas overhanging the water, swayed with sensuous grace to the rhythm of the breeze. Iramamowe and three other young men were the first to don their festive attire and to paint themselves with *onoto* before heading toward the host's *shabono*. Iramamowe returned shortly, carrying a basket filled with roasted meat and baked plantains.

"Ohooo, the Mocototeri have so much more," he said, distributing the food among us.

Before the women began to beautify themselves they assisted their men with the pasting of white down on their hair and tying feathers and monkey fur around their arms and heads. I was given the task of decorating the children's faces and bodies with the prescribed *onoto* designs.

Our laughter and chatter were interrupted by the shouts of an approaching Mocototeri.

"He looks like a monkey," Ritimi whispered.

I nodded in agreement, barely able to conceal my giggles. The man's short bowed legs and long disproportionate arms seemed even more pronounced as he stood next to Etewa and Iramamowe, who looked imposing with their white down-covered heads, the long multicolored macaw feathers streaming from their armbands, and their bright-red waist belts.

"Our headman wants to start the feast. He wants you to come soon," the Mocototeri said in the same formal high-pitched voice as the man who had come to the *shabono* to invite us to the feast. "If you take too long to prepare yourselves, there will be no time to talk."

With their heads held high, their chins slightly pushed up, Etewa, Iramamowe, and three young men, also properly painted and decorated, followed the Mocototeri. Although they pretended indifference, the men were aware of the admiring glances of the rest of us as they strutted toward the *shabono*.

Overcome by last-minute nervousness, the women hurried through the last touches of their toilette, adding a flower or feather here, a dab of *onoto* there. How they looked was entirely up to the judgment of the others, for there were no mirrors.

Ritimi fastened the waist belt around me, making sure the wide fringe was centered properly. "You're still so thin," she said, touching my breasts, "even though you eat so much. Don't eat today the way you eat at our *shabono* or the Mocototeri will think we don't give you enough."

I promised to eat very sparingly, then burst into laughter as I remembered that this was the same advice my mother used to give me as a child whenever I was invited to spend the weekend with friends. She too had been embarrassed by my voracious appetite, thinking that people might believe I was not properly fed at home or, worse yet, that they might think I had a tapeworm.

Just before we set out toward the Mocototeri *shabono*, old Hayama admonished her great-grandchildren, Texoma and Sisiwe, to behave properly. Raising her voice so that the other children who had come with us could also hear her, she stressed how important it was to minimize any chance for the Mocototeri women to criticize them once they had departed. Old Hayama insisted the children try to urinate and defecate for one last time behind the bushes, for once inside the *shabono* no one would clean up after them or take them outside if they had to go.

Upon reaching the Mocototeri clearing, the men formed a line, holding their weapons vertically to their upraised haughty faces. We stood behind them with the children.

A group of shouting women ran out of the huts as soon as they saw me. I was neither afraid nor repelled as they touched, kissed, and licked my face and body. But Ritimi seemed to have forgotten how the Iticoteri had first greeted me when I arrived at their settlement, for she kept mumbling under her breath that she would have to retrace the *onoto* designs on my skin.

Holding my arm in a strong grip, one of the Mocototeri women pushed Ritimi aside. "Come with me, white girl," she said.

"No," Ritimi shouted, pulling me closer to her. Her smile did not detract from the sharp angry tone of her voice. "I've brought the white girl for you to look at. No one must take her away from me. We are like each other's shadows. I go where she goes. She goes where I go." Trying to outstare her opponent, Ritimi's eyes held the woman's fixed gaze, daring her to challenge her words.

The woman opened her tobacco-filled mouth in gaping laughter. "If you have brought the white girl to visit, you must let her come into my hut."

Someone from behind the group of women approached us. With arms crossed over his chest, he pushed his hips forward with a little swagger as he came to stand beside me. "I'm the headman of the Mocototeri," he said. As he smiled his eyes were but two shining slits amidst the red designs of his deeply wrinkled face. "Is the white girl your sister that you protect her so?" he asked Ritimi.

"Yes," she said forcefully. "She is my sister."

Shaking his head in disbelief, the headman studied me. He seemed totally unimpressed. "I can see that she is white, but she doesn't look like a real white woman," he finally said. "Her feet are bare like ours; she does not wear strange clothes on her body except for this." He pulled at my torn, loose underpants. "Why does she wear this under an Indian waist belt?"

"Pantiis," Ritimi said importantly; she liked the English word better than the Spanish, which she had also learned. "That's what white people call it. She has two more of them. She wears pantiis because she is afraid that spiders at night and centipedes during the day might crawl inside her body."

Nodding as if he understood my fear, the headman touched my short hair and rubbed his fleshy palm over my shaven tonsure. "It's the color of the young *assai* palm fronds." He moved his face close to mine until our noses touched. "What strange eyes—they are the color of rain." His scowl disappeared in a smile of delight. "Yes, she must be white; and if you call her sister, then no one will take her away from you," he said to Ritimi.

"How can you call her sister?" the woman who still held my arm asked. There was earnest perplexity written all over her painted face as she gazed at me.

"I call her sister because she is like us," Ritimi said, putting her arm around my waist.

"I want her to come and stay in my hut," the woman said. "I want her to touch my children."

We followed the woman into one of the huts. Bows and arrows were leaning against the sloping roof. Bananas, gourds, and bundles of meat wrapped in leaves were strung from the rafters. Machetes, axes, and an assortment of clubs lay in the corners. The ground was littered with twigs, branches, fruit skins, and shards of earthenware vessels.

Ritimi sat with me in the same cotton hammock. As soon as I had finished the juice made from soaked palm fruit the woman had given me, she placed a small baby in my lap. "Caress him."

Turning and twisting in my arms, the infant almost fell to the ground. And when he stared into my face he began to bawl.

"You better take him," I said, handing the woman the child. "Babies are afraid of me. They first have to get to know me before I can touch them."

"Is that so?" the woman asked, eyeing Ritimi suspiciously as she rocked the baby in her arms.

"Our babies don't scream." Ritimi cast contemptuous glances at the infant. "My own and my father's children even sleep with her in the same hammock."

"I'll call the older children," the woman said, gesturing toward the little girls and boys peeking from behind the bundles of plantains stacked against the sloping roof.

"Don't," I said. I knew that they would be frightened too. "If you force them to come, they too will cry."

"Yes," said one of the women who had followed us into

the hut. "The children will sit with the white girl as soon as they see that their mothers are not afraid to touch her palm-fiber hair and pale body."

Several women had gathered around us. Tentatively at first, their hands explored my face, then my neck, arms, breasts, stomach, thighs, knees, calves, toes; there was not a part of me they left unexamined. Whenever they discovered a mosquito bite or a scratch, they spat on it, then rubbed the spot with their thumbs. If the bite was recent, they sucked out the poison.

Although I had become accustomed to Ritimi's, Tutemi's, and the Iticoteri's children's lavish shows of affection, which never lasted more than a moment, I felt uncomfortable under the exploring touch of so many hands on my body. "What are they doing?" I asked, pointing to a group of men squatting outside the hut next to us.

"They are preparing the *assai* leaves for the dance," said the woman who had placed the baby in my lap. "Do you want to look at that?"

"Yes," I said emphatically, wanting to shift the attention away from myself.

"Does Ritimi have to accompany you everywhere you go?" the woman asked as Ritimi got up from the hammock with me.

"Yes," I said. "Had it not been for her I would not be visiting your *shabono*. Ritimi has taken care of me since I arrived in the forest."

Ritimi beamed at me. I wished I had expressed words to that effect sooner. Not once during the rest of our stay did any of the Mocototeri women question Ritimi's proprietary manner toward me.

The men outside the hut were separating the still closed, pale yellow leaves of the young *assai* palm with sharp little sticks. One of the men rose from his squatting position as we approached. Taking the tobacco wad from his mouth, he wiped the dribbling juice from his chin with the back of his hand and held the palm frond over my head. Smiling, he pointed to the fine gold veins in the leaf, barely visible against the light of the setting sun. He touched my hair, replaced the wad in his mouth, and without saying a word, continued separating the leaves.

Fires were lit in the middle of the clearing as soon as it was dark. The Iticoteri men touched off an explosion of wild cheering from their hosts as they lined up, weapons in hand, around the fires. Two at a time, the Iticoteri danced around the clearing, slowing down in front of each hut, so all could admire their attire and their dancing steps.

Etewa and Iramamowe made up the last pair. Shouts reached a higher pitch as they moved in perfectly matched steps. They did not dance around the huts but stayed close to the fires, wheeling and spinning at an ever accelerating speed, their rhythm dictated by the leaping flames. Etewa and Iramamowe stopped abruptly in their tracks, held their bows and arrows vertically next to their faces, then aimed them at the Mocototeri men standing in front of their huts. Laughing uproariously, the two men resumed their dance while the onlookers broke out in exultant, approving shouts.

The Iticoteri men were invited by their hosts to rest in their hammocks. While food was served, a group of Mocototeri burst into the clearing. *"Haii, haiii, haiiii,"* they shouted, moving to the clacking of their bows and arrows, to the swishing sound of the fringed, undulating *assai* palm fronds.

I could hardly make out the dancing figures. At times they seemed fused together, then they leapt apart, fragments of dancing arms, legs, and feet visible from between the swaying palm fronds—black, birdlike silhouettes with giant wings as they moved away from the light of the fires, blazing copper figures, no longer man or bird, as their bodies glistening with sweat glowed in the flames.

"We want to dance with your women," the Mocototeri demanded. When there was no response from the Iticoteri, they jeered. "You are jealous of them. Why don't you let your poor women dance? Don't you remember we let you dance with our women at your feast?"

"Whoever wants to dance with the Mocototeri, may do so," Iramamowe shouted, then admonished the men, "But you will not force any of our women to dance if they don't wish to do so."

"*Haii, haiii, haiiii,*" the men yelled euphorically, welcoming the Iticoteri women as well as their own.

"Don't you want to dance?" I asked Ritimi. "I will go with you."

"No. I don't want to lose you in the crowd," she said. "I don't want anyone to hit you on the head."

"But that was an accident. Besides, the Mocototeri are not dancing with fire logs," I said. "What could they possibly do with palm fronds?"

Ritimi shrugged her shoulders. "My father said the Mocototeri are not to be trusted."

"I thought one only invites one's friends to a feast."

"Enemies too," Ritimi said, giggling. "Feasts are a good time to find out what people are planning to do."

"The Mocototeri are very friendly," I said. "They have fed us very well."

"They feed us well because they don't want anyone to say they are stingy," Ritimi said. "But as my father has told you, you are still ignorant. You obviously don't know what's going on if you think they are friendly." Ritimi patted my head as if I were a child, then continued, "Didn't you notice that our men didn't take *epena* this afternoon? Haven't you realized how watchful they are?"

I had not noticed and was tempted to add that I thought

the Iticoteri's behavior was not very friendly but remained quiet. After all, as Ritimi had pointed out, I did not understand what was going on. I observed the six Iticoteri men dancing around the fires. They were not moving with their usual abandon and their eyes kept darting back and forth, keenly watching all that went on around them. The rest of the Iticoteri men were not lounging in their host's hammocks but were standing outside the huts.

The dance had lost its enchantment for me. Shadows and voices took on a different mood. The night now seemed packed with an ominous darkness. I began to eat what had been served to me earlier. "This meat tastes bitter," I said, wondering if it was poisoned.

"It's bitter because of the *mamucori*," Ritimi said casually. "The spot where the poisoned arrow hit the monkey hasn't been washed properly."

I spat out the meat. Not only was I afraid of being poisoned, but I felt nauseous as I remembered the sight of the monkey boiling in the tall aluminum pot, a layer of fat and monkey hairs floating on the surface.

Ritimi put the piece of meat back on my calabash plate. "Eat it," she urged me. "It's good—even the bitter part. Your body will get used to the poison. Don't you know that fathers always give their sons the part where the arrow hit? If they are shot in a raid by a poisoned arrow they won't die because their bodies will be used to the *mamucori*."

"I'm afraid that before I get hit by a poisoned arrow, I will die from eating poisoned meat."

"No. One doesn't die from eating *mamucori*," Ritimi assured me. "It has to go through the skin." She took the already chewed piece from my calabash, bit off a chunk, then pushed the remaining half into my gaping mouth. Smiling mockingly, she exchanged her dish with mine. "I don't want you to choke," she said, eating the rest of the cooked monkey breast with exaggerated gusto. Still chewing, she pointed toward the clearing and asked if I could see the woman with the round face dancing by the fire.

I nodded, but I did not recognize which one she meant. There were about ten women dancing close to the fire. They all had round faces, dark slanted eyes, voluptuous bodies the color of honey in the light of the flames.

"She is the one who had intercourse with Etewa at our feast," Ritimi said. "I've bewitched her already."

"When did you do that?"

"This afternoon," Ritimi said softly, and began to giggle. "I blew the *oko-shiki* I had collected from my garden on her hammock," she added with satisfaction.

"What if someone else sits in her hammock?"

"It makes no difference. The magic is only meant to harm her," Ritimi assured me.

I had no chance to find out more about the bewitching for at that moment the dancing ceased and the tired, smiling dancers returned to the various huts to rest and eat.

The women who joined us around the hearth were surprised Ritimi and I had not danced. Dancing was as important as painting the body with *onoto*—it kept one young and happy.

Shortly the headman stepped into the clearing and announced in a thunderous voice, "I want to hear the Iticoteri women sing. Their voices are pleasing to my ears. I want our women to learn their songs."

Giggling, the women nudged each other. "You go, Ritimi," one of Iramamowe's wives said. "Your voice is beautiful."

That was all the encouragement Ritimi needed. "Let's all go together," she said, standing up.

Silence spread over the *shabono* as we walked out into the clearing with our arms around each other's waists. Facing the headman's hut, Ritimi began to sing in a clear,

melodious voice. The songs were very short; the last two
lines were repeated as a chorus by the rest of us. The other
women sang too, but it was Ritimi's songs, one in particular, that the Mocototeri headman insisted she repeat until
his women had learned it.

When the wind blows the palm leaves,
I listen to their melancholy sound with the silent frogs.
High in the sky, the stars are all laughing,
But cry tears of sadness as the clouds cover them.

The headman walked toward us and, addressing me,
said, "Now you must sing for us."

"But I don't know any songs," I said, unable to repress
my giggles.

"You must know some," the headman insisted. "I've
heard stories of how much the whites like to sing. They
even have boxes that sing."

In the third grade in Caracas I had been told by the
music teacher that besides having a dreadful voice I was
also tone deaf. However, Professor Hans, as he expected to
be addressed, was not insensitive to my desire to sing. He
allowed me to remain in the class provided I stayed in the
last row and sang very softly. Professor Hans did not
bother much with the required religious and folk songs we
were supposed to be learning but taught us Argentinian
tangos from the thirties. I had not forgotten those songs.

Looking at the expectant faces around me, I stepped
closer to the fire. I cleared my throat and began to sing,
oblivious to the jarring notes escaping my throat. For a
moment I felt I was faithfully reproducing the passionate
manner in which Professor Hans had sung his tangos. I
clutched my hands to my breast, I closed my eyes as if
transported with the sadness and tragedy of each line.

My audience was spellbound. The Mocototeri and Iticoteri had come out of their huts to watch my every gesture.

The headman stared at me for a long time, then finally said, "Our women cannot learn to sing in this strange manner."

The men sang next. Each singer stood alone in the middle of the clearing, both hands resting high on his upright bow. Sometimes a friend accompanied the performer; then the singer rested his arm over his companion's shoulder. One song in particular, sung by a Mocototeri youth, was the favorite of the night.

> *When a monkey jumps from tree to tree*
> *I shoot it with my arrow.*
> *Only green leaves drop down.*
> *Swirling around, they gather at my feet.*

The Iticoteri men did not lie down in their hammocks but talked and sang with their hosts throughout the night. I slept with the women and children in the empty huts around the main entrance of the *shabono*.

In the morning I stuffed myself with the papayas and pineapples one of the Mocototeri girls had brought for me from her father's garden. Ritimi and I had discovered them earlier on our way into the bush. She had advised me not to ask for the fruit—not because it was not proper, but because the fruit was unripe. But I did not mind their sour taste or even the slight stomachache that followed. I had not eaten familiar fruits for months. Bananas and palm fruit were like vegetables to me.

"You had a wretched voice when you sang," a young man said, squatting next to me. "Ohoo, I didn't understand your song, but it sounded hideous."

Speechless, I glared at him. I did not know whether to laugh or insult him in turn.

Putting her arms around my neck, Ritimi burst into

laughter. She looked at me askance, then whispered in my ear, "When you sang I thought the monkey meat had given you a bellyache."

Squatting on the same spot in the clearing where they had started out last night, a group of Iticoteri and Mocototeri men were still talking in the formal, ritualized manner proper to the *wayamou*. Bartering was a slow, involved affair during which equal importance was given to the items for trading and the exchange of information and gossip.

Close to noon, some Mocototeri women began criticizing their husbands for the items they had exchanged, stating that they needed the machetes, aluminum pots, and cotton hammocks themselves. "Poisoned arrowheads," one of the women shouted angrily. "You could make them yourself if you weren't so lazy." Without paying the slightest attention to the women's remarks, the men continued their hagglings.

13

It was past noon when we left the Mocototeri settlement, our baskets filled with the accustomed plantains, palm fruits, and meat given to departing guests.

Shortly before nightfall, three Mocototeri men caught up with us. One of them raised his bow as he spoke. "Our headman wants the white girl to stay with us." He stared at me down the shaft of his drawn arrow.

"Only a coward points his arrow at a woman," Iramamowe said, stepping in front of me. "Why don't you shoot, you useless Mocototeri?"

"We haven't come to fight," the man remarked, returning his bow and arrow to an upright position. "We could have ambushed you some time ago. All we want is to frighten the white girl so she'll come with us."

"She cannot stay with you," Iramamowe said. "Milagros brought her to our *shabono*. If he had wanted her to stay with you, he would have taken her to your settlement."

"We want her to come with us," the man persisted. "We will bring her back before the rains start."

"If you make me angry, I shall kill you on the spot." Iramamowe pounded his chest. "Remember, you cowardly Mocototeri, that I'm a fierce warrior. The *hekuras* in my

chest are always at my command, even without *epena*."
Iramamowe moved nearer to the three men. "Don't you
know that the white girl belongs to the Iticoteri?"

"Why don't you ask her where she wants to stay?" the
man said. "She liked our people. Maybe she wants to live
with us."

Iramamowe began to laugh—a rumbling laughter that
did not reveal whether he was amused or outraged. He
stopped abruptly. "The white girl does not like the way
the Mocototeri look. She said you all resemble monkeys."
Iramamowe turned toward me. There was such a pleading
expression in his eyes that it was all I could do not to
giggle.

I felt a tinge of remorse as I looked into the bewildered
faces of the three Mocototeri. For an instant I felt tempted
to deny Iramamowe's words. But I could not ignore his
anger, nor had I forgotten Arasuwe's apprehension at my
going to the feast. I crossed my arms over my chest, lifted
my chin, and without looking at them directly said, "I
don't want to go to your settlement. I don't want to eat
and sleep with monkeys."

The Iticoteri burst into loud guffaws. The three men
turned around abruptly, then disappeared on the path
leading into the thicket.

We made camp not too far from the river in a cleared
area of the forest, where the remains of temporary shelters
still stood. We did not cover them with new leaves, for old
Kamosiwe assured us that it would not rain that night.

Iramamowe did not eat, but sat, glum and intense, in
front of the fire. There was a tension about him as if he
were expecting the three men to reappear at any moment.

"Is there any danger the Mocototeri might come back?"
I asked.

Iramamowe was some time before giving me an answer.
"They are cowards. They know that my arrows will kill

them on the spot." He stared fixedly on the ground, his lips set in a straight line. "I'm considering what would be the best way to return to our *shabono*."

"We should divide up our party," old Kamosiwe suggested, gazing at me with his one eye. "There is no moon tonight; the Mocototeri will not return. Perhaps tomorrow they will ask again for the white girl. We can tell them that they frightened her away, that she asked to be taken back to the mission."

"Are you sending her back?" Ritimi's voice hung in the darkness, charged with anxiety.

"No," the old man said cheerfully. The grayish bristles on his chin, his one eye that never missed anything, his slight wrinkled body gave him the appearance of a wicked elf. "Etewa should return to the *shabono* with Ritimi and the white girl by way of the mountains. It's a longer route but they won't be slowed down by children and old people. They will reach our settlement no later than a day or two after we do. It is a good route, not traveled much." Old Kamosiwe got up and sniffed the air. "It will rain tomorrow. Build a shelter for the night," he said to Etewa, then squatted, a smile on his lips, his one sunken eye staring at me. "Are you afraid to return to the *shabono* by way of the mountains?"

Smiling, I shook my head. Somehow I could not envision myself to be in real danger.

"Were you afraid when the Mocototeri aimed his arrow at you?" old Kamosiwe asked.

"No. I knew the Iticoteri would protect me." I had to refrain myself from adding that the incident had seemed comical to me rather than dangerous. I did not fully realize at the time that in spite of the obvious bluffing, characteristic of any critical circumstance, the Mocototeri and Iticoteri were perfectly serious in their threats and demands.

Old Kamosiwe was delighted with my reply. I had the feeling his pleasure derived not so much from the fact that I had not been frightened but rather by my trust in his people. He talked to Etewa long into the night. Ritimi fell asleep holding my hand in hers, a blissful smile on her lips. Watching her dream, I knew why she looked so happy. For a few days she would have Etewa practically to herself.

In the *shabono* men hardly ever showed any outward affection toward their wives. It was considered a weakness. Only toward the children were the men openly tender and loving; they indulged, kissed, and caressed them lavishly. I had seen Etewa and even the fierce Iramamowe carry the heavy loads of wood for their women only to drop them as soon as they approached the *shabono*. When there had been no other man near, I had seen Etewa save a special piece of meat or fruit for Ritimi or Tutemi. Protected by the darkness, I had seen him press his ear against Tutemi's womb to listen to the strong kicks of his unborn child. In the presence of others he never mentioned that he was to be a father.

Ritimi and I were awakened by Etewa hours before dawn. Quietly we left the camp, following the sandy bank of the river. Except for our hammocks, a few plantains, and the three pineapples the Mocototeri girl had given me, our baskets were empty. Old Kamosiwe had assured Etewa that he would find plenty of game. There was no moon, yet the water shone black, reflecting the faint glow of the sky. At intervals the sound of a nocturnal bird darted through the stillness, a faint cry heralding the oncoming dawn. One by one, the stars faded; the contours of trees became distinct as the rosy light of dawn descended all the way to the shadows at our feet. I was astonished at the width of the river, at the silence of its flowing waters, so still they did not seem to move. Three macaws formed a triangle in the sky, painting the stationary clouds with their red, blue, and yellow feathers as the orange glowing sun rose over the treetops.

Etewa opened his mouth in a yawn that seemed to force its way up from the farthest depths of his lungs. He squinted; the light of the sun was too bright for eyes that had not slept enough.

We unfastened our baskets. Ritimi and I sat on a log from where we watched Etewa draw his bow. Slowly, he raised his arms and arched his back, pointing his arrow high in the air. Motionless, he stood for an interminable time, a stone figure, each taut muscle carefully etched, his gaze attentive to the birds crossing the sky. I did not dare ask why he was waiting so long to let his arrow go.

I did not hear the arrow travel through the air—only a flashing cry that dissolved into a flapping of wings. For an instant the macaw, a mass of feathers held together by the red-tinted arrow, was suspended in the sky before it plunged downward, not too far from where Etewa stood.

Etewa made a fire over which we roasted the plucked bird and some plantains. He ate only a small portion, insisting that we finish the rest so we would have enough strength for the arduous climb over the hills.

We did not miss the sunlight on the river path as we turned into the thicket. The penumbra of vines and trees was soothing to our tired eyes. Decaying leaves looked like patches of flowers against the background of greenness. Etewa cut branches from the dark, wild cocoa trees. "With this wood one makes the best fire drills," he said, stripping the branches of their bark with his sharp knife, which was made from the lower incisor of an agouti. Then he cut the green, yellow, and purple pods individually attached to the stunted cacao trunks by short leafless stems. He split the fruits open and we sucked the sweet gelatinous flesh surrounding the seeds, which we wrapped in leaves.

"Cooked," Ritimi explained, "the *pohoro* seeds are delicious." I wondered if they would taste like chocolate.

"There must be monkeys and weasels nearby," Etewa explained, showing me the discarded, chewed-up fruit skins on the ground. "They like the *pohoro* fruit as much as we do."

A bit further on Etewa stopped in front of a twisted vine, which he marked with his knife. *"Mamucori,"* he said. "I will return to this spot when I need to make fresh poison."

"Ashukamaki?" I exclaimed as we stopped beneath a tree, its trunk encrusted with glossy, waxlike leaves. But it was not the liana used to thicken curare. Etewa pointed out that those leaves were long and jagged. He had stopped because of the various animal bones on the ground.

"Harpy eagle," he said, gesturing to the nest at the top of the tree.

"Don't kill the bird," Ritimi pleaded. "Perhaps it's the spirit of a dead Iticoteri."

Ignoring his wife, Etewa climbed up the tree. Upon reaching the nest he lifted out a shrieking white fluffy chick. We heard the loud cries of its mother as Etewa threw the chick on the ground. He propped himself against the trunk and a branch, then aimed his arrow at the circling bird.

"I'm glad I shot the bird," Etewa said, motioning us to follow him to the spot where the dead eagle crashed through the trees. "It eats only meat." He turned toward Ritimi, then added softly, "I listened to its cry before I aimed my arrow—it wasn't the voice of a spirit." He plucked the soft white feathers from the bird's breast, the long gray ones from its wings, then wrapped them in leaves.

The afternoon heat filtering through the leaves made me so drowsy that all I wanted to do was sleep. Ritimi had dark smudges under her eyes, as if she had dabbed coal on the tender skin. Etewa's pace slackened. Without saying a word, he headed toward the river. We stood motionless in the wide, shallow waters, held in suspension by the heat and the glare. We stared at the reflected clouds and trees, then lay down on a bank of ochre-colored sand in the middle of the river. Blues faded into green and red from the tannin of the submerged roots. Not a leaf stirred, not a cloud moved. Even the dragonflies hovering over the water seemed motionless in their transparent vibrations. Turning on my stomach, I let my hands lie flat on the river's surface as if I could hold the languid harmony reigning between the reflection in the river and the glow in the sky. I slid on my stomach until my lips touched the water, then drank the mirrored clouds.

Two herons that had taken flight at our arrival returned. Poised on their long legs, with necks sunk between their feathers, they watched us through blinking, half-closed lids. I saw silvery bodies jump up in the air, seeking the intoxicating heat shimmering over the water. "Fish," I exclaimed, my lethargy momentarily gone.

Chuckling, Etewa pointed with his arrow to a flock of shrieking parrots crossing the sky. "Birds," he shouted, then reached for the bamboo quiver on his back. He took out an arrowhead, tasted it with the tip of his tongue to see if the poison was still good. Satisfied by its bitter taste, he fastened the sharp point to one of his arrow shafts. Next he tested his bow by letting go of the string. "It's not well stretched," he said, untying it at one end. He twisted the string several times, then threaded it again. "We will stay here for the night," he said, wading through the water. He climbed up on the opposite bank, disappearing behind the trees.

Ritimi and I remained on the sandy bank. She unwrapped the feathers and spread them on a stone for the sun to kill the lice. Excitedly she pointed to a tree on the bank on which clusters of pale flowers hung like fruit. She cut whole branches, then offered me the flowers to eat. "They are sweet," she pointed out upon noticing my reluctance to eat them.

Trying to explain that the flowers reminded me of strongly perfumed soap, I fell asleep. I awoke with the sounds of dusk sweeping up the light of the day, the rustling of the breeze cooling the trees, the calls of birds settling for the night.

Etewa had returned with two curassows and a bundle of palm fronds. I helped Ritimi collect firewood along the riverbank. While she plucked the birds, I assisted Etewa with building the shelter.

"Are you sure it's going to rain?" I asked him, looking at the clear, cloudless sky.

"If old Kamosiwe said it's going to rain, then it will," Etewa said. "He can smell rain the way others can smell food."

It was a cozy little hut. The front pole was higher than the two in the back but not high enough for us to stand up. The poles were connected with long sticks, giving the shelter a triangular shape. Both the roof and the back were covered with palm fronds. We covered the ground with *platanillo* leaves, for the poles were not strong enough to support three hammocks.

Actually, Etewa did not build the shelter so much for Ritimi's and my comfort as for his. If he got wet in the rain, he might cause the child in Tutemi's womb to be born dead or deformed.

Ritimi cooked the birds, several plantains, and the cacao seeds over the fire Etewa built inside the hut. I mashed one of our pineapples. The mixture of flavors, textures, reminded me of a Thanksgiving dinner.

"It must be like *momo* nuts," Ritimi said after I had explained about cranberry sauce. "*Momo* is also red; it needs to be boiled for a long time until it's soft. It also has to soak in water until all the poison is leached out."

"I don't think I'd like *momo* nuts."

"You will," Ritimi assured me. "See how much you like the *pohoro* seeds. *Momo* nuts are even better."

Smiling, I nodded. Although the roasted cacao seeds did not taste like chocolate, they were as delicious as fresh cashews.

Etewa and Ritimi were asleep the moment they lay back on the *platanillo* leaves. I stretched out next to Ritimi. In her sleep she reached over, hugging me close to her. The warmth of her body filled me with a soothing laziness; her rhythmic breathing lulled me into a pleasant drowsiness. A succession of dreamlike images drifted through my mind, sometimes slow, sometimes fast, as if someone were projecting them in front of me: Mocototeri men brachiating from tree to tree glided past me, their cries indistinguishable from the howler monkeys. Crocodiles with luminous eyes, barely above the surface of the water, blinked sleepily, then suddenly opened their giant jaws ready to swallow me. Anteaters with threadlike viscous tongues blew bubbles in which I saw myself captive together with hundreds of ants.

I was awakened by a sudden gust of wind; it brought with it the smell of rain. I sat up and listened to the heavy drops pattering on the palm fronds. The familiar sounds of crickets and frogs provided a continuous pulsating background hum to the plaintive cries of nocturnal monkeys, the flutelike calls of forest partridges. I was sure I heard steps and then the snapping of twigs.

"There is someone out there," I said, reaching over to Etewa.

He moved to the front pole of the shelter. "It's a jaguar looking for frogs in the marshes." Etewa turned my head slightly to the left. "You can smell him."

I sniffed the air repeatedly. "I can't smell a thing."

"It's the jaguar's breath that smells. It's strong because he eats everything raw." Etewa turned my head once more, this time to the right. "Listen, he is returning to the forest."

I lay down again. Ritimi awoke, rubbed her eyes, and smiled. "I dreamt that I walked up in the mountains and saw the waterfalls."

"We will go that way tomorrow," Etewa said, unfastening the *epena* pouch from around his neck. He poured some of the powder in his palm, then with one deep breath drew it into his nostrils.

"Are you going to chant to the *hekuras* now?" I asked.

"I will beg the spirits of the forest to protect us," Etewa said, then began to chant in a low voice. His song, carried on the night breeze, seemed to traverse the darkness. I was certain it reached the spirits dwelling in the four corners of the earth. The fire died down to a red glimmer. I no longer heard Etewa's voice, but his lips were still moving as I fell into a dreamless sleep.

I was awakened shortly by Ritimi's soft moans and touched her shoulder, thinking she was having a nightmare.

"Do you want to try it?" she murmured.

Surprised, I opened my eyes and looked into Etewa's smiling face; he was making love to her. I watched them for a while. The motion of their bodies was so closely adjusted they barely moved.

Etewa, not in the least embarrassed, moved out of Ritimi and knelt in front of me. Lifting my legs, he stretched them slightly. He pressed his cheeks against my calves; his touch was like the playful caress of a child. There was no embrace; there were no words. Yet I was filled with tenderness.

Etewa switched to Ritimi again, resting his head between her shoulder and mine.

"Now we truly are sisters," Ritimi said softly. "On the outside we don't look the same, but our insides are the same now."

I snuggled against her. The river breeze brushing through the shelter was like a caress.

The rosy light of dawn descended gently over the treetops. Ritimi and Etewa headed toward the river. I stepped outside the shelter and breathed in the new day. At dawn the darkness of the forest is no longer black but a bluish green, like an underground cave that is illuminated by a light filtering through some secret crack. A sprinkling of dew, like soft rain, wet my face as I pushed leaves and vines out of my way. Little red spiders with hairy legs hastily respun their silvery webs.

Etewa found a honeycomb inside a hollow trunk. After squeezing the last drop in our mouths, he soaked the comb in a water-filled calabash and later we drank the sweet water.

We climbed overgrown paths bordering small cascades and stretches of river that swept by at dizzying speeds, causing a breeze that blew our hair and swayed the bamboo on the shore.

"This is the scene of my dream," Ritimi said, extending her arms as if to embrace the wide expanse of water hurtling down before us into a deep wide pool.

I edged my way onto the dark basalt rocks protruding around the falls. For a long time I stood beneath it, my hands raised to break the thunderous force of the water descending from heights already warmed by the sun.

"Come out, white girl," Etewa shouted. "The spirits of the rushing water will make you ill."

Later in the afternoon we made camp by a grove of wild banana trees. Amidst them I discovered an avocado tree. It had only one fruit; it was not pear shaped, but round, as big as a cantaloupe, and shone as if it were made out of wax. Etewa lifted me so I could reach the first branch, then slowly I climbed toward the fruit hanging at the tip of the highest limb. My greed to reach the green ball was so great I ignored the brittle branches cracking under my weight. As I pulled the fruit toward me the branch I was standing on gave way.

Etewa laughed till tears rolled down his cheeks. Ritimi, also laughing, scraped the mashed avocado from my stomach and thigh.

"I could have hurt myself," I said, piqued by their indifference and mirth. "Maybe I broke a leg."

"No, you didn't," Etewa assured me. "The ground is soft with dead leaves." He scooped some mashed fruit in his hand and urged me to taste it. "I told you not to stay under the falls," he added seriously. "The spirits of the rushing water made you ignore the danger of dry branches."

By the time Etewa had built the shelter all trace of day had vanished. The forest was clouded in a whitish mist. It did not rain, but the dew on the leaves fell in heavy drops at the slightest touch.

We slept on the *platanillo* leaves, warmed by each other's bodies and by the low fire that Etewa kept alive throughout the night by periodically pushing the burning logs closer to the flame with his foot.

We left our camp before dawn. Thick mist still shrouded the trees and the cry of frogs reached us as if from a great distance. The higher we climbed, the scantier the vegetation became until at last there was nothing but grasses and rocks.

We reached the top of a plateau eroded by winds and

rains, a relic from another age. Below, the forest was still asleep under a blanket of fog. A mysterious, pathless world whose vastness one could never guess from the outside. We sat on the ground and silently waited for the sun to rise.

An overwhelming sense of awe brought me to my feet as the sky in the east glowed red and purple along the horizon. The clouds, obedient to the wind, opened to let the rising disk through. Pink mist rolled over the treetops, touching up shadows with deep blue, spreading green and yellow all over the sky until it changed into a transparent blue.

I turned to look behind me, to the west, where clouds were changing shape, giving way to the expanding light. To the south, the sky was tinted with fiery streaks and luminous clouds piled up, pushed by the wind.

"Over there is our *shabono*," Etewa said, pointing into the distance. He grasped my arm and turned me around, into a northerly direction. "And over there is the great river, where the white man passes by."

The sun had lifted the blanket of fog. The river shone like a golden snake cutting through the greenness until it lost itself in an immensity of space that seemed to be part of another world.

I wanted to speak, to cry out loud, but I had no words with which to express my emotions. Looking at Ritimi and Etewa, I knew they understood how deeply I felt. I held out my arms as if to embrace this marvelous border of forest and sky. I felt I was at the edge of time and space. I could hear the vibrations of the light, the whispering of trees, the cries of distant birds carried by the wind.

I suddenly knew that it was out of choice and not out of lack of interest that the Iticoteri had never been curious about my past. For them I had no personal history. Only thus could they have accepted me as something other than an oddity. Events and relationships of my past had begun to blur in my memory. It was not that I had forgotten them; I had simply stopped thinking about them, for they had no meaning there in the forest. Like the Iticoteri, I had learned to live in the present. Time was outside of me. It was something to be used only at the moment. Once used, it sank back into itself and became an imperceptible part of my inner being.

"You have been so quiet for so long," Ritimi said, sitting on the ground. Pulling her knees up, she clasped them, then rested her chin on them and gazed at me.

"I've been thinking of how happy I am to be here," I said.

Smiling, Ritimi rocked herself gently to and fro. "One day I will collect wood and you will no longer be at my side. But I will not be sad, because this afternoon, before we reach the *shabono,* we will paint ourselves with *onoto* and we will be happy watching a flow of macaws chase the setting sun."

PART FOUR

14

Women, I had been told, were not to concern themselves with any aspect of the *epena* ritual. They were not supposed to prepare it, nor were they allowed to take the hallucinogenic snuff. It was not even proper for a woman to touch the cane tube through which the powder was blown, unless a man specifically asked her to fetch it for him.

To my utter astonishment one morning, I saw Ritimi bent over the hearth, attentively studying the dark reddish *epena* seeds drying over the embers. Without acknowledging my presence, she proceeded to rub the dried seeds between her palms over a large leaf containing a heap of bark ashes. With the same confidence and expertise I had seen in Etewa, she periodically spat on the ashes and seeds as she kneaded them into a pliable uniform mass.

As she transferred the doughy mixture onto a hot earthenware shard, Ritimi looked up at me, her smile clearly revealing how delighted she was by my bafflement. "Ohooo, the *epena* will be strong," she said, shifting her gaze back to the hallucinogenic dough bursting with loud popping sounds on the piece of terra-cotta. With a smooth stone she ground the fast-drying mass until it all blended into a very fine powder, which included a layer of dust from the earthenware shard.

"I didn't know women knew how to prepare *epena*," I said.

"Women can do anything," Ritimi said, funneling the brownish powder into a slender bamboo container.

Waiting in vain for her to satisfy my curiosity, I finally asked, "Why are you preparing the snuff?"

"Etewa knows I prepare *epena* well," she said proudly. "He likes to have some ready whenever he returns from a hunt."

For several days we had eaten nothing but fish. Not being in the mood for hunting, Etewa, together with a group of men, had dammed a small stream, in which they placed crushed, cut-up pieces of *ayori-toto* vine. The water had turned a whitish color, as if it were milk. All the women had to do was to fill their baskets with the asphyxiated fish that rose to the surface. But the Iticoteri were not too fond of fish and soon the women and children began to complain about the lack of meat. Two days had passed since Etewa and his friends had set out for the forest.

"How do you know Etewa is returning today?" I asked, and before Ritimi answered, hastily added, "I know, you can feel it in your legs."

Smiling, Ritimi picked up the long narrow tube and blew through it repeatedly. "I'm cleaning it," she said with a mischievous glint in her eyes.

"Have you ever taken *epena*?"

Ritimi leaned closer to whisper in my ear, "Yes, but I did not like it. It gave me a headache." She looked around furtively. "Would you like to try some?"

"I don't want a headache."

"Maybe it's different for you," she said. Standing up, she casually put the bamboo container and the three-foot-long cane into her basket. "Let's go to the river. I want to see if I mixed the *epena* well."

We walked along the bank, quite a distance from where

the Iticoteri usually came to bathe or to draw water. I squatted on the ground in front of Ritimi, who meticulously began introducing a small amount of *epena* into one end of the cane. Delicately, she flicked the tube with her forefinger, scattering the powder along its length. I felt drops of sweat running down my sides. The only time I had ever been drugged was when I had had three wisdom teeth removed. At the time I had wondered if it would not have been wiser to bear the pain instead of the gruesome hallucinations the drug had induced in me.

"Lift your head slightly," Ritimi said, holding the slender tube toward me. "See the little *rasha* nut at the end? Press it against your nostril."

I nodded. I could see that the palm seed had been tightly attached to the end of the cane with resin. I made sure the small hole that had been drilled into the hollowed-out fruit was inside my nose. I ran my hand along the fragile length of the smooth cane. I heard the sharp sound of compressed air shooting through the tube. I let go of it as a piercing pain seared into my brain. "That feels terrible!" I groaned, pounding the top of my head with my palms.

"Now the other one," laughed Ritimi as she placed the cane against my left nostril.

I felt as if I were bleeding, but Ritimi assured me it was only mucus and saliva dribbling uncontrollably from my nose and mouth. I tried to wipe myself clean but was unable to lift my heavy hand.

"Why don't you enjoy it instead of being so fussy about a little slime running into your belly button?" Ritimi said, grinning at my clumsy efforts. "I'll wash you later in the river."

"There is nothing to enjoy," I said, beginning to sweat profusely from every pore. I felt nauseous and there was an odd heaviness in my limbs. I saw points of red and yellow light everywhere. I wondered what Ritimi found so funny. Her laughter reverberated in my ears as if it came from inside my head. "Let me blow some in your nose," I suggested.

"Oh, no. I have to watch over you," she said. "We cannot both end up with a headache."

"This *epena* has to give more than a headache," I said. "Blow some more into my nose. I want to see a *hekura*."

"*Hekuras* don't come to women," Ritimi said between fits of laughter. She placed the cane against my nose. "But perhaps if you chant they'll come to you."

I felt each grain travel up my nasal passage, exploding in the top of my skull. Slowly, a delicious lassitude spread through my body. I turned my gaze to the river, almost expecting a mythical creature to emerge from its depths. Ripples of water began to grow into waves splashing back and forth with such force that I scurried backward on my hands and knees. I was certain the water was trying to trap me. Shifting my eyes to Ritimi's face, I was bewildered by her alarmed expression.

"What is it?" I asked. My voice trailed off as I followed the direction of her gaze. Etewa and Iramamowe stood in front of us. With great difficulty I stood up. I touched them to make sure I was not hallucinating.

Unfastening the large bundles slung over their backs, they handed them to the other hunters standing behind on the trail. "Take the meat to the *shabono*," Iramamowe said hoarsely.

The thought that Etewa and Iramamowe would eat so little of the meat filled me with such sadness I began to cry. A hunter gives away most of the game he kills. He would rather go hungry than risk the chance of being accused of stinginess. "I'll save you my portion," I said to Etewa. "I prefer fish to meat."

"Why are you taking *epena*?" Etewa's voice was stern, but his eyes were sparkling with amusement.

"We had to check if Ritimi mixed the powder properly," I mumbled. "It's not strong enough. Haven't seen a *hekura* yet."

"It's strong," Etewa retorted. Putting his hands on my shoulders, he made me squat on the ground in front of him. "*Epena* made from seeds is stronger than the kind made from bark." He filled the cane with the snuff. "Ritimi's breath does not have much strength." A devilish grin creased his face as he placed the tube against my nostril and blew.

I fell backward, cradling my head, which reverberated with Iramamowe's and Etewa's uproarious laughter. Slowly I stood up. My feet felt as though they were not touching the ground.

"Dance, white girl," Iramamowe urged me. "See if you can lure the *hekuras* with your chant."

Mesmerized by his words, I held out my arms and began to dance with small jerky steps, the way I had seen the men dance when in an *epena* trance.

Through my head ran the melody and words of one of Iramamowe's *hekura* songs.

> *After days of calling the hekura of*
> *the hummingbird,*
> *she finally came to me.*
> *Dazzled, I watched her dance.*
> *I fainted on the ground*
> *and did not feel as she*
> *pierced my throat*
> *and tore out my tongue.*
> *I did not see how my blood*
> *flowed into the river,*
> *tinting the water red.*

She filled the gap with precious feathers.
That is why I know the hekura songs.
That is why I sing so well.

Etewa guided me to the edge of the river, then splashed water on my face and chest. "Don't repeat his song," he warned me. "Iramamowe will get angry. He will harm you with his magic plants."

I wanted to do as he told me, yet I was compelled to repeat Iramamowe's *hekura* song.

"Don't repeat his song," Etewa pleaded. "Iramamowe will make you deaf. He will make your eyes bleed." Etewa turned toward Iramamowe. "Do not bewitch the white girl."

"I won't," Iramamowe assured him. "I'm not angry at her. I know she is still ignorant of our ways." Framing my face with his hands, he forced me to look into his eyes. "I can see the *hekuras* dancing in her pupils."

In the light of the sun Iramamowe's eyes were not dark, but light, the color of honey. "I can also see the *hekuras* in your eyes," I said to him, studying the yellow specks on his iris. His face radiated a gentleness that I had never seen before. As I tried to tell him that I finally understood why his name was Jaguar's Eye, I collapsed against him. I was vaguely aware of being carried in someone's arms. As soon as I was in my hammock, I fell into a deep sleep from which I did not awaken until the following day.

Arasuwe, Iramamowe, and old Kamosiwe had gathered in Etewa's hut. Anxiously, I looked from one to the other. They were painted with *onoto;* their perforated earlobes were decorated with short, feather-ornamented pieces of cane. When Ritimi sat next to me in my hammock, I was certain she had come to protect me from their wrath. Before giving any of the men a chance to speak, I began weaving excuses for having taken *epena*. The faster I talked, the safer I felt. A steady flow of words, I thought, was the surest way of dispelling their anger.

Arasuwe finally cut into my incoherent chatter. "You talk too fast. I can't understand what you are saying."

I was disconcerted at the friendliness of his tone. I was certain it was not a result of my talking. I glanced at the others. Except for a vague curiosity, their faces revealed nothing. I leaned against Ritimi and whispered, "If they aren't upset, why are they all in the hut?"

"I don't know," she said softly.

"White girl, have you ever seen a *hekura* before yesterday?" Arasuwe asked.

"I've never seen a *hekura* in my life," I rapidly assured him. "Not even yesterday."

"Iramamowe saw *hekuras* in your eyes," Arasuwe insisted. "He took *epena* last night. His personal *hekura* told him she had taught you her song."

"I know Iramamowe's song because I've heard it so often," I almost shouted. "How could his *hekura* have taught me? Spirits don't come to women."

"You don't look like an Iticoteri woman," old Kamosiwe said, gazing at me as if he were seeing me for the first time. "The *hekuras* could easily be confused." He wiped the tobacco juice dribbling down the side of his mouth. "There have been times when *hekuras* have come to women."

"Believe me," I said to Iramamowe, "the reason I know your song is because I've heard you sing it so many times."

"But I sing very softly," Iramamowe argued. "If you really know my song, why don't you sing it now?"

Hoping this would bring the *epena* incident to an end, I began to hum the melody. To my utter distress, I could not remember the words.

"You see," Iramamowe exclaimed triumphantly. "My

hekura taught you my song. That's why I didn't get angry
at you yesterday, why I didn't blow into your eyes and ears,
why I didn't hit you with a burning log."

"It must be so," I said, forcing a smile. Inwardly I shuddered. Iramamowe was well known for his quick temper,
revengeful nature, and cruel punishments.

Old Kamosiwe spat his tobacco wad on the ground, then
reached for a banana hanging directly above him. Peeling
it, he stuffed the fruit whole in his mouth. "A long time
ago there was a woman *shapori*," he mumbled, still chewing. "Her name was Imaawami. Her skin was as white as
yours. She was tall and very strong. When she took *epena*,
she sang to the *hekuras*. She knew how to massage away
pain and how to suck out sickness. There was no one like
her to hunt for the lost souls of children and to counteract
the curses of enemy shamans."

"Tell us, white girl," Arasuwe said, "have you known a
shapori before you came here? Have you ever been taught
by one?"

"I've known shamans," I said. "But they have never
taught me anything." In great detail I described the kind of
work I had been engaged in prior to my arrival at the
mission. I talked about doña Mercedes and how she had
permitted me to watch and record the interaction between
herself and her patients. "Once doña Mercedes let me take
part in a spiritual séance," I said. "She believed that I
might be a medium. Curers from various areas had gathered at her house. We all sat in a circle chanting for the
spirits to come. We chanted for a very long time."

"Did you take *epena*?" Iramamowe asked.

"No. We smoked big, fat cigars," I said, and almost giggled at the memory. There had been ten people in doña
Mercedes's room. Rigidly we had all sat on stools covered
with goat skin. With obsessive concentration we had

puffed at our cigars, filling the room with smoke so thick
we could hardly see each other. I was too busy getting sick
to be transported into a trance. "One of the curers asked
me to leave, saying that the spirits would not come as long
as I stayed in the room."

"Did the *hekuras* come after you left?" Iramamowe
asked.

"Yes," I said. "Doña Mercedes told me the following day
how the spirits entered into the head of each curer."

"Strange," Iramamowe murmured. "But you must have
learned many things if you lived at her house."

"I learned her prayers and incantations to the spirits,
and also the types of plants and roots she used for her
patients," I said. "But I was never taught how to communicate with spirits or how to cure people." I looked at
each of the men. Etewa was the only one who smiled. "According to her, the only way to learn about curing was to
do it."

"Did you start curing?" old Kamosiwe asked.

"No. Doña Mercedes suggested I should go to the
jungle."

The four men looked at one another, then slowly turned
to me and almost in a chorus asked, "Did you come here to
learn about shamans."

"No!" I shouted, then in a subdued tone added, "I came
to bring Angelica's ashes." Choosing my words very carefully, I explained how it was my profession to study people, including shamans—not because I wanted to become
one, but because I was interested in learning about the
similarities and differences between various shamanistic
traditions.

"Have you been with other *shapori* besides doña Mercedes?" old Kamosiwe asked.

I told the men about Juan Caridad, an old man I had

met years before. I got up and reached for my knapsack, which I kept inside a basket tied to one of the rafters. From the zipped side pocket, which because of the odd lock had escaped the women's curiosity, I pulled out a small leather pouch. I emptied its contents into Arasuwe's hands. Suspiciously, he gazed at a stone, a pearl, and the uncut diamond I had been given by Mr. Barth.

"This stone," I said, taking it from Arasuwe's hand, "was given to me by Juan Caridad. He made it jump out of the water before my eyes." I caressed the smooth, deep golden-colored stone. It fitted perfectly in my palm. It was oval-shaped, flat on one side, a round bulge on the other.

"Did you stay with him the way you did with doña Mercedes?" Arasuwe asked.

"No. I didn't stay with him for very long," I said. "I was afraid of him."

"Afraid? I thought you were never afraid," old Kamosiwe exclaimed.

"Juan Caridad was an awesome man," I said. "He made me have strange dreams in which he would always appear. In the mornings he would give me a detailed account of what I had dreamt."

The men nodded knowingly at each other. "What a powerful *shapori*," Kamosiwe said. "What did he make you dream about?"

I told them that the dream that had frightened me the most had been, up to a point, an exact sequential replica of an event that had taken place when I was five years old. Once, while I was returning from the beach with my family, my father decided, instead of driving directly home, to take a detour through the forest to look for orchids. We stopped by a shallow river. My brothers went with my father into the bush. My mother, afraid of snakes and mosquitoes, remained in the car. My sister dared me to wade with her along the shallow riverbank. She was ten years older than I, tall and thin, with short curly hair so bleached by the sun it appeared white. Her eyes were a deep velvety brown, not blue or green like most blondes'. As she squatted in the middle of the stream, she told me to watch the water between her feet, which to my utter bewilderment turned red with blood. "Are you hurt?" I asked. She did not say a word as she stood up. Smiling, she beckoned me to follow her. I remained in the water, petrified, as I watched her climb up the opposite bank.

In my dream I experienced the same fear, but I told myself that now that I was an adult there was nothing to be afraid of. I was about to follow my sister up the steep bank when I heard Juan Caridad's voice urging me to remain in the water. "She is calling you from the land of the dead," he said. "Don't you remember that she is dead?"

No matter how much I begged him, Juan Caridad absolutely refused to discuss how he succeeded in appearing in my dreams or how he knew that my sister had died in a plane crash. I had never talked to him about my family. He knew nothing about me except that I had come from Los Angeles to learn about curing practices.

Juan Caridad did not get angry when I suggested that he probably was familiar with someone who knew me well. He assured me that no matter what I said or what I accused him of, he would not discuss a subject he had sworn to remain silent about. He also urged me to return home.

"Why did he give you the stone?" old Kamosiwe asked.

"Can you see these dark spots and the transparent veins crisscrossing the surface?" I said, holding the stone close to his one eye. "Juan Caridad told me that they represent the trees and the rivers of the forest. He said the stone revealed that I would spend a long time in the jungle, that I should keep it as a talisman to protect me from harm."

The four men in the hut were silent for a long time. Arasuwe handed me the uncut diamond and the pearl. "Tell us about these."

I talked about the diamond Mr. Barth had given me at the mission.

"And this?" old Kamosiwe asked, picking up the small pearl from my hand. "I've never seen such a round stone."

"I've had it for a long time," I said.

"Longer than the stone Juan Caridad gave you?" Ritimi asked.

"Much longer," I said. "The pearl was also given to me by an old man when I arrived at Margarita Island, where I had gone with some classmates for a holiday. As we disembarked from the boat, an old fisherman came directly toward me. Placing the pearl in my hand, he said, 'It was yours from the day you were born. You lost it, but I found it for you at the bottom of the sea.' "

"What happened then?" Arasuwe asked impatiently.

"Nothing much," I said. "Before I recovered from my surprise, the old man was gone."

Kamosiwe held the pearl in his hand, letting it roll back and forth. It looked strangely beautiful in his dark, calloused palm, as if it belonged there. "I would like you to have it," I said to him.

Smiling, Kamosiwe looked at me. "I like it very much." He held the pearl against the sunlight. "How beautiful it is. There are clouds inside the stone. Did the old man who gave it to you look like me?" he asked as all four men were walking out of the hut.

"He was old like you," I said as he turned toward his hut. But the old man had not heard me. Holding the pearl high above his head, he pranced around the clearing.

*   *   *

No one said a word about my having taken *epena*. On some evenings, however, when the men gathered outside their huts to inhale the hallucinogenic powder, some youths would jokingly cry out, "White girl, we want to see you dance. We want to hear you sing Iramamowe's *hekura* song." But I did not try the powder again.

15

I never found out where Puriwariwe, Angelica's brother, lived. I wondered if someone actually called him when he was needed or if he intuited it. Whether he would stay in the *shabono* for days or weeks, no one knew. There was something reassuring about his presence, about the way he chanted to the *hekuras* at night, urging the spirits to protect his people, especially the children, who were the most vulnerable of all, from the spells of an evil *shapori*.

One morning the old *shapori* walked directly into Etewa's hut. Sitting in one of the empty hammocks, he demanded I show him the treasures I kept hidden in my knapsack.

I was tempted to retort that I kept nothing hidden, but remained silent as I unfastened my basket from the rafter. I knew he was going to ask me for one of the stones and fervently wished it would not be the one Juan Caridad had given me. Somehow I was certain it was the stone that had brought me to the jungle. I feared that if Puriwariwe were to take it from me, Milagros would arrive and take me back to the mission. Or worse, something dreadful might happen to me. I believed implicitly in the stone's protective powers.

Intently the old man studied both the diamond and the stone. He held the diamond against the light. "I want this one," he said, smiling. "It holds the colors of the sky." Stretching in the hammock, the old man placed the diamond and the other stone on his stomach. "Now, I want you to tell me about the *shapori* Juan Caridad. I want to hear of all the dreams in which this man appeared."

"I don't know if I can remember them all." Glancing at his thin, wrinkled face and emaciated body, I had the vague feeling I had known him longer than I could remember. There was a familiar, tender response in me as his smiling eyes held my gaze. Lying comfortably in my hammock, I began to speak with an easy fluency. Whenever I did not know the Iticoteri word, I filled in with a Spanish one. Puriwariwe did not seem to mind. I had the impression he was more interested in the sound and rhythm of my words than in their actual meaning.

When I finished with my narration, the old man spat out the wad of tobacco Ritimi had prepared for him prior to leaving for work in the gardens. In a soft voice he spoke of the woman shaman Kamosiwe had already told me about. Not only was Imaawami considered a great *shapori*, but she was also believed to have been a superb hunter and warrior who had raided enemy settlements together with the men.

"Did she have a gun?" I asked, hoping to learn more about her identity. Since I first heard about her, I had been obsessed with the possibility that she might have been a captive white woman. Maybe as far back as the time when the Spaniards first came looking for El Dorado.

"She used a bow and arrows," the old shaman said. "Her *mamucori* poison was of the best kind."

No matter how I phrased my question, I was unable to learn whether Imaawami was a real person or a being that belonged to a mythological epoch. All the *shapori* was willing to say was that Imaawami existed a long time ago. I was certain the old man was not being evasive; it was common for the Iticoteri to be vague about past events.

On some evenings, after the women had cooked the last meal, Puriwariwe would sit by the fire in the middle of the clearing. Both young and old gathered around him. I always looked for a spot close to him, for I did not want to miss a word of what he said. In a low, monotonous, nasal tone, he talked about the origin of man, of fire, of floods, of the moon and the sun. Some of these myths I already knew. Yet each time they were recounted it was as if I were listening to a different story. Each narrator embellished, improved upon it according to his own vision.

"Which one is the real myth of creation?" I asked Puriwariwe one evening after he finished the story of Waipilishoni, a woman shaman who had created blood by mixing *onoto* and water. She had given life to the woodlike bodies of a brother and sister by making them drink this substance. The evening before the *shapori* had told us that the first Indian was born out of the leg of a manlike creature.

For an instant Puriwariwe regarded me with a perplexed expression. "They are all real," he finally said. "Don't you know that man was created many times throughout the ages?"

I shook my head in amazement. He touched my face and laughed. "Ohoo, how ignorant you still are. Listen carefully. I will tell you of all the times the world was destroyed by fires and floods."

A few days later, Puriwariwe announced that Xorowe, Iramamowe's oldest son, was to be initiated as a *shapori*. Xorowe was perhaps seventeen or eighteen years old. He had a slight, agile body and a narrow, delicately featured face in which his deep brown eyes seemed overly large and glowing. Taking only a hammock, he moved into the small hut that had been built for him in the clearing. Since it was believed that *hekuras* fled from women, no females were allowed near the dwelling—not even Xorowe's mother, grandmother, or his sisters.

A youth who had never been with a woman was chosen to take care of the initiate. It was he who blew *epena* into Xorowe's nostrils, who saw that the fire was never out, and made sure each day that Xorowe had the proper amount of water and honey, the only food the initiate was allowed. The women always left enough wood outside the *shabono,* so the boy did not have to search too far. The men were responsible for finding honey. Each day the *shapori* urged them to go farther into the forest for new sources.

Xorowe spent most of the time inside the hut lying in his hammock. Sometimes he sat on a polished tree trunk Iramamowe had placed outside the dwelling, for he was not supposed to sit on the ground. Within a week, Xorowe's face had darkened from the *epena.* His once glowing eyes were dull and unfocused. His body, dirty and emaciated, moved with the clumsiness of a drunkard.

Life went on as usual in the *shabono,* except for the families living closest to Xorowe's hut, who were not allowed to cook meat on their hearths. According to Puriwariwe, *hekuras* detested the smell of roasting meat, and if they so much as caught a whiff of the offensive odor, they would flee back to the mountains.

Like his apprentice, Puriwariwe took *epena* day and night. Tirelessly, he chanted for hours, coaxing the spirits into Xorowe's hut, begging the *hekuras* to cut open the young man's chest. Some evenings Arasuwe, Iramamowe, and others accompanied the old man in his chants.

During the second week, in an uncertain, quivering voice, Xorowe joined in the singing. At first he only sang the *hekura* songs of the armadillo, tapir, jaguar, and other large animals, which were believed to be masculine spirits. They were the easiest to entice. Next he sang the *hekura* songs of plants and rocks. And last he sang the songs of the female spirits—the spider, snake, and hummingbird. They were not only the most difficult to lure but, because of their treacherous and jealous nature, were hard to control.

Late one night, when most of the *shabono* was asleep, I sat outside Etewa's hut and watched the men chant. Xorowe was so weak one of the men had to hold him up so Puriwariwe could dance around him. "Xorowe, sing louder," the old man urged him. "Sing as loud as the birds, as loud as the jaguars." Puriwariwe danced out of the *shabono* into the forest. "Xorowe, sing louder," he shouted. "The *hekuras* dwelling in all the corners of the world need to hear your song."

Three nights later, Xorowe's joyful cries echoed through the *shabono:* "Father, Father, the *hekuras* are approaching. I can hear their humming and buzzing. They are dancing toward me. They are opening my chest, my head. They are coming through my fingers and my feet." Xorowe ran out of the hut. Squatting before the old man, he cried, "Father, Father, help me, for they are coming through my eyes and nose."

Puriwariwe helped Xorowe to his feet. They began to dance in the clearing, their thin emaciated shadows spilling across the moonlit ground. Hours later, a despairing scream, the cry of a panic-stricken child, pierced the dawn. "Father, Father, from today on let no woman come near my hut."

"That's what they all say," Ritimi mumbled, getting out of her hammock. She stocked the fire, then buried several plantains under the hot embers. "When Etewa decided to be initiated as a *shapori,* I had already gone to live with him," she said. "The night he begged Puriwariwe to let no woman near him I went to his hut and drove the *hekuras* away."

"Why did you do that?"

"Etewa's mother urged me to do it," Ritimi said. "She was afraid he would die. She knew Etewa liked women too much; she knew he would never become a great *shapori*." Ritimi sat in my hammock. "I will tell you the whole story." She snuggled comfortably against me, then began to speak in a low whisper. "The night the *hekuras* entered Etewa's chest, he cried out just as Xorowe did tonight. It is the female *hekuras* who make such a fuss. They want no woman in the hut. Etewa sobbed bitterly that night, crying out that an evil woman had passed near his hut. I felt quite sad when I heard him say that the *hekuras* had left him."

"Did Etewa know it was you who had been in his hut?"

"No," Ritimi said. "No one saw me. If Puriwariwe knew, he didn't say. He was aware Etewa would never be a good *shapori*."

"Why did he get initiated in the first place?"

"There is always the possibility that a man may become a great *shapori*." Ritimi rested her head against my arm. "That night many men stayed up chanting for the *hekuras* to return. But the spirits had no desire to come back. They had left not only because Etewa had been soiled by a woman, but because the *hekuras* were afraid he would never be a good father to them."

"Why does a man get soiled when he goes with a woman?"

"*Shapori* do," Ritimi said. "I don't know why, because men as well as *shapori* enjoy it. I believe it's the female *hekuras* who are jealous and afraid of a man who enjoys women too often." Ritimi went on to explain how a sexually active man had little desire to take *epena* and chant to the spirits. Male spirits, she explained, were not posses- sive. They were content if a man took the hallucinogenic snuff before and after a hunt or a raid. "I'd rather have a good hunter and warrior than a good *shapori* for a husband," she confessed. "*Shapori* don't like women much."

"What about Iramamowe?" I asked. "He is considered a great *shapori,* yet he has two wives."

"Ohoo, you are so ignorant. I have to explain everything to you." Ritimi giggled. "Iramamowe does not sleep with his two wives often. His youngest brother, who has no woman of his own, sleeps with one of them." Ritimi looked around to make sure no one was overhearing us. "Have you noticed that Iramamowe often goes into the forest by himself?"

I nodded. "But so do other men."

"And so do women," Ritimi aped me, mispronouncing the words the way I had. I had great difficulty imitating the proper Iticoteri nasal tone, which probably was a result of their usually having tobacco wads in their mouths. "That's not what I mean," she said. "Iramamowe goes into the forest to find what great *shapori* seek."

"What is that?"

"The strength to travel to the house of thunder. The strength to travel to the sun and come back alive."

"I've seen Iramamowe sleep in the forest with a woman," I confessed.

Ritimi laughed softly. "I will tell you a very important secret," she whispered. "Iramamowe sleeps with a woman the way a *shapori* does. He takes a woman's energy away but gives nothing in return."

"Have you slept with him?"

Ritimi nodded. But no matter how much I coaxed and pleaded with her, she would not elaborate any further.

A week later, Xorowe's mother, sisters, aunts, and cousins started to wail in their huts. "Old man," the mother cried, "my son has no more strength. Do you want to kill him of hunger? Do you want to kill him from lack of sleep? It is time you left him alone."

The old *shapori* paid no attention to their cries. The following evening Iramamowe took *epena* and danced in front of his son's hut. He alternated between jumping high in the air and crawling on all fours, imitating the fierce growls of a jaguar. He stopped abruptly. With his eyes fixed on some point directly in front of him, he sat on the ground. "Women, women, do not despair," he cried out in a loud, nasal voice. "For a few more days Xorowe has to remain without food. Even though he appears weak, and his movements are clumsy, and he moans in his sleep, he will not die." Standing up, Iramamowe walked toward Puriwariwe and asked him to blow more *epena* into his head. Then he returned to the same spot where he had been sitting.

"Listen carefully," Ritimi urged me. "Iramamowe is one of the few *shapori* who has traveled to the sun during his initiation. He has guided others on their first journey. He has two voices. The one you just heard was his own; the other one is that of his personal *hekura*."

Now Iramamowe's words sprang from deep in his chest; like stones rumbling down a ravine, the words tumbled into the silence of people gathered in their huts. Huddled together in an atmosphere heavy with smoke and anticipation, they seemed to be barely breathing. Their eyes glittered with longing for what the personal *hekura* of Iramamowe had to say, for what was about to take place in the mysterious world of the initiate.

"My son has traveled into the depths of the earth and burned in the hot fires of their silent caves," said Iramamowe's rumbling *hekura* voice. "Guided by the *hekura* eyes, he has been led through cobwebs of darkness, across rivers and mountains. They have taught him songs of birds, fishes, snakes, spiders, monkeys, and jaguars.

"Although his eyes and cheeks are sunken, he is strong. Those who have descended into the silent burning caves, those who have traveled beyond the forest mist, will return with their personal *hekura* in their chest. Those are the ones who will be guided to the sun, to the luminous huts of my brothers and sisters, the *hekuras* of the sky.

"Women, women, do not cry out his name. Let him go on his journey. Let him depart from his mother and sisters, so he can reach this world of light, which is more exhausting than the world of darkness."

Spellbound, I listened to Iramamowe's voice. No one talked, no one moved, no one looked anywhere but at his figure, sitting rigidly in front of his son's hut. After every pause, his voice rose to a higher pitch of intensity.

"Women, women, do not despair. On his path he will meet those who have withstood the long nights of mist. He will meet those who have not turned back. He will meet those who have not trembled in fear by what they have witnessed during their journey. He will meet those who had their bodies burned and cut up, those who had their bones removed and dried in the sun. He will meet those who did not fall into the clouds on their way to the sun.

"Women, women, do not disturb his balance. My son is about to reach the end of his journey. Do not watch his dark face. Do not look into his hollow eyes that shine with no light, for he is destined to be a solitary man." Iramamowe stood up. Together with Puriwariwe he entered Xorowe's hut, where they spent the rest of the night chanting softly to the *hekuras*.

A few days later, the youth who had taken care of Xorowe during his long weeks of initiation washed him with warm water and dried him with fragrant leaves. Then he painted his body with a mixture of coals and *onoto*—wavy lines extending from his forehead down his cheeks and shoulders. The rest of his body was marked with evenly distributed round spots that reached to his ankles.

For a moment Xorowe stood in the middle of the clearing. His eyes shone sadly from their hollow sockets, filled with an immense melancholy, as if he had just realized he was no longer his former human self, but only a shadow. Yet there was an aura of strength about him that had not been there before, as if the conviction of his newfound knowledge and experience were more enduring than the memory of his past. Silently Puriwariwe led him into the forest.

16

"White girl!" Ritimi's six-year-old son shouted, running along the manioc rows. Out of breath, he stopped in front of me, then cried out excitedly, "White girl, your brother..."

"My what?" Dropping my digging stick, I ran toward the *shabono*. I stopped at the edge of the cleared strip of forest around the wooden palisade circling the *shabono*. Although it was not considered a garden, gourds, cotton, and an assortment of medicinal plants grew there. According to Etewa, the reason for this cleared strip was that enemies could not possibly trespass silently through this kind of vegetation as they could a forest cover.

No unusual sounds came from the huts. Crossing the clearing toward the group of people squatting outside Arasuwe's hut, I was not surprised to see Milagros.

"Blond Indian," he said in Spanish, motioning me to squat beside him. "You even smell like one."

"I'm glad you are here," I said. "Little Sisiwe said you were my brother."

"I spoke to Father Coriolano at the mission." Milagros pointed to the writing pads, pencils, sardine cans, boxes of crackers, and sweet biscuits the Iticoteri were passing around. "Father Coriolano wants me to take you back to the mission," Milagros said, looking at me thoughtfully.

I could think of nothing to say. Picking up a twig, I drew lines on the dirt. "I can't leave yet."

"I know." Milagros smiled, but there was a trace of sadness about his lips. His voice was quite gentle, ironic. "I told Father Coriolano you were doing much work. I convinced him how important it is for you to finish this remarkable research you are conducting."

I could not repress my giggles. He sounded like a pompous anthropologist. "Did he believe you?"

Milagros pushed the writing pads and pencils toward me. "I assured Father Coriolano that you are well." From a small bundle Milagros pulled out a box containing three bars of Camay soap. "He also gave me these for you."

"What am I to do with them?" I asked, sniffing the scented bars.

"Wash yourself!" Milagros said emphatically, as if he really believed I had forgotten what soap was for.

"Let me smell it," Ritimi said, lifting a bar from the box. She held it against her nose, closed her eyes and took one long breath. "Hum. What are you going to wash with it?"

"My hair!" I exclaimed. It occurred to me that perhaps the soap would kill the lice.

"I'll wash mine too," Ritimi said, rubbing the bar on her head.

"Soap only works with water," I explained. "We have to go to the river."

"To the river!" cried the women who had gathered around the men as they stood up.

Laughing, we ran down the path. Men returning from the gardens just gaped at us, whereas the women accompanying them turned around and ran after us, toward Ritimi, who was holding the precious soap in her upraised hand.

"You have to get your hair wet," I called out from the water. The women remained on the bank, looking doubtfully at me. Grinning, Ritimi handed me the soap. Soon my head was covered with a thick lather. I scrubbed hard, enjoying the dirty suds squishing through my fingers, down my neck, back, and chest. With a halved calabash I rinsed my hair, using the soapy water to wash my body. I began to sing an old Spanish commercial advertising Camay soap—one I used to hear on the radio as a child. "For a heavenly array, there is nothing like *jabon* Camay."

"Who wants to be next?" I asked, wading toward the bank where the women stood. I felt I was glowing with cleanliness.

Stepping back, the women smiled, but none volunteered. "I will, I will," little Texoma shouted, running into the water.

One by one, the women came closer. Awed, they watched attentively as the suds seemed to grow out of the child's head. I worked up a stiff lather and shaped Texoma's hair until spikes stuck out all around her head. Hesitantly, Ritimi touched her daughter's hair. A timid smile crinkled the corners of her mouth. "Ohoo, what beauty!"

"Keep your eyes closed until I've rinsed out all the soap," I admonished Texoma. "Close them tight. It hurts if the suds run into your eyes."

"For a heavenly array," Texoma cried out as the soapy water ran down her back. "There is nothing like . . ." She looked at me and I filled in the rest. "Sing that song again. I want my hair to turn the color of yours."

"It won't turn my color," I said. "But it will smell good."

"I want to be next!" the women began shouting.

Except for the pregnant ones, who were afraid that the magic soap might harm their unborn children, I washed at least twenty-five heads. However, not wanting to be outdone, the pregnant women decided to wash their hair in the accustomed manner—with leaves and mud from the bottom of the river. To them too I had to sing the silly Camay soap commercial. By the time we were all scrubbed, my voice was hoarse.

The men, gathered around Arasuwe's hut, were still listening to Milagros's account of his visit to the outside world. They sniffed our hair as we squatted beside them. An old woman crouching next to a youth, pushed his head between her legs. "Sniff this, I washed it with Camay soap." She began to hum the melody of the commercial.

The men and women burst into guffaws. Still laughing, Etewa shouted, "Grandmother, no one wants your vagina, even if you fill it with honey."

Cackling, the woman made an obscene gesture, then went inside her hut. "Etewa," she shouted from her hammock, "I've seen you lying between the legs of even older hags than myself."

After the laughter subsided, Milagros pointed to the four machetes placed on the ground in front of him. "Your friends left these at the mission before departing for the city," he said. "They are for you to give away."

I looked at him helplessly. "Why so few?"

"Because I couldn't carry more," Milagros said cheerfully. "Don't give them to the women."

"I will give them to the headman," I said, gazing at the expectant faces around me. Grinning, I pushed the four machetes in front of Arasuwe. "My friends sent these for you."

"White girl, you are clever," he said, checking the sharp point of one of the machetes. "This one I will keep for myself. One is for my brother Iramamowe, who has protected you from the Mocototeri. One is for Hayama's son, from whose garden and game you eat the most." Arasuwe looked at Etewa. "One should be for you, but since you were given a machete not too long ago at one of our feasts I will give the machete to your wives, Ritimi and Tutemi. They take care of the white girl as if she were their own sister."

For a moment there was absolute silence; then one of the men stood up and addressed Ritimi. "Give me your machete so I can cut down trees. You don't need to do the work a man does."

"Don't give it to him," Tutemi said. "It's easier to work in the gardens with a machete than with a digging stick."

Ritimi looked at the machete, picked it up, then handed it to the man. "I will give it to you. The worst sin of all is not to give away what others ask of you. I don't want to end up in *shopariwabe*."

"Where is that?" I whispered to Milagros.

"*Shopariwabe* is a place like the missionaries' hell."

I opened one of the sardine cans. After popping one of the silvery oily fish into my mouth, I offered the can to Ritimi. "Try one," I coaxed her.

She looked at me uncertainly. Between thumb and forefinger, she daintily lifted a piece of sardine into her mouth. "Ugh, what an ugly taste," she cried, spitting it out.

Milagros took the can from my hand. "Save them. They are for the journey back to the mission."

"But I'm not going back yet," I said. "They will spoil if we save them for long."

"You should return before the rains," Milagros said gravely. "Once they start, it will be impossible to cross rivers or walk through the forest."

I could not help the smug grin. "I have to stay at least until Tutemi's child is born," I said. I was sure the baby would arrive during the rains.

"What shall I tell Father Coriolano?"

"What you told him already," I said mockingly. "That I'm doing remarkable work."

"But he expects you to return before the rains," Milagros said. "It rains for months!"

Smiling, I took one of the boxes of crackers. "We better eat these—they will spoil with the humidity."

"Don't open the other sardine cans," Milagros said in Spanish. "The Iticoteri won't like them. I will eat them myself."

"Aren't you afraid to go to *shopariwabe*?"

Without answering, Milagros passed the already opened can around. Most of the men only smelled the contents, then handed it to the next person. The ones who were daring enough to taste the sardines, spit them out. The women did not bother either smelling or trying them. Milagros smiled at me when the can was returned to him. "They don't like sardines. I will not go to hell if I eat them all by myself."

The crackers were no success either, except with a few children, who licked off the salt. But the sweet biscuits, even though they tasted rancid, were eaten with smacking sounds of approval.

Ritimi appropriated the writing pads and pencils. She insisted I teach her the same kind of designs with which I had decorated my burned notebook. Dutifully, she practiced writing the Spanish and English words I had taught her. She was not interested in learning how to write, even though she eventually learned to draw all the letters of the alphabet, including a few Chinese ideograms I had once been taught in a calligraphy class. To Ritimi they remained designs that she painted sometimes on her body, preferring the letters S and W.

Milagros stayed for a few weeks at the *shabono*. He went hunting with the men and helped them in the gardens. Most of the time, however, he spent lounging in his hammock, doing nothing but play with the children. At all hours one could hear their shrieks of delight as Milagros balanced the younger ones high in the air on his upraised feet. In the evenings he entertained us with stories about the *nape,* the white men he had met through the years, the places he had visited, and the eccentric customs he had observed.

Nape was a term applied to all foreigners—that is, all who were not *Yanomama.* The Iticoteri made no distinction between nationalities. To them a Venezuelan, Brazilian, Swede, German, or American, regardless of their color, were *nape.*

Seen through Milagros's eyes, these white men appeared peculiar even to me. It was his sense of humor, his knack for the absurd, and his dramatic rendition that transformed the most mundane, insignificant event into an extraordinary happening. If ever anyone in the audience dared to doubt the veracity of his account, Milagros, in a very dignified manner, would turn to me. "White girl, tell them if I'm lying." No matter how much he had exaggerated, I never contradicted him.

17

Tutemi joined Ritimi and me in the gardens. "I think my time is coming," she said, dropping her wood-filled basket on the ground. "My arms have no strength. My breathing is not deep. I can no longer bend easily."

"Are you in pain?" I asked, seeing Tutemi's face twist into a grimace.

She nodded. "I'm also afraid."

Gently Ritimi probed the girl's stomach, first on the sides, then the front. "The baby is kicking hard. It's time for it to come out." Ritimi turned to me. "Go get old Hayama. Tell her that Tutemi is in pain. She will know what to do."

"Where will you be?"

Ritimi pointed straight ahead. I cut through the forest, jumping over fallen trunks, heedless of thorns, roots, and stones. "Come quickly," I shouted, gasping for air, in front of Hayama's hut. "Tutemi is having her child. She's in pain."

Picking up her bamboo knife, Ritimi's grandmother first went to see an old man living in a hut across the clearing. "I'm sure you heard the white girl," Hayama said. Seeing the old man nod, she added, "If we need you, I will send her to get you."

I walked in front of Hayama, impatiently waiting every

fifty paces for her to catch up. Leaning heavily on the piece of broken bow she used as a cane, she seemed to be moving even more slowly then usual. "Is the old man a *shapori?*" I asked.

"He knows all there is to know about a child that does not want to be born."

"Tutemi has only pains."

"When there is pain," Hayama said deliberately, "it means that the child doesn't want to leave the womb."

"I don't think it means that at all." I was unable to disguise the argumentative tone of my voice. "It's normal for the first child to be difficult," I affirmed, as if I really knew. "White women have pains with almost every child."

"It's not normal," Hayama affirmed. "Maybe white babies don't want to see the world."

Tutemi's moans came muffled through the underbrush. She was crouching on the *platanillo* leaves Ritimi had spread on the ground. Dark shadows circled her feverish eyes. Minute drops of perspiration shone above her brow and on her upper lip.

"The water has already broken," Ritimi said. "But the baby doesn't want to come."

"Let us go farther into the forest," Tutemi begged. "I don't want anyone at the *shabono* to hear my screams."

Tenderly, old Hayama pushed the young woman's bangs back from her forehead and wiped the sweat from her face and neck. "It will be better in a moment," she said soothingly, as if speaking to a child. Each time the contractions came, Hayama pressed hard on Tutemi's stomach. After what I judged to be an interminably long time, Hayama told me to get the old *shapori*.

He was prepared. He had taken *epena* and over the fire a dark concoction was boiling. With a stick he flicked the mucus from his nose, then poured the brew into a gourd.

"What is it made of?"

"Roots and leaves," he said, but did not mention the name of the plant. As soon as we reached the three women, he urged Tutemi to empty the gourd to the last drop. While she drank, he danced around her. In a high nasal voice, he pleaded with the *hekura* of the white monkey to release the neck of the unborn child.

Slowly, Tutemi's face relaxed, and her eyes lost their frightened expression. "I think the baby will come now," she said, smiling at the old man.

Hayama held her from behind, stretching Tutemi's arms over her head. While I was wondering whether it was the concoction or the shaman's dance that had induced such a state of relaxation, I missed the actual birth. I put my hand over my mouth to stifle a scream as I saw the umbilical cord wrapped around the neck of the purple-skinned boy. Hayama cut the cord, then put a leaf on the navel to absorb the blood. She rubbed her forefinger in the afterbirth, then smeared the finger against the child's lips.

"What is she doing?" I asked Ritimi.

"She is making sure the boy will learn to speak properly."

Before I had a chance to blurt out that the child was dead, the most disconcerting human cry I have ever heard echoed through the forest. Ritimi picked up the screaming infant and motioned me to follow her to the river. She filled her mouth with water, waited for a moment for it to warm up, then squirted it over the baby. Imitating her, I helped her rinse his little body clean of slime and blood.

"Now he has three mothers," Ritimi said, handing the baby to me. "Whoever washes a newborn baby is responsible for it should something happen to the mother. Tutemi will be happy that you have helped wash her child."

Ritimi filled a large *platanillo* leaf with mud, while I cradled the boy in uncertain arms. I had never held a newborn baby before. Looking in awe at the purplish wrinkled face, at his tiny fists, which he tried to push into his mouth, I wondered what miracle had made him live.

Hayama wrapped the placenta into a tight bundle of leaves and placed it under a small elevated windscreen the old man had built under a tall ceiba. It was to be burned in a few weeks. With the mud we covered all traces of blood on the ground to prevent wild animals and dogs from sniffing around.

With the child safely in her arms, Tutemi led the way back to the *shabono*. Before entering her hut, she placed him on the ground. We who had witnessed the birth had to step three times over the baby, thus marking his acceptance into the settlement.

Etewa did not look up from his hammock; he had been resting there since learning that his youngest wife was in labor. Tutemi entered the hut with their newborn son and sat by the hearth. After squeezing her nipple, she pushed it inside the baby's mouth. Avidly, the boy began to suck, opening his still unfocused eyes from time to time as if imprinting on his mind this source of food and comfort.

Neither parent ate anything that day. On the second and third day Etewa caught a basketful of small fish, which he cooked and fed to Tutemi. Thereafter both of them slowly resumed a normal diet. The day after giving birth, Tutemi returned to work in the gardens with the newborn baby strapped on her back. Etewa, on the other hand, remained resting in his hammock for a week. Any physical effort on his part was believed to be deleterious to the infant's health.

On the ninth day Milagros was asked to pierce the boy's earlobes with long *rasha* palm thorns, which were kept in the holes. After cutting the sharp points close to the lobes, Milagros coated each end with resin so the child would not pull the blunted thorns out. On that same day, the infant was also given the name of Hoaxiwe, for it was a white monkey that had wanted to keep the child in the womb. It was only a nickname. By the time the boy started walking, he would be given his real name.

18

It was not quite dawn when Milagros leaned over my hammock. I felt his calloused hand brushing my forehead and cheeks. I could hardly see his features in the darkness. I knew he was leaving. I waited for him to speak, but fell asleep without finding out whether he had actually wanted to say something.

"The rains will come soon," old Kamosiwe announced that evening. "I've seen the size of the young turtles. I've been listening to the croaking of the rain frogs."

Four days later, in the early afternoon, the wind blew with terrifying force through the trees and the *shabono*. The empty hammocks swung back and forth like boats on a tempestuous sea. The leaves on the ground swirled in spiraling dances that died as suddenly as they had begun.

I stood in the middle of the clearing, watching the gusts of wind coming from every direction. Pieces of bark flattened against my shins. Kicking my legs, I tried to shake the bark off, but it stuck to me as if it had been glued on. Giant black clouds darkened the sky. The steady far-off roar of approaching rain grew louder as it moved across the forest. Thunder rumbled through the clouds and the flickering of white lightning flashed through the afternoon darkness. The groans of a falling tree, hit by lightning, echoed through the forest with the mournful clamor of other uprooted trees crashing to the ground.

Shrieking, the women and children huddled together behind the plantains stacked against the sloping roof. Seizing a log from the fire, old Hayama rushed into Iramamowe's hut. Desperately, she began to beat one of the poles. "Wake up!" she screamed. "Your father is not here. Wake up! Defend us from the *hekuras*." Hayama was addressing Iramamowe's personal *hekura*, for he was out hunting with several other men.

Thunder and lightning receded into the distance as the clouds broke open above us. The rain came in a solid sheet, so dense we could not see across the clearing. Moments later, the sky was clear. I accompanied old Kamosiwe to look at the roaring river. Masses of earth toppled from the banks, gouged out by the raging torrent. Each landslide was followed by the tearing of vines, which snapped with the sound of breaking bowstrings.

A great stillness settled over the forest. Not a bird, insect, or frog could be heard. Suddenly, without any warning, a growl of thunder seemed to come directly out of the sun, cracking over our heads. "But there are no clouds," I shouted, falling on the ground as if struck.

"Don't defy the spirits," Kamosiwe warned me. Cutting two large leaves, he motioned me to take cover. Squatting side by side, we watched the rain cascade down from a clear sky. Gusts of wind shook the forest until the curtain of dark clouds hid the sun once more.

"Storms are caused by the dead whose bones have not been burned, whose ashes have not been eaten," old Kamosiwe said. "It's these unfortunate spirits, longing to be cremated, who heat up the clouds until fires light up the sky."

"Fires that will finally burn them," I completed his sentence.

"Ohoo, you are not so ignorant anymore," Kamosiwe said. "The rains have started. You will be with us for many days—you will learn so much more."

Smiling, I nodded. "Do you think Milagros has reached the mission?"

Kamosiwe looked at me askance, then broke into a hoarse, raspy laughter, the laughter of a very old man, resounding eerily in the noise of the rain. He still had most of his teeth. Strong and yellowish, they stood out from his receding gums like pieces of aged ivory. "Milagros did not go to the mission. He went to see his wife and children."

"At which settlement does Milagros live?"

"In many."

"Does he have a wife and children in all of them?"

"Milagros is a talented man," Kamosiwe said, his one dark eye shining with a devilish glint. "He has a white woman somewhere."

Filled with anticipation, I looked at Kamosiwe. I was finally going to learn something about Milagros. But the old man remained silent. When he put his hand in mine, I knew his mind had wandered elsewhere. Slowly, I massaged his gnarled fingers.

"Old man, are you really Milagros's grandfather?" I asked, hoping to bring him back to the subject of Milagros.

Startled, Kamosiwe looked into my face, his one eye scrutinizing me intently as if he had thought of something. Mumbling, he gave me his other hand to massage.

Absentmindedly, I watched his one eye rolling into his socket as he drowsed. "I wonder how old you really are?"

Kamosiwe's eye came to rest on my face, clouded with memories. "If you lay out the time I've lived, it would reach all the way to the moon," Kamosiwe murmured. "That's how old I am."

We stayed under the leaves, watching the dark clouds

disperse across the sky. Mist drifted through the trees, filtering the light to a ghostly gray.

"The rains have started," Kamosiwe repeated softly as we walked back to the *shabono*. The fires in the huts produced more smoke than heat, but the rainy air created a misty warmth. I stretched in my hammock and fell asleep to the distant and confused sounds of the storming forest.

The morning was cold and damp. Ritimi, Tutemi, and I stayed in our hammocks the whole day, eating baked plantains and listening to the rain pound on the palm-thatched roofs.

"I wish Etewa and the others had returned last night from the hunt," Ritimi mumbled from time to time, looking at the sky, which changed only from a faint white to gray.

The hunters returned late in the afternoon of the following day. Iramamowe and Etewa walked directly into old Hayama's hut carrying her youngest son Matuwe in a litter made from bark strips. Matuwe had been injured by a falling branch. Carefully, the two men transferred him to his own hammock. His leg hung limply down and his shinbone threatened to pierce the swollen purple skin.

"It's broken," old Hayama said.

"It's broken," I repeated with the rest of the women in the hut. I had adopted the habit of stating the obvious. It was a way of expressing concern, love, sympathy all at once.

Matuwe gasped in pain as Hayama set the leg straight. Ritimi held his foot outstretched while the old woman made a splint with broken pieces of arrow shafts. Deftly, she arranged them along each side of the leg, inserting cotton fibers in between the skin and cane. Around the splint, extending all the way from the ankle to the middle of his thigh, Hayama bound fresh strips of a thin, resistant bark.

Totemi and Xotomi, the man's young wife, giggled each time Matuwe moaned. They were not amused, but were trying to cheer him up. "Oh, Matuwe, it doesn't hurt," Xotomi tried to convince him. "Remember how glad you were when your head was bleeding after you had been hit with a club at the last feast."

"Stay still," Hayama said to her son. Fastening a liana rope over one of the rafters, she tied one end to his ankle, the other to his thigh. "Now you cannot move your leg," she said, inspecting her work with satisfaction.

About two weeks later, Hayama removed the bark and cane splint. The purple bruised leg had turned green and yellowish but was no longer swollen. She probed around the bone lightly. "It's growing together," she announced, then proceeded to massage the leg with warm water. Every day, for almost a month, she went through the same routine of unfastening the cast, massaging the leg, then tying it back to the rafter.

"The bone is mended," Hayama affirmed one day, breaking the cane splint into small pieces.

"But my leg is not healed!" Matuwe protested in alarm. "I cannot move it properly."

Hayama calmed him, explaining that his knee had become stiff from having had his leg stretched out for so long. "I'll continue massaging your leg until you can walk as you did before."

The rains brought with them a sense of tranquillity, of timelessness, as day and night blurred into each other. No one worked much in the gardens. For endless hours we lay or sat in our hammocks conversing in that odd way people do when it rains, with long pauses and absentminded stares into the distance.

Ritimi tried to make a basket weaver out of me. I started out with what I thought was the easiest kind—the large

U-shaped basket used for carrying wood. The women had great fun watching my awkward attempts at trying to master the simple twining technique. I then concentrated my efforts on something I believed to be more manageable— the flat, disklike baskets used for storing fruit or separating the ashes from the bones of the dead. Although I was quite pleased with the finished product, I had to agree with old Hayama that the basket did not look the way it was supposed to.

Grinning at her, I remembered the time a school friend had done her best to teach me how to knit. In the most relaxed manner, while watching TV, talking, or waiting for an appointment, she knitted beautiful sweaters, mittens, and skiing caps. I sat tensely beside her, with tight shoulders, my stiff fingers holding the needles only inches away from my face, cursing every time I dropped a stitch.

I was not ready to give up basketry. One had to try at least three times, I told myself, as I began to make one of the flat fishing baskets.

"Ohoo, white girl." Xotomo giggled uncontrollably. "You didn't twine it tight enough." She put her fingers through the loosely woven vine strips. "The fish will slip through the holes."

Finally I resigned myself to the simple task of splitting the bark and vines needed for weaving into the most perfectly even strands, which were much in demand. Emboldened by my success, I made a hammock. I cut strands about seven feet long, tied the ends firmly together, reinforcing them with intertwined bark rope below the binding. I joined the liana strands loosely with transverse cotton yarn, which I had dyed red with *onoto*. Ritimi was so enchanted with the hammock, she replaced Etewa's old one with it.

"Etewa, I made a new hammock for you," I said as he came in from working in the gardens.

He looked at me skeptically. "You think it will hold me?"

I clicked my tongue in affirmation, showing him how well I had reinforced the ends.

Hesitantly he sat in the hammock. "It seems strong," he said, stretching fully. I heard the rubbing of the vine rope against the pole, but before I could warn him Etewa and the hammock were on the ground.

Ritimi, Tutemi, Arasuwe, and his wives, watching from the hut next to us, burst into guffaws, immediately attracting a large crowd. Slapping each other on their thighs and shoulders, they doubled up with laughter. Later I asked Ritimi if she had tied the hammock loosely on purpose.

"Naturally," she said, her eyes shining with loving malice. She assured me that Etewa was not in the least upset. "Men enjoy being outwitted by a woman."

Although I had my doubts as to whether Etewa had actually enjoyed the incident, he certainly held no grudge against me. He advertised throughout the *shabono* how well he was resting in his new hammock. I was besieged with requests. Sometimes I made as many as three hammocks a day. Several men busied themselves supplying me with cotton, which they separated by hand from the seeds. With a whorl stick they spun the fibers into thread, and twisted them into the strong yarn which I loosely wove in between the strands.

With a finished hammock draped over my arm, I entered Iramamowe's hut one afternoon. "Are you going to make arrows?" I asked him. He had climbed up a pole in his hut and was reaching for cane stored under the rafters of the roof.

"Is this hammock for me?" he asked, handing me the cane. He took the hammock, fastened it, then sat astride on it. "It's well made."

"I made it for your eldest wife," I said. "I'll make you one if you teach me how to make arrows."

"It isn't time to make arrows," Iramamowe said. "I was only checking if the cane is still dry." He regarded me mockingly, then burst into laughter. "The white girl wants to make arrows," he shouted at the top of his voice. "I will teach her and take her hunting with me." Still laughing, he motioned me to sit beside him. He spread the cane on the ground, then sorted the shafts according to size. "The long ones are best for hunting. Short ones are best for fishing and killing the enemy. Only a good marksman will use long ones for whatever he pleases. They are often flawed and their trajectory is imprecise."

Iramamowe selected a short and a long shaft. "In here I will fit the arrowhead," he said, splitting one end of each cane. Firmly he tied them together with cotton thread. He cut a few feathers in half, then attached them to the other end by means of resin and cotton thread. "Some hunters decorate their shafts with their personal designs. I only do so when I go raiding. I like my enemy to know who killed him."

Like most Iticoteri men, Iramamowe was a superb raconteur, animating his stories with precise onomatopoeia, dramatic gestures, and pauses. Step by step, he took his listener through the hunt: how he first spotted the animal; how before releasing his arrow he blew on it the powdered roots of one of his magic plants to immobilize his victim, thus making sure his arrow would not fail to hit its target; and how, once hit, the animal resisted dying.

With his eyes fixed on me, he emptied the contents of his quiver on the ground. In great detail he explained about all the arrowheads he had. "This is one of the palm-wood points," he said, handing me a sharp piece of wood. "It's made from splinters. The ringlike grooves cut into the point are smeared with *mamucori*. They break inside the animal's body. It's the best point for hunting monkeys." He smiled, then added, "And for killing the enemy." Next he held up a long, wide point, sharpened along its edges and decorated with meandering lines. "This one is good for hunting jaguars and tapirs."

The excited barking of dogs, mingled with the shouts of people, interrupted Iramamowe's explanation. I followed him as he rushed toward the river. An anteater the size of a small bear had taken refuge from the barking dogs in the water. Etewa and Arasuwe had wounded the animal on the neck, stomach, and back. Raised on its hind legs, it pawed the air desperately with its powerful front claws.

"Want to finish it off with my arrow?" Iramamowe asked.

Unable to avert my gaze from the animal's long tongue, I shook my head. I was not sure whether he was serious or joking. The animal's tongue hung out of a narrow muzzle, dripping a sticky liquid in which dead ants swam. Iramamowe's arrow hit the anteater's tiny ear and instantly the animal collapsed. The men tied ropes around the massive body, then hoisted it up the bank, where Arasuwe quartered the animal so the men could carry the heavy pieces to the *shabono*.

The men singed off the hair, then placed the various pieces on a wooden platform built over the fire. As soon as Hayama wrapped the innards in *pishaansi* leaves, she buried them in the embers.

"An anteater," the children cried out. Clapping their hands in delight, they danced around the fire.

"Wait until it's cooked properly," old Hayama warned the children, whenever one poked at the tightly wrapped bundles. "You will get sick if you eat meat that isn't well done. It has to cook until no more juice drips from the leaves."

The liver was done first. Hayama cut me a piece before

the children got to it. It was tender, juicy, and unpleasantly sour, as if it had been marinated in rancid lemon
juice.

Later Iramamowe brought me a piece of the roasted
hind leg. "Why didn't you want to try my arrow?" he
asked.

"I might have hit one of the dogs," I said evasively,
biting into the tough meat. It too tasted sour. I looked up
into Iramamowe's face and wondered if he had been aware
that I did not want to be even vaguely compared to
Imaawami, the woman shaman who knew how to call the
hekuras and hunted like a man.

On stormy afternoons the men took *epena* and chanted to
the *hekura* of the anaconda to twist herself around the
trees so as to prevent the wind from breaking their trunks.
During one particularly vicious storm, old Kamosiwe
rubbed white ashes over his wrinkled body. In a hoarse,
raspy voice he called out to the spider, his personal *hekura*,
to spin her protective silvery threads around the plants in
the gardens.

Suddenly his voice changed to a higher pitch, as shrill as
the piercing shriek of a parakeet. "I was once an old child
who climbed to the tallest treetop. I fell and was transformed into a spider. Why do you disturb my peaceful
sleep?"

Reverting again to his old man's voice, Kamosiwe rose
from his squatting position. "Spider, I want to blow your
sting on those *hekuras* who break and tear the plants in
our gardens." With his *epena* cane, he blew all around the
shabono, aiming the spider sting against the destructive
spirits.

The following morning I accompanied Kamosiwe into
the gardens. Smiling, he pointed to the small hairy spiders
busily reweaving their webs. Minute drops of moisture

clung to the tenuous silvery threads. In the sunshine they glistened like jade pearls, reflecting the greenness of leaves. We walked through the steaming forest toward the river. Squatting next to each other we silently watched the broken lianas, trees, and masses of leaves speeding by in the muddy waters. Back in the *shabono,* Kamosiwe invited me into his hut to share with him his specialty—roasted ants dipped in honey.

A favorite pastime during these rainy nights was for a woman to ridicule her husband for a wrongdoing through a song. A quarrel ensued whenever the woman hinted that her man was better fit to carry a basket than a bow. These disputes always ended up as public arguments, in which others took an active part by expressing their own opinions. Sometimes hours after the quarrel had ended someone would shout across the clearing with a fresh insight into the particular problem, thus renewing the squabble.

PART FIVE

19

Whenever the sun pierced through the clouds, I went with the women and men to work in the gardens. The weeds were much easier to pull from the soaked ground, but I had little energy. Like old Kamosiwe, I just stood amidst the high blades of the manioc plants and soaked up the light and warmth of the sun. Counting the birds, which had not appeared for days, crossing the sky, I wished for the hot rainless days. After so many weeks of rain, I longed for the sun to stay long enough to lift the mist.

One morning I felt so dizzy I could not get out of my hammock. I lowered my head toward my knees and waited for the spell to pass. I did not have the strength to lift my head and answer Ritimi's anxious words, which were lost in the loud persistent noise around me. It must be the river, I thought. It was not too far away, but then I realized the noise came from another direction. Desperately, as if my life depended on it, I tried to think where the sound actually came from. It came from within me.

For days I heard nothing but drumming in my head. I wanted to open my eyes. I could not. Through my closed lids I saw the stars burn brighter instead of fading in the sky. Panic seized me at the thought that it would be night forever, that I was descending deeper and deeper into a world of shadows and disconnected dreams.

Waving from misty riverbanks, Ritimi, Tutemi, Etewa, Arasuwe, Iramamowe, Hayama, old Kamosiwe drifted by me. Sometimes they jumped from cloud to cloud, sweeping the mist with leafy brooms. Whenever I called them, they melted into the fog. Sometimes I could see the light of the sun, shining red and yellow, between branches and leaves. I forced my eyes to stay open and realized it had only been the fire dancing on the palm-thatched roof.

"White people need food when they are sick," I distinctly heard Milagros's shouts. I felt his lips on mine as he pushed masticated meat into my mouth.

Another time I recognized Puriwariwe's voice. "Clothes make people ill." I felt him pull my blanket away. "I need to cool her down. Get me white mud from the river." I felt his hands coil around my body, covering me with mud from the top of my head to the tip of my toes. His lips left a trail of coldness on my skin as he sucked the evil spirits out of me.

My hours of wakefulness and sleep were filled with the *shapori*'s voice. Wherever I focused my eyes in the darkness, his face appeared. I heard the song of his *hekura*. I felt the sharp hummingbird's beak cut open my chest. The beak turned into light. Not the light of the sun or the light of the moon but the dazzling radiance of the old *shapori*'s eyes. He urged me to look into his deep pupils. His eyes appeared lidless, extending toward his temples. They were filled with dancing birds. The eyes of a madman, I thought. I saw his *hekuras* suspended in dewdrops, dancing in the shiny eyes of a jaguar, and I drank the watery tears of the *epena*. A violent tickling in my throat tightened my stomach until I vomited water. It flowed out of the hut, out of the *shabono*, down the path to the river, melting with the night of smoke and chanting.

Opening my eyes, I sat up in my hammock. I distinctly saw Puriwariwe running outside the hut. He stretched his arms to the night, his fingers spread wide as if summoning the energy of the stars. Turning around, he looked at me. "You are going to live," he said. "The evil spirits have left your body." Then he disappeared into the shadows of the night.

After weeks of violent storms, the rains abated to an even, almost predictable pattern. Dawns would arrive opaque and misty, but by midmorning white fluffy clouds would drift across the sky. Hours later the clouds would gather above the *shabono*. They would hang so low that they appeared to be suspended from the trees, ominously darkening the afternoon sky. A heavy downpour would follow, fading to a light drizzle that often continued far into the night.

I did not work much in the gardens during those rainless mornings but usually accompanied the children into the swamps that had formed around the river. There we would catch frogs and pry out crabs from underneath stones.

The children, on all fours, eyes and ears alert to the slightest motion and sound, pounced with uncanny agility on the unsuspecting frogs. With eyes that looked almost transparent because of the diffused light, the little girls and boys worked with the precision of evil gnomes as they pulled the fiber loops around the frogs' necks until the last croak died down. Smiling, with the candor only children have when unaware of their cruelty, they would cut open the frogs' feet so that all the blood, which was believed to be poisonous, could flow out. After the frogs had been skinned, each child would wrap his catch in *pishaansi* leaves and cook them over the fire. With manioc gruel, they tasted delicious.

Mostly, I just sat on a rock in the tall bamboo grass and watched rows of shiny black and yellow scarabs climb with careful, almost imperceptible slowness up and down the light green stems. They looked like creatures of another world, protected by their brilliant armor of obsidian and gold. On windless mornings it was so quiet in the bamboo grass that I could hear the beetles sucking sap from the tender shoots.

Early one morning, Arasuwe sat at the head of my hammock. There was a cheerful glow on his face, extending from his high cheekbones to his lower lip, where a wad of tobacco protruded. The concentration of wrinkles around his eyes deepened as he grinned, adding a reassuring warmth to his expression. I fixed my gaze on his thick, ribbed nails as he cupped his brown hand to catch the last drops of honey from a calabash. He extended his hand toward me and I dipped my finger in his palm. "This is the best honey I've had for a long time," I said, licking my finger with relish.

"You can come with me downriver," Arasuwe said. He went on to explain that with two of his wives and his two youngest sons-in-law, one of which was Matuwe, he was going to an abandoned garden where months earlier they had felled several palm trees to harvest the tasty palm hearts. "Do you remember how much you liked the crisp, crunchy shoots?" he asked. "By now the decaying pith in the dead trunks must be filled with fat worms."

As I was pondering on how to express that I would not like the grubs as much as I had enjoyed the palm hearts, Ritimi came to sit beside me. "I will also go to the gardens," she said. "I have to watch over the white girl."

Arasuwe blew his nose, flicking the mucus away with his forefinger, then laughed. "My daughter, we are going by canoe. I thought you didn't like traveling on water."

"It's better than walking through a swampy forest," Ritimi said flippantly.

Ritimi came instead of Arasuwe's youngest wife. For a short distance we walked along the riverbank until we reached an embankment. Hidden underneath the thicket was a long canoe.

"It looks like one of the large troughs you use for making soup," I said, eyeing the bark contraption suspiciously.

Proudly, Arasuwe explained that both were made in exactly the same fashion. The bark of a large tree was loosened in one piece by pounding the trunk with clubs. Then the ends were heated over a fire to make them pliable enough to be folded back and pinched into a flat-nosed basin, and finally the ends were lashed together with vines. A crude framework of sticks was added to give the boat its stability.

The men pushed the canoe into the water. Giggling, Arasuwe's second wife, Ritimi, and I climbed inside. Afraid to upset the tublike craft, I did not dare move from my crouching position. Arasuwe maneuvered the canoe with a pole into the middle of the river.

With their backs turned to their mother-in-law, the two young men sat as far away from her as they could. I wondered why Arasuwe had brought them at all. It was considered incestuous for a man to be familiar with his wife's mother, especially if the woman was still sexually active. Men usually avoided their mothers-in-law altogether, to the extent that they did not even look at them. And under no circumstances did they say their names aloud.

The current seized us, carrying us swiftly down the gurgling, muddy river. There were stretches when the waters were calm, reflecting the trees on either side of the bank with exaggerated intensity. Gazing at the mirrored leaves, I had the feeling we were ripping through an intricately laced veil. The forest was silent. From time to time we caught sight of a bird gliding across the sky. Without flapping its wings, it seemed to be flying asleep. The ride was over all too soon. Arasuwe beached the canoe in the sand amidst black basalt rocks.

"Now we have to walk," he said, looking at the dark forest ascending in front of us.

"What about the canoe?" I asked. "We should turn it upside down so the afternoon rain won't fill it with water."

Arasuwe scratched his head, then burst into laughter. He had mentioned on different occasions that I was far too opinionated—not necessarily because I was a woman, but because I was young. Old people, regardless of sex, were respected and held in esteem. Their advice was sought and followed. It was the young ones who were discouraged from voicing their judgments. "We will not use the boat to get back," Arasuwe said. "It's too hard to pole upriver."

"Who is going to take it back to the *shabono*?" I could not help asking, afraid we would have to carry it.

"No one," he assured me. "The boat is only good for going downstream." Grinning, Arasuwe turned the canoe upside down. "Maybe someone else will need it to go farther downriver."

It felt good to move my cramped legs. We walked silently through the wet, marshy forest. Matuwe was in front of me. He was thin and long legged. His quiver hung so low on his back that it bumped back and forth on his buttocks. I began to whistle a little tune. Matuwe turned around. His scowling face made me giggle. I had the overwhelming temptation to poke his buttocks with the quiver but controlled my impulse. "Don't you like your mother-in-law?" I asked, unable to refrain myself from teasing him.

Grinning shyly, Matuwe blushed at my impudence for having spoken Arasuwe's wife's name aloud in front of him. "Don't you know that a man cannot look at, talk to, or be near his mother-in-law?"

His stricken tone made me feel guilty for having teased him. "I didn't know," I lied.

Upon arriving at the site, Ritimi assured me that it was the same abandoned garden she and Tutemi had taken me to after our first encounter in the forest. I did not recognize the place. It was so overgrown with weeds, I had a hard time finding the temporary shelters I knew to stand around the plantain trees.

Slashing the weeds with their machetes, the men looked for the fallen palm tree trunks. After uncovering them, they dug out the decaying pith, then broke it open with their bare hands. Ritimi and Arasuwe's wife shrieked ecstatically as they saw the wriggling grubs, some as big as Ping-Pong balls. Squatting beside the men, they helped bite off each larva's head, pulling it away together with the intestines. The white torsos were collected in *pishaansi* leaves. Whenever Ritimi damaged a grub, which she did quite often, she ate it raw on the spot, smacking her lips in approval.

Despite their mocking pleas that I help them prepare the grubs, I could not bring myself to touch the squirming blobs, let alone to bite off their heads. Borrowing Matuwe's machete, I cut down banana fronds with which to cover the roofs of the badly weathered shelters.

Arasuwe called me as soon as some of the larvae were roasting on the fire. "Eat it," he urged, pushing one of the bundles in front of me. "You need the fat—you haven't had enough lately. That's why you have diarrhea," he added in a tone that begged no argument.

I grinned sheepishly. With a resoluteness I did not feel, I opened the tightly bound package. The shrunken, whitish grubs were swimming in fat; they smelled like burnt bacon. Watching the others, I first licked the *pishaansi* leaf, then carefully popped a grub into my mouth. It tasted wonderfully similar to the burned gristly fat around a New York steak.

At dusk, soon after we had settled into one of the repaired huts, Arasuwe announced in a solemn tone that we had to return to the *shabono*.

"You want to travel at night?" Matuwe asked incredulously. "What about the roots we wanted to dig up in the morning?"

"We cannot stay here," Arasuwe reiterated. "I can feel it in my legs that something is about to happen at the *shabono*." Closing his eyes, he swung his head to and fro as if the slow, rhythmic movement could provide him with an answer as to what he should do. "We have to reach the *shabono* by dawn," he said determinedly.

Ritimi distributed among our baskets the nearly forty pounds of grubs the men had recovered from the decaying palm trunks, placing the smallest amount into mine. Arasuwe and his two sons-in-law took the half-burned logs from the fire, then we set out in single file. To keep the makeshift torches glowing, the men blew on them periodically, dispersing a shower of sparks amidst the damp shadows. At times the almost full moon cut through the leaves, casting an eerie, bluish-green light on the path. The tall tree trunks stood like columns of smoke dissolving in the humid air, as if intent on eluding the embrace of vines and parasitic growths hanging across space. Only the trees' crowns were perfectly outlined against the moving clouds.

Arasuwe stopped often, cocking his ear to the slightest sound, his eyes darting back and forth in the darkness. He breathed deeply, dilating his nostrils, as if he could detect something besides the smell of wetness and decay. When he looked at us women, his eyes appeared anxious. I wondered if the memories of raids, ambushes, and God knows what other dangers rushed through his mind. But I did not dwell for too long on the headman's worried expression. I was too concerned in making sure the exposed roots of the giant ceibas were not bulging anacondas digesting a tapir or a peccary.

Arasuwe waded into a shallow river. He cupped his hand behind his ear as if trying to catch the faintest sound. Ritimi whispered that her father was listening to the echoes of the current, to the murmur of the spirits that knew of the dangers lying ahead. Arasuwe placed his hands on the surface of the water and for a moment held the reflected image of the moon.

As we walked on, the moon faded into a misty, barely discernible image. I wondered if the lonely clouds traversing the sky were trying to keep abreast of us in their journey toward morning. Little by little, the calls of monkeys and birds faded, the night breeze ceased, and I knew dawn was not far away.

We arrived at the *shabono* at that time of still indeterminate grayness when it is no longer night and not yet morning. Many of the Iticoteri were still asleep. Those who were up greeted us, surprised to see us back so soon.

Relieved that Arasuwe's fears had been unfounded, I lay down in my hammock.

I was awakened abruptly when Xotomi sat beside me. "Eat this quickly," she urged, handing me a baked plantain. "Yesterday I saw the kind of fish you and I like best." Without waiting to hear whether or not I was too tired to go, she handed me my small bow and short arrows. The thought of eating fish instead of grubs quickly dispelled my fatigue.

"I want to come too," little Sisiwe said, following us.

We headed upriver, where the waters formed wide pools. Not a leaf stirred, not a bird or frog could be heard.

Squatting on a rock, we watched the early rays of the sun filter through the mist-enshrouded canopy of leaves. As if strained through a gauzy veil, the faint rays lit the dark waters of the pool.

"I heard something," little Sisiwe whispered, holding on to my arm. "I heard a branch snap."

"I heard it too," Xotomi said softly.

I was sure it was not an animal but the unmistakable sound of a human who steps with caution, then stops at the noise he has made.

"There he is," Sisiwe shouted, pointing across the river. "It's the enemy," he added, then fled toward the *shabono*.

Grabbing my arm, Xotomi pulled me to the side. I turned around. All I saw were the dewy ferns on the opposite bank. At that same instant Xotomi let out a piercing scream. An arrow had hit her in the leg. I dragged her into the bushes by the side of the path, insisting we crawl farther into the thicket until we were hidden completely.

"We will wait here until the Iticoteri come to rescue us," I said, examining her leg.

Xotomi wiped the tears from her cheeks with the back of her hand. "If it's a raid, the men will stay in the *shabono* to defend the women and children."

"They will come," I said with a confidence I was far from feeling. "Little Sisiwe went for help." The barbed point had pierced through her calf. I broke the arrow, pulled the head from the ghastly wound that was bleeding from both sides, then wrapped my torn underpants around her leg. Blood soaked through the thin cotton instantly. Worried that the arrow might have been poisoned, I carefully undid the makeshift bandage and examined the wound once again to see if the flesh around it was getting dark. Iramamowe had explained to me that a wound caused by a poisoned arrow invariably darkened. "I don't think the arrowhead was smeared with *mamucori*," I said.

"Yes. I also noticed," she said, smiling faintly. Leaning her head to one side, she motioned me to be still.

"Do you think there is more than one man?" I whispered when I heard the sound of a twig snapping.

Xotomi looked at me, her eyes wide with fear. "There usually are."

"We can't wait here like frogs," I said, taking my bow and arrows. Quietly, I crawled toward the path. "Show your face, you coward, you monkey! You have shot at a woman!" I yelled in a voice that did not sound like my own. For good measure I added the words I knew an Iticoteri warrior would say: "I will kill you on the spot when I see you!"

No farther than twelve feet from where I stood a blackened face peeked from behind the leaves. His hair was wet. I had an irrational desire to laugh. I was sure he had not taken a bath but had slipped crossing the river, for the water was only waist high. I pointed my arrow at him. For an instant I was at a loss as to what to say next. "Drop your weapons on the path," I finally shouted. Then for good measure I added, "My arrows are poisoned with the best *mamucori* the Iticoteri make. Drop your weapons," I repeated. "I'm aiming at your stomach, right where death lies."

Wide-eyed, as if he were apprehending an apparition, the man stepped out on the trail. He was not much taller than I but powerfully built. His bow and arrows were clutched tightly in his hands.

"Drop your weapons on the ground," I repeated, stomping my right foot for emphasis.

With careful slowness, the man placed his bow and arrows on the path in front of him.

"Why did you shoot at my friend?" I asked as I saw Xotomi crawling out to the path.

"I did not want to shoot at her," he said, his eyes fixed

on the torn, bloodied makeshift bandage wrapped around Xotomi's leg. "I wanted to shoot at you."

"At me!" I felt helpless in my anger. I opened and closed my mouth repeatedly, unable to utter a single word. When I finally regained my speech, I stammered insult upon insult in all the languages I knew, including Iticoteri, which had the most descriptive profanities of all.

Transfixed, the man stood in front of me, seemingly more surprised by my foul language than at the arrow I still held pointed at him. Neither one of us noticed Arasuwe and Etewa approach.

"A Mocototeri coward," Arasuwe said. "I ought to kill you on the spot."

"He wanted to kill me," I said in a cracking voice. I felt all my courage melt away, leaving me shaking. "He shot Xotomi in the leg."

"I didn't want to kill you," the Mocototeri said, eyeing me supplicantly. "I only wanted to hit your leg so as to prevent you from running away." He turned to Arasuwe. "You can be assured of my good intentions; my arrows are not poisoned." He looked at Xotomi. "I hit you accidentally when you dragged the white girl away," he mumbled, as if not fully accepting that he had missed.

"How many more of you are here?" Arasuwe asked, squatting beside his daughter. Not for a moment did he take his eyes from the Mocototeri as he ran his fingers over the wound. "It's not bad," he said, straightening up.

"There are two more." The Mocototeri imitated the call of a bird and was immediately answered by similar cries. "We wanted to take the white girl with us. Our people want her to stay at our *shabono*."

"How do you think I could have walked if I was injured?" I asked.

"We would have carried you in a hammock," the man said promptly, smiling at me.

Shortly, two other Mocototeri emerged from the thicket. Grinning, they stared at me, not in the least embarrassed or afraid for having been caught.

"How long have you been here?" Arasuwe asked.

"We have been watching the white girl for several days," one of the men said. "We know she likes to catch frogs with the children." The man smiled broadly as he turned toward me. "There are many frogs around our *shabono*."

"Why have you waited so long?" Arasuwe asked.

In the frankest manner the man observed that there had always been too many women and children around me. He had hoped to capture me at dawn when I went to relieve myself, for he had heard that I preferred going far into the forest by myself. "But we didn't see her go, not even once."

Grinning, Arasuwe and Etewa looked at me, as if waiting for me to elaborate on the matter. I stared back at them. Since the rains had started, I had noticed a lot more snakes around the usual places set aside for bodily functions, but I was not going to discuss with them where I went instead.

With the same enthusiasm as if he were telling a story, the Mocototeri went on to explain that they had not come to kill any of the Iticoteri or to abduct any of their women. "All we wanted was to take the white girl with us." The man laughed, then uttered, "Wouldn't it have surprised you and your people if suddenly the white girl had disappeared without leaving a trace?"

Arasuwe conceded that indeed it would have been quite a feat. "But we would have known it was the Mocototeri who had taken her. You were careless enough to leave footprints in the mud. I saw plenty of evidence as I was scouting around the *shabono* that Mocototeri had been here. Last night I had the certainty something was amiss—that's why I returned so promptly from our trip to the old gardens." Arasuwe paused for a moment, as if giving the three men time for his words to sink in, then declared, "Had you taken the white girl with you, we would have raided your settlement and taken her back, as well as some of your women."

The man who had shot Xotomi in the leg picked up his bow and arrows from the ground. "Today was a good time, I thought. There was only one woman and a child with the white girl." He looked helplessly at me. "But I hit the wrong person. There must be powerful *hekuras* in your settlement protecting the white girl." He shook his head, as if full of doubt, then fixed his gaze on Arasuwe. "Why does she use a man's weapon? We saw her one morning at the river with the women, shooting fish like a man. We did not know what to think of her. That is why I failed to hit her. I no longer knew what she was."

Arasuwe commanded the three men to walk toward the *shabono*.

I was overwhelmed with the absurdity of the whole situation. Only the thought that Xotomi had been hurt kept me from laughing, yet a convulsive smile kept rising to my lips. I tried to keep a sober expression but I could feel my mouth twitching. I carried Xotomi piggyback, but she laughed so hard her leg started to bleed again.

"It will be easier if I lean against you," she said. "My leg doesn't hurt too much."

"Are the Mocototeri prisoners?" I asked.

She looked at me uncomprehendingly for an instant, then finally said, "No. Only women are taken captive."

"What will happen to them at the *shabono*?"

"They will be fed."

"But they are enemies," I said. "They shot you in the leg. They ought to be punished."

Xotomi looked at me, then shook her head as if knowing that it was beyond her to make me understand. She asked me if I would have killed the Mocototeri if he had not dropped his weapons on the ground.

"I would have shot him," I said loud enough for the men to hear. "I would have killed him with my poisoned arrows."

Arasuwe and Etewa glanced back. The stern expression on their faces relaxed into a smile. They knew my arrows were not poisoned. "Yes, she would have shot you," Arasuwe told the Mocototeri. "The white girl is not like our women. Whites kill very fast."

I wondered if I actually would have shot my arrow at the Mocototeri. I certainly would have kicked him in the groin or stomach had he not dropped his bow and arrows. I was aware of the folly of trying to overpower a stronger opponent, but I saw no reason a small person could not startle an unsuspecting assailant with a quick punch or kick. That, I was sure, would have given me enough time to run away. A kick would certainly have shocked the unaware Mocototeri even more than my bow and arrows. That thought gave me much comfort.

Arriving at the *shabono,* we were met by the Iticoteri men staring at us down the shaft of their drawn arrows. The women and children were hiding inside the huts. Ritimi came running toward me. "I knew you would be fine," she said, helping me carry her half-sister into old Hayama's hut.

Ritimi's grandmother washed Xotomi's leg with warm water, then poured *epena* powder into the wound. "Don't get out of your hammock," she admonished the girl. "I will get some leaves to wrap around your calf."

Exhausted, I went to rest in my hammock. Hoping to fall asleep, I pulled the sides over me. But I was awakened shortly by Ritimi's laughter. Leaning over me, she covered my face with resounding kisses. "I heard how you scared the Mocototeri."

"Why did only Arasuwe and Etewa come to rescue us?" I asked. "There might have been many Mocototeri men."

"But my father and husband didn't come to rescue you," Ritimi informed me candidly. She made herself comfortable in my hammock, then explained that no one in the *shabono* had realized I had gone with Xotomi and little Sisiwe to catch fish. It was purely accidental that Arasuwe and Etewa had found Xotomi and myself. Arasuwe, following his premonitions, had gone to scout the *shabono*'s surroundings upon returning from our night-long trek. Although he suspected that something was amiss, he had not actually known there were Mocototeri outside. Her father, Ritimi declared, was only performing his headman's duty and checking to see if there was evidence of intruders. It was a task a headman had to perform by himself, for usually no one was willing to accompany him on such a dangerous mission. No one was expected to.

Only lately had I come to realize that although Arasuwe had been introduced to me by Milagros as the headman of the Iticoteri, it was an uncertain title. The powers of a headman were limited. He wore no special insignia to distinguish him from the other men, and all adult males were involved in important decisions. Even if a judgment had been reached, each man was still free to do what he pleased. Arasuwe's importance stemmed from his kinship following. His brothers, numerous sons, and sons-in-law gave him power and support. As long as his decisions satisfied the people of his *shabono*, there was little dispute as to his authority.

"How come Etewa was with him?"

"That was totally unforeseen," Ritimi said, laughing. "He was probably returning from a clandestine rendezvous with one of the women of the *shabono* when he stumbled upon his father-in-law."

"You mean no one would have come to rescue us?" I asked incredulously.

"Once the men know that the enemy is around, they will not purposely go outside. It's too easy to be ambushed."

"But we could have been killed!"

"Women are hardly ever killed," Ritimi stated with utter conviction. "They would have captured you. But our men would have raided the Mocototeri settlement and brought you back," she argued with astounding simplicity, as if it were the most natural course of events.

"But they shot Xotomi's leg." I felt like crying. "They intended to maim me."

"That's only because they didn't know how to capture you," Ritimi said, putting her arms around my neck. "They know how to deal with Indian women. We are easy to abduct. The Mocototeri must have been at their wits' end with you. You should be happy. You are as brave as a warrior. Iramamowe is certain you have special *hekuras* protecting you, so powerful they even deviated the arrow intended for you into Xotomi's leg."

"What will happen to the Mocototeri?" I asked, looking into Arasuwe's hut. The three men were sitting in hammocks, eating baked plantains as if they were guests. "It is strange how you treat the enemy."

"Strange?" Ritimi looked at me, puzzled. "We treat them right. Didn't they reveal their plan? Arasuwe is glad they didn't succeed." Ritimi mentioned that the three men would probably stay with the Iticoteri for some time—especially if they suspected that there was a good chance their settlement was to be raided by the Iticoteri. The two *shabonos* had been raiding back and forth for many years, as far back as her grandfather's and great-grandfather's time and even before. Ritimi pulled my head toward her and whispered in my ear, "Etewa has been wishing to take revenge on the Mocototeri for a long time."

"Etewa! But he was so happy to go to their feast," I said, bewildered. "I thought he liked them. I know Arasuwe believes they are a treacherous lot—even Iramamowe. But Etewa! I was sure he was delighted to dance and sing at their party."

"I told you once that one doesn't go to a feast only to dance and sing but to find out what other people's plans are," Ritimi whispered. She looked at me anxiously. "Etewa wants his enemy to think that he has no intention of avenging his father."

"Was his father killed by the Mocototeri?"

Ritimi put her hand to my lips. "Let us not talk about it. It's bad luck to mention a person who has been killed in a raid."

"Is there going to be a raid?" I managed to ask before Ritimi pushed a piece of baked plantain in my mouth.

She only smiled at me but did not answer. The thought of a raid made me feel extremely uncomfortable. I had a hard time swallowing the plantain. Somehow I had associated raids with the past. The few times I had asked Milagros about them, he had been vague with his answers. Only now did I wonder if there had been regret in Milagros's voice when he stated that the missionaries had been quite successful in their attempt to put an end to intervillage feuding.

"Is there going to be a raid?" I asked Etewa as he entered the hut.

He looked at me, his face set in a scowl. "That's not a question for a woman to ask."

20

It was dusk when Puriwariwe walked into the *shabono*. I had not seen him since my illness, since the night he had stood in the middle of the clearing, arms outstretched as if pleading with the darkness. From Milagros I learned that for six consecutive days and nights the old *shapori* had taken *epena*. The old man had been on the verge of collapsing under the weight of the spirits he had called into his chest. Yet perseveringly he had beseeched the *hekuras* to cure me from the onslaught of a tropical fever.

Ritimi had also emphasized that it had been a particularly hard struggle to cure me in that the *hekuras* resent being called in the rainy season. "It was the *hekura* of the hummingbird that saved you," she had explained. "In spite of its small size, the hummingbird is a powerful spirit. It's used by an accomplished *shapori* as a last resort."

I had not been comforted in the least when Ritimi had wrapped her arms around my neck, assuring me that if I had died my soul would not have wandered aimlessly in the forest but would have ascended peacefully to the house of thunder, for my body would have been burned and my pulverized bones would have been eaten by her and her relatives.

I joined Puriwariwe in the clearing. "I'm well now," I said, squatting beside him.

He looked at me with veiled, almost dreamy eyes, then ran his hand over my head. It was a small dark hand that moved rapidly, yet felt heavy and slow. A vague tenderness softened his features, but he did not say a word. I wondered if he knew that I had felt the beak of a humming-bird cutting into my chest during my illness. I had told no one.

A group of men, their faces and bodies painted black, gathered around Puriwariwe. They blew *epena* into each other's noses and listened to his chant, pleading with the *hekuras* to come out of their hiding places in the mountains. The men's black figures were more like shadows, barely illuminated by the fires of the huts. Softly, they repeated the shaman's songs. I felt a chill run up my spine as the quickened pace of their unintelligible words became more menacing and forceful.

Upon returning to the hut I asked Ritimi what the men were celebrating.

"They are sending *hekuras* to the Mocototeri settlement to kill the enemy."

"Will the enemy really die?"

Drawing up her knees, she looked pensively beyond the palm fringe of the hut into the pitch-dark sky, bereft of moon and stars. "They will die," she said softly.

Convinced there was not going to be a real raid, I dozed off and on in my hammock, listening to the chanting outside. More than hearing the men, I visualized the fragments of sound, endlessly rising and falling, as being carried away by the smoke from the hearths.

Hours later I got up and sat outside the hut. Most of the men had retired to their hammocks. Only ten remained in the clearing, Etewa among them. With closed eyes, they repeated Puriwariwe's song. His words came to me clearly through the humid air:

> Follow me, follow my vision.
> Follow me over the treetops.
> Look at the birds and butterflies; such colors you
> will never see on the ground.
> I'm rising into heaven, toward the sun.

The *shapori*'s song was interrupted abruptly by one of the men. "I've been struck by the sun—my eyes are burning," he shouted as he stood up. He looked helplessly around in the darkness. His legs gave way under him and he collapsed with a thud on the ground. No one took any notice.

Puriwariwe's voice became more insistent, as if he were trying to raise the men collectively toward his vision. He repeated his song again and again to those still squatting around him. Urging the men not to get sidetracked in the dew of their visions, he warned them of spearlike bamboo leaves and poisonous snakes lurching from behind trees and roots on the path to the sun. Above all, he urged the men not to pass into human sleep but to step from the darkness of the night to the white darkness of the sun. He promised them that their bodies would be soaked with the glow of the *hekuras*, that their eyes would shine with the sun's precious light.

I remained outside the hut until the dawn erased the shadows on the ground. Expecting to find some visible evidence of their journey to the sun, I walked from man to man, peering intently into each face.

Puriwariwe watched me curiously, a mocking grin on his haggard face. "You'll find no outward indication of their flight," he said as if he had read my thoughts. "Their eyes are dull and red from the night's vigil," he added, pointing to the men who were staring indifferently into the distance, totally unconcerned with my presence. "That precious light you expect to see reflected in their pupils, only shines inside them. Only they can see it."

Before I had a chance to ask him about his journey to the sun, he had walked out of the *shabono* into the forest.

In the days that followed, a gloomy oppressive mood enveloped the settlement. At first it was only a vague feeling, but I finally became obsessed with the certainty I was being purposely kept in the dark about some impending event. I became morose, distant, and irritable. I struggled against my sensation of isolation. I tried to hide my ill-focused apprehension, yet I felt as if I were being attacked by unidentifiable forces. Whenever I asked Ritimi or any of the other women if there was some approaching change, they would not even acknowledge my question. Instead they would comment on some silly incident, hoping to make me laugh.

"Are we going to be raided?" I finally asked Arasuwe one day.

He turned his perplexed face toward me as if he were trying to untangle my words.

I felt confused, nervous, and close to tears. I told him that I was not stupid, that I had noticed how the men were constantly on the alert and how the women were afraid to go by themselves into the gardens or to fish in the river. "Why can't someone tell me what is going on?" I yelled.

"There is nothing going on," Arasuwe said calmly. Folding his arms behind his neck, he stretched comfortably in his hammock. He began to talk about something unrelated to my question, chuckling frequently at his own tale. But I was not to be soothed. I did not laugh with him. I did not even pay attention to his words. He seemed totally bewildered as I stomped back to my hut.

I was miserable for days, feeling alternately resentful and sorry for myself. I did not sleep well. I kept repeating to myself that I, who had so totally embraced this new life, was suddenly treated like a stranger. I felt angry and betrayed. I could not accept that Arasuwe had not taken me into his confidence. Not even Ritimi had been willing to put me at ease. If only Milagros were here, I wished fervently. Surely he would dispel my anxiety. He would tell me everything.

One night, when I could not quite lose myself in sleep but hovered in a half-waking state, I was suddenly hit by an insight. It did not come in words, but translated itself as a whole process of thoughts and memories that flashed like pictures before me and put everything into a proper perspective.

I felt elated. I began to laugh with relief that turned into sheer joy. I could hear my laughter echo through the huts. Sitting up in my hammock, I noticed that most of the Iticoteri were laughing with me.

Arasuwe squatted by my hammock. "Have the spirits of the forest made you mad?" he inquired, holding my head between his hands.

"Quite mad," I said, still laughing. I looked into his eyes; they shone in the darkness. I gazed at Ritimi, Tutemi, and Etewa standing next to Arasuwe, their curious, sleepy faces aglow with laughter. Words blurted out of me in an unending procession, piling onto one another with astonishing velocity. I was speaking in Spanish, not because I wanted to conceal anything, but because my explanation would not have made sense in their language. Arasuwe and the others listened as if they understood, as if they sensed my need to unburden myself of the turmoil within me.

I realized that I was, after all, an outsider, and my demand to be informed of events not even the Iticoteri talked about among themselves was due to my feelings of self-importance. What had turned me into an intolerable individual was the thought of being left out—excluded from something I believed I had a right to know. I had not questioned why I believed I had the right to know. It had made me miserable, blinding me to all the joyful moments I had so much cherished before. The gloom and oppressiveness I had felt was not outside but within me, communicating itself to the *shabono* and its people.

I felt Arasuwe's calloused hand on my shaven tonsure. I did not feel ashamed of my feelings, but was glad to realize that it was up to me to restore the sense of magic and wonder at being in a different world.

"Blow *epena* in my nose," Arasuwe said to Etewa. "I want to make sure the evil spirits stay away from the white girl."

I heard murmuring, a rustling of voices, a soft laughter, then Arasuwe's monotonous chant. I fell into a peaceful sleep, the best I had had for days. Little Texoma, who had not come into my hammock for days, awoke me at dawn. "I heard you laugh last night," she said, snuggling against me. "You had not laughed for so many days, I was afraid you would not laugh ever again."

I gazed into her bright eyes as if I might find in them the answer that would enable me in the future to laugh away all the anxiety and turmoils of my spirit.

An unusual stillness enshrouded the *shabono* as the shades of night closed in around us. The lulling touch of Tutemi's fingers as she searched my head for lice almost put me to sleep. The women's noisy chatter subsided to whispers as they went about preparing the evening meals and nursing their babies. As if obeying an unspoken command, the children forsook their vociferous evening games and gathered in Arasuwe's hut to listen to old Kamosiwe's tales. He seemed to be totally engrossed in his own words, gesturing dramatically with his hands as he talked. Yet his own eye was fixed intently on the long tubes of sweet potatoes sticking out from the embers. I watched in awe as the old man picked the roots out of the fire with his bare hand. Not waiting for the potatoes to cool, he crammed them into his mouth.

From where I sat I could see the waning moon appear over the treetops, obscured by the traveling clouds that shone white against the dark sky. The night stillness was pierced by an eerie sound—something between a scream and a growl. The next instant Etewa, his face and body painted black, materialized out of the shadows. He stood in front of the fires that had been lit in the clearing and clacked his bow and arrows high above his head. I did not see from which hut the others appeared, but eleven more men, their faces and bodies equally blackened, joined Etewa in the clearing.

Arasuwe pushed and pulled each of them until they all stood in a perfectly straight line, then, after positioning the last man in place, he joined them. The headman began to sing in a deep, nasal tone. The others repeated the last line of his song in a chorus. I could distinguish each separate voice in the murmured harmony, though I understood none of the words. The longer they sang, the angrier the men seemed to become. At the end of each song, they let out the most ferocious screams I had ever heard. Oddly, I had the feeling that the louder they yelled, the more remote was their rage, as if it was no longer part of their black-painted bodies.

Abruptly they became silent. The faint light of the fires accentuated the wrathful expression on their rigid, mask-like faces, the feverish glow in their eyes. I could not see if

Arasuwe gave the command, but in unison they shouted, "How I will enjoy watching my arrow hit the enemy. How I will enjoy seeing his blood splash all over the ground."

Holding their weapons above their heads, the warriors broke the line and gathered into a tight circle. They began to shout, first softly, then in such piercing voices that I felt a chill run down my spine. They were silent once more, and Ritimi whispered in my ear that the men were listening to the echo of their screams so they could determine from which direction it came. The echoes, she explained, carried the spirits of the enemy.

Groaning, clacking their weapons, the men began to prance about the clearing. Arasuwe calmed them down. Two more times they gathered into a tight circle and shouted with all their might. Instead of walking into the forest, as I had expected and feared, the men moved toward the huts standing close to the entrance of the *shabono*. They lay down in the hammocks and forced themselves to vomit.

"Why are they doing that?" I asked Ritimi.

"While they chanted, they devoured their enemies," she said. "Now they have to get rid of the rotten flesh."

I sighed with relief, yet I felt oddly disappointed that the raid had been acted out symbolically. Shortly before dawn, I was awakened by the wailing of women. I rubbed my eyes to make sure I was not dreaming. As if no time had elapsed, the men stood outside in exactly the same straight formation they had assumed earlier in the night. Their cries had lost their fierceness, as if the wails of the women had dampened their wrath. They flung the plantain bundles, which had been stacked at the *shabono*'s entrance, over their shoulders, then marched dramatically down the path leading to the river.

Old Kamosiwe and I followed the men at a distance. I thought it was raining, but it was only dew dripping from leaf to leaf. For a moment the men stood still, their shadows perfectly outlined against the light sand of the riverbank. The half-moon had traveled across the sky, shimmering faintly through the misty air. As if the sand had sucked in their shadows, the men vanished before my eyes. All I heard was the sound of rustling leaves, of snapping branches receding into the forest. The mist closed in on us like an impenetrable wall, as though nothing had happened, as if all I had seen was only a dream.

Old Kamosiwe, sitting beside me on a rock, touched my arm lightly. "I no longer hear the echoes of their steps," he said, then slowly walked into the water. I followed him. I shivered with coldness. I felt the little fish that hide beneath the submerged roots brush against my legs, but I could not see them in the dark waters.

Old Kamosiwe giggled as I rubbed him dry with leaves. "Look at the *sikomasik,*" he said rapturously, pointing to the white mushrooms growing on a rotten tree trunk.

I picked them up for him, wrapping them in leaves. When roasted over the fire, they were considered a delicacy, particularly by the old people.

Kamosiwe held the end of his broken bow toward me; I pulled him up the slippery path leading to the *shabono.* The mist did not rise the whole day, as if the sun were afraid to witness the men's journey through the forest.

21

Little Texoma sat next to me on the log in the bamboo grass. "Aren't you going to catch any frogs?" I asked her.

She looked at me woefully. Her eyes, usually so bright, were dull. Slowly they filled with tears.

"What makes you sad?" I asked, cradling her in my arms. Children were never left to cry for fear that their soul might escape through their mouths. Lifting her on my back, I headed toward the *shabono*. "You are as heavy as a basket full of ripe plantains," I said in an effort to make her laugh.

But the little girl did not even smile. Her face remained pressed against my neck; her tears rolled unchecked down my breasts. Carefully, I laid her down in her hammock. She clung to me tenaciously, forcing me to lie beside her. Soon she was asleep. It was not a peaceful sleep. From time to time her little body trembled as if she were in the throes of some dreadful nightmare.

With Tutemi's baby strapped to her back, Ritimi entered the hut. She began to cry as she looked at the sleeping child next to me. "I'm sure one of the evil Mocototeri *shapori* has lured her soul away." Ritimi wept with such heartbreaking sobs, I left Texoma's hammock and sat next to her. I did not know quite what to say. I was sure Ritimi

was not only crying for her little daughter, but also for
Etewa, who had been gone with the raiding party for almost a week. Since her husband's departure, she had not
been her usual self. She had not worked in the gardens;
neither had she accompanied any of the women to gather
berries or wood in the forest. Listless and dejected, she
moped around the *shabono*. Most of the time she lay in her
hammock, playing with Tutemi's baby. No matter what I
did or said to cheer her up, I was unable to erase the
forlorn expression on her face. The rueful little smile with
which Ritimi responded to my efforts only made her look
all the more despondent.

I put my arms around her neck and planted loud kisses
on her cheek, reassuring her all the time that Texoma had
nothing but a cold. Ritimi was not to be consoled. Weeping did not bring her any release or tire her out but only
intensified her distress.

"Maybe something has happened to Etewa," Ritimi
said. "Maybe a Mocototeri has killed him."

"Nothing has happened to Etewa," I stated. "I can feel
it in my legs."

Ritimi smiled slightly, as if doubting my words. "But
why is my little daughter sick?" she insisted.

"Texoma is sick because she got chilled playing in the
swamps with the frogs," I stated matter-of-factly. "Children get sick very fast and recuperate just as speedily."

"Are you sure that's the way it is?"

"Absolutely sure," I said.

Ritimi looked at me doubtfully, then said, "But none of
the other children are sick. I know Texoma has been bewitched."

Not knowing how to answer, I suggested that it would
be best to call Ritimi's uncle. Moments later I returned
with Iramamowe. During his brother Arasuwe's absence,
Iramamowe assumed the duties of a headman. His bravery

made him the most qualified man to defend the *shabono* from potential raiders. His reputation as a shaman insured the settlement of protection against evil *hekuras* sent by enemy sorcerers.

Iramamowe looked at the child, then asked me to fetch his *epena* cane and the container with the hallucinogenic powder. He had a young man blow the snuff into his nose, then chanted to the *hekuras,* pacing up and down in front of the hut. From time to time he jumped high in the air, yelling at the evil spirits—which he believed had lodged in the child's body—to leave Texoma alone.

Gently Iramamowe massaged the child, starting with her head, down her chest, her stomach, all the way to her feet. He flicked his hands repeatedly, shaking off the evil *hekuras* he had drawn out of Texoma. Several other men took *epena* and chanted with Iramamowe throughout the night. He alternately massaged and sucked the disease from her little body.

However, the child was not any better the following day. Motionless, she lay in her hammock. Her eyes were red and swollen. She refused all food, including the water and honey I offered her.

Iramamowe diagnosed that her soul had wandered from her body and proceeded to build a platform with poles and lianas in the middle of the clearing. He fastened *assai* palm leaves in his hair; he drew circles around his eyes and mouth with a mixture of *onoto* and coals. Prancing around the platform, he imitated the cries of the harpy eagle. With a branch from one of the bushes growing around the *shabono* he swept the ground thoroughly in an effort to locate the wandering soul of the child.

Unable to find the soul, he gathered several of Texoma's playmates around him. He decorated their hair and faces the same as his, then lifted them onto the platform. "Examine the ground from above," he told the children. "Find your sister's soul."

Imitating the cries of the harpy eagle, the children jumped up and down on the precariously built structure. They swept the air with the branches the women had handed them; but they too were unable to catch the lost soul.

Taking the branch Ritimi gave me, I joined the others in the quest. We swept the paths leading to the river, to the gardens, and to the swamps, where Texoma had been catching frogs. Iramamowe exchanged his branch for mine. "You carried her to the *shabono,*" he said. "Maybe you can find her soul."

Without any thoughts as to the futility of the task, I swept the ground with the same eagerness as the others. "How does one know the soul is nearby?" I asked Iramamowe as we retraced our steps back to the *shabono.*

"One just knows," he said.

We searched in every hut, sweeping under hammocks, around each hearth, and behind stacks of plantains. We lifted baskets from the ground. We moved bows and arrows leaning against the sloping roof. We scared spiders and scorpions out of their nests in the thatched roof. I gave up the hunt when I saw a snake slithering from behind one of the rafters.

Laughing, old Hayama cut the reptile's head off with one swift blow of Iramamowe's machete. She wrapped the still wriggling, headless snake in *pishaansi* leaves, then placed it on the fire. Hayama also collected the spiders falling on the ground. These too were wrapped in leaves and roasted. Old people were particularly fond of the soft bellies. The legs Hayama saved, to be ground later. The powder was believed to heal cuts, bites, and scratches.

By dusk little Texoma showed no signs of improvement.

Motionless, she lay in her hammock, her eyes staring vacantly at the thatched roof. I was filled with an indescribable sense of helplessness as Iramamowe once again bent over the child to massage and suck out the evil spirits.

"Let me try to cure the child," I said.

Iramamowe smiled almost imperceptibly, focusing his gaze alternately on me and Texoma. "What makes you think you can cure my grand-niece?" he asked with deliberate thoughtfulness. There was no mockery in his tone—only a vague curiosity. "We have not found her soul. A powerful enemy *shapori* has lured it away. Do you think you can counteract an evil sorcerer's curse?"

"No," I hastily assured him. "Only you can do that."

"What will you do then?" he asked. "You said once that you never cured anyone. What makes you think you can now?"

"I will help Texoma with hot water," I said. "And you will cure her with your chants to the *hekuras*."

Iramamowe deliberated for a moment; gradually his thoughtful expression relaxed. He held his hand over his mouth as if he were hiding an urge to giggle. "Did you learn much from the *shapori* you knew?"

"I remember some of the ways they cured," I answered, but did not mention that the cure I intended for Texoma was my grandmother's way of dealing with a fever that had not broken. "You said you have seen *hekuras* in my eyes. If you chant to them, maybe they will help me."

An easy smile came and lingered around Iramamowe's lips. He seemed almost convinced by my reasoning. Yet he shook his head as if full of doubt. "Curing is not done this way. How can I ask the *hekuras* to help you? Will you also want to take *epena*?"

"I won't need to take the snuff," I assured him, then remarked that if a powerful *shapori* could command his *hekuras* to steal the soul of a child, then an accomplished sorcerer like himself could certainly command his spirits, which according to him were already acquainted with me, to come to my aid.

"I will call the *hekuras* to assist you," Iramamowe declared. "I will take *epena* for you."

While one of the men blew the hallucinogenic substance into Iramamowe's nostrils, Ritimi, Tutemi, and Arasuwe's wives brought me calabashes filled with hot water that old Hayama had heated in the large aluminum pots. I soaked my cut-up blanket in the hot water and, using the legs of my jeans as gloves, I wrung each thin strip of cloth until not a drop of moisture was to be squeezed out. Carefully, I wrapped them around Texoma's body, then covered her with the heated palm fronds some of the older boys had cut for me.

I could hardly move among the crowd gathered in the hut. Silently they watched my every motion, intent and alert, so as not to miss anything. Iramamowe squatted beside me, chanting tirelessly into the night. As the hours passed, the people retired to their hammocks. I was not put off by their show of disapproval, but kept changing the compresses as soon as they cooled off. Ritimi sat silently in her hammock, her interlaced fingers resting limply on her lap in an attitude of supreme hopelessness. Whenever she glanced at me she broke into tears.

Texoma seemed oblivious to my ministrations. What if she had something other than a cold? I thought. What if she got worse? My assurance faltered. I mumbled a prayer for her with a fervor I had not had since I was a child. Looking up, I noticed Iramamowe gazing at me. He seemed anxious, as if aware of the mixture of feelings—magic, religion, and fear—fighting inside me. Determinedly, he went on chanting.

Old Kamosiwe came and joined us. He squatted close to the hearth. The cold of dawn had not yet crept into the hut, but the mere fact that there was a fire made him huddle over it instinctively. Softly, he began to chant. His murmured song filled me with comfort; it seemed to carry the voices of past generations. The rain prattled on the thatched roof with a determined vigor, then relaxed into a light drizzle that plunged me into a kind of stupor.

It was almost dawn when Texoma began tossing in her hammock. Impatiently she tore at the wet pieces of blanket, at the palm fronds wrapped around her. With eyes opened wide in surprise, she sat up, then smiled at old Kamosiwe, Iramamowe, and myself crouching beside her hammock. "I'm thirsty," she said, then gulped down the water and honey I gave her.

"Will she be well?" Ritimi asked hesitantly.

"Iramamowe lured her soul back," I said. "The hot water has broken her fever. Now she needs to be kept warm and sleep peacefully."

I walked into the clearing and stretched my cramped legs. Old Kamosiwe, leaning against a pole, looked like a child with his forearms tightly wrapped around his chest to keep warm. Iramamowe stopped beside me on the way to his hut. We did not talk, but I was certain we shared a moment of absolute understanding.

22

At the sound of approaching steps, Tutemi motioned me to lower myself beside the moldy leaves of the squash vines. "It's the raiding party," she whispered. "Women are not supposed to see from which direction the warriors return."

Unable to curb my curiosity, I slowly stood up. There were three women with the men; one of them was pregnant.

"Don't look," Tutemi pleaded, pulling me down. "If you see the path on which the raiders return, the enemy will capture you."

"How beautiful the men look with the bright feathers streaming from their armbands and the *onoto* designs on their bodies," I said. "But Etewa is missing! Do you think he has been killed?" I asked in dismay.

Tutemi looked at me, a dazed expression on her face. There was no nervousness in her movements as she separated the large squash leaves to peek at the retreating figures. Her anxious face beamed with a smile as she grabbed my arm. "Look, there is Etewa." She pulled my head close to hers so I could see where she was pointing. "He is *unucai.*"

Trailing a distance behind the others, Etewa walked

slowly, with his shoulders hunched forward as if he were burdened by a heavy weight on his back. He was not adorned with feathers or paint. Only short little sticks of arrow cane were stuck through his pierced earlobes and one arrow cane stick was tied to each wrist like a bracelet.

"Is he ill?"

"No! He is *unucai*," she said admiringly. "He has killed a Mocototeri."

Unable to share Tutemi's excitement, I could only stare at her in dumb incredulity. I felt my eyes fill with tears and turned my gaze away from her. We waited until Etewa was out of sight, then slowly headed toward the *shabono*.

Tutemi quickened her pace upon hearing the welcoming shouts from the men and women in the huts. Surrounded by the exultant Iticoteri, the raiders stood proudly in the clearing. Turning away from her husband, Arasuwe's youngest wife approached the three captive women, who had not been included in the jubilant greetings. Silently they stood apart, their apprehensive gazes fixed on the approaching Iticoteri woman.

"Painted with *onoto*—how disgusting," Arasuwe's wife yelled. "What else can one expect from a Mocototeri woman? Do you think you have been invited to a feast?" Glaring at the three women, she picked up a stick. "I will beat you all. If I had been captured, I would have run away," she shouted.

The three Mocototeri huddled closer to each other.

"At least I would have arrived crying pitifully," Arasuwe's wife hissed, pulling the hair of one of the women.

Arasuwe stepped in between his wife and the Mocototeri. "Leave them alone. They have cried so much they have soaked the path with their tears. We made them stop. We didn't want to listen to their wails." Arasuwe took the stick away from his wife. "We demanded they paint their faces and bodies with *onoto*. These women will be happy here. They will be treated well!" He turned to the rest of the Iticoteri women who had gathered around his wife. "Give them something to eat. They are hungry like us. We haven't eaten for two days."

Arasuwe's wife was not intimidated. "Were your men killed?" she asked the three women. "Did you burn them? Have you eaten their ashes?" She faced the pregnant woman. "Was your husband also killed? Do you expect an Iticoteri man to become a father to your child?"

Pushing his wife roughly away, Arasuwe announced, "Only one man was killed. He was shot by Etewa's arrow. He was the man who killed Etewa's father the last time the Mocototeri raided us so treacherously." Arasuwe turned to the pregnant woman. There was no sympathy in his eyes or in his voice as he continued, "You were captured by the Mocototeri some time ago. You have no brothers among them who will rescue you. You are now an Iticoteri. Do not cry any longer." Arasuwe went on to explain to the three captives that they would be better off with his people. The Iticoteri, he stressed, had enjoyed meat almost every day as well as plenty of roots and plantains throughout the rainy season. No one had gone hungry.

One of the captives was only a young girl, perhaps ten or eleven years old. "What will happen to her?" I asked Tutemi.

"Like the others, she will be taken as a wife," Tutemi said. "I was probably her age when I was abducted by the Iticoteri." A wistful little smile curved her lips. "I was lucky Ritimi's mother-in-law chose me as a second wife for Etewa. He has never beaten me. Ritimi treats me like a sister. She does not quarrel with me, nor does she make me work too . . ." Tutemi broke in midsentence as Arasuwe's youngest wife resumed her shouting at the Mocototeri women.

"How disgusting to come all painted. All you need is to stick flowers in your ears and start to dance." She followed the three women into her husband's hut. "Did the men rape you in the forest? Is that why you stayed away so long? You must have enjoyed it." Pushing the pregnant woman, she added, "Did they also sleep with you?"

"Shut up!" Arasuwe yelled, "or I'll beat you till I draw blood." Arasuwe turned to the women who had followed behind. "You should rejoice that your men have returned unharmed. You should be content that Etewa has killed a man, that we have brought three captives. Go to your huts and prepare food for your men."

Grumbling, the women dispersed to their respective hearths.

"Why is only Arasuwe's wife so upset?" I asked Tutemi.

"Don't you know?" she asked, smiling maliciously. "She is afraid he will take one of the women as his fourth wife."

"Why does he want so many?"

"He is powerful," Tutemi stated categorically. "He has many sons-in-law who bring plenty of game and help him work in the gardens. Arasuwe can feed many women."

"Were the captives raped?" I asked.

"One was." Tutemi was momentarily puzzled by my shocked expression, then went on to explain that a captured woman was usually raped by all the men in the raiding party. "It's the custom."

"Did they also rape the young girl?"

"No," Tutemi said casually. "She is not yet a woman. Neither did they rape the pregnant one—they are never touched."

Ritimi had remained in her hammock throughout the whole commotion. She told me she had no reason to get worked up about the Mocototeri women, for she knew Etewa would not take a third wife. I was happy to notice that her sadness and dejection, which had been so much a part of her during the last few days, had vanished.

"Where is Etewa?" I asked. "Is he not coming to the *shabono*?"

Ritimi's eyes appeared almost feverish with excitement as she explained that her husband, since he had killed an enemy, was searching for a tree not too far from the settlement on which he could hang his old hammock and quiver. However, before he could do so, he had to strip the tree's trunk and branches of its bark.

Ritimi's eyes expressed a deep concern as she faced me. She warned me against gazing at such a tree. She was certain I would not confuse it with the kind that is stripped of its bark to make troughs and canoes. Those trees, she explained, still looked like trees. Whereas the ones stripped by a man who has killed looked like a ghostly shadow, all white among the greenness around them, with hammock and quiver, bow, and arrows dangling from the peeled branches. Spirits—evil ones in particular—liked hiding in the vicinity of such places. I had to promise Ritimi that if I ever found myself in the neighborhood of such a tree, I would run from the spot as fast as possible.

In a voice so low I thought she was talking to herself, Ritimi confided her fears to me. She hoped Etewa would not collapse under the weight of the man he had killed. The *hekuras* of a slain man lodge themselves in the killer's chest, where they remain until the dead man's relatives have burned the body and eaten the pulverized bones. The Mocototeri would postpone for as long as possible the burning of the body in the hope that Etewa would die from weakness.

"Will the men talk about the raid?" I asked.

"As soon as they have eaten," Ritimi said.

With his bow and arrows in hand, Etewa walked across

the clearing toward the hut where Iramamowe's son had been initiated as a shaman. The men who had been with Etewa on the raid covered the sides of the hut with palm fronds. Only a small entrance was left open at the front. They brought him a water-filled calabash and built a fire inside.

Etewa was to remain in the hut until Puriwariwe would announce that the dead Mocototeri had been burned. Day and night Etewa had to be on the alert in case the dead man's spirit came prowling about the hut in the form of a jaguar. Were Etewa to talk, touch a woman, or eat during those days, he would die.

Old Hayama, accompanied by her daughter-in-law, came into our hut. "I want to find out what's going on at Arasuwe's place," the old woman said, sitting beside me. Xotomi sat on the ground, reclining her head against my legs, dangling from my hammock. A purple scar—a reminder of the arrow wound—marred the smooth line of her calf. That did not worry Xotomi; she was grateful the wound had not become infected.

"Matuwe caught one of the women," Hayama said proudly. "It's a good time for him to get another wife. I'd better select the right one for him. I'm sure he will make a mistake if it's left up to him to make the choice."

"But he has a wife," I stammered, looking at Xotomi.

"Yes," the old woman agreed. "But if he is to have a second wife, this is the best time. Xotomi is young. It will be easy for her to be friends with another woman now. Matuwe should take the youngest of the three captives." Hayama brushed her hand over Xotomi's shaven tonsure. "The girl is younger than you. She will obey you. If you menstruate, she can cook for us. She can help you in the gardens and with the gathering of wood. I'm getting too old to work much."

Xotomi examined the three Mocototeri women in

Arasuwe's hut. "If Matuwe is to take another wife, I wish him to take the young girl. I will like her. She can warm his hammock when I'm pregnant."

"Are you?" I asked.

"I'm not certain," she said, smiling smugly.

Hayama had told me some time ago that a pregnant woman usually waited three to four months, sometimes even longer, before telling her husband of her state. The man was a tacit accomplice in this deception, for he also dreaded the restrictive food and behavior taboos. Whenever a woman suffered a miscarriage or gave birth to a deformed child, she was never at fault. It was the husband who was always blamed. In fact, if a woman repeatedly bore a sickly infant, she was encouraged to conceive by another man. Her own husband, however, had to obey the taboos and raise the baby as his own.

Hayama went over to Arasuwe's hut. "I will take this Mocototeri girl with me. She will make a fine wife for my son," she said, taking the girl by the hand. "She will live with me in my hut."

"I captured a woman," Matuwe said. "I don't want this child. She is too thin. I want a strong woman who will bear healthy sons."

"She will grow strong," Hayama said calmly. "She is still green, but soon she will be ripe. Look at her breasts. They are already large. Besides," she added, "Xotomi will not mind if you take her." Hayama faced the men gathered inside and outside Arasuwe's hut. "No one is to touch her. I will take care of her until she becomes my son's wife. From today on she is my daughter-in-law."

No objections were raised by the men as Hayama took the girl into our hut. Shyly, the Mocototeri sat on the ground, close to the hearth. "I will not beat you," Xotomi said, taking the girl's hand in hers. "But you must do what I tell you."

Matuwe grinned sheepishly at us across the hut. I wondered if he was proud to have two wives or actually embarrassed to be forced into taking a child when he had captured a woman.

"What will happen to the other captives?" I asked.

"Arasuwe will take the pregnant one," Hayama declared.

"How do you know?" Without waiting for her answer, I asked about the third one.

"She will be given to someone as a wife after she has been taken by any of the men in the *shabono* who wish to do so," Hayama said.

"But she has already been raped by the raiders," I said indignantly.

Old Hayama burst into laughter. "But not by the men who didn't participate in the raid." The old woman patted my head. "Don't look so stricken. It is the custom. I was captured once. I was raped by many men. I was lucky and found a chance to escape. No, don't interrupt me, white girl," Hayama said, putting her hand over my mouth. "I didn't run away because I had been raped. I forgot that very fast. I escaped because I had to work too hard and was not given enough food."

As the old woman had predicted, Arasuwe took the pregnant woman for himself.

"You have three wives already," the youngest one shouted, her face contorted in anger. "Why do you want another one?"

Giggling nervously, Arasuwe's two other wives watched from their hammocks as the youngest pushed the pregnant woman on the burning coals of the hearth. Arasuwe jumped out of his hammock, took a burning log from the fire, and handed it to the fallen Mocototeri woman. "Burn my wife's arm," he urged the Mocototeri woman as he held his youngest wife pinned against one of the poles in the hut. Sobbing, the pregnant woman covered her burned shoulder with her hand.

"Burn me!" Arasuwe's wife dared her, twisting away from her husband's grip. "If you do, I will burn you alive —but no one will eat your bones. I shall scatter them in the forest, so we can piss on them . . ." She stopped, her eyes widened in genuine astonishment as she discovered the extent of the woman's injured shoulder. "You are really burnt! Does it hurt much?"

Looking up, the Mocototeri wiped the tears from her face. "I'm in great pain."

"Oh, you poor woman." Solicitously, Arasuwe's wife helped her to stand up, guiding her over to her own hammock. She took leaves from a calabash and gently placed them on the woman's shoulder. "It will heal very fast. I will make sure of it."

"Don't weep any longer," Arasuwe's oldest wife said, sitting next to the Mocototeri woman. She patted her leg affectionately. "Our husband is a good man. He will treat you well. I will make sure no one in the shabono mistreats you."

"What will happen when the baby is born?" I asked Hayama.

"That's hard to say," the old woman conceded. She remained quiet for a moment as if deep in thought. "She may kill it. Yet if it is a boy Arasuwe might ask his oldest wife to raise him as if it were his own."

Hours later, Arasuwe began his tale about the events of the raid. He talked in a slow, nasal tone. "We traveled slowly the first day and stopped to rest often. Our backs ached from the heavy loads of plantains. That first night we hardly slept, for we didn't have enough firewood to keep warm. The rain fell with such force the night sky seemed to melt with the darkness around us. The following day we walked somewhat faster, arriving in the vicinity of the Mocototeri settlement. We were still far enough away that the enemy hunters would not discover our presence that night, yet close enough that we didn't dare light a fire in our camp.''

I could only see Arasuwe's face in profile. Fascinated, I watched the red and black designs on his cheeks moving animatedly with the rhythm of his speech, as if they had a life of their own. The feathers in his earlobes added a softness to his stern, tired face, a playfulness that belied the horror of his tale.

"For a few days we carefully watched the comings and goings of our enemy. Our aim was to kill a Mocototeri without alarming their *shabono* of our presence. One morning we saw the man who had killed Etewa's father walk into the thicket after a woman. Etewa shot him in the stomach with one of his poisoned arrows. The man was so dazed he did not even shout. By the time he recovered from his surprise, Etewa had shot a second arrow in his stomach and another in his neck, right behind his ear. He fell on the ground, dead.

"Walking like a stunned man, Etewa headed home, accompanied by my nephew. Meanwhile Matuwe had found the woman hiding in the thicket. He threatened to kill her if she so much as opened her mouth to cough. Matuwe, together with my youngest son-in-law, headed toward our settlement with the reluctant woman. We were all to meet later at a predetermined location. As the rest of us were deciding whether to split into even smaller groups, we saw a mother with her little son, a pregnant woman, and a young girl, all heading into the forest. We could not resist the temptation. Quietly, we followed them." Leaning back in his hammock, hands locked behind his head, Arasuwe regarded his spellbound audience.

Taking advantage of the headman's pause, one of the

men who had been on the raid stood up. Motioning the people to make space for him to move, he opened his narration with exactly the same words Arasuwe used. "We traveled slowly the first day."

But that was all his and the headman's narratives had in common. Gesticulating a great deal, the man mimicked with exaggerated flare the moods and expressions of different members of the raiding party, thus adding a touch of humor and melodrama to Arasuwe's dry, matter-of-fact rendition. Encouraged by his audience's laughter and cheers, the man told at great length about the two youngest members of the raiding party. They were no older than sixteen or seventeen. Not only had they complained of sore feet, the cold, and their aches and pains, but they had been afraid of prowling jaguars and spirits on the second night when they had all slept without lighting a fire. The man interspersed his account with detailed information on the variety of game and ripening wild fruit—color, size, and shape—he had spotted on the way.

Arasuwe resumed his own report as soon as the man paused. "When the three women and the girl were far enough from the *shabono*," the headman continued, "we threatened to shoot them if they tried to run away or scream. The small boy managed to sneak into the bushes. We did not pursue him, but retreated as fast as possible, making sure not to leave footprints behind. We were sure that as soon as the Mocototeri discovered the dead man they would follow us.

"Just before dusk, the mother of the boy who had sneaked away cried out in pain. Sitting on the ground, she pressed her foot between her hands. She wept bitterly, complaining that a poisonous snake had bitten her. Her heartbreaking wails saddened us so much we did not even make sure there had been a snake. 'What good has it been,' she sobbed, 'for my little son to run away if he no longer has a mother to take care of him?' Screaming that she could not bear the pain any longer, the woman hobbled into the bushes. It took us a moment to realize we had been tricked. We searched the forest thoroughly, but we couldn't discover in which direction she had fled."

Old Kamosiwe laughed heartily. "It's good that she tricked you. It never pays to abduct a woman who has left behind a small child. They cry until they become ill and, worse, they almost always escape."

The men talked until the rainy dawn enshrouded the *shabono*. In the middle of the clearing stood the solitary hut where Etewa was enclosed. It was so quiet and apart— so close, yet so far removed from the voices and laughter.

A week later, Puriwariwe visited Etewa. As soon as he had eaten a baked plantain and honey, the old man asked Iramamowe to blow *epena* into his head. Chanting, Puriwariwe danced around Etewa's hut. "The dead man has not yet been burned," he announced. "His body has been placed in a trough. It is rotting high up in a tree. Do not break your silence yet. The *hekuras* of the dead man are still in your chest. Prepare your new arrows and bow. Soon the Mocototeri will burn the rotting flesh for the worms are already crawling out of the carcass." The old *shapori* circled Etewa's hut once more, then danced across the clearing into the forest.

Three days later, Puriwariwe announced that the Mocototeri had burned the dead man. "Take out the sticks from your earlobes, untie the ones from your wrists," he said, helping Etewa stand up. "In a few days take your old bow and arrows to the same peeled tree on which you hung your hammock and quiver."

Puriwariwe led Etewa into the forest. Arasuwe, together with some of the men who had been on the raid, followed behind.

They returned in the late afternoon. Etewa's hair had been cut, his tonsure shaven. His body had been washed and painted afresh with *onoto*. Cane rods, decorated with red macaw feathers, had been inserted in his earlobes. He also wore the new fur armbands, adorned with feathers, and the thick cotton waist belt Ritimi had made for him. Arasuwe offered Etewa a basket full of tiny fish he had cooked for him in *pishaansi* leaves.

Three days later, Etewa ventured for the first time by himself into the forest. "I've shot a monkey," he announced hours later, standing in the clearing. As soon as a group of men had gathered around him, he gave them precise information as to where the animal could be found.

To insure the aid and protection of the *hekuras* during future hunts, Etewa went two more times by himself into the forest. On each occasion he returned without the kill, then informed others where they could locate it. Etewa did not eat of the monkey and the two peccaries he had shot.

One afternoon he returned with a curassow hung from his back. He scalped the bird, saving the strip of skin where the curly black feathers were attached. It would serve as an armband. The wing feathers he saved for feathering his arrows. He cooked the almost two-foot-long bird on a wooden platform he had built over the fire. Tasting to see if the curassow was done thoroughly, he then proceeded to divide it between his children and two wives.

"Is the white girl your child or your wife?" old Hayama shouted from her hut as Etewa handed me a piece of the dark breast meat.

"She is my mother," Etewa said, joining the laughing Iticoteri.

Days later, Arasuwe supervised the cooking of plantain pap. Etewa emptied a small gourd into the soup. Ritimi told me they were the last of the powdered bones of

Etewa's father. Tears rolled down the men's and women's cheeks as they swallowed the thick soup. I took the calabash ladle Etewa offered me and cried for his dead father.

As soon as the trough was empty, Arasuwe shouted at the top of his voice, "What a *waiteri* man we have amongst us. He has killed his enemy. He has carried the dead man's *hekuras* in his chest without succumbing to hunger or loneliness during his confinement."

Etewa walked around the clearing. "Yes, I am *waiteri*," he sang. "The *hekuras* of a dead man can kill the strongest warrior. It is a heavy burden to carry them for so many days. A person can die of sorrow." Etewa began to dance. "I no longer think about the man I killed. I dance with the shadows of the night, not with the shadows of death." The longer he danced, the lighter and faster his steps became, as though through the movements he was finally able to shake off the burden he had borne in his chest.

Many an evening the events of the raid were retold by the men. Even old Kamosiwe had a version. All the stories had in common with the original one was that Etewa had killed a man, that three women had been captured. In time only a vague memory of the actual facts remained, and it became a tale of the distant past like all the other stories the Iticoteri were so fond of telling.

PART SIX

PART SIX

23

The pressure of tiny feet kneading on my stomach woke me from my reveries. As if only a moment had passed, the memories of the bygone days, weeks, and months had drifted through my mind in vivid detail. Words of protest died on my lips as Tutemi lowered Hoaxiwe on top of me. I cradled the baby in my arms, lest he awaken little Texoma, who had fallen asleep in my hammock while waiting for me to get up. I reached for Hoaxiwe's frog skulls threaded on a liana string hanging at the head of my hammock and rattled them in front of him. Gurgling with delight, the baby tried to reach them.

"Are you awake?" Texoma mumbled, touching my cheek lightly. "I thought you were going to sleep the whole day."

"I've been thinking about all I've seen and learned since I first came here," I said, taking her small hand in mine. The narrow palm, the long, delicately shaped fingers were oddly mature for a five-year-old child and contrasted sharply with her dimpled face. "I didn't realize the sun's already up."

"You didn't even notice my brother and cousins leaving your hammock as soon as the plantains were baked," Texoma said. "Were you thinking very hard?"

"No," I laughed. "It was more like dreaming. It seems as if no time has passed since the day I arrived at the *shabono*."

"To me it's like a long time," Texoma said seriously, caressing her half-brother's soft hair. "When you first arrived, this tiny baby was still sleeping inside Tutemi's belly. I remember well the day my mothers found you." Giggling, the little girl buried her face in my neck. "I know why you wept that day. You were afraid of my great-uncle Iramamowe—he has an ugly face."

"That day," I whispered conspiringly, "I was afraid of all the Iticoteri." Feeling a warm wetness on my stomach, I held Hoaxiwe away from me. Etewa, sitting astride his hammock, smiled in amusement as he watched the arc of his son's urine spanning over the fire.

"Of all of us?" Texoma asked. "Even of my father and grandfather? Even of my mothers and old Hayama?" Bending over my face, she gazed at me with an expression of incredulity, almost of anguish, as if she were searching for something in my eyes. "Were you also afraid of me?"

"No. I wasn't afraid of you," I assured her, bouncing the laughing Hoaxiwe on my thighs.

"I wasn't afraid of you either." Sighing with relief, Texoma lay back in the hammock. "I didn't hide like most of the children did when you first walked into our hut. We had heard that whites were tall and hairy like monkeys. But you looked so little, I knew you couldn't be a real white."

As soon as her basket was securely fastened to her back, Tutemi lifted her baby from my lap. Expertly she placed him in the wide, softened-bark sling she wore across her chest. "Ready," she said, smiling, then looked questioningly at Etewa and Ritimi.

Grinning, Etewa picked up his machete and his bow and arrows.

"Will you come later?" Ritimi asked me as she adjusted the long, slender rod stuck through the septum of her nose. The corners of her mouth, free of the usual smooth sticks, turned up in a smile, dimpling her cheeks. As if sensing my indecision, Ritimi did not wait for my reply but followed her husband and Tutemi to the gardens.

"Hayama is coming," Tutemi whispered. "She is wondering why you haven't come to eat her baked plantain." The little girl slid from the hammock and ran toward a group of children playing outside.

Muttering, Hayama walked through Tutemi's hut. Her loose skin hung in long vertical wrinkles down her thighs and belly. Her face was set in a stern mien as she handed me a half-gourd filled with plantain mush. Sighing, she sat in Ritimi's hammock, letting her hand trail along the ground as she rocked herself to and fro, apparently entranced by the rhythmic squeaking of the liana knot against the pole. "It's too bad I've not been able to fatten you up," the old woman said after a long silence.

I assured her that her plantains had worked wonders— that given a bit more time I might even become fat.

"There isn't much time," Hayama said softly. "You are leaving for the mission."

"What?" I cried, struck by the definiteness of her tone. "Who says so?"

"Before he left, Milagros made Arasuwe promise that if we were to move to one of our old gardens deeper in the forest, we were not to take you." The nostalgic, almost dreamy gaze of her eyes softened Hayama's expression as she reminded me of the various families who several weeks before had left for the old gardens. Believing they were to return soon, I had not paid much attention to their departure at the time. Hayama went on to explain that Arasuwe's household, as well as those of his brothers, cousins, sons, and daughters, had not yet followed the others for the simple reason that the headman was waiting to hear from Milagros.

"Is the *shabono* going to be abandoned?" I asked. "What about the gardens here? They were only recently expanded. What will happen to all the new plantain shoots?" I said excitedly.

"They will grow." Hayama's face crinkled with cheerful amusement. "The old people and many of the children will remain here. We will build temporary shelters close to the plantain patches, for no one likes to live in a solitary *shabono*. We will take care of the gardens until the others return. By then the bananas and *rasha* fruit will be ripe and once again it will be time to feast."

"But why are so many Iticoteri leaving?" I asked. "Isn't there enough food here?"

Hayama did not actually say that there was a food shortage, yet she stressed the fact that old gardens, which have not been visited for a long time, become a feeding ground for monkeys, birds, agouti, peccary, and tapir. Men have an easy time hunting and the women still find plenty of roots and fruits in such gardens to last until the game has been exhausted. "Besides," Hayama went on, "a temporary move is always good, especially after a raid. If I weren't too old, I would also go."

"Like a holiday," I said.

"Yes. A holiday!" Hayama laughed, once I explained what was meant by the word. "Oh, how much I'd like to go and sit in the shade, stuffing myself with *kafu* fruit."

Kafu trees were prized for their bark and bast fibers. The clusters of fruit, each about ten inches long, hang on a common stalk. The gelatinous, fleshy fruit is filled with tiny seeds and tastes like an overripe fresh fig.

"If I can't move with Arasuwe and his family to the old gardens," I said, squatting at the head of Hayama's hammock, "then I will stay here with you. There is no reason for me to return to the mission. We'll await the return of the others together."

Hayama's eyes shone with an unnatural brightness as they rested on my face. In a slow, deliberate tone, she made it clear that, although it was not customary to raid an empty *shabono* or to kill old people and children, the Mocototeri would undoubtedly make trouble if they were to learn, which the old woman assured me they would, that I had been left behind in an unprotected settlement.

I shuddered, remembering how several weeks before a group of Mocototeri men, armed with clubs, had arrived at the *shabono* demanding the return of their women. After both groups had shouted threats and insults at each other, Arasuwe told the Mocototeri that he had purposely freed one of the abducted women on his way home. He stressed the fact that not for an instant had he been taken in by the woman's trick of having been bitten by a snake. However, after more bickering on both sides, the headman reluctantly handed over the girl old Hayama had chosen as a second wife for her youngest son. Threatening to retaliate at a later date, the Mocototeri left.

It was Etewa who had explained to me that although the Mocototeri had had no intention of starting a shooting war—they had left their bows and arrows hidden in the forest—the headman had acted wisely in returning the girl so promptly. The Iticoteri were outnumbered, as several men had already left for the abandoned gardens.

"When will Arasuwe join the others in the old gardens?" I asked Hayama.

"Very soon," she said. "Arasuwe has sent several men to find Milagros. Unfortunately, they have been unable to get in touch with him so far."

I smiled to myself. "It seems that regardless of what Arasuwe promised, I'll end up going with Ritimi and Etewa," I said smugly.

"You won't," Hayama assured me, then grinned maliciously. "It's not only from the Mocototeri we have to protect you, but a *shapori* might abduct you on the way to the gardens and keep you as his woman in a faraway hut."

"I doubt it," I said, giggling. "You told me once that no man would want me this skinny." I told the old woman about the incident in the mountains with Etewa.

Pressing her folded arms across her hanging bosom, Hayama laughed until tears rolled down her wrinkled cheeks. "Etewa would take any woman that's available," she said. "But he's afraid of you." Hayama leaned over her hammock, then whispered, "A *shapori* isn't an ordinary man. He wouldn't want you for his pleasure. A *shapori* needs the femaleness in his body." She lay back in the hammock. "Do you know where that femaleness is?"

"No."

The old woman looked at me as if she thought I was slow-witted. "In the vagina," she finally said, almost choking on her laughter.

"Do you think that Puriwariwe might abduct me?" I asked mockingly. "I'm sure that he's too old to care about women."

Genuine amazement widened her eyes. "Haven't you seen? Hasn't anyone told you that that old *shapori* is stronger than any man in the *shabono*?" she asked. "There are nights when that old man goes from hut to hut, sticking his cock inside every woman he can find. And he doesn't get tired. At dawn, when he returns to the forest, he's as ready as ever." Hayama assured me that Puriwariwe could not possibly abduct me, for he no longer needed anything. She warned me, however, that there were other shamans, less powerful than the old man, who might.

Closing her eyes, she sighed loudly. I thought she had fallen asleep, but, as if sensing my motion to get up, the old woman turned to me abruptly. She placed both her hands on my shoulders, then asked me in a voice that shook with emotion, "Do you know why you like being with us?"

I looked at her uncomprehendingly, and as I opened my mouth to respond Hayama went on to say, "You are happy here because you have no responsibilities. You live like us. You have learned to speak quite well and know many of our customs. To us you are neither child or adult, man or woman. We make no demands on you. If we did, you would resent it." Hayama's eyes were so dark as they held my gaze, they made me uncomfortable. In her wrinkled face they seemed too large and bright, as if glowing with an inexhaustible inner energy. After a long pause, she added provokingly, "Were you to become a woman *shapori,* you would be very unhappy."

I felt threatened. Yet, as I stammered inanities to defend myself, I suddenly realized that she was right and I was seized by a desperate desire to laugh.

Gently the old woman pressed her fingers over my lips. "There are powerful *shapori* living in remote places where the *hekuras* of animals and plants dwell," Hayama said. "In the dark of night, those men consort with beautiful female spirits."

"I'm glad I'm not a beautiful spirit," I said.

"No. You are not beautiful." Hayama with her cajoling laugh and mocking gaze made it impossible for me to take offense at her uncomplimentary remark. "Yet to many of us you are strange." There was great tenderness in her voice as she tried to make me understand why the Mocototeri wanted to take me to their *shabono.* Their interest in me was not due to the usual reasons Indians befriend whites—to get machetes, cooking pots, and clothes—but because the Mocototeri believed I had powers. They had heard of how I had cured little Texoma, about the *epena* incident, and how Iramamowe had seen *hekuras* reflected in my eyes. They had even seen me use a bow and arrow.

All my endeavors to make the old woman realize that it required no special powers, only common sense, to help a child with a cold were in vain. I argued that even she herself could be considered to have healing powers—she set bones and smeared secret concoctions made from animal parts, roots, and leaves on bites, scratches, and cuts. But my reasonings were futile. To her there was a vast difference between setting a bone and coaxing the lost soul of a child back into its body. That, she stressed, only a *shapori* could do.

"But Iramamowe brought her soul back," I asserted. "I only cured her cold."

"He didn't," Hayama insisted. "He heard you chant."

"That was a prayer," I said feebly, realizing that a prayer was in no way different from Iramamowe's *hekura* chants.

"I know whites are not like us," Hayama interrupted me, determined to prevent me from arguing further. "I'm talking about something different altogether. Had you been born an Iticoteri, you would still be different from Ritimi, Tutemi, or me." Hayama touched my face, running her long, bony fingers over my forehead and cheeks. "My sister Angelica would never have asked you to accompany her into the forest. Milagros would never have brought you to stay with us if you were like the whites he knows." She regarded me thoughtfully, then, as if struck with an afterthought, added, "I wonder if any other whites would have been as happy as you have been with us."

"I'm sure they would have," I said softly. "There aren't many whites who have a chance to come here."

Hayama shrugged her shoulders. "Do you remember the story about Imawaami, the woman *shapori*?" she asked.

"That's a myth!" Afraid that the old woman was trying to make some connection between Imawaami and myself, I hastily added, "It's like the story of the bird who stole the first fire from the alligator's mouth."

"Maybe," Hayama said dreamily. "Lately, I have been thinking about the stories my father, grandfather, and even my great-grandfather used to tell about the white men they had seen traveling along the big rivers. There must have been whites journeying through the forest long before my great-grandfather's time. Perhaps Imawaami was one of them." Hayama moved her eager face close to mine, then continued in a whisper. "It must have been a *shapori* who captured her, believing the white woman was a beautiful spirit. But she was more powerful than the *shapori*. She stole his *hekuras* and became a sorceress herself." Hayama looked at me provokingly, as if daring me to contradict her.

I was not surprised by the old woman's reasoning. The Iticoteri were in the habit of bringing their mythology up to date, or of incorporating facts into their myths. "Do Indian women ever become *shapori*?" I asked.

"Yes," Hayama said promptly. "Female *shapori* are strange creatures. Like men, they hunt with bow and arrows. They decorate their bodies with the spots and broken circles of a jaguar. They take *epena* and lure the *hekuras* into their chests with their songs. Women *shapori* have husbands who serve them. But if they have children, they once again become ordinary women."

"Angelica was a *shapori*, wasn't she?" I was unaware I had thought out loud. The thought came with the certainty of a revelation. I recalled the time Angelica had awakened me from a nightmare at the mission, the way her incomprehensible song had soothed me. It had not resembled the melodious song of the Iticoteri women but the monotonous chant of the shamans. Like them, Angelica seemed to possess two voices—one that orginated from somewhere deep inside her, the other from her throat. I remembered the days of walking with Milagros and Angelica through the forest and how Angelica's remarks about the spirits of the forest lurking in the shadows—that I should always dance with them, but never let them become a burden—had enchanted me. I clearly visualized how Angelica had danced that morning—her arms raised above her head, her feet moving with quick jerky steps in the same manner that the Iticoteri men danced when in an *epena* trance. Until now I had never thought it in the least odd that Angelica, as opposed to the other Indian women at the mission, had considered it very natural for me to have come to hunt in the jungle.

Hayama's words awoke me from my musings. "Did my sister tell you she was a *shapori*?" A profound grief filled Hayama's eyes; tears gathered at their corners. The drops never rolled down her cheeks but lost themselves in a network of wrinkles.

"She never told me," I murmured, then lay down in my hammock. With one leg on the ground I pushed myself back and forth, adjusting the rhythm of my hammock to Hayama's so that the vine knots would squeak in unison.

"My sister was a *shapori*," Hayama said after a long silence. "I don't know what happened to her after she left our *shabono*. While she was with us, she was a respected *shapori*, but she lost her powers when she had Milagros." Hayama sat up abruptly. "His father was a white man."

Afraid that my curiosity might escape through my eyes, I closed them. I did not dare breathe, lest the smallest sound put an end to the old woman's reveries. There was no way of learning which country Milagros's father had come from. Regardless of their origins, any non-Indian was considered a *nape*.

"Milagros's father was a white man," Hayama repeated. "A long time ago, when we lived closer to the big river, a *nape* came to stay at our settlement. Angelica believed she could get his power. Instead she got pregnant."

"Why didn't she abort?"

A broad grin crossed Hayama's lined face. "Perhaps Angelica was too confident," the old woman murmured. "Maybe she believed she could still be a *shapori* after having a child by a white man." Hayama's mouth opened wide with laughter, revealing yellowish teeth. "There is nothing white about Milagros," she said mischievously. "Even though my sister took him away. In spite of all he learned from the white man, Milagros will always be an Iticoteri." Hayama's eyes shone with a strong, unwavering stare, and her face revealed a certain indefinable, pent-up triumph.

The thought that I would soon be returning to the mission filled me with apprehension. On several occasions since my illness I had tried to imagine what it would be like to return to Caracas or to Los Angeles. How would I react to seeing relatives and friends? During those moments, I had known I would never leave of my own accord.

"When will Milagros take me back to the mission?" I asked.

"I don't think Arasuwe will wait for Milagros. The headman can no longer postpone his departure," Hayama said. "Iramamowe will take you back."

"Iramamowe!" I exclaimed in disbelief. "Why not Etewa?"

Patiently, Hayama explained that Iramamowe had been near the mission on several occasions; he knew the way better than any of the Iticoteri. There was also the possibility of Etewa being discovered by Mocototeri hunters, in which case he would be killed and I would be abducted. "Iramamowe, on the other hand," Hayama assured me, "can make himself invisible in the forest."

"But I can't!" I protested.

"You will be guarded by Iramamowe's *hekuras*," Hayama said with utter conviction. Cumbersomely, the old woman stood up, rested for a moment with her hands on her thighs, then took my arm and slowly walked me over to her own hut. "Iramamowe has protected you before," Hayama reminded me, then eased herself into her hammock.

"Yes," I agreed. "But I can't go to the mission without Milagros. I need sardines and crackers."

"That stuff will only make you sick," she said contemptuously. Hayama assured me that I would not suffer from hunger on the way, for Iramamowe's arrows would hit plenty of game. Besides, she would give me a basketful of plantains.

"I'm too weak to carry such a heavy load," I objected, knowing that Iramamowe would carry nothing besides his bow and arrows.

Hayama regarded me with gentle mockery. She stretched in her hammock, opened her mouth in an interminable yawn, and promptly fell asleep.

I walked into the clearing. A group of children, mostly little girls, were playing with a puppy. Each girl tried to make the animal suck from her flat nipples.

Except for a few old people resting in their hammocks and several menstruating women crouching near the hearths, most of the huts were deserted. I went from dwelling to dwelling, wondering if they knew I was soon to leave. An old man offered me his tobacco wad. Smiling, I declined. "How can anyone refuse such a treat?" his eyes seemed to say as he reinserted the wad between his lower lip and gum.

Late in the afternoon I walked into Iramamowe's hut. His oldest wife, who had just returned from the river, was hanging two water-filled gourds on the rafters. We had become good friends since the time her son Xorowe had been initiated as a *shapori* and had spent many afternoons talking about him. Occasionally Xorowe returned to the *shabono* to cure people afflicted with colds, fevers, and diarrhea. He chanted to the *hekuras* with the same zeal and strength as the more experienced shamans did. Yet, according to Puriwariwe, it would still be some time before Xorowe could send his own spirits to cause harm among an enemy settlement. Only then would he be accepted as a full-fledged sorcerer.

Iramamowe's wife poured some water into a small calabash, then added some honey. Greedily, I watched the runny paste, studded with bees in the various stages of their metamorphic process. After stirring it thoroughly with her finger she offered me the gourd. Smacking my lips between each sip, I finished the drink and licked the bottom clean. "What a delight," I exclaimed. "I'm sure it's from the *amoshi* bees." They were a stingless variety and greatly prized for their dark aromatic honey.

Smiling in agreement, Iramamowe's wife motioned me to sit beside her in her hammock. She examined my back for flea and mosquito bites. Discovering two recent ones, she sucked out the poison. The light entering the hut grew dimmer. It seemed that such a long time had passed since I had talked with Hayama that morning. Drowsily, I closed my eyes.

I dreamt I was with the children by the river. Thousands of butterflies fluttered out of the trees, swirling through the air like autumn leaves. They alighted on our hair, faces, and bodies, covering us with the tenuous golden light of dusk. Despondently I gazed at their wings, like delicate hands waving farewell. "You cannot be sad," the children were saying. I looked into each face and kissed the laughter on their lips.

24

Instead of the bamboo knife she always used, Ritimi trimmed my hair with a sharp grass blade. Frowning with concentration, she made sure the hair was cut evenly all around my head.

"Not my tonsure," I said, covering the top of my head with my folded hands. "It hurts."

"Don't be so cowardly," Ritimi laughed. "You don't want to arrive at the mission looking like a barbarian."

I could not make her understand that among whites I would be considered an oddity with a bald spot on the top of my head. Ritimi insisted that it was not merely for aesthetic reasons but practical ones as well that she needed to shave the crown of my head.

"Lice," she pointed out, "like that particular spot best. I'm certain Iramamowe will not delouse you in the evenings."

"Maybe you should shave my hair completely," I suggested. "That's the best way to get rid of them."

Horrified, Ritimi stared at me. "Only the very sick have their heads shaved. You would look ugly."

Nodding in agreement, I submitted to her ministrations. Upon finishing, she rubbed the bald spot with *onoto*.

Then, she very carefully painted my face with the red paste. She drew a wide straight line just below my bangs and wavy ones across my cheeks with dots between each of the lines. "What a shame I did not pierce your nose and the corners of your mouth when you first arrived," she said disappointedly. Removing the polished slender stick from her septum, she held it under my nose. "How beautiful you would have looked," she sighed with comical resignation, and proceeded to paint my back with wide *onoto* lines rounding toward my buttocks. On the front, starting below my breasts, she drew wavy lines all the way to my thighs. Lastly she encircled my ankles with broad red bands. Looking down my legs, I had the feeling I was wearing socks.

Tutemi tied a newly made cotton belt around my waist, the front fringe resting on my pubis. Pleased at my appearance, she clapped her hands and jumped up and down excitedly. "Oh, the ears!" she cried, motioning Ritimi to hand her the white feather tufts held together on a thin string. Tutemi tied them on my earrings. Around my upper arms and below my knees she fastened red-dyed cotton strands.

Encircling my waist with her arm, Ritimi took me from hut to hut, so I could be admired by the Iticoteri. For one last time I saw myself reflected in the women's shiny eyes and delighted in the men's mocking smiles. Yawning, old Kamosiwe stretched his skinny arms until they seemed about to be pulled from their sockets. He opened his one eye, studying my face as if he were trying to memorize my features. With slow, deliberate movements, he unfastened the small pouch he wore around his neck and took out the pearl I had given him. "Whenever I let this stone roll on my palm, I will think of you."

Unwilling to believe that never again would I stand there in the *shabono,* that never again would I awake to the children's laughter as they climbed into my hammock at dawn, I wept.

There were no good-byes. I simply followed Iramamowe and Etewa into the forest. Ritimi and Tutemi were behind me, as if we were going to collect firewood. Silently we walked along the path the whole day, stopping only momentarily to snack.

The sun was setting behind the horizon of trees when we came to a halt beneath the dark shadows of three giant ceibas. They had grown so close together that they appeared to be one. Ritimi fastened the basket she had been carrying for me on my back. It was packed with plantains, roasted monkey meat, a honey-filled calabash, several empty gourds, my hammock, and my knapsack, which contained my jeans and a torn shirt.

"You won't grow sad if you paint your body with *onoto* each time you bathe in the river," Ritimi said, tying a small gourd around my waist. It had been polished with abrasive leaves. Smooth and white, it hung from my cotton belt like a giant teardrop.

The forest, the three smiling faces, blurred before me. Without another word, Ritimi led the way into the thicket. Only Etewa turned around before melting into the shadows. A grin lit his face as he waved the way he had so often seen Milagros do when he bid me farewell.

I gave free rein to the vast desolation inside me. It did not make me feel any better but only heightened my despondency. Yet, in spite of my wretchedness, I was strangely aware of the three ceibas in front of me. As if in a dream, I recognized the trees. I had been on this very spot before. Milagros had squatted in front of me. Impassively, he had watched the rain wash my face and body of Angelica's ashes. Today it was Iramamowe squatting on the same spot, gazing at the tears rolling uncontrollably down my cheeks.

"It was here that I first saw Ritimi, Tutemi, and Etewa," I said. Suddenly I realized it had been Ritimi's deliberate choice to accompany me this far. I understood all she had left unsaid, how deeply she felt. She had given me back a basket and a gourd, the two items I was carrying that distant day. Only now the gourd was not filled with ashes, but with *onoto*, a symbol of life and happiness. A quiet loneliness, humble and accepting, filled my heart. I carefully dried my tears so as not to erase the *onoto* designs.

"Perhaps one day Ritimi will find you on this spot again," Iramamowe said, his habitually stern face softened by a fleeting smile. "Let's walk a bit farther before we rest for the night." Lifting the heavy bunch of plantains from my basket, he flung it over his shoulder. He was slightly swaybacked and his belly stuck out.

Iramamowe must have felt the same urge to walk as I did. My feet seemed to move of their own accord, knowing exactly where to step in the darkness. I never lost sight of Iramamowe's arrow quiver, immobilized under the load of plantains. Moving through the darkness, I had the illusion that it was not I but the forest that was leaving.

"We'll sleep here," Iramamowe said, inspecting the weathered lean-to that stood away from the path. He built a small fire inside, then hung his hammock next to mine.

I lay awake, watching the stars and the faint moon through the opening of the hut. Mist thickened the darkness until there was no light left. Trees and sky formed one mass through which I imagined bows falling from the clouds like heavy rain and *hekuras* rising from invisible crevices in the earth; they danced to the sound of a shaman's song.

The sun was high over the treetops when Iramamowe woke me. After finishing a baked plantain and a piece of monkey meat, I offered him my calabash with honey.

"You'll need it for the days of walking," he said. A

friendly glance softened his words of refusal. "We will find more on the way," he promised, reaching for his machete and his bow and arrows.

We walked at a steady pace, much faster than I remember ever having walked in my life. We crossed rivers, we moved up and down hills that bore no familiar landmark. Days spent walking, nights spent sleeping chased each other with predictable swiftness. My thoughts did not reach beyond each day or night. There was nothing between them but a short-lived dawn and dusk during which we ate.

"I know this place!" I exclaimed one afternoon, breaking the long silence. I pointed to the dark rocks jutting from the earth. They formed a perpendicular wall along the river's edge. But the longer I gazed at the river and trees, already purple in the twilight, the less sure I felt I had been there before. I climbed over a tree trunk that extended all the way into the water. The day had been deadly still, but now the leaves began to stir gently, sending forth a fresh whisper along the river. Arching branches and creepers brushed the water's surface, burying themselves in the dark liquid that harbored no fish and discouraged mosquitoes. "Are we close to the mission?" I asked, turning to Iramamowe.

He did not answer. After a moment, as if annoyed by the silence he was unwilling to break, he motioned me to follow.

I felt tired—each step was an effort—yet I could not remember having gone very far that day. I lifted my head as I heard the cry of a bird. A yellow leaf, like a giant butterfly, fluttered from a branch. As if afraid to fall and rot on the ground, the leaf clung to my thigh. Iramamowe held out his hand behind him, gesturing me to remain still. Stealthily he stalked along the riverbank. "We will eat meat tonight," he whispered, then disappeared in the uncertain light, his body but a line against the shimmering river's surface.

Lying down on the dark sand, I watched the sky ablaze for a moment as the earth swallowed the sun. I drank the last of the honey Iramamowe had found that morning, then fell asleep with its sweetness on my lips. Awakened by the sound of crackling flames, I turned on my stomach. On a small platform built over the fire Iramamowe was roasting an almost two-foot-long agouti.

"It's not good to sleep at night without the protection of a fire," he said, facing me. "The spirits of the forest might bewitch you."

"I am so tired," I yawned, moving closer to the fire. "I could sleep for days."

"It will rain during the night," Iramamowe announced as he planted the three poles that would make our shelter around the roasting meat. I helped him cover the roof and sides with the wild banana fronds he had cut while I slept. He fastened the hammocks close to the fire, so we could push the logs to the flames without having to get up.

The agouti tasted like roast pork, tender and juicy. What we did not finish Iramamowe tied to a stick high above the fire. "We'll eat the rest in the morning." Grinning, as if pleased with himself, he stretched fully in his hammock. "It will give us strength to climb the mountains."

"Mountains?" I asked. "I only went over hills when I came with Angelica and Milagros." I bent over Iramamowe. "The only time I climbed up a mountain was when I returned to the *shabono* with Ritimi and Etewa from the Mocototeri feast. Those mountains were close to the *shabono*." I touched his face. "Are you sure you know the way to the mission?"

"What a question to ask," he said, closing his eyes and

crossing his arms over his chest. His bristly eyebrows slanted toward his temples. There were a few hairs at the edge of his upper lip. The skin over his high cheekbones was stretched taut, only a faint trace of the *onoto* designs still recognizable. As if annoyed by my scrutiny, he opened his eyes; they reflected the light of the fire, but his gaze revealed nothing.

I lay down in my hammock. I ran my fingers along my forehead and cheeks, wondering if the *onoto* lines and dots had also faded on my face. Tomorrow I'll bathe in the river, I thought. And my uneasiness, which is probably nothing but exhaustion, will vanish as soon as I paint myself anew with *onoto*. Yet, no matter how I tried to reassure myself, I was unable to still my mounting distrust. My body and mind were tight with a vague premonition I could not put into words. The air became chilly. Leaning over, I pushed one of the logs closer to the flames.

"It will be even colder in the mountains," Iramamowe mumbled. "I will make us a drink from plants that will keep us warm."

Reassured by his words, I began to inhale and exhale with exaggerated depth, deliberately pushing all thoughts away, until I was aware of nothing but the sound of the rain, the smoke-warmed air, the smell of damp earth. And I slept a calm, untroubled sleep that lasted throughout the night.

In the morning we bathed in the river, then painted each other's faces and bodies with *onoto*. Iramamowe was specific about the designs he desired: A serpentine line across his forehead, extending down to his jaws, then around his mouth; a circle between his brow, at the corners of his eyes, and two on each cheek. On his chest he wanted wavy lines, running all the way to his navel, and on his back the lines had to be straight. A smile of gentle mockery softened his face as he covered me from head to foot with uniform circles.

"What do they mean?" I asked eagerly. Ritimi had never decorated me thus.

"Nothing," he said, laughing. "This way you don't look so skinny."

At first the ascent up the narrow trail was easy. The undergrowth was free of serrated grasses and thorny weeds. A warm mist enshrouded the forest, creating a diaphanous light through which the crowns of the tall palm trees seemed to hang suspended from the sky. The sound of waterfalls echoed eerily through the misty air, and each time I brushed against a branch or leaf tiny drops of moisture clung to me. The afternoon rain, however, turned the path into a muddy menace. I bruised my toes repeatedly on the roots and stones beneath the slippery surface.

We made camp late in the afternoon, halfway up the summit. Exhausted, I sat on the ground and watched Iramamowe pound three strong poles into the earth. I did not have the strength to help him cover the triangular structure with palm fronds and giant leaves.

"Are you coming back this way on your return to the *shabono*?" I asked, wondering why he was reinforcing the hut so well. It appeared altogether too sturdy for a one-night shelter.

Iramamowe gave me a sidelong glance but did not answer.

"Is there going to be a storm tonight?" I asked in an exasperated tone.

An irrepressible smile played around his lips and his face looked uncannily childish as he squatted beside me. A mischievous sparkle, as if he were planning some prank, shone in his eyes. "Tonight you will sleep well," he finally said, then proceeded to build a fire inside the cozy hut. He fastened my hammock in the back; his own he hung close to the narrow entrance. "Tonight we will not feel the cold air," he said, looking for the gourd in which were soaking the shredded leaves and pale yellow flowers of a plant he had found the previous day, growing over some rocks in a sunny spot along the river's edge. He unsealed the calabash, added more water, then placed it over the fire. Softly he began to chant, his eyes fixed on the dark simmering liquid.

Trying to figure out the words of his song, I fell asleep. I was awakened shortly by him. "Drink this," he urged, holding the gourd close to my lips. "It has been cooled by the mountain dew."

I took a sip. It tasted like herb tea, bitter but not unpleasantly so. After a few more gulps, I pushed the calabash toward him.

"Drink it all," Iramamowe said coaxingly. "It will keep you warm. You will sleep for days."

"Days?" I emptied the gourd, smiling at his remark as if it were a joke. A faint touch of malice seemed to be lurking somewhere within him. By the time it fully dawned on me that he was not being facetious, a pleasant numbness seeped through my body, melting my anxiety into a comforting heaviness that made my head feel as if it were lead. I was sure it would break off my neck. The image of my head rolling on the ground, a ball with two glass eyes, threw me into spasms of laughter.

Crouching by the fire, Iramamowe watched me with growing curiosity. Slowly, I stood up. I've lost my physicality, I thought. I had no control over my legs as I tried to place one foot in front of the other. Dejected, I slumped on the ground, next to Iramamowe. "Why don't you laugh?" I asked, surprised at my own words. What I really wanted to know was if the sound of drops prattling on the thatched roof was a storm. I wondered if I had actually spoken, for the words kept reverberating in my head like a distant echo. Afraid to miss his answer, I moved closer to him.

Iramamowe's face became taut as the cry of a nocturnal monkey broke the night's stillness. His nostrils flared, his full lips set in a straight line. His eyes, piercing into mine, grew larger, shining with a deep loneliness, a gentleness that contrasted oddly with his severe masklike face.

As if I were animated by a slow-motion mechanism, I crawled to the edge of the hut, each of my movements a gigantic effort. I felt as if all my tendons had been replaced with elastic strings. I relished the sensation of being able to stretch in any direction, into the most absurd postures I could imagine.

From the pouch hanging around his neck, Iramamowe poured *epena* into his palm. He drew the hallucinogenic powder deep into his nostrils, then began chanting. I felt his song inside me, surrounding me, drawing me toward him. Without any hesitation I drank from the gourd he once again held to my lips. The dark liquid no longer tasted bitter.

My sense of time and distance became distorted. Iramamowe and the fire were so far away, I feared I had lost them across the wide expanse of the hut. Yet the next instant, his eyes were so close to mine I saw myself reflected in their dark pupils. I was crushed by the weight of his body and my arms folded beneath his chest. He whispered words into my ears that I could not hear. A breeze parted the leaves, revealing the shadowy night, the treetops brushing the stars—countless stars, massed together as if in readiness to fall. I reached out; my hand grasped leaves adorned with diamond drops. For an instant, they clung to my fingers, then disintegrated like dew.

Iramamowe's heavy body held me; his eyes sowed seeds of light inside me; his gentle voice urged me to follow him through dreams of day and night, dreams of rainwater and bitter leaves. There was nothing violent about his body imprisoning mine. Waves of pleasure mingled with visions of mountains and rivers, faraway places where *hekuras* dwell. I danced with the spirits of animals and trees, gliding with them through mist, through roots and trunks, through branches and leaves. I sang with the voices of birds and spiders, jaguars and snakes. I shared the dreams of all those who feed on *epena,* on bitter flowers and leaves.

I no longer knew if I was awake or dreaming. At moments I vaguely remembered old Hayama's words about shamans needing the femaleness in their bodies. But those memories were neither clear nor lasting; they remained dim, unexamined premonitions. Iramamowe always knew whenever I was about to fall into real sleep, whenever my tongue was ready to ask, whenever I was about to weep.

"If you can't dream, I'll make you," he said, taking me in his arms and rubbing away my tears against his cheek. And my desire to refuse the gourd sitting by the fire like a forest spirit vanished. Greedily I drank the dark bearer of visions until once again I was suspended in a timelessness that was neither day or night. I was one with the rhythm of Iramamowe's breath, with the beat of his heart, as I merged with the light and the darkness inside him.

A time came when I felt I was moving through an undergrowth of trees, leaves, and motionless vines. I knew I was not walking; yet I was descending from the cold forest, sunk in mist. My feet were tied and my upside-down head shook as though it were being emptied. Visions flowed from my ears, nostrils, and mouth, leaving a faint line on the steep path. And for one last instant I glimpsed *shabonos* inhabited by men and women shamans of another time.

When I awoke, Iramamowe was crouched by the fire, his face alight with the flames and a faint streak of moon shining into the hut. I wondered how many days had elapsed since the night he had first offered me the bitter-tasting brew. There was no gourd by the fire. I was certain we were no longer in the mountains. The night was clear. The soft breeze stirring the treetops disentangled my thoughts and I drifted into a dreamless sleep as I listened to the monotonous sound of Iramamowe's *hekura* songs.

The persistent growling of my stomach awoke me. I felt dizzy as I stood on uncertain legs in the empty hut. My body was painted with wavy lines. How strange it had all been, I thought. I felt no regret; I was not filled with hate or repulsion. It was not that I was numbed emotionally. Rather I felt the same indescribable sensation I experienced upon awakening from a dream that I could not quite explain.

Near the fire lay a bundle containing roasted frogs. I sat on the ground and gnawed on the tiny bones until they were clean. Iramamowe's machete reclining against one of the poles reassured me that he was somewhere close by.

Following the sound of the river, I walked through the tangled growth. Startled to see Iramamowe beaching a small canoe only a short distance away, I hid behind some bushes. I recognized the craft as being one made by the Maquiritare Indians. I had seen that kind, made from a hollowed tree trunk, at the mission. The thought that we might be close to one of their settlements, or perhaps even to the mission, made my heart beat faster. Iramamowe gave no indication of having heard or seen me approach. Furtively, I returned to the shelter, wondering how he came into possession of the canoe.

Moments later, with a vine rope and a large bundle slung over his back, Iramamowe walked into the hut. "Fish," he said, dropping the rope and bundle on the ground.

I blushed, and embarrassed at my blushing, laughed.

Unhurriedly, he balanced the wrapped fish between the logs, making sure enough heat but no direct flames reached the *platanillo* leaves. Totally engrossed in the sound of the simmering fish, he remained squatting by the fire. As soon as all the juices were cooked away, he removed the bundle from the logs with a forked stick and opened it. "It's good," he said, scooping a handful of white, flaky meat into his mouth, then pushed the bundle toward me.

"What happened in the mountains?" I asked.

Startled by my belligerent tone, his mouth gaped open. A piece of unchewed fish fell into the ashes. Automatically, without checking the dirt sticking to it, he put the morsel back into his mouth, then reached for the liana rope on the ground.

An irrational fear seized me. I was convinced that Iramamowe was going to tie me up and carry me farther into the forest. I was no longer aware that only a short while before I had been certain we were near a Maquiritare settlement, or even the mission. All I could think of was old Hayama's story about shamans who kept captive women hidden in faraway places. I was convinced Iramamowe would never take me back to the mission. The thought that had he wanted to keep me hidden in the forest he would not have brought me down from the mountains did not cross my mind at that moment.

I did not trust his smile, nor the gentle glint in his eyes. I picked up the water-filled gourd standing by the fire and offered it to him. Smiling, he dropped the rope. I moved closer as if I intended to bring the calabash to his lips. Instead, I smashed it between his eyes with all my strength. Caught totally unawares, he fell backward, staring at me in dumb incredulity as the blood ran down on both sides of his nose.

Heedless of thorns, roots, and the sharp grass, I sped

through the thicket toward the place where I had seen the canoe. But I miscalculated where Iramamowe had anchored it, for when I reached the river there was nothing but stones strewn along the bank; the craft was farther upriver. With a swiftness I hardly believed myself capable of, I leaped from rock to rock. Gasping for breath, I slumped beside the canoe, pushed halfway up the sandy bank. A cry escaped my throat when I saw Iramamowe standing in front of me.

Squatting, he opened his mouth and laughed. His laughter came in bursts, extending from his face to his feet with such force the ground shook beneath me. Tears ran down his cheeks, mingling with the blood from the gash between his brows. "You forgot this," he said, dangling my knapsack in front of me. He opened it, then handed me my jeans and shirt. "Today you will reach the mission."

"Is this the river on which the mission stands?" I asked, staring at his bloodstained face. "I don't recognize this place."

"You have been here with Angelica and Milagros," he assured me. "The rains change the rivers and the forest the way the clouds change the sky."

I pulled up my jeans; loosely they hung from my waist, threatening to slide over my hips. The damp moldy-smelling shirt made me sneeze. I felt awkward and turned uncertain eyes to Iramamowe. "How do I look?"

He walked around me, examining me meticulously from every angle. Then, after a moment's deliberation, he squatted once more and pronounced with a laugh, "You look better painted with *onoto*."

I squatted beside him. The wind was still; there was no movement on the river. Shadows from the tall trees reached across the water, darkening the sand at our feet. I wanted to apologize for smashing the gourd in his face and to explain my suspicions. I wanted him to tell me of the days in the mountains, but was reluctant to break the silence.

As if cognizant and amused by my dilemma, Iramamowe lowered his face to his knees and laughed softly, as if sharing his mirth with the drops of blood falling between his wide spread toes. "I wanted to take the *hekuras* I once saw in your eyes," he murmured. He went on to say that not only he but also Puriwariwe, the old *shapori,* had seen the *hekuras* within me. "Every time I lay with you and felt the energy bursting inside you, I hoped to lure the spirits into my chest," Iramamowe said. "But they didn't want to leave you." He turned his eyes to me, intense with protest. "The *hekuras* would not answer my call; they would not heed my songs. And then I became afraid that you might take the *hekuras* from my body."

Anger and an indescribable sadness rendered me speechless for a moment. "Did we stay longer than a day and a night in the mountains?" I finally asked, my curiosity getting the better of me.

Iramamowe nodded, but did not say for how long we had remained in the hut. "When I was certain that I could not change your body, when I realized that the *hekuras* would not leave you, I carried you in a sling to this place."

"Had you changed my body would you have kept me in the forest?"

Iramamowe looked at me sheepishly. A smile of relief parted his lips, yet his eyes were veiled with a vague regret. "You have the soul and shadow of an Iticoteri," he murmured. "You have eaten the ashes of our dead. But your body and head is that of a *nape.*" A silence punctuated his last sentence before he softly added, "There will be nights when the wind will bring your voice mingled with the cries of monkeys and jaguars. And I will see your shadow dancing on the ground, painted by the moonlight. On those nights I will think of you." He stood up and pushed the canoe into the water. "Stay close to the bank—otherwise the current will take you too swiftly," he said, motioning me to climb inside.

"Aren't you coming?" I asked, alarmed.

"It's a good canoe," he said, handing me a small paddle. It had a beautifully shaped handle, a rounded shaft, and the oval blade was shaped like a pointed concave shield. "It will take you safely to the mission."

"Wait!" I cried before he let go of the craft. My hands trembled as I fumbled with the zippered side pocket of my knapsack. I took out the leather pouch and handed it to him. "Do you remember the stone the shaman Juan Caridad gave me?" I asked. "It's yours now."

Something between shock and surprise seemed to momentarily paralyze his face. Slowly his fingers closed over the pouch and his features relaxed into a smile. Without a word, he pushed the canoe into the water. Folding his arms across his chest, he watched me drift downriver. I turned my head often, until he was out of sight. There was a moment when I thought I still saw his figure, but it was only the wind playing with the shadows that tricked my eyes.

25

The trees on either side of the banks, the clouds traveling across the sky shadowed the river. Hoping to shorten the time between the world left behind and the one now awaiting me, I paddled as fast as I could. But I soon got tired and then only used the small paddle to push myself free whenever I got too close to the bank.

At times the river was clear, reflecting the lush greenness with exaggerated intensity. There was something peaceful about the darkness of the forest and the deep silence around me. The trees seemed to be nodding in farewell as they bent slightly with the afternoon breeze, or perhaps they were only lamenting the passing of day, of the sun's last rays fading in the sky. Shortly before twilight deepened, I maneuvered the canoe toward the opposite bank, where I had seen stretches of sand amidst the dark rocks.

As soon as the craft hit the sand, I jumped out and dragged the canoe farther up the bank, close to the forest edge, where drooping vines and branches formed a safe, dark nook. I turned around and gazed at the distant mountains, violet in the dusk, and I wondered if I had been up there for more than a week before Iramamowe carried me to the hut where I had awakened that morning. I climbed to the highest rock and scanned the landscape for the lights of the mission. It had to be farther than Iramamowe estimated, I thought. Only darkness crept from out of the river, crawling up the rocks as the last vestiges of sunlight disappeared from the sky. I was hungry but did not dare explore the sandy river shore for turtle eggs.

I could not decide whether I should place my knapsack under my head as a pillow or wrap it around my cold feet as I lay inside the canoe. Through the tangled mass of branches above me I saw the clear sky, filled with innumerable tiny stars shining like golden specks of dust. As I drifted off to sleep, my feet tucked in my knapsack, I hoped that my feelings, like the light of the stars spanning the sky, would reach those I had loved in the forest.

I awoke shortly. The air was filled with the sounds of crickets and frogs. I sat up, then looked around me as if I could dispel the darkness. Shafts of moonlight spilled through the branches, painting the sand with grotesque shadows that seemed to come alive with the rustling of wind. Even with my eyes closed, I was painfully conscious of the shadows brushing against the canoe. And each time a cricket interrupted its continuous chirping I opened my eyes, waiting for the sound to resume. Dawn finally silenced the cries, murmurs, and whistling of the forest. The mist-coated leaves looked as if they had been sprinkled with fine silver dust.

The sun rose over the treetops, tinting the clouds orange, purple, and pink. I bathed, washed my clothes with the fine river sand, spread them over the canoe to dry, then painted myself with *onoto*.

I was glad I had not arrived at the mission the day before, as I had first hoped, but that I still had time to watch the clouds change the sky. To the east, heavy clouds gathered, darkening the horizon. Lightning flashed in the distance, thunder followed after long intervals, and white lines of rain moved across the sky toward the north, keeping ahead of me. I wondered if alligators were basking in the sun amid the driftwood scattered on the bank. I had not floated downriver for long before the waters widened. The current became so strong I had a hard time keeping from swirling around in the shallow waters along the bank beset with rocks.

For an instant I thought I was hallucinating when I saw on the opposite bank a long dugout slowly pushing its way upriver. I stood up, frantically waving my shirt in the air, then cried with sheer happiness as the dugout crossed the wide expanse of water and headed toward me. With calculated precision, the almost thirty-foot-long canoe beached just a few paces away.

Smiling, twelve people climbed out of the canoe—four women, four men, and four children. They looked odd in their Western clothes and the purple designs on their faces. Their hair was cut like mine, but the crown of their head was not shaved.

"Maquiritare?" I asked.

Nodding, the women bit their lips as if trying to contain their giggles. Their chins quivered until they burst into uncontrollable laughter that was echoed by the men. Hastily, I put on my jeans and shirt. The oldest woman came closer. She was short and sturdy, her sleeveless dress revealing round fat arms and long breasts, which hung to her waist. "You are the one who went into the forest with the old Iticoteri woman," she said, as if it were the most natural thing in the world to have found me paddling downriver in a dugout made by her people. "We know about you from the father at the mission." After formally shaking my hand, the old woman introduced me to her husband, their three daughters, their respective husbands and children.

"Are we close to the mission?" I asked.

"We left early this morning," the old woman's husband said. "We have been visiting relatives who live nearby."

"She has become a real savage," the youngest of the three daughters cried, pointing to my cut feet with such an expression of outrage that it was all I could do not to giggle. She searched my canoe and shook the empty knapsack. "She has no shoes," she said in disbelief. "She is a real savage!"

I looked at her bare feet.

"Our shoes are in the canoe," she affirmed, and proceeded to bring an assortment of footwear from the boat. "See? We all have shoes."

"Do you have any food with you?" I asked.

"We do," the old woman assured me, then asked her daughter to put the shoes back into the canoe and bring one of the bark boxes.

The box was lined with *platanillo* leaves and filled with cassava bread. I huddled over the food, almost hugging it as I dunked piece after piece into a water-filled calabash before popping it into my mouth. "My stomach is full and happy," I said after I had eaten halfway down the box.

The Maquiritare regretted that they had no meat but only sugarcane with them. The old man cut a foot-long piece, peeled the bamboolike bark with his machete, then handed it to me. "It will give you strength," he said.

I chewed and sucked on the pale hard fibers until they were dry and tasteless. The Maquiritare had heard about Milagros. One of the sons-in-law knew him personally, but none of them knew where Milagros was.

"We will take you to the mission," the old man said.

I made a feeble attempt to convince him that it was not necessary for him to retrace his steps, but my words lacked conviction. Eagerly I boarded the craft, sitting between the

women and children. To take advantage of the full speed
of the current, the men steered the canoe right into the
middle of the river. They paddled without saying a word
to each other, yet each man was so attuned to the others'
rhythm that they were able to anticipate each other's precise needs in advance. I remembered Milagros had once
mentioned to me that the Maquiritare were not only the
greatest boat builders of the Orinoco area, but also the best
navigators.

Exhaustion pressed heavily on my eyes. The rhythmic
splashing of the paddles made me so drowsy, my head kept
lolling forward and sideways. The bygone days and nights
drifted through my mind like fragmented dreams of another time. It seemed all so vague, so far away, as if it had
all been an illusion.

It was noon when I was awakened by Father Coriolano,
who had come into the room to bring me a mug filled with
coffee. "Eighteen hours of sleep is a good start," he said.
His smile held the same reassuring warmth with which he
had greeted me the day before as I stepped out of the
Maquiritare's boat.

My eyes were still heavy with sleep as I sat on the canvas
cot. My back was stiff from resting in a flat position.
Slowly, I sipped the hot black brew, so strong and thickened with sugar it made me nauseous.

"I also have chocolate," Father Coriolano said.

I straightened the calico shift I had been given to sleep
in and followed him into the kitchen. With the flair of a
chef preparing a fancy meal, he stirred two tablespoons of
dried milk powder, four of Nestlé's chocolate powder, four
of sugar, and a few grains of salt into a pot of water boiling
on a kerosene stove.

He drank my unfinished coffee while I spooned the

delicious-tasting chocolate. "I can radio your friends in Caracas to pick you up with their plane anytime you want."

"Oh, not yet," I said faintly.

The days passed slowly. In the mornings I wandered around the gardens along the riverbank and at noon I sat under the large mango tree that bore no fruit outside the chapel. Father Coriolano did not ask me what my plans were or how long I intended to stay at the mission. He seemed to have accepted my presence as something inevitable.

In the evenings I spent hours talking to Father Coriolano and to Mr. Barth, who often came to visit. We chatted about the crops, the school, the dispensary—always impersonal subjects. I was grateful that neither of them asked me where I had been for over a year, what I had done, or what I had seen. I would not have been able to answer—not because I wanted to be secretive, but because there was nothing to say. If we exhausted our conversation, Mr. Barth would read us articles from newspapers and magazines, some over twenty years old. Regardless of whether we were listening or not, he rattled on as he pleased, now and then interrupting himself to roar with laughter.

In spite of their humor and affable nature, there were evenings when shadows of loneliness crossed their faces as we sat in silence listening to the rain pattering on the corrugated roof or to the solitary cry of a howler monkey settling for the night. It was then that I wondered if they too had learned the secrets of the forest—secrets of misty caves, of the sound of sap running through branches and trunks, of spiders spinning their silvery webs. At those times I wondered if that was what Father Coriolano had tried to warn me about when he had talked of the dangers of the forest. And I wondered if it was this that kept them from returning to the world they had left behind.

At night, enclosed in the four walls of my room, I felt a vast emptiness. I missed the closeness of the huts, the smell of people and smoke. Carried by the sound of the river flowing outside my window, I dreamt I was with the Iticoteri. I heard Ritimi's laughter, I saw the children's smiling faces, and there was always Iramamowe, squatting outside his hut calling to the *hekuras* that had eluded him.

Walking along the river's edge one afternoon, I was overcome by an uncontrollable sadness. The noise of the river was loud, drowning out the voices of the people chatting nearby. It had rained at noon and the sun peeked through the clouds without properly shining. Aimlessly I walked up and down the sandy beach. Then in the distance I saw the lonely figure of a man approaching. Dressed in khaki pants and a red checkered shirt, he looked indistinguishable from any of the Westernized Indians around the mission. Yet there was something familiar about the man's swaggering gait.

"Milagros!" I cried, then waited until he stood before me. His face looked unfamiliar under the torn straw hat through which his hair stuck out like blackened palm fibers. "I'm so glad you came."

Smiling, he motioned me to squat beside him. He brushed his hand over the top of my head. "Your hair has grown," he said. "I knew you would not leave until you saw me."

"I'm going back to Los Angeles," I said. There had been so many things I wanted to ask him, but now that he was beside me, I no longer saw the need to have anything explained. We watched the twilight spread over the river and the forest. The darkness filled with the sounds of frogs and crickets. A full moon ascended the sky. It grew smaller as it climbed and covered the river with silver ripples. "Like a dream," I murmured.

"A dream," Milagros repeated. "A dream you will always dream. A dream of walking, of laughter, of sadness." There was a long pause before he continued. "Even though your body has lost our smell, a part of you will always keep a bit of our world," he said, gesturing toward the distance. "You will never be free."

"I didn't even thank them," I said. "There is no thank you in your language."

"Neither is there good-bye," he added.

Something cold, like a drop of rain or dew, touched my forehead. When I turned to face him, Milagros was no longer by my side. From across the river, out of the distant darkness, the wind carried the Iticoteri's laughter. "Good-bye is said with the eyes." The voice rustled through the ancient trees, then vanished, like the silvery ripples on the water.

GLOSSARY

ASHUKAMAKI
(*Ah shuh kah mah kee*)

A vine used to thicken the curare poison.

AYORI-TOTO
(*Ah yo ree toh toh*)

A vine used to poison fish.

EPENA (*Eh peh nah*)

A hallucinatory snuff derived from either the bark of the *epena* tree or the seeds of the hisioma tree. Both substances are prepared and taken in the same fashion.

HEKURAS (*Heh kuh rahs*)

Tiny humanoid spirits that dwell in rocks and mountains. Shamans contact the *hekuras* by taking the hallucinatory snuff *epena*. Through chants the shamans lure the *hekuras* into their chests. Successful shamans can control these spirits at will.

MAMUCORI
(*Mah muh ko ree*)

A thick vine used to make the curare poison.

MOMO (*Moh moh*)

A nutlike edible seed.

NABRUSHI (*Nah bru shee*) A six-foot-long club used for fighting.

NAPE (*Nah peh*) A foreigner. Anyone who is not an Indian, regardless of color, race, or nationality.

OKO-SHIKI (*Oh koh shee kee*) Magical plants used for malevolent purposes.

ONOTO (*Oh no toh*) A red vegetable dye derived from the crushed, boiled seeds of the *Bixa orellana*. The dye is used for decorating the face and body as well as baskets, arrowheads, and ornaments.

PISHAANSI (*Pee sha han see*) A large leaf used for wrapping meat, for cooking, or as a receptacle.

PLATANILLO (*Plah tah neeyo*) A large, broad, sturdy leaf used for wrapping and as ground cover.

POHORO (*Ph oh roh*) Wild cacao.

RASHA (*Rah sha*) The cultivated spiny-trunked peach palm. Highly valued for its fruit, which it produces for fifty years and longer. After the plantain, it is probably the most important plant in the gardens. These palms are owned individually by whoever planted them.

SHABONO (*Sha boh noh*) A permanent *Yanomama* settlement consisting of a circle of huts around an open clearing.

SHAPORI (*Sha poh ree*) A shaman, witch doctor, sorcerer.

SIKOMASIK
  (*See kouw mah seek*)

A whitish edible mushroom that grows on decaying tree trunks.

UNUCAI (*Uh nuh kah ee*)

A man who has killed an enemy.

WAITERI (*Wah ee teh ree*)

A brave, courageous warrior.

WAYAMOU (*Wah yah mow*)

The formal, ritualized ceremonial language used by the men when bartering.

After Midnight

*Also by Diana Palmer
in Large Print:*

After the Music
Diamond Girl
Heart of Ice
Heather's Song
Roomful of Roses
September Morning
Abducted Hearts (Published in Spanish as
      Corazones secuestrados)
Desperado

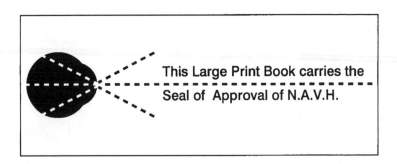

This Large Print Book carries the
Seal of Approval of N.A.V.H.

After Midnight

Diana Palmer

Thorndike Press • Waterville, Maine

Copyright © 1993 by Susan Kyle.

Published in 2004 by arrangement with
Harlequin Books, S.A.

Thorndike Press® Large Print Romance.

The tree indicium is a trademark of Thorndike Press.

The text of this Large Print edition is unabridged.
Other aspects of the book may vary from the original edition.

Set in 16 pt. Plantin by Myrna S. Raven.

Printed in the United States on permanent paper.

Library of Congress Cataloging-in-Publication Data

Palmer, Diana.
    After midnight / Diana Palmer.
      p. cm.
    ISBN 0-7862-6342-3 (lg. print : hc : alk. paper)
    1. Women political consultants — Fiction. 2. South Carolina — Fiction. 3. Islands — Fiction. 4. Large type books. I. Title.
PS3566.A513A67 2004
813′.54—dc22   2003071123

After Midnight

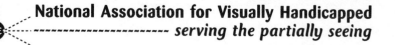
National Association for Visually Handicapped
-------------------- *serving the partially seeing*

As the Founder/CEO of NAVH, the only national health agency solely devoted to those who, although not totally blind, have an eye disease which could lead to serious visual impairment, I am pleased to recognize Thorndike Press★ as one of the leading publishers in the large print field.

Founded in 1954 in San Francisco to prepare large print textbooks for partially seeing children, NAVH became the pioneer and standard setting agency in the preparation of large type.

Today, those publishers who meet our standards carry the prestigious "Seal of Approval" indicating high quality large print. We are delighted that Thorndike Press is one of the publishers whose titles meet these standards. We are also pleased to recognize the significant contribution Thorndike Press is making in this important and growing field.

Lorraine H. Marchi, L.H.D.
Founder/CEO
NAVH

★ Thorndike Press encompasses the following imprints: Thorndike, Wheeler, Walker and Large Pr int Press.

Chapter One

Seabrook had been the Seymour family's vacation spot for twenty years. It was a beautiful small community island offering a marina, golf course, a private club and a welcome break from the hectic pace of the resorts.

This particular stretch of it was connected with some of the wealthiest Charleston families. Nicole Seymour didn't have a million dollars, but the Seymour name granted her entry into the wealthiest circles of society as only the oldest South Carolinian names could. This beach property had originally been purchased by her father on speculation. But when the planned community started taking shape in 1992, he held on to his acreage and built a cottage on it for family vacations. At his death, it had gone to Nicole and her brother, Republican Congressman Clayton Myers Seymour, Representative of the First Congressional District of South Carolina.

The Seymours of Charleston were one of the most respected families in the state and it wasn't surprising that when Nikki's brother had first announced his candidacy for the House of Representatives seat from his district three years ago, he was immediately supported by the local Republican vanguard. He was elected without even a runoff in the general election two years ago, to Clayton's surprise and Nikki's delight.

Nikki's social standing made her the perfect hostess for Clayton. During his three years in Washington, D.C., her brother had done a good job. So had Nikki, helping to curry favor for him, because she had a knack for presenting unpopular points of view. She was in the process of organizing dinner parties and reelection fund-raising galas for Clayton. He'd just announced his candidacy for reelection, and it promised to be a tough race. Clayton not only had Republican opposition from his own party, but the field of Democratic candidates included Sam Hewett, a well-known and liked businessman who had a virtual empire behind him, not to mention the clout of a very dangerous tabloid paper out of New York. In fact, Sam's campaign administrative assistant was one of the sons of the tabloid owner.

Nikki had just put the finishing touches

on the organization of another gala for Clayton in Washington, D.C., in September, after the general primary election. She hoped with all her heart that it would also serve as a celebration of Clayton's hoped-for victory in the primary. Those preparations, coupled with her participation in the world-famous Spoleto Festival in Charleston had exhausted her. She was weak from a bout of pneumonia that she'd just recovered from. Now that the festival was almost over, Nikki was recuperating at the family retreat. Clayton wouldn't need her for a few days and she relished the peace and quiet of the beach house. This particular section of the island was fairly isolated, dotted with only a few houses, most of which were very old and belonged to families with old money. The two surrounding the Seymour cottage were owned by families from other areas of the state, and were usually unoccupied until late June.

She stretched as the sun beat down on the deck where she was comfortably sprawled on a padded lounger. She was tall and slender, perfectly proportioned. Her body was as sensual as her slanted pure green eyes and the bow curve of her pretty mouth. She sparkled when she was happy, an enchanted columnist had said by way of description — and despite her height, she had the mischievous disposition of a pixie. With her thick black hair cut in a wedge around her soft oval face, she even had the look of one. But behind the beauty was a quick mind and an impeccable reputation. If others thought her a bit too wary and cautious, Nikki knew these qualities had helped thwart political enemies when they laid traps for her brother.

Her small breasts lifted and fell slowly as she lay breathing in the delicious sea air. It was early June, and unseasonably cool. A lot of renovation had been done since Hurricane Hugo passed through Charleston and the coastal areas in September of 1989, and Nikki and Clayton's beach house had been one of the ones damaged by high winds. Although they had made the most necessary repairs, many decorative accents had yet to be restored. Unlike many of their neighbors, the Seymours didn't have unlimited funds from which to renovate. Nikki and Clayton were working on a five-year plan to restore the beach house to its former glory.

The sound of a float-plane caught her attention. She shaded her eyes and watched its silvery glitter as it landed not far from

10

her house. This area had no shortage of tycoons. In fact, Kane Lombard had recently bought the old Settles place a few houses down the beach from Nikki and Clayton's, not far from where the plane had landed. Lombard was a Houston oilman who headed a conglomerate which included Charleston's newest automobile manufacturing company. Nikki had heard that personal tragedy seemed to follow the man, culminating months ago in the violent death of his wife and son in Lebanon during a business trip.

Three weeks ago, he'd moved into the beach house property and his yacht had a slip at the marina. Nikki had seen a photograph of it in the Charleston paper's society section.

Nikki had never met him, and there were no full-face or close-up photos of him in newspapers, except for one that Nikki had seen in *Forbes Magazine*. Even the tabloids couldn't catch him on film. Of course, his family did own one of the biggest tabloids in the country. The Lombards of Houston, like the Seymours of Charleston, came from old money. The difference was, the Lombards still had their money. They lived in New York now, not Texas, where they maintained their exclusive tabloid.

The sound of the plane faded and Nikki stretched again. She felt restless. She knew all the right people and she had a comfortable income from the sculptures she did for local galleries. But she was empty inside. Sometimes it bothered her that she was so completely alone except for her brother.

She had been married, briefly; a marriage that destroyed all her illusions and made her question her own sexuality. Her father needed a favor from a U.S. senator by the name of Mosby Torrance, a South Carolinian. Mosby had been under siege because of, among other things, his long-standing bachelor standing. Mosby had agreed to the favor, which would save Nikki's father from certain bankruptcy, but only in return for Nikki's hand in marriage.

Nikki shivered, remembering her delight. Mosby was fourteen years her senior, an Adonis of a man, with blond hair and blue eyes and a trim, athletic figure. She'd been swept off her feet, and nothing would have stopped her from agreeing to the union. She'd only been eighteen years old. Naive. Innocent. Stupid.

Her father might have suspected, but he never really knew about Mosby until it was

12

much too late. Nikki had emerged from the marriage six months later, so shaken that the divorce was final before she was completely rational again.

She never could admit what she'd endured to her father or brother, but afterward, Clayton was especially kind to her. They grew very close, and when their father died, she and her brother continued to share the huge Charleston house near the Battery. As he entered politics, Nikki was his greatest support. She learned to organize, to be a hostess, to charm and coax money from prospective supporters. She did whatever Clayton needed her to do to help him, both at his Charleston office and in Washington, D.C., where she had gained some repute as a hostess. She always created just the right mix of people at banquets and cocktail parties, with motifs and themes that radiated excitement and interest. She was very successful at her endeavors. But the old fears and lack of self-confidence kept her free of relationships of any sort. She couldn't trust her judgment ever again. She could live without a man in her life, she'd decided. But she was twenty-five and lonely. So lonely.

The sun was getting too warm. She stood up and slipped a silky blue caftan

13

over her green-and-gold bathing suit, loving the feel of it against her soft, tanned skin. A movement on the beach caught her eye and she went to the railing to look out over the ocean. Something black was there, bobbing, in the surf. She frowned and leaned over to get a better look, shading her eyes from the sunlight. A head! It was a person!

Without even thinking, she darted down the steps and ran across the beach, stumbling as the thick sand made her path unwieldy. Her heart raced madly as she began to think of the possibilities. Suppose it was a body washing up on the beach? What if she found herself in the wake of a murder? Or worse, what if it were a drowning victim? She had no lifesaving training, a stupid thing to admit to when she had a holiday home on the beach! She made a mental note even in her panic to sign up for lifesaving courses at the Red Cross.

As she reached the surf, she realized that the body in the water was a man's. It was muscular and husky and very tall-looking with darkly tanned skin and dark hair. She knelt quickly beside it and felt for a pulse. She found it. Her breath sighed out and she realized only then that she'd been holding it.

She managed to roll the man over onto his belly, just out of the surf. Turning his face to one side, she began to push in the center of his back, a maneuver she'd seen on one of the real-life rescue series on TV. The man began to cough and retch, and she kept pumping. Seconds later, he jerked away from her and sat up, holding his forehead. He was a big man for all his leanness. Thank God, she wasn't going to have to try and drag him any farther out of the surf!

"Are you all right?" she asked worriedly.

"My head . . . hurts," he choked, still coughing.

She hesitated for a second before she began to look through his thick wet hair. She found a gash just above his temple. The blood had congealed and it didn't look very deep, but he'd been unconscious.

"I think I'd better call an ambulance," she began. "You could have a concussion."

"I don't need an ambulance," he said firmly. He coughed again. "I fell off a Jet Ski and hit my head. I remember that." He scowled. "Funny. I can't remember anything else!"

Nikki sat very still. The hem of her caftan was soaked from the rising surf. She gnawed on her lower lip, a habit from

15

childhood, while she struggled with the question of what to do next.

"Would you like to come up to my beach house and rest for a bit?" she asked in her softly accented voice.

He lifted his head and looked at her, and she felt a shock all the way through her. He seemed very familiar. She couldn't quite place him, but he looked like someone she knew. Could she have met him at the Spoleto Festival?

"I must be visiting someone around here," he began slowly. "I couldn't have come far."

"You're disoriented," she said. "When you've rested, perhaps you'll remember who you are. I believe amnesia of this kind is very temporary."

"Are you a nurse?"

Her eyebrows lifted. "Why not a doctor?" she asked.

"Why not a nurse?" he asked, his eyes and his tone challenging.

She threw up her hands. "You're going to be one of those sharp, difficult people, I can tell. Here, let's see if we can get you underway. Oh, for a wheelbarrow . . ." She eyed him. "Make that a front-end loader."

"If you're trying out for stand-up

comedy," he murmured, "don't give up your day job."

His deep voice was unaccented. If anything it sounded midwestern. He was wearing a waterproof Rolex watch and the swimming trunks he had on were designer marked. He was no transient. And he was much too old to be a college student on summer vacation, she thought wickedly as she noted the streaks of gray at his temples. He had to be almost forty. Certainly he was older than her brother.

She felt uncomfortable with the close physical contact that was necessary now, but she forced herself to yield to the situation. He couldn't very well stay down here on the beach all day.

She eased under his arm and slid her hand around his back. His skin was olive tan and silky, rippling with muscle. He was fit for a man of his age, she thought, her eyes dropping involuntarily to the broad chest with an incredibly thick mass of curling black hair that ran in a wedge from his collarbone all the way down into the low-slung swimming trunks around his lean hips. Most men, since her marriage, repelled Nikki. This man, strangely, didn't. She already felt comfortable with him, as if the sight of his almost nude

17

body was familiar to her.

Of course, he had the kind of body that even a disinterested woman couldn't help but admire right down to long, tanned, powerful legs with just enough hair to be masculine and not offensive. She drew his arm over her shoulder, holding it by the hand. He had nice hands, too, she thought. Very lean and big, with oval nails immaculately kept. No jewelry at all. She wondered if that was deliberate. Where his watch had shifted, there was no white line, so his tan must be of the year-round variety.

"Easy does it," she said gently. The feel of all the muscle so close was really disturbing. She hadn't been so close to a man since her tragic marriage. He attracted her and she immediately forced her mind to stop thinking in that direction. He needed her. That was all she must consider now.

"I can walk by myself," he said gruffly, and then stumbled as he tried to prove it.

Nikki managed not to smile. "One step at a time," she repeated. "You're injured, that's all. It's bound to affect your balance."

"Are you sure your first name isn't Florence?" he muttered. "Maybe it's Polyanna."

"You're very offensive for a man the ocean spit out," she remarked. "Obviously you left a bad taste in its mouth."

He didn't smile, but his chest tightened a little. Nikki guessed he was repressing a laugh. "Maybe so."

"Do you feel sleepy or nauseous?" she persisted.

"No. Dizzy, though."

She nodded, her mind running quickly through possibilities. She needed to get a look at his eyes to tell if the pupils were equal or overly dilated, but that could wait.

"Are you a nurse?" he asked again.

"Not really. I've had some first-aid training, and," she added with a mischievous glance upward, "a little experience with beached whales. Speaking of which . . ."

"Stop right there while you're ahead," he advised. "God, what a headache!" His big hand went to his head and he groaned.

Nikki was getting more nervous by the minute. Head injuries could be quickly fatal. She didn't have the expertise to deal with something this serious, and she had no telephone. What if he died?

He glanced sideways and saw the troubled look on her face. He glowered even more. "I'm not going to drop dead on the beach," he said irritably. "Are you always this transparent?"

"In fact, I've been told I have a poker face," she said without thinking. She looked up into his dark eyes and found herself staring into them with something approaching recognition. How frightening, she thought dimly, to be like that with a stranger, and especially such an unfriendly one!

"You have green eyes, 'Florence Nightingale,' " he said. "Green like a cat's."

"I scratch like one, too, so watch out," she murmured with far more bravado than courage.

"Point taken." He eased the pressure of his arm around her and went the last few steps up to the deck under his own power. He stopped, holding his head and breathing deliberately, for a few seconds.

"I could do with a cup of coffee," he said after a minute.

"So could I." She eased him through the sliding glass doors and into the kitchen, watching him lower his huge frame into a chair at the kitchen table. "Are you going to be all right?"

"I'm sure that I'm tough as nails normally." He rested his elbows on the clean surface of the oak table and held his head in his hands. "Do you often find strange men washed up on your beach?"

"You're my first," she replied. "But considering the size of you, I'm hoping for an ocean liner tomorrow."

He lifted an eyebrow at her as she busied herself filling the drip coffeemaker.

"Have you lived here long?" he asked, making conversation.

"We've had the place a few years."

"We?"

"The, um . . . man who lives here and I," she replied noncommittally. It wouldn't do to tell him she was single and on her own. "He normally drives down on Friday evenings," she lied.

He didn't seem to register the information. Perhaps he didn't know what day it was.

"Today is Friday," she said, just in case. "My friend is very nice, you'll like him." She glanced over her shoulder at him. "Any nausea yet? Drowsiness?"

"I haven't got a concussion," he replied tersely. "I'm not sure how I know that I'd recognize the symptoms. Perhaps I've had it before."

"Perhaps you haven't." She picked up the telephone and dialed.

"What are you doing?" he asked curtly.

"Phoning a friend. He's a doctor. I want

21

to . . . Hello, Chad?" she said when the person answered. "I've just rescued a swimmer who was suffering from a bang on the head. He's conscious and very lucid," she added with a meaningful glare at her houseguest. "But he won't let me call an ambulance. Could you stop by here when you get back from the golf course and just reassure me that he isn't going to drop dead on my floor."

Chad Holman laughed. "Sure. No sweat. Let me ask you a couple of questions."

He did and she fielded them to her guest, who replied reluctantly.

"I think he'll do until I get there," Chad reassured her. "But if he drops off and you can't wake him or if he has any violent vomiting, call the ambulance anyway."

"Will do. Thanks."

"Any time."

She hung up, feeling relieved now that she had a professional opinion on her guest's condition. "Well, I don't want any dead bodies in my living room, especially not one I can't even drag!" she informed him mischievously.

He scowled at her. "Dead bodies. Dead . . ." He shook his head irritably. "I keep getting flashes, but I can't grasp anything! Damn it!"

22

"The coffee's almost ready. Maybe a jolt of caffeine will start your brain working again," she suggested.

She perched on a stool at the counter, her long bare legs drawing his eyes. She glared at him.

"Don't get any ideas about why you're here, if you please," she said, her voice soft but vaguely menacing just the same.

"Don't worry. I'm absolutely sure that I don't like green-eyed women," he returned shortly. He sat back in the chair with a rough sigh and shifted, one big hand idly rubbing the thick hair on his chest. He made her very self-conscious and nervous. He looked aggressively masculine, whether he was or not. She fidgeted.

"I can find you something to put on, if you like," she said after a minute.

"That would be nice. Your male friend leaves things here, I suppose? To remind you that you cohabit with him?"

She didn't like the sarcasm, but she didn't rise to it. She slipped easily off the stool. "The shirt may be a bit tight, but he's got some baggy shorts with an elastic waist that probably will fit you. I won't be a minute."

She darted into Clayton's bedroom and borrowed the biggest oversize shirt he owned, a three-colored one, and a pair of big tan shorts. They hung on her brother, but they were probably going to be a tight fit on the giant she'd found washed up on the beach.

She carried the clothes back in to him. "The bathroom is through there," she said, nodding down the hall. "Third door on the right. You'll find a razor and soap and towels if you'd like to clean up. Are you hungry?"

"I think I could eat," he said.

"I'll make an omelet and toast."

He got to his feet very slowly, the clothes in one large hand. He hesitated as he turned to leave the room, looking very big and threatening to Nikki. "I don't remember anything. But I'm not a cruel man, if it helps. I do know that."

"It helps." She managed a smile.

"I'm not used to accepting help from strangers," he added.

"Good thing. I'm not used to offering it to strangers. Of course, there's a first time . . ."

". . . for everything," he finished for her. "Thanks."

He left the room and Nikki got out eggs and condiments, proceeding to make an omelet.

He showered and shaved before he changed into the dry clothes and joined her in the kitchen. He was still barefoot, but the shorts did fit. The shirt showed off muscles that had obviously not been obtained by any lengthy inactivity. He was fit and rippled, very athletic. Nikki had to remind herself not to look at him too hard.

"What do you like in your coffee?" she asked as she poured it into thick white mugs and set them on the spotless green-and-white checked tablecloth.

He frowned as he sat down. "I think I like cream."

"I'd have thought you were a man who never added anything to his coffee," she murmured with amusement.

"Why?"

"I don't know. You seem oddly familiar to me, as if I know you. But I don't believe that I've ever seen you before," she said quietly.

He shrugged. "Maybe I have that kind of face."

Her eyebrows arched. "You?"

He smiled, just faintly. "Thanks." He sipped his coffee and pursed his lips. "Very nice. Just strong enough."

"I make good coffee. It's my only real accomplishment, except for omelets. I'm much too busy to learn how to cook."

"What does your poor friend eat?" he asked.

"He lives on fast food and restaurant chow, but he isn't home much."

"What does he do?"

She studied him. "He's in energy," she said, which was the truth. He sat on the Energy and Commerce Committee that dealt with it.

"Oh. He works for a power plant?"

"That's pretty close," she agreed, hiding the amusement in her eyes as she thought about the power that particular committee wielded nationally.

"And what do you do?"

"*Moi?*" she laughed. "Oh, I sculpt."

"What?"

"People."

He looked around at the furniture, but the only artwork of any kind that was visible were some prints she'd purchased.

"I sell my work in galleries," she told him.

He decided to reserve judgment on that reply. The house was a dump, and she had to know it. She obviously had little money and lived with a man who had even less. He knew that he couldn't afford to trust her. He wished he knew why he was certain of that. "Do you have any of your work here?"

"A bust or two," she said. "I'll show you later, if you like."

He sampled the omelet. "You're good."

"Thanks." She studied his face. It was pale, and he seemed to be having a hard time keeping his eyes open. "You're drowsy."

"Yes. I don't know how I know it, but I'm pretty sure that I haven't been sleeping well lately."

"Woman trouble?" she asked with a knowing smile.

He frowned. "I'm not sure. Perhaps." He looked up. "I can't possibly stay here . . ."

"Where would you go?" she asked reasonably. "You can't wander up and down the beach here, the police will pick you up for vagrancy. Do you remember where you live?"

"I don't even know my name," he confessed heavily. "You can't imagine how intimidating that is."

"You're right." She searched his tanned face, his dark eyes. He looked incredibly tired. "Why don't you have an early night? I'll send Chad in to check you out when he swings by. He's a friend," she added. "He'll do it as a favor, so you don't have to worry about his fee. Things will look so much better in the morning. You might remember who you are."

"God, I hope so," he said gruffly. "The man . . . who lives here. You said he'd be here later?"

She nodded, her eyes as steady as if she'd been telling the truth, and he was fooled.

"Then it will be all right, I suppose. I appreciate your trust. I could be anybody."

"So could I," she said in a menacing tone, grinning.

He got the point. When she showed him to the guest bedroom, he fell on the bed without bothering to turn back the covers. Within seconds, he was sound asleep.

He was still sleeping when Chad stopped by to check him. Nikki waited in the living room until the doctor came out, bag in hand, gently closing the door.

"He's all right," he assured her with a grin, his blond good looks fairly intimidating to her because he still reminded her a little of her ex-husband. "A little disorientation, but that will pass quickly. There's been no real damage. By morning he should remember his name and after he gets past the very terrible headache he's going to have, he should be all right. I'm leaving some tablets for him when he wakes up groaning." He produced them from his bag and handed them to Nikki. "Otherwise, you know what to look for. If you get in trouble all you have to do is call me. Okay?"

"Okay. Thanks, Chad."

He shrugged. "What are friends for?" he asked with a big grin. He left, closing the door gently behind him.

Later, when Nikki went back to check on her houseguest, he was lying on his back, completely nude in the soft glow from the night-light on the wall.

Nikki stood and just stared at him helplessly, feeling her body tingle and burn with old familiar longings that she desperately tried to bank down. This man attracted her as even Mosby hadn't — in the beginning. She looked at the long, muscular lines of his tanned body with aching need.

He must sunbathe nude, she thought idly. He was magnificent. Even that part of him that was most male didn't offend or repel her. She was surprised at her own lack of inhibitions as she stared at him, feeling vaguely like a Peeping Tom. He did look vaguely familiar as well. That bothered her. Not as much, of course, as his body did in stark nudity.

Oddly, she found men revolting for the most part. This one was special. She loved the way his big body looked without clothes. She wondered how that hand, almost the size of a plate, would feel smoothing over her soft skin in the darkness.

The thought pulled her up short. She turned and went out of the bedroom, closing the door gently behind her.

Chapter Two

Nicole slept fitfully that night, haunted by images of her houseguest sprawled in magnificent abandon on the bed in the guest room. She woke up earlier than usual. She slipped into a neat blue patterned sundress before she went to the kitchen, barefoot, to make breakfast. It was a good thing that she had plenty of provisions, she thought. Judging by his size and build, the man in the guest room was a man with a more than ample appetite.

She'd just dished up scrambled eggs to go with the sweet rolls and sausages when the man came into the living room from Clayton's bedroom. He was wearing the shorts she'd found for him, an old pair that Clay had worn, with the shirt whose edges didn't quite meet in front. He looked out of sorts, and vaguely confused.

"Are you all right?" she asked immediately.

He glowered at her. "I feel like an overdrawn account. Otherwise, I suppose I'll do." He spoke without any particular accent, although there was a faint residual drawl there. His was not a Charleston accent, though, she mused; and she ought to know, because her own was fairly thick.

"I do have some aspirin, if you need them," she said.

"I could use a couple, thanks."

She went to get them while he sat down at the table and poured coffee into his cup and hers. He shook out a couple of aspirin tablets into his big hand and swallowed them with coffee.

"You've remembered, haven't you?" she persisted.

"I've remembered a few things," he confessed. "Not a lot." He felt for his watch and frowned. Hadn't he had one when he went into the water? A diver's watch?

"Oh, I almost forgot!" She jumped up and reached onto the counter by the stove, producing the missing wristwatch. "Here. This was still on your wrist and almost unfastened when I found you. I stuck it in my robe pocket and didn't notice it until this morning when I started to put the robe in the laundry. Good thing I didn't wash it," she laughed. "However do you tell time with something so complicated?"

She didn't recognize a diver's watch. Did that mean she didn't realize how expensive it was?

He took it from her. "Thanks," he said slowly.

"It still works, doesn't it?" she asked idly as she ate her eggs. "I didn't know they made waterproof watches."

"It's a diver's watch," he informed her, and then waited for her reaction.

"I see. Do you skin-dive?" she asked brightly.

He did, occasionally, when he wasn't sailing his yacht. He didn't want to mention that. "Sometimes," he said.

"I wanted to learn, but I'm too afraid of water," she told him. "I can't even swim properly."

"Then why have a beach house?" he asked curiously. "Or isn't it yours?"

She saw the way he was looking at her and interpreted it correctly. That watch wasn't cheap, and he'd apparently remembered more than he wanted her to know. So he thought she was a gold digger, did he? She was going to enjoy this.

"Well, no, it belongs to . . ." She stopped suddenly, not wanting to give too much away. His face was all too familiar, more so this morning. "It belongs to the man who owns this place. He lets me stay here when I like."

He glanced around and his expression spoke volumes.

"The hurricane got it," she said quickly. "He hasn't had time to do many repairs." That, at least, was true. But it didn't sound that way to her guest. In fact, he looked even more suspicious.

He didn't say anything else. He concentrated on the meal Nikki had prepared. His dark eyes slid over her pretty face and narrowed.

"What's your name?" he asked curiously.

"Nikki," she replied. Even if he knew of her family, he wouldn't know of the nickname, which was used only by family and very close friends. "Do you remember yours?"

He studied her thoughtfully while he wavered between the truth and a lie. She was obviously a transient here, in her boyfriend's house. He was new to the area. It was highly unlikely that she'd even know who he was if he introduced himself honestly. He kept a low profile. In his income bracket, it paid to do that.

He laughed at his own caution. This woman probably didn't even know what the CEO of a corporation was. "It's McKane," he said offhandedly. "But I'm usually called Kane."

Fortunately, Nikki had her eyes on her coffee cup. She didn't show it, but inside she panicked. The familiar face she couldn't place before now leaped into her consciousness vividly. She knew that name all too well, and now she remembered where she'd seen the face, in a business magazine of Clayton's. Kane Lombard was reclusive to the point of being a hermit, and the photograph of him had been a rarity for such a successful businessman.

Her brother had just had a very disturbing run-in with Kane Lombard over an environmental issue in Charleston. Lombard, she knew, was backing the leading Democratic contender for Clayton's House seat.

Her mind worked rapidly. She didn't dare let Lombard know who she was, now. They'd spent the night together, albeit innocently. Wouldn't that tidbit do Clayton a lot of good in a national election? In some parts of the country, especially this one, morality was still enough to make or break a politician; even his sister's morality. And Lombard was helping the opposition.

Her fingers closed around her coffee cup and she lifted her eyes with a schooled expression on her face. Everything would be all right. All she had to do was ease him out of here without letting on that she knew him. Since he didn't travel in the same circles as Clayton and herself, chances were good that she'd never see him up close again anyway.

"It's a nice name. I like it." She smiled as if she genuinely didn't recognize him.

He relaxed visibly. His firm mouth tugged into a smile. "Thanks for taking care of me," he added. "It's been a long time since anyone had to do that."

"Nobody's invulnerable," she reminded him. "But next time, you might check that there aren't any rocks around when you decide to use the Jet Ski."

"I'll do that."

He finished his coffee and reluctantly, she thought, got to his feet. "I'll return your friend's clothes. Thanks for the loan."

"I can run you home, if you like," she offered, knowing full well that he wouldn't risk letting her see where he lived. He thought she was an opportunist. She could have laughed out loud at the very idea.

"No, thanks," he said quickly, smiling to soften the rejection. "I need the exercise. You've been very kind." His eyes were shrewd. "I hope I can repay you one day."

"Oh, that's not necessary," she assured him as she stood. "Don't we all have a moral duty to help each other out when we're in need?" She looked at her slender, well-kept hands. "I'm sure you'd do the same for me."

That last bit was meant to rattle him, but it didn't work. She looked up, impishly, and he was just watching her with a lifted eyebrow and a faintly indulgent smile.

"Of course I would," he assured her. But he was wary again, looking for traps, even while his eyes were quietly bold on her soft curves.

"It was nice meeting you," she added.

"Same here." He gave her a last wistful appraisal and went with long, determined strides toward the front door. He walked as if he'd go right over anything in his path, and Nikki envied him that self-confidence. She had it, to a degree, but in a standing fight, he was going to be a hard man to beat. She'd have to remember and warn Clayton not to underestimate Lombard; and do it without revealing that the source of her information was the man himself.

The rambling beach house where Kane lived was in the same immaculate shape he'd left it. His housekeeper had been in, apparently unconcerned that he was missing. That shouldn't surprise him. Unless he paid people, no one seemed to notice if he lived or died.

He chided himself for that cynical thought. Women did agonize over him from time to time. He had a mistress who pretended to care in return for the expensive presents he gave her with careless affection. But no one cared as much as his son had. He closed his eyes and tried not to remember the horror of his last sight of the young boy.

There was a portrait of his son with his late wife on the side table. He looked at that, instead, remembering David as a bright young man with his mother's light hair and eyes and her smile. Although he and Evelyn had grown apart over their years together, David had been loved and cherished by both of them. See what you get for sticking your nose in where it doesn't belong, he thought. Just a routine business trip, you said, and they could go with you. Then all hell broke loose the day they arrived, and he and his family were caught innocently in the cross fire.

He'd blamed himself bitterly for all of it, but time was taking away some of the sting. He had to go on, after all.

The new automotive plant in an industrial Charleston suburb had certainly been a step in the right direction. Planned long before the death of his family, it had just begun operation about the time they were buried. Now it was the lynchpin of his sanity.

He changed into a knit shirt and shorts, idly placing his borrowed clothing to be washed before he returned it. Nikki's sparkling green eyes came to mind and made him smile. She was so young, he mused, and probably a madcap when she set her mind to it. For a moment he allowed himself to envy her lover. She had a pretty body, slender and winsome. But he had Chris when he needed a woman desperately, and there was no place for a permanent woman in his life. He made sure that Chris knew it, so that she wouldn't expect too much. Marriage was out.

He picked up the telephone and dialed the offices of the Charleston plant. What he needed, he told himself, was something to occupy his mind again.

"Get Will Jurkins on the line," he replied to his secretary's polite greeting.

"Yes, sir," she said at once.

A minute later, a slow voice came on the line. "How's the vacation going, Mr. Lombard?"

"So far, so good," Kane said carelessly. "I want to know why you've terminated that contract with the Coastal Waste Company?"

There was a pause. Jurkins should have realized that his superior would fax that information up to Kane Lombard. Sick or not, Ed Nelson was on the ball, as many plant managers were not. "Well . . . uh, I had to."

"Why?"

The word almost struck him. Jurkins wiped his sweaty brow, glancing around from his desk to the warehouse facility where dangerous materials were kept before they were picked up by waste disposal companies. It was considered less expensive to hire that done rather than provide trucks and men to do it. The city could handle toxic substances at its landfill, but Lombard International had contracted CWC to do it since its opening.

"I believe I mentioned to you, Mr. Lombard, that I noticed discrepancies in their invoices."

"I don't remember any such conversation."

Jurkins kept his head, barely. "Listen, Mr. Lombard," he began in a conciliatory tone, "you're a busy man. You can't keep up with all the little details of a plant this size. You sit on the board of directors of three other corporations and the board of trustees of two colleges, you belong to business organizations where you hold office. I mean, how would you have the time to sift through all the day-to-day stuff here?"

Kane took a breath to stem his rush of temper. The man was new, after all, as chief of the waste disposal unit. And he made sense. "That's true. I haven't time to oversee every facet of every operation. Normally, this would be Ed Nelson's problem."

"I know that. Yes, I do, sir. But Mr. Nelson's had kidney stones and he had to have surgery for them last week. He's sort of low. Not that he doesn't keep up with things," he added quickly. "He's still on top of the situation here." That wasn't quite true, but the wording gave Lombard the impression that Nelson had agreed with Jurkins's decision to replace CWC.

Kane relaxed. Jurkins was a native of Charleston. He'd know the ins and outs of sanitation, and surely he'd already have a handle on the proper people to do a good job. "All right," he said. "Who have you contracted with to replace CWC?"

"I found a very reputable company, Mr. Lombard," he assured his boss. "Very reputable, indeed. In fact, two of the local automotive parts companies use them. It's Burke's."

"Burke's?"

"They're not as well-known as CWC, sir," Jurkins said. "They're a young company, but very energetic. They don't cost an arm and a leg, either."

Kane's head was hurting. He didn't have time for this infernal runaround. He'd ask Nelson when he got back to the office the following week.

"All right, Jurkins. Go ahead and make the switch. I'll approve it, if there's any flak," he said. "Just make sure they do what they're supposed to. Put Jenny back on the line."

"Yes, sir! Have a good vacation, sir, and don't you worry, everything's going along just fine!"

Kane made a grunting sound and waited for his secretary to come back on the line. When she did, he began shooting orders at her, for faxes to be sent up to his machine, for contract estimates, for correspondence. He hadn't a secretary here and he hesitated to ask for Jenny to join him, because she had a huge crush on him which he didn't want to encourage. He could scribble notes on the letters for answers and fax them back to her. Yes, that would work.

While Kane was debating his next move, a relieved Will Jurkins pushed back his sweaty red hair and breathed a long sigh, grinning cagily at the man standing beside him.

"That was a close one," he told the man. "Lombard wanted to know why I made the switch."

"You're getting enough out of this deal to make it worth the risk," came the laconic reply. "And you're in too deep to back out."

"Don't I know it," Jurkins said uneasily. "Are you sure about this? I don't want to go to jail."

"Will you stop worrying? I know what I'm doing." He slipped the man a wad of large bills, careful not to let himself be seen.

Jurkins grimaced as he counted the money and quickly slipped it into his pocket. He had a child with leukemia and his medical insurance had run out. He was out of choices and this cigar-smoking magician had offered him a small fortune just to switch sanitation firms. On the surface, there was nothing wrong with it. But he was uneasy, because Burke's sanitation outfit had already been in trouble with the environmental people for some illegal dumping.

"Burke's is not very reliable," he began, trying again. "And I already made one major mistake here, letting that raw sewage get dumped accidentally into the river. If they catch Burke putting anything toxic in a bad place, it will look pretty bad for Lombard International."

"Burke's needs the business," the raspy-voiced man said. "Trust me. It's just to help him out. There's no way it will be traced back to you. You need the money don't you?" When Jurkins nodded, the man patted him on the shoulder and smiled, waving the cigar around. "Nobody will know. And I was never here. Right?"

"Right."

Jurkins watched the man leave by the side door. He went into the parking lot and climbed into a sedate gray BMW. A car like that would cost Jurkins a year's salary. He wondered what his benefactor did for a living.

Clayton Seymour had gone down the roster of Republican representatives over a new bill which affected cable television rates. He and his legislative committee —

44

not to mention part of his personal staff — were helping his friend, the minority whip, gather enough representatives together for a decisive vote on the issue. But he was going blind in the process. He looked out his window at the distant Washington, D.C., skyline and wished he was back home in Charleston and going fishing. He maintained only two district offices, whereas most of the other House members had anywhere from two to eight.

Each of those offices back home in South Carolina had full-time and part-time staffers who could handle requests from constituents. In addition, he'd appointed a constituent staff at his Washington office, along with his legislative, institutional, and personal staff. It sounded like a lot of people on the payroll, but there were actually only a handful involved and they were eminently qualified. Most had master's degrees. His district director had a Ph.D. and his executive legislative counsel was a Harvard graduate.

He was ultimately satisfied with the job he'd done. During his term in office, he'd remained within his budget. It was one of many feathers in his political cap. In addition, he had seats on the Energy and Commerce Committee and the Ways and

Means Committee, among others. He worked from twelve to fourteen hours a day and occasionally took offense at remarks that members of Congress were overpaid layabouts. He didn't have time to lay about. In the next congress, over eleven thousand new pieces of legislation were predicted for introduction. If he was reelected — *when* he was reelected — he was going to have to work even harder.

His executive administrative assistant in charge of his personal and constituent staff, Derrie Keller, knocked on the door and opened it all in the same motion. She was tall and pretty, with light blond hair and green eyes and a nice smile. Everybody was kind to her because she had such a sweet nature. But she also had a bachelor's degree in political science, and was keen-minded, efficient, and tough when the situation called for it. She headed the personal staff, and when she went to Charleston with Clayton, that position also applied to whichever of the two district offices she visited.

"Ah, Derrie," he said on a long-suffering sigh. "Are you going to bury me in paperwork again?"

She grinned. "Want to lie down, first, so we can do it properly?"

46

"If I lie down, three senators and a news-paperman will come in and stand on me," he assured her. He sat upright in his chair. He was good-looking — tall, dark-haired and blue-eyed, with a charismatic personality and a perfect smile.

Women loved him, Derrie thought; particularly a highly paid Washington lobbyist who practiced law named Bett Watts. The woman was forever in and out of the office, tossing out orders to anyone stupid enough to take them. Derrie wasn't. She was simply biding her time until her tunnel-visioned boss eventually noticed that she was a ripe fruit hanging low on the limb, waiting for him to reach up and . . .

"Are you going to stand there all day?" he prompted impatiently.

"Sorry." She put the letters on his desk. "Want coffee?"

"You can't bring me coffee," he said absently. "You're an overpaid public official with administrative duties. If you bring me coffee, secretarial unions will storm the office and sacrifice me on the White House lawn."

She knew this speech by heart. She just smiled. "Cream and sugar?"

"Yes, please," he replied with a grin.

She went out to get it, laughing at his irrepressible overreaction. He always made her laugh. She couldn't resist going with him to political rallies where he was scheduled to speak, because she enjoyed him so much. He was in constant demand as an after-dinner speaker.

"Here you go," she said a minute later, reappearing with two steaming cups. She put hers down and sat in the chair beside his desk with her pad and pen in hand.

"Thanks." He was studying another piece of legislation on which a vote would shortly be taken. "New stuff on the agenda today, Derrie. I'll need you to direct one of the interns to do some legwork for me."

"Is that the lumbering bill?" she asked, eyeing the paper in his lean hands.

"Yes," he said, mildly surprised. "Why?"

"You're not going to vote for it, are you?"

He scowled as he lifted his cup of coffee, fixed with cream just as he liked it, and looked at her while he sipped it gingerly. "Yes, I am," he replied slowly.

She glared at him. "It will set the environment back ten years."

"It will open up jobs for people who can't get any work."

"It's an old forest," she persisted. "One

48

of the oldest untouched forests in the world."

"We can't afford to leave it in its pristine condition," he said, exasperated. "Listen, why don't you meet with all those lobbyists who represent the starving mothers and children of lumbermen out west? Maybe you can explain your position to them better than I could. Hungry kids really get to me."

"How do you know they were really starving and not just short a hot lunch?"

"You cynic!" he exclaimed. He sat forward in his chair. "Hasn't anybody ever explained basic economics to you? Ecology is wonderful, I'm all for it. In fact, I have a very enviable record in South Carolina for my stand against toxic waste dumps and industrial polluters. However, this is another issue entirely. People are asking us to set aside thousands of acres of viable timber to save an owl, when people are jobless and homeless and facing the prospect of going on the welfare rolls — which is, by the way, going to impact taxpayers all the way from Oregon to D.C."

"I know all that," she grumbled. "But we're cutting down all the trees we have and we're not replacing them fast enough.

In fact, how can you replace something that old?"

"You can't replace it," he agreed. "You can't replace people, either, Derrie."

"There are things you're overlooking," she persisted. "Have you read all the background literature on that bill?"

"When I have time?" he exploded. "My God, you of all people should know how fast they throw legislation at me! If I read every word of every bill . . ."

"I can read it for you. If you'll listen I'll tell you why the bill is a bad idea."

"I have legislative counsel to advise me," he said tersely, glaring at her. "My executive legislative counsel is a Harvard graduate."

Derrie knew that. She also liked Mary Tanner, an elegant African American woman whose Harvard law degree often surprised people who mistook her for a model. Mary was beautiful.

"And Mary is very good," she agreed. "But you don't always listen to your advisors."

"The people elected me, not my staff," he reminded her with a cold stare.

She almost challenged that look. But he'd been under a lot of pressure, and she had a little time left before the vote to

50

work on him. She backed down. "All right. I'll work my fingers to the bone for you, but I won't quit harping on the lumber bill," she warned. "I don't believe in profit at the expense of the environment."

"Then you aren't living in the real world."

She gave him a killing glare and walked out of the room. It was to her credit that she didn't slam the door behind her.

Clayton watched her retreat with mixed emotions. Usually, Derrie agreed with him on issues. This time, she was fighting tooth and nail. It amused him, to see his little homebody of an assistant ready to scratch and claw.

The telephone rang and a minute later, Derrie's arctic voice informed him that Ms. Watts was on the line.

"Hello, Bett," he told the caller. "How are you?"

"Worn," came the mocking reply. "I can't see you tonight. I've got a board meeting, followed by a cocktail party, followed by a brief meeting with one of the senior senators, all of which I really must get through."

"Don't you ever get tired of lobbying and long for something different?" he probed.

"Something like giving fancy parties and placating political adversaries?" Bett asked sarcastically.

Clayton felt himself going tense. "I know you don't like my sister," he said curtly. "But a remark like that is catty and frankly intolerable. Call me back when you feel like rejoining the human race."

He put the phone down and buzzed Derrie. "If Ms. Watts calls back, tell her I'm indisposed indefinitely!" he said icily.

"Does she like virgin forests, too?"

He slammed the phone down and took the receiver off the hook.

Clayton phoned Nikki that evening. He didn't mention Bett's nasty remark or his fight with Derrie, which had resulted in her giving him an icy good-night and leaving him alone with cold coffee and hot bills. He had to depend on his district director for coffee, and Stan couldn't make it strong enough.

"I'm not going to be able to turn loose for at least two weeks," he said sadly. "I'd love to spend some time with you before we get our feet good and wet in this campaign, but I've got too much on my plate."

"Take some time off. Congress won't be in session much longer."

"I know that. I am a U.S. Representative," he reminded her dryly. "Which is all the more reason for me to push these so-and-so's into getting down here to vote when our bill comes up. I can't leave."

"In that case, don't expect me to wail for you."

"Would I? Anyway, you need the rest more than I do," he said on a laugh. "How's everything going?"

"Fine," she said. "Nothing exciting. A big fish washed up on the beach . . ."

"I hope you didn't try to save it," he muttered. "You're hell to take on a fishing trip, with your overstimulated protective instincts."

"I let this one go," she said, feeling vaguely guilty that she was keeping a secret from him. It was the first time, too. "It wasn't hurt very badly. It swam away and I'll never see it again." That much was probably true.

"Well, stay out of trouble, can't you?"

"Clay, I'll do my very best," she promised.

"Get some rest. You'll need it when autumn comes and the campaigning begins in earnest."

"Don't I know it," she chuckled. "Good night."

53

"Good night."

She hung up the phone and went to lounge on the deck, watching the white-caps curl rhythmically in to the white beach. The moon shone on them and as she sipped white wine, she thought that she'd never felt quite so alone. She wondered what Mr. Lombard was doing.

Chapter Three

Kane Lombard was sitting on his own deck with a highball, thinking about Nikki. It had been a productive day. Most days were, because the job was everything to him. But now, as he contemplated the moonlight sparkle on the ocean, he felt unfulfilled.

He was thirty-eight years old. He'd had a wife, and a son. There had been a twelve-year marriage which, while not perfect, at least gave him a sense of security. At least he'd been in love when he married, even if things had gone sour a few years later. Now he was among the ranks of the single men again, but without the youth and idealism that made marriage a viable prospect. He was jaded and somewhere along the way, he'd lost all his illusions about people. About life. He was like those waves, he thought, being aimlessly thrown onto the beach and then forgotten. When he died, there would be nothing to leave behind, nothing to show that Kane Lombard had lived on this planet.

That wasn't totally true, he chided himself as he swallowed a sip of the stinging highball. He had the company to leave behind. The name would probably be changed somewhere down the line, though. Names didn't last long.

He leaned back on the chaise lounge and closed his eyes. Nikki. Her name was Nikki, and she had black hair and green eyes and the face of an angel. He liked the way she looked, the way she laughed, as if life still had wonderful things to offer. He knew better, but she made him optimistic. He needed someone like that.

Not permanently, of course, he told himself. He needed an affair. Just an affair. Would she be willing? She seemed to find him attractive enough. If he took her out and bided his time, would she be receptive? He sloshed the liquid in the glass, listening to the soft chink of the ice cubes against the watery roar of the ocean. Perhaps she was lonely, too. God knew, there was no monopoly on loneliness. Like the air itself, it permeated everything. His eyelids felt heavy. He closed them, just for a minute . . .

It was dawn when he woke, still lying on the chaise lounge, with the chill morning air in his face. The glass, long since forgotten, had fallen gently to the deck and was dry now, the ice and whiskey melted and evaporated on the wood floor. He got up, stretching with faint soreness. His head was much better, but there were still vestiges of a headache. He stared out over the ocean, and was jarred from his thoughts when the telephone rang.

His housekeeper was apparently in residence, because the ringing stopped, to be replaced by her loud, stringent voice.

"Telephone, Mr. Lombard!" she called.

"I'll take it out here," he returned gruffly.

She handed him the phone and he nodded curtly as he took it, waving her away. "Yes?" he asked.

"I'm Todd Lawson, Mr. Lombard," a deep voice replied. "I work for your father and brothers in New York at the *Weekly Voice*," he prompted when there was a long pause on the other end of the line.

Kane recognized the name. Lawson was his father's star reporter, if a man who was better at creating news than gathering it could be called a journalist.

"Yes, I know you," Kane said. "What do you want?"

"Your father sent me to Charleston to do a little prospecting. He wants me to see what I can find on the Republican U.S. Representative incumbent, Seymour. I've

57

just checked into a hotel here. Any ideas about a good place to start looking for skeletons?"

"I can't help you. I haven't lived in Charleston long enough to know many people. I only know Seymour through the mails and the telephone," he added curtly. "If I put a step wrong, he'll be over me like tarpaper, I know that. We had a sewage leak a couple of weeks ago, accidental, and he's been after my neck ever since. He went on television to point fingers at me as a perfect example of a money-hungry anticonservationist." He shook his head. "He's gung ho on this industrial pollution issue. It's his number one priority, they say."

"Interesting that he's fighting for the lumber bill out west," Lawson murmured, tongue in cheek.

"The habitat of an owl out west apparently doesn't do him as much political good as digging out industrial polluters on his doorstep."

"You said it."

"Keep me posted, will you?"

"You bet."

He put down the receiver. Seymour was an odd bird, he thought. The man had little material wealth, but his old

Charleston heritage had helped put him in office. The backing of Senator Mosby Torrance hadn't hurt, either. The junior U.S. senator from South Carolina was a personable man with an equally impeccable reputation, even if he had a failed marriage behind him. Mosby's marriage had been very brief, Kane understood, and rather secretive, but that had been because of his bride's tender age, his sources told him. He couldn't quite remember, but it seemed that there had been some connection with the Seymours before that. He'd have to remember and tell Lawson. It wasn't important enough to try to reach the reporter, even if he knew where to look. No matter. Lawson would call back.

In the campaign headquarters of Sam Hewett, candidate for the Democratic nomination to the U.S. House of Representatives for the district that included Charleston, South Carolina, a heated discussion was taking place between Hewett and his advisors.

"You can't risk a personal attack on Seymour at this point," Norman Lombard muttered through a cloud of cigar smoke. His dark eyes lanced the candidate, who was tall and thin and rather nervous. "Let

59

us take care of anything in that line. My father owns the biggest tabloid in America and my brothers and I are solidly behind you, financially and every other way. You just shake hands and make friends. For now, worry about nothing more than the Democratic nomination. When the time comes, we'll have enough to slide you past Seymour at the polls."

"What if I can't gather enough support?" Hewett asked uneasily. "I'm not that well-known. I don't have the background that Seymour does!"

"You'll have the name identification when we get through with you," Norman said, chuckling. "My dad knows how to get the publicity. You'll get the votes. We guarantee it."

"You won't do anything illegal?" the candidate asked.

The question seemed to be perennial in Hewett's mind. Lombard sighed angrily and puffed on his cigar. "We won't have to," he assured the other man for the tenth time. "A little mud here, a little doubt there, and we'll have the seat in our grasp. Just relax, Sam. You're a shoo-in. Enjoy the ride."

"I want to win honestly."

"The last person who won honestly was

George Washington," Lombard joked cynically. "But never mind, we'll do our best to keep your conscience quiet. Now, get out there and campaign, Sam. And stop worrying, will you? I promise you, it will all work out for the best."

Hewett wasn't as certain as his advisor appeared, but he was a newcomer to politics. He was learning more than he wanted to about the election process every day. He'd been idealistic and enthusiastic at the outset. Now, he was losing his illusions by the minute. He couldn't help but wonder if this was what the founding fathers had in mind when they outlined the electoral process. It seemed a real shame that qualifications meant nothing at all in the race; it was a contest of personalities and high-tech advertising and money, not issues. But on that foundation, the election rested. He did want to win, he told himself. But for the first time, he wasn't sure why.

It had thrilled him when the Lombards backed him as a candidate. It had been Kane Lombard's idea initially. Kane liked Sam because they were both yachtsmen, and because Sam supported tax cuts and other incentives that would help his fledgling automobile manufacturing industry in Charleston. Mainly, Sam thought, it was

61

because Clayton Seymour had taken an instant dislike to Kane and had done everything possible to put obstacles in his path when the auto manufacturing firm first located in Charleston. The antagonism had been mutual. Now, with Kane's latest bad luck in having a sewage spill into the river, Seymour had attacked him from every angle.

Sam didn't like dirty politics. He wanted to win the election, but not if it meant stooping to the sort of tactics Seymour and his mentor Mosby Torrance were using against Kane. The double-dealing at city hall had been shocking to Sam, with both politicians using unfair influence to delay building permits and regulatory requirements.

Privately, Sam thought a lot of their resentment was due to the national reputation of the tabloid Kane's father and brothers owned in New York. It was increasingly focusing on politics and it had done some nasty exposes on pet projects of Senator Torrance. It had also made some veiled threats about going on a witch-hunt to drag out scandals in Congress, beginning with southern senators and representatives. That had been about the time Kane announced the building of his plant.

It had also coincided with Seymour's bid for reelection.

Having Kane so close to home was making Seymour and Torrance nervous. Sam began to wonder what they had to hide.

Nicole had driven her small used red sports car into the village market near the medical center to get milk and bread — the eternal necessities — and fresh fruit. She'd just walked onto her porch when she heard the sound of a car pulling to a stop behind her.

She turned, and found Kane Lombard climbing out of a ramshackle old Jeep. She wondered just for an instant where he'd borrowed such a dilapidated vehicle before the sight of him in jeans and a white knit shirt made her heart start beating faster.

He smiled at the picture she made in cutoff denim shorts and a pink tank top. That dark tan gave her an almost continental look.

"You tan well," he remarked.

"Our ancestors were French Huguenots, who came to Charleston early in the seventeenth century to escape religious persecution in Europe," she told him. "I'm told that our olive complexion comes from them."

"I brought back the things you loaned me." He handed her a bundle. "Washed and pressed," he added.

"With your own two hands?" she teased.

He liked the way her eyes sparkled when she smiled. She made him feel young again. "Not quite." He stuck his hands in his pockets and studied her closely, with pursed lips. "Come for a ride."

Her heart skipped. She couldn't really afford to get mixed up with her brother's enemy, she told herself firmly. Really she couldn't.

"Just let me put these things away," she said.

He followed her inside and wandered around the living room while she put the perishable things into the refrigerator and the bread in the bread box.

"I should change . . ." she began.

"Why?" He turned, smiling at her. "You look fine to me."

"In that case, I'm ready."

She locked the door, grateful that she hadn't any photographs setting around that might clue him in to her relationship with Clayton. Nor was there anything expensive or antique in the beach house. She and Clayton didn't keep valuables here, and the beach house remained in the name of their cousin who also had access to it. That kept nosey parkers from finding Clayton when he was up here on holiday. Records on land ownership were not hard to obtain, especially for someone like Kane Lombard.

He unlocked the passenger door and helped her inside. "It's not very neat in here," he said, apologizing. "I use this old rattletrap for fishing trips, mostly. I like to angle for bass down on the Santee-Cooper River."

"You don't look like a fisherman," she remarked. She clipped her seat belt into place, idly watching his hard, dark face and wondering at the lines in it, the silvery hair at his temples. He was older than she'd first thought.

"I hate fishing, as a rule," he replied. He started the Jeep and reversed it neatly, wheeling around before he sped off down the beach highway. The sun was shining. It was a glorious morning, with seagulls and pelicans scrounging for fish in the surf while a handful of residents walked in the surf and watched the ocean.

"Then, why do it?" she asked absently.

"My father loves it. He and I have very

little in common, otherwise. I go fishing with him because it gives me an excuse to see him occasionally — and my younger brothers."

"How many do you have?"

"Two. No sisters. There are just the three of us. We drove my mother crazy when we were kids." He glanced at her. "Do you have family?"

"Not many, not anymore," she said, her voice very quiet and distant.

"I'm sorry. It must be lonely for you."

"It's not bad," she replied. "I have friends."

"Like the one who lets you share the beach house with him?" he asked pointedly.

She smiled at him, unconcerned. "Yes. Like him."

Kane made a mental note to find out who owned that beach house. He wanted to know the name of the man with whom Nikki was involved. It didn't occur to him then that his very curiosity betrayed his growing involvement with her.

All along the beach, people were beginning to set up lawn chairs and spread towels in the sun. It was a warm spring day, with nothing but a sprinkling of clouds overhead.

"I love the ocean," Nikki said softly, smiling as her wide green eyes took in her surroundings. "I could never live inland. Even the freighters and fishing boats fascinate me."

"I know what you mean," he agreed. "I've lived in port cities all my life. You get addicted to the sight and sound of big ships."

He must mean Houston, but she couldn't admit that she knew where he was from. "Do you live here?" she asked.

"I'm on holiday," he said, which was true enough. "Do you stay here, all the time?"

"No," she confessed. "I live farther down the coast."

"In Charleston?" he probed.

"Sort of."

"What does sort of mean?"

"I live on the beach itself." She did. She lived in one of the graceful old homes on the Battery, which was listed in the National Register of Historic Places and which was open to tourists two weeks a year.

He could imagine in what kind of house she normally lived. He hadn't seen her in anything so far that didn't look as if she'd found it in a yard sale. He felt vaguely sorry for her. She had no one of her own except her indifferent lover, and her material possessions were obviously very few. He'd noticed that she drove a very dilapidated red MG Midget, the model that was popular back in the 60s.

"Feel like a cup of coffee?" he asked, nodding toward a small fast-food joint near the beach, with tables outside covered by faded yellow umbrellas.

"Yes, I do, thanks," she told him.

He parked the Jeep and they got out. Nikki strolled to the beachside table and sat down while Kane ordered coffee. He hadn't needed to be told how Nikki took hers. He brought it with cream and sugar, smiling mischievously at her surprise.

"I have a more or less photographic memory," he told her as he slid onto the seat across from her.

"I'll remember that," she said with a grin.

He lifted his head and closed his eyes, letting the sea breeze drift over his darkly tanned face. It had a faintly leonine look, broad and definite, with a straight nose that was just short of oversized, a jutting brow with thick eyebrows, and a wide, thin-lipped mouth that managed to be sexy and masculine all at once. His eyes were large and brown, his pupils edged in black.

They were staring at her with faint amusement.

"You look Spanish," she blurted out, embarrassed at having been caught looking at him.

He frowned slightly, smiling. "My great-grandmother was a highborn Spanish lady," he replied. "She was visiting relatives near San Antonio, where my great-grandfather was a ranch foreman. As the story goes, they were married five days after they met, leaving a raging scandal behind them when they moved to Houston to prospect for oil."

"How interesting! And did they find any?"

"My great-grandfather was prospecting up around Beaumont when Spindletop blew its stack in 1901," he told her. "He made and lost a fortune in two months' time." He didn't add that his great-grandfather had quickly recouped his losses and went on to found an oil company.

"Poor man." She looked up from the coffee she was sipping. "His wife didn't leave him because he lost everything, did she?"

"She wasn't the type. She stuck by him, all the way."

"That doesn't happen very often any-

69

more, does it? Women sticking by men, I mean," she added wistfully. "Now, marriages are expendable. Nobody does it for keeps."

He scowled. "You're very cynical for someone so young."

"I'm twenty-five," she told him. "Not young at all for this day and age." She studied her brightly polished fingernails, curled around the foam cup. "For the rest, it's a cynical world. Profit even takes precedence over human life. I'm told that in the Amazon jungles, they kill the natives without compunction to get them off land the government wants to let big international corporations develop."

He stared at her. "Do you really think that with all the people this planet has to support, we can afford to allow primitive cultures to sit on that much arable land?"

Her green eyes began to glitter. "I think that if we develop all the arable land, we're going to have to eat concrete and steel a few years down the line."

He was delighted. Absolutely delighted. For all her beauty, there was a brain under that black hair. He moved his coffee cup around on the scarred surface of the table and smiled at her. "Progress costs," he countered.

"It's going to cost us the planet at the rate we're destroying our natural resources," she said sweetly. "Or aren't you aware that about one percent of us is feeding the other ninety-nine percent? You have to have flat, rich land to plant on. Unfortunately the same sort of land that is best suited to agriculture is also best suited to building sites."

"On the other hand," he pointed out, "without jobs, people won't be able to afford seed to plant. A new business means new jobs, a better standard of living for the people in the community. Better nutrition for nursing mothers, for young children."

"That's all true," she agreed, leaning forward earnestly. "But what about the price people pay for that better standard of living? When farm mechanization came along, farmers had to grow more food in order to afford the equipment to make planting and harvesting less time-consuming. That raised the price of food. The pesticides and fertilizers they had to use, to increase production, caused the toxic byproducts to leach into the ground, and pollute the water table. We produced more food, surely, but the more food you raise, the more the population grows. That increases the amount of food you *have* to raise to feed the increasing numbers of people! It's a vicious circle."

"My God, you talk like an economist," he said.

"Why not? I studied it in college."

"Well, well." He grinned at her. "What did you take your degree in?"

"I didn't finish," she said sadly. "I dropped out after three and a half years, totally burned out. I'll go back and finish one day, though. I only lack two semesters having enough units to graduate, with a major in history and a minor in sociology."

"God help the world when you get out," he murmured. "You could go into politics with a brain like yours."

She was flattered and amused, but she didn't let him see the latter. He mustn't know how wrapped up she already was in politics.

"You're not bad yourself."

"I took my degree in business administration," he said. "I did a double minor in economics and marketing."

"Do you work in business?" she asked with deliberate innocence.

"You might say so," he said carelessly. "I'm in marketing."

"It must be exciting."

"Sometimes," he dodged. He finished

his coffee. "Do you like to walk on the beach?" he asked. "I enjoy it early in the morning and late in the afternoon. It helps me clear my mind so that I can think."

"Me, too," she said.

"Kindred spirits," he said almost to himself, and she smiled.

He put the garbage in the receptacle and impulsively slid his hand into Nikki's.

It was the first deliberate physical contact between them, and sparks flew as his big, strong fingers linked sensuously between her slender ones. She felt their warm touch and tingles worked all the way down her body. She hadn't felt that way in years. Not since Mosby . . .

She caught her breath and looked up at him with something like panic in her green eyes.

"What is it, Nikki?" he asked gently.

His deep voice stirred her even more than the touch of his hand. She felt him, as if they were standing locked together. Her eyes looked into his and she could almost taste him.

"Nothing," she choked after a minute. She pulled her fingers from his grasp firmly, but hesitantly. "Shall we go?"

He watched her move off ahead of him, her hands suddenly in her pockets, the small fanny pack around her waist drooping over one rounded hip. She looked frightened. That was an odd sort of behavior from a woman who'd let him share her home for a night, he thought idly. She hadn't been afraid of him then.

She paused when he caught up with her, feeling guilty and not quite herself. She looked up at him with a rueful, embarrassed smile.

"I don't trust men, as a rule," she confessed. "Most of them have one major objective when they start paying attention to a woman. I've never been accused of misleading anyone. That's why I'm going to tell you right now, and up front, that I don't sleep around, ever."

"At least you're honest," he said as they continued to walk toward the beach.

"Always," she assured him. "I find it's the best policy."

"Do you sleep with the man who owns the beach house?"

"What I do with him is none of your business," she said simply.

"Fair enough." He put his hands in his pockets and looked down at her while they strolled along the white sand. Whitecaps rolled, foaming onto the nearby shore, and above head the seagulls danced on the wind with black-tipped white wings spread to the sun.

"You're very big," she remarked.

He chuckled. "Tall. Not big."

"You are," she argued. "I'm five foot five and you tower over me."

"I'm barely six foot two," he told her. "You're a shrimp, that's why I seem big to you."

"Watch your mouth, buster, I'm not through growing yet," she said pertly, cutting her sparkling eyes up at him.

He chuckled. "Smart mouth."

"Smart, period, thank you so much."

"Now that we both know you won't sleep with me, can we hold hands? Mine are cold."

"I might have suspected there would be an ulterior motive," she mentioned. But all the same, she took her left hand out of her pocket and let him fold it under his warm fingers.

"You aren't cold," she protested.

"Sure I am. You just can't tell." His fingers tightened, and he smiled at the faint flush on her cheeks as the exercise began to tell on her. "You ninety-seven-pound-weakling," he chided. "Can't you keep up with me?"

"Normally I could run rings around

you," she said heavily. "But I'm getting over a bout of pneumonia."

He stopped abruptly, scowling. "Idiot! You don't need to be out in this early morning chill! Why didn't you say something?"

His concern made her heart lift. "It's been a week since I got out of bed," she assured him. "And I haven't been sitting home idle all that time."

"You haven't done much exercising, either, have you?"

"Not really," she admitted. The help she'd given with the Spoleto Festival had involved a lot of telephone calls and assistance that she could give sitting down. Her strength was still lagging behind her will.

"What a waif and stray it is, and it hasn't much of a mind at times, either," he murmured softly.

She started to take offense when he moved suddenly and swept her into his warm, strong arms. He turned and started walking back the way they'd come.

Nikki was totally breathless with surprised delight. It was the first time in her life that she'd experienced a man's strength in this way. She wasn't sure she liked the feeling of vulnerability it gave her, and that doubt was in her eyes when they met his at close range.

"I can see the words right there on the tip of your tongue," he said softly, his deep voice faintly accented and very tender as he smiled at her. "But don't say them. Put your arms around me and lie close to my chest while I carry you."

Shades of a romantic movie, she thought wildly. But the odd thing was that she obeyed him without question, without hesitation. There was a breathy little sigh escaping from her. She dropped her eyes to his throat, where thick hair showed in the opening, and she felt a sweet swelling in her body as he drew her relentlessly closer. Her face ended up in the hot curve of his throat, her arms close around his neck.

"Nikki," he said in a rough, husky voice, and his arms suddenly contracted, crushing her soft breasts against the wall of his chest as he turned toward the car.

It was no longer a teasing or tender embrace. Her nails were biting into his shoulders as he walked, and she felt the closeness in every single pore of her body. Her breasts had gone hard-tipped, her heart was throbbing. Low in her stomach, she felt a heat and hunger that was totally without precedent.

"Oh, baby," he whispered suddenly, and

she felt his open mouth quite suddenly on the softness of her throat where her tank top left it bare to her collarbone.

She closed her eyes with a shaky gasp. The wind blew her hair around her face and cooled the heat in her cheeks. He was warm and strong and he smelled of spices. She wanted him to strip her out of her clothes and put his warm, hard mouth on her breasts and her belly and the inside of her thighs. She wanted him to put her down on the beach and make love to her under the sky.

With a total disregard for safety and sanity, her hand tangled in the thick, wavy hair at the back of his head and she pulled his mouth down to the soft curve under her collarbone.

Chapter Four

Kane's head was spinning, but when Nikki coaxed his mouth down, he came to his senses with a jolt. It was a public beach, for God's sake, and he was a man who didn't need this sort of complication!

He jerked his face up and put her down abruptly. He stepped back, trying not to show how shaken he was. It had been a long time since he'd felt anything so powerful. He looked into her dazed, misty, half-closed green eyes.

She was shaken, too, and unable to hide it. His lips had almost been touching her bare skin when he'd withdrawn them. She felt as if she'd been left in limbo, but she had to keep her head.

"Thank you," she said. "I knew that you could save me from myself," she managed with irrepressible spirit.

He smiled in spite of himself. "I suppose I did. But I'd never have believed it of myself. I'm not one to throw away opportunities, and you have a mouth like a ripe apple."

"I'm thrilled that you think so."

He burst out laughing, absolutely delighted. "In that case, don't you want to come with me to a quiet, deserted place?"

"Of course I do." She pushed back her disheveled hair. "But we've already agreed that it wouldn't be sensible."

"You agreed. I didn't."

She was having trouble with her legs. They didn't want to move. And the throbbing need in her body was getting worse, not better. How ironic of her to suddenly explode with passion for a man after all this time, and the man had to be her brother's worst enemy in the world!

"Stop tempting me to do sordid things," she told him firmly. She pushed back her disheveled hair. "I'll have you know that I'm a virtuous woman."

"That may not last if you spend much time around me. How about going sailing with me?"

Her hand poised above her hair. "Sailing?"

"Your eyes lit up. Do you like sailing?" he asked.

"I love it!"

He chuckled. "I'll pick you up early tomorrow." He paused. "If you're free?"

She knew what he was asking. He meant, would her "live-in lover" mind?

"He isn't jealous," she said with a slow smile.

"Isn't he?"

His dark eyes sketched her face and he began to worry. He knew he was losing his grasp on reality, to take this sort of chance. She appealed to him physically. That was all. There was an added threat. What if she found out who he was?

His own apprehension amused him. What if she did, for God's sake? What could she do, blackmail him because they'd spent an innocent night together?

"The man I live with and I . . . we have an . . . open relationship," she assured him.

"I hope you aren't entertaining ideas that I might be willing to take his place," he said slowly. "I enjoy your company, and I find you very attractive. But I'm not in the market for a lover. I already have one."

Why should that shock her? She shifted a little and averted her eyes to the beach. She wasn't shopping for a lover, either. Not with her past. So wasn't it just as well that he didn't want one?

"That suits me," she replied absently. "I don't care for purely physical relationships. I wouldn't mind a friend, though," she added suddenly, her green eyes linking with his as she smiled. "I have very few of those."

"I doubt if anyone can boast more than one true friend," he said cynically. "Okay. Friends it is."

"And no funny stuff on the sailboat," she said, returning to her former mood with mercurial rapidity. "You can't lash me to the mast and ravish me, or strip me naked and use me to troll for sharks. You have to promise."

He grinned. "Fair enough."

"Then I'll see you tomorrow."

"I don't think we can avoid it," he agreed. "Come on. I'll take you home."

That evening, sitting alone on the deck, her conscience nagged at her. It didn't help that Clayton telephoned to tell her about the progress he was making.

"I've won over a new ally," he told her, and mentioned the congressman's name. "How's that for a day's work?!"

"Great!" she said, laughing. "Uh, how's the owl controversy?"

"It's a real hoot," he muttered. "Derrie and I aren't speaking because of it. Here I am a conservation candidate, voting against a little owl and a bunch of old trees just because it will mean new jobs and economic prosperity. She thinks I'm a lunatic."

"Was the moon full?"

"Cut it out. You're my sister. Blood is thicker than water."

"Probably it is, but what does that have to do with anything?"

He scowled. "I can't think of a single thing. How are you? Getting some rest?"

"Enough." She hesitated. "I . . . met someone."

"Someone? A man? A real, honest to God man?"

"He looks like one. He's taking me sailing."

"Nikki, I'm delighted! Who is he?"

She crossed her fingers on her lap. "Just an ordinary man," she lied. "He's into . . . cars."

"Oh. A mechanic? Well, there's nothing wrong with being a mechanic, I guess. Can he sail well enough not to drown you?"

"I think he could do anything he set his mind to," she murmured dreamily.

"Is this really you?" he teased. "You were off men for life, the last time we spoke."

"Oh, I am," she agreed readily. "It's just that this one is so different." She added, "I haven't ever met anyone quite like him."

"Is he a ladies' man?"

"I don't know. Perhaps."

"Nikki," he began, hesitating. She'd had a rough experience at an early age. She was vulnerable. "Listen, suppose I come up for a few days?"

"No!" She cleared her throat and lowered her voice. "I mean, there's no need to do that."

"You're worrying me," he said.

"You can't protect me from the world, you know. I have to stand on my own two feet sometime."

"I guess you do," he said, sounding resigned and not too happy. "Okay, sis. Have it your way. But I'm as close as the telephone if you need me. Will you remember that?"

"You can bet on it."

"Then I'll speak to you soon."

When he hung up, Nikki let out the breath she'd been holding. That was all she needed now, to have Clayton come wandering up to the house and run head-on into his worst enemy. Things were getting complicated and she was certain that she needed to cut off the impossible relationship before it began. But she couldn't quite manage it. Already, Kane had gotten close to her heart. She hoped that it wouldn't break completely in the end.

She wondered how Kane was going to keep her in the dark about his wealth. If he took her sailing in a yacht, even a moron would notice that it meant he had money.

The next day he solved the problem adroitly by mentioning that he couldn't rent the sailboat he'd planned to take her out in, so they were going riding in a motorboat instead. It was a very nice motorboat, but nothing like the yacht he usually took onto the ocean.

Nikki smiled to herself and accepted the change of conveyance without noticeable effect.

"I know I said I'd take you out on a sailboat," he explained as he helped her into the boat, "but they're not very safe in high winds. It's pretty windy today."

It was, but she hardly thought a yacht would be very much affected. On the other hand, it wouldn't do for her "ordinary" houseguest to turn up in a million-dollar-plus sailing ship, and he must have realized that.

"Oh, I like motorboats," she said honestly, her eyes lighting up with excitement as Kane eased into the driver's seat and turned the key. The motor started right up and ran like a purring cat.

He glanced at her with a wry smile. "Are

you a good sailor?"

"I guess we'll find out together," she returned.

He chuckled and pulled away from the pier.

The boat had a smooth glide on the water's surface, and the engine wasn't overly loud. Nikki put up a hand to her windblown hair, laughing as the faint spray of water teased her nose.

"Aren't you ever gloomy?" he asked with genuine curiosity.

"Oh, why bother being pessimistic?" she replied. "Life is so short. It's a crime to waste it, when every day is like Christmas, bringing something new."

She loved life. He'd forgotten how. His dark eyes turned toward the distant horizon and he tried not to think about how short life really was, or how tragically he'd learned the lesson.

"Where are we going?" Nikki asked.

"No place in particular," he said. He glanced at her with faint amusement. "Unless," he added, "you like to fish."

"I don't mind it. But you hate it!" she laughed.

"Of course I do. But I have to keep my hand in," he added. "So that I don't disgrace the rest of my family. The gear and tackle are under that tarp. I thought we'd ease up the river a bit and settle in a likely spot. I brought an ice chest and lunch."

"You really are full of surprises," she commented.

His dark eyes twinkled. "You don't know the half of it," he murmured, turning his concentration back to navigation.

He found a leafy glade and tied the boat up next to shore. He and Nikki sat lazily on the bank and watched their corks rise and fall and occasionally bob. They ate cold cut sandwiches and potato chips and sipped soft drinks, and Nikki marveled at the tycoon who was a great fishing companion. Not since her childhood, when she'd gone fishing with her late grandfather, had she enjoyed anything so much. She'd forgotten how much fun it was to sit on the river with a fishing pole.

"Do you do this often?" she wanted to know.

"With my brothers and my father. Not ever with a woman." His broad shoulders lifted and fell. "Most of them that I know don't care for worms and hooks," he mused. "You're not squeamish, are you?"

"Not really. About some things, maybe," she added quietly. "But unless you're shooting the fish in a barrel, they have a sporting chance. And I do love fried bass!"

"Can you clean a fish?"

"You bet!"

He chuckled with delight. "In that case, if we catch anything, I'm inviting myself to supper." His eyes narrowed. "If you have no other plans."

"Not for two weeks, I haven't," she said.

He seemed to relax. His powerful legs stretched out in front of him and he tugged on the fishing pole to test the hook. "Nothing's striking at my bait," he grumbled. "I haven't had a bite yet. We'll give it ten more minutes and then we're moving to a better spot."

"The minute we move, a hundred big fish will feel safe to vacation here," she pointed out.

"You're probably right. Some days aren't good ones to fish."

"That depends on what you're fishing for," she said, concentrating on the sudden bob of her cork. "Watch this . . . !"

She pulled suddenly on the pole, snaring something at the end of the line, and scrambled to her feet. Whatever she'd hooked was giving her a run for her money. She pulled and released, pulled and released, worked the pole, moved up the bank, muttered and clicked her tongue until finally her prey began to tire. She watched Kane watching her and laughed at his dismal expression.

"You're hoping I'll drop him, aren't you?" she challenged. "Well, I won't. Supper, here you come!"

She gave a hard jerk on the line and the fish, a large bass, flipped up onto the bank. While Kane dealt with it, she baited her hook again. "I've got mine," she told him. "I don't know what you'll eat, of course."

He sat down beside her and picked up his own pole. "We'll just see about that," he returned.

Two hours later, they had three large bass. Nikki had caught two of them. Kane lifted the garbage and then the cooler with the fish into the boat. Nikki forgave herself for feeling vaguely superior, just for a few minutes.

Kane had forgotten his tragedies, his business dealings, his worries in the carefree morning he was sharing with Nikki. Her company had liberated his one-track mind from the rigors that plagued men of his echelon. He was used to being by himself, to letting business occupy every waking hour. Since the death of his family, he'd substituted making money for everything else. Food tasted like cardboard to him. Sleep was infrequent and an irritating necessity. He hadn't taken a vacation or even a day off since the trip he'd taken with his wife and son that had ended so tragically.

Perhaps that very weariness had made him careless and caused his head injury. But looking at Nikki, so relaxed and happy beside him, he couldn't be sorry about it. She was an experience he knew he'd never forget. But, like all the others, he'd taste her delights and put her aside. And in two weeks after he left her, he wouldn't be able to recall her name. The thought made him restless.

Nikki noticed his unease. She wondered if he was as attracted to her emotionally as he seemed to be physically. It had worried her when he'd admitted that he had a lover. Of course, he thought she did, too, and it couldn't have been further from the truth. But it could be, she was forced to admit, remembering the feel of his big arms around her. He could be her lover. She trembled inside at the size and power of his body. Mosby had never been able to bring himself to make love to her at all. He'd only been able to touch her lightly and without passion. She hadn't known what it was to be kissed breathless, to be a slave to her body's needs, until this stranger had come along. There were many reasons that would keep her from becoming intimate with him. And the first was the faceless lover who clung to him in the darkness. She didn't know how to compete with another woman, because she'd never had to.

She forced her wandering mind back to the fishing. This had been one of the most carefree days of her life. She was sad to see it end. Kane had agreed to come to supper, but she was losing him now to other concerns. His mind wasn't on the fish, or her. She wondered what errant thought had made him so preoccupied.

"I have to make a telephone call, or I'd help you clean the fish," he said when he left her at the front door of her beach house with the cooler.

"Business?" she asked.

His face showed nothing. "You might call it that." He didn't say anything else. He smiled at her distractedly and left with a careless wave of his hand.

Nikki went in to clean the fish, disturbed by his sudden remoteness. What kind of business could he have meant?

Kane listened patiently while the angry

voice at the other end of the telephone ranted and railed at him.

"You promised that we could go to the Waltons' party tonight!" Chris fumed. "How can you do this to me? What sort of deal are you working on that demands a whole evening of your time?"

"That's hardly your concern," he said in a very quiet voice. Her rudeness and lack of compassion were beginning to irritate him. She was a competent psychologist, and he couldn't fault her intellect. But their mutual need for safe intimacy had been their only common bond. Chris wanted a man she could lead around by the nose in any emotional relationship. Kane wasn't the type to let anyone, man or woman, dictate to him. He'd tired of Chris. Tonight, she was an absolute nuisance.

"When will you phone me, then?" she asked stiffly.

"When I have time. It might be as well if we don't see as much of each other in the future."

There was a hesitation, then a stiff, "Perhaps you're right. You're a wonderful lover, Kane, but I always have the feeling that you're going over cost overruns even when we're together."

"I'm a businessman," he reminded her.

"You're a business," she retorted. "A walking, talking industry, and I still say you should be in therapy. You haven't been the same since . . ."

He didn't want to hear any more. "I'll phone you. Good night."

He put the receiver down before she could say anything else. He'd had quite enough of her psychoanalysis. She did it all the time, even when she was in bed with him; especially when she was in bed with him, he amended. If he was aggressive, she labeled him a repressed masochist. If he was tender, he was pandering to her because he felt superior. Lately, she inhibited him so much that he lost interest very quickly when he was in bed with her, to the point of not being able to consummate lovemaking. That really infuriated her. She decided that his real problem was impotence.

If her barbs hadn't been so painful, they might have been amusing. He'd never been impotent in his life with anyone except Chris. Certainly he was more capable than ever when he just looked at Nikki. But, then, Nikki apparently didn't have any reason to hate and despise men. She was very feminine along with her intelligence, and she didn't tease viciously.

He got up and changed from jeans and jersey into dress slacks and a comfortable yellow knit shirt. Fried fish with Nikki was suddenly much more enticing than a prime rib and cocktails with Chris.

He selected a bottle of wine from the supply he'd imported and carried it along with him. He wondered if Nikki knew anything about fine white wine. She was an intelligent girl, but she hadn't the advantages of wealth. Probably she wouldn't know a Chardonnay from a Johannisberg Riesling. That was something he could teach her. He didn't dare think about tutoring her in anything else just yet. She could become even more addicting than alcohol if he let her. Chris was all the trouble he needed for the present.

Nikki had cleaned and fried the fish and was making a fruit salad and a poppyseed dressing to go with it when Kane knocked briefly and let himself into the cottage.

She glanced over her shoulder and smiled at him. "Come on in," she invited. She was wearing a frilly floral sundress that left most of her pretty, tanned back bare while it discreetly covered her breasts in front. She was barefoot at the kitchen table and Kane felt his body surge at the picture of feminine beauty she presented. How long had it been, he tried to recall, since he'd seen a woman in his own circle of friends wearing anything less masculine than a pin-striped business suit? Nikki dressed the way he liked to see a woman dress, not flaunting her curves but not denying it, either. She dressed as if she had enough confidence in her intellect not to have to hide her womanhood behind it.

"I've just finished the salad and dressing. Want to set the table?" she asked brightly.

He hesitated. He couldn't remember ever doing that in his life. Even as a child, there had always been maids who worked in the kitchen.

"The plates are there," she nodded toward a cupboard with her head. "You'll find utensils in the second drawer. Place mats and napkins are in the third drawer." She noticed his expression and his hesitation with faint amusement. "You do know how to set a table?"

"Not really," he admitted.

"Then it's high time you learned," she said. "Someday you may get married, and think how much more desirable you'll be if you know your way around a kitchen."

He didn't react to the teasing with a smile. He stared at her with a curious remoteness and she remembered belatedly the dead wife she wasn't supposed to know about.

"I don't want to marry anyone," he said unexpectedly. "Especially a woman I've only just met," he added without being unkind.

"Well, certainly you don't want to marry me right now," she agreed. "After all, you don't even know me. Sadly, once you discover my worthy traits and my earthy longings, you'll be clamoring to put a ring on my finger. But I'll have to turn you down, you know. I already have a commitment."

His face went hard and his eyes glittered. He turned away from her and began searching in drawers. "Some commitment," he muttered. "The man doesn't even come to check on you. What if a hurricane hit? What if some criminal forced his way in here and raped you, or worse?"

"He phones occasionally," she said demurely.

"What a hell of a concession," he returned. "How do you stand all that attention?"

"I really don't need your approval."

"Good thing. You won't get it. Not that I have any plans other than supper," he added forcefully, glaring at her as he began to put things on the table in strange and mysterious order.

She didn't bother to answer the gibe. "You really should take lessons in how to do a place setting," she remarked, noting that he had the forks in the middle of the plate and the knives lumped together.

"I don't want to make a career of it."

"Suit yourself," she told him. "Just don't blame me if you're never able to get a job as a busboy in one of the better hotels. Heaven knows, I tried to teach you the basics."

He chuckled faintly. She turned and began to put the food on the table. Afterward, she rearranged the place settings until they were as they should be.

"Show-off," he accused.

She curtsied, grinning at him. "Do sit down."

He held the chair out for her, watching when she hesitated. "I am prepared to stand here until winter," he observed.

With a long sigh, she allowed him to seat her. "Archaic custom."

"Courtesy is not archaic, and I have no plans to abandon it." He sat down across from her. "I also say grace before meals — another custom which I have no plans to abandon."

She obediently bowed her head. She liked him. He wasn't shy about standing up for what he believed in.

Halfway through the meal, they wound up in a discussion of politics and she didn't pull her punches.

"I think it's criminal to kill an old forest to save the timbering subsidy," she announced.

His thick eyebrows lifted. "So you should. It is criminal," he added.

She put down her fork. "You're a conservationist?"

"Not exclusively, but I do believe in preservation of natural resources. Why are you surprised?" he added suspiciously.

That was an answer she had to avoid at all costs. She forced a bright, innocent smile to her face. "Most men are in favor of progress."

He studied her very intently for a moment, before he let the idea pass. "I do favor it, but not above conservation, and it depends on what's being threatened. Some species are going to become extinct despite all our best efforts, you do realize that?"

"Yes," she said. "But it seems to me that we're paving everything these days. It's a travesty!"

"I've heard of development projects that

were stopped because of the right sort of intervention by concerned parties. But it isn't a frequent occurrence," he remarked.

"I hate a world that equates might with right."

"Nevertheless, that's how the system works. The people with the most money and power make the rules. It's always been that way, Nikki. Since the beginning of civilization, one class leads and other classes serve."

"At the turn of the century, industrialists used to trot out Scientific Darwinism to excuse the injustices they practiced to further their interests," she observed.

"Scientific Darwinism," he said, surprised. "Yes, the theory of survival of the fittest extended from nature to business." He shook his head. "Incredible."

"It's still done," she pointed out. "Big fish eat little fish, companies which can't compete go under . . ."

"And now we can quote Adam Smith and a few tasty morsels from *The Wealth of Nations*, complete with all the dangers of interfering in business. Let the sinking sink. No government intervention."

She stared at him curiously. "Are you by any chance a closet history minor?" she queried with a smile.

2057/31

"I took a few courses, back in the dark ages," he confessed. "History fascinates me. So does archaeology."

"Me, too," she enthused. "But I know so little about it."

"You could go back to school for those last two semesters," he suggested. "Or, failing that, you could take some extension courses."

She hesitated. "That would be nice."

But she didn't have the means. She didn't have to say it. He knew already. She'd ducked her head as she spoke, and she looked faintly embarrassed.

She had to stop spouting off, she told herself firmly. Her tongue would run too far one day and betray her brother to this man. She hadn't lied about college, though. Part of the terms of her settlement with Mosby Torrance at their divorce was that he would pay for her college education. And he had. She'd worked very hard for her degree. The pain she'd felt at her bad experience had spurred her to great heights, but she hadn't been able to finish. She'd had to drop out just after her junior year to help Clayton campaign. Kane didn't know that.

"What do you do for a living?" he asked suddenly.

She couldn't decide how to answer him. She couldn't very well say that she hostessed for her brother. On the other hand, she did keep house for him.

"I'm a housekeeper," she said brightly, and smiled.

He'd hoped she might have some secret skill that she hadn't shared with him. She seemed intelligent enough. But apparently she had no ambition past being her boyfriend's kept woman. That disappointed him. He liked ambitious, capable women. He was strong himself and he disliked women whom he could dominate too easily or overwhelm.

"I see," he said quietly.

He looked disappointed. Nikki didn't add anything to what she'd said. It was just as well that he lost interest in her before things got complicated, she told herself. After all, she could hardly tell him who she really was.

Chapter Five

Nikki put the dishes away while Kane wandered around the living room, looking at the meager stock of books in the shelves. She sounded like she was well-read, but the only books he noted were rather weathered ones on law.

"They were my father's," she told him. "He wanted to be a lawyer, but he couldn't afford the time."

Or the money, Kane thought silently. He glanced at her. "Don't you have books of your own?"

"Plenty. They're not here, though. The house tends to flood during storms and squalls, so we . . . I —" she caught herself "— don't leave anything really valuable here."

As if she probably had anything valuable. His dark eyes slid over her body quietly, enjoying its soft curves but without sending blatant sexual messages her way.

"You don't look at me as other men do," she said hesitantly. His eyebrows arched and she laughed self-consciously. "I mean," she amended, "that you don't make me feel inferior or cheap. Women are rather defensive when men wolf whistle and make catcalls. Perhaps they don't realize how threatening it can be to a woman when she's by herself. Or perhaps they do."

"You're very attractive. I suppose a man who lacks verbal skills uses the only weapons he has."

"Weapons." She tasted the word and made a face. "They are, aren't they? Weapons to demean and humiliate."

He moved closer. "You're destroying my illusions," he told her. "I was just thinking that you were unique — a woman comfortable in her femininity."

"Oh, I am," she said. "I enjoy being a woman. But there are looks and words that make me uncomfortable. I dislike harassment."

"Would you believe that men can be made just as uncomfortable by aggressive women?" he asked softly.

She laughed a little. "I suppose so. But one doesn't think of women making men uncomfortable."

"You'd be amazed," he confessed.

Her thin eyebrows drew slightly together. "Is she aggressive?"

He stilled. "She?"

"The woman you . . . your lover."

She was perceptive, he thought. Too perceptive. He smiled, but it wasn't a pleasant smile. "Yes," he said. "She's learned how to make me impotent, in fact, and she seems to enjoy it."

She flushed. "Sorry." She sat down on the sofa, busying herself with arranging the pillows.

"Oh, hell, I'm sorry, too," he said gruffly. He sat down in the armchair across from her, his arms crossed on his knees as he stared at her until she met his dark eyes. "You're remarkably inhibited for a woman your age."

"Am I?" She smiled vacantly.

It should have discouraged him. It didn't. His eyes narrowed as his mind started adding up discrepancies between her flirtatious nature and her reaction to blatant comments. "The man you're living with," he began. "You are lovers, aren't you?"

She stared at him while her mind struggled with answers that wouldn't give her completely away.

His lips parted and he let out a slow breath. "There's only one answer that fits this whole setup," he said quietly. "The man you share this beach house with . . . is he gay?"

She shifted uncomfortably. She couldn't let him think that about the owner of the beach house, in case he found out somewhere down the road that it belonged to Clayton Seymour. On the other hand, her face had already given away the fact that she didn't sleep with the owner of the beach house.

"No," she said shortly. "He most certainly is not gay."

His eyes narrowed. "Then how can you be committed to him when he's never here? Or are you just a one-night stand he can't shake off?"

She got to her feet, her eyes blazing. "You make a great deal of assumptions for a man who knows nothing about my situation."

He got up, too. He shrugged, sticking his hands in his pockets as he studied her. "You don't add up. All I want is a straight answer. Do you have a lover or not?"

He'd put it in such a way that she could answer it if she wanted to, without implicating her brother. "I'm no maiden," she said — and it was true, because she'd been married to Mosby.

"I hardly supposed you were," he returned. His eyes slowly wandered over her. "I want you," he said bluntly.

She stared at him levelly. Well, what had she expected, professions of love eternal and a sparkly diamond? She drew in a slow breath. "For how long?"

"Until we get tired of each other," he said.

He was ruthless. She'd suspected that he was, but it was disconcerting to have proof. It was a good thing that she hadn't dashed in headfirst. She studied the floor at her feet, her eyes idly on her sandals and her pink-tipped toes. "I told you at the outset that I don't sleep around."

"Yes, you did. But I'm offering you more than that. I've given you the impression that I'm poor. I'm not." He moved closer, his powerful body intimidating as he stood just in front of her, so that the scent of his cologne teased her nostrils. "Nikki, I can pay for you to finish college. I can buy you a place of your own, one that you won't have to share."

She was almost shaking with indignation. Had he no idea what she was like. He knew that she was intelligent, but that counted for nothing. It was a body he wanted in bed, nothing more. She felt cheap, and she didn't like it.

She lifted cold green eyes to his, and he seemed taken aback by the hostility he saw in them. "I don't have a price tag," she told him very evenly.

A cynical smile brushed his hard mouth. "Don't you? Suppose I produced a wedding ring? Would that change your mind?"

At the mention of the words, nightmarish memories made her eyelids flicker. She turned away. "I have no interest in marriage," she said stiffly.

"Then you're a rarity in the world." He grew more impatient and irritated by the second. She wasn't reacting as he'd expected. "Most women would trade themselves for the right offer."

Her hands clenched at her sides while she struggled for composure. She'd had years of practice at the polite, meaningless smile she used on overbearing people. She dredged it up now.

"Then perhaps you'd better fall back on the few you already know," she said. "I'd like for you to leave now."

"I thought I was doing you a favor by being honest," he replied, because he saw her clenched hands.

She was finding that out. "You're absolutely right, you did. It's marvelous to find out that my intelligence and my personality count for nothing with you, that as far as you're concerned, I'm just a slab of meat after all."

He scowled. "You weren't exactly a shrinking violet yesterday."

"One kiss and you think you're irresistible?" she asked, wide-eyed.

That did it. His eyes blazed with dark rage. "Who the hell do you think you are?" he demanded.

"Only a woman you've propositioned, don't let it worry you. I'm sure you'll trip over willing bodies on your way back to your own house. Do drive carefully. Thank you for the fishing trip. And goodbye," she added, smiling.

How he hated that damned plastic smile! He turned on his heel and strode angrily to the front door. He couldn't remember ever having felt such a violent hatred of a woman.

He went home in a stupor, uncertain why he'd made such a blatant proposition to someone for whom he was beginning to feel a rare tenderness. He didn't understand his own behavior.

It was worse when he remembered how she'd clung to him on the beach the day before, and how much he'd wanted to make love to her right there on the sand. He felt frankly threatened by his own confusion. His desire for her was growing by the second. He needed a woman tonight, badly, to get Nikki out of his thoughts.

But calling Chris was out of the question. He had two other women friends with whom he could satisfy these inconvenient longings. The problem was, they were halfway in love with him. He couldn't take one of them to bed without encouraging her. Damn the luck, he thought furiously. It was Nikki who'd aroused him, but she was the one woman in the world he didn't dare go to for satisfaction. What a joke fate had played on him!

Nikki cleaned up the house and went to sit on the deck. It was stormy-looking. There were dark clouds over the ocean, and she hoped the predictions of that tropical depression turning into a full fledged tropical storm were false. She had enough storms in her life.

She wondered if any other woman had ever rejected Kane Lombard after such a blatant proposition. Probably not, once they knew who he was. He had money all right, but what hurt the most was that he'd assumed that because he thought Nikki had none, he felt justified in using money as bait to get her into bed with him.

She dashed away angry tears. She

doubted if he'd gone home to spend the night alone. He had a little black book. His photograph wasn't well-known, but he made the gossip columns, just the same. There had been stories in the media about his flings with women, after his wife's untimely death. He'd been almost a playboy, if the gossip columns could be believed. He wouldn't have to go far to find consolation, she knew, and she hated him for that, too.

Mosby had rejected her because he didn't like women. Kane had only wanted to have an affair with her. She seemed destined to spend her life alone.

She tried to tell herself that it was just as well. After all, she had no self-confidence. After her sad interlude with Mosby, she didn't trust her judgment anyway. But Kane wasn't like Mosby.

Well, it was for the best. She didn't want to become addicted to a man her brother hated and that had already been in danger of happening. She was halfway in over her head and she might be grateful to him for calling it quits, she told herself. He might have just saved her heart from being completely broken. One day, Kane Lombard would have found out her real identity. But her depression lasted far into the night, and the next day, just the same.

Clayton had flown back to Charleston for the weekend, taking a sulky Derrie with him. She'd had a date with a promising Washington politician for a play and Clayton had deliberately conned her into this trip and out of D.C. For some reason that he didn't quite understand, he didn't want his executive assistant dating anyone.

It had needled him, that acerbic comment from Bett, the woman he'd been dating casually, about his sister. Bett didn't like Derrie, either. She considered Southern women too helpless and man-loving to be real, and she held them in contempt for what she felt was behavior demeaning to women. Derrie, on the other hand, held Bett in contempt for denying her womanhood while trying to become a man with breasts.

"Couldn't you stop glaring at me?" Clayton asked with a hopeful smile. "Your eyebrows are going to grow in that position and you'll look like a wrestler."

Derrie tossed back her blond hair. "Good! Then I can work for myself and make a lot of money."

"You wouldn't enjoy a job that didn't let you spar with me," he said smugly. "You'd be miserable."

"I don't know. I might adopt one of those poor little spotted owls whose houses you're going to help cut down!"

Now he was glaring back. "I'm not personally going to evict one single feathered resident of the northwest forest."

"You're going to vote for a bill that does," she returned. She squared her shoulders, obviously setting down to fight.

"We have to provide jobs for the loggers," he began halfheartedly.

"Great idea. If you want to keep those men working, fund programs to retrain them. You'll have to do it eventually, when all the forests are gone."

"Forests are being replanted," he said curtly. "You're not listening."

"I am. You're not. Forests are being cut down much faster than they can be replaced. Before you sit on that issue with your full weight, it wouldn't hurt to read a few contrary opinions on it." Her chin lifted. "While we're on the subject, it might be just as well if you talked to a few people besides Ms. Watts about it. She is a lobbyist. They aren't paying her to tell you both sides of the issue — only theirs. And she's working for the timber industry."

"I hadn't forgotten," he said, his voice growing strained.

"Do remember when you vote," she added, getting out of her seat once the plane was down, "that the American taxpayers aren't getting the benefit of having Ms. Watts in bed with them. So they might not appreciate her position in the same way you do."

He got up in one lightning motion, more angry than he could ever remember being. "One day, so help me, Derrie . . . !" he burst out furiously.

"Oh, am I not supposed to know that you're sleeping with her?" she asked with feigned innocence. "Why, how could I not know, when she's advertised your relationship to everyone who works in the building!"

His jaw clenched. Derrie was exaggerating. She must be. "That's unfair."

"I wouldn't call it that, when she pulled a pair of her lacy pink panties out of your middle desk drawer in front of an aide and two administrative assistants," she said with fierce distaste. "Didn't she tell you she'd done it? My, my. How thoughtless."

While he was absorbing that blow, she turned and walked down the aisle toward the exit. Still vibrating with rage and sudden uncertainty about his entire position, Clayton left the bags for his assistant and started toward the front of the plane. But he didn't hurry. He wasn't anxious to catch up with her until he cooled down.

Mark Davis, a junior member of Clayton Seymour's staff and a former investigative journalist, had uncovered an interesting little tidbit with some help from Senator Torrance's district director, John Haralson. He was savoring it in the privacy of his apartment while he poured the remains of a bottle of gin into a glass of ice and water. Haralson had all but given him the low-down, swearing him to secrecy about how he'd obtained his information. Haralson had said that he didn't want to be directly connected with it, so he was giving the credit to Davis.

"Nice," he mused to himself. "Very, very nice." He'd connected with a representative from the biggest and best of the local waste disposal companies. The Coastal Waste Company man had told him that Kane Lombard had, without reason, suddenly dissolved his contract with the solid waste disposal group and replaced them with what was a little-known local company.

The CWC representative was still fuming about the incident, which had been inexplicable — his company had an impeccable reputation all over the southeast for its handling of dangerous waste disposal. CWC had drivers who were specially trained for the work. They used vehicles designated for only the purpose of handling toxic materials, and the vehicles were double insulated for safety. The drivers were trained in how to handle an accident, what to do in case of a leakage. The company had even been spotlighted on the national news for the excellence of its work. And now without reason, Kane Lombard had fired them. The damage to their reputation was at the head of their concern.

Had they tried to contact Lombard to find out his reason, Mark had asked. Of course they had, the CWC representative replied. But Lombard had refused to answer the call. That, too, was odd. He was a man known for not dodging controversy or argument.

What was very interesting was the name of the new solid waste contractor. Burke. There had been a local concern under that name which had been sued only a year back for dumping chemicals from an electroplating company directly into a vacant field instead of the small town's landfill. The contaminants had gotten into a stream on the property and some cattle on a neighboring piece of land had died. The farmer had seen something suspicious in the stream and had it chemically analyzed. His attorney had asked some questions and learned that a neighbor had seen Burke and his truck in the vicinity several times.

It hadn't been hard to connect the electroplating residue with Burke, since there was only one electroplating company in the county and none of its refuse was permitted at the landfill. The farmer had taken Burke to court and the city attorney had an inquiry underway. But the impending litigation hadn't stopped Burke. He was still hauling off waste in two dilapidated old trucks, and he wasn't seen taking any of his shipments into the city's landfills. Which raised the question of where he was taking it.

Mark smiled as he kicked off his shoes, put his glass on the bedside table, and sprawled on the bed. Lombard had already barely escaped a charge for letting sewage from the plant leak into the river. He was already on every environmentalist's list of prospective targets. Haralson had said that he had a hunch about a dumping site, but he'd have to have outside help to do any more digging.

116

If they could link Burke to Lombard's company and then to some illegal dumping site, the resulting explosion should be enough to knock the man's socks off. Lombard would be in over his head in no time, and the fact that Clayton would have brought the charges would help him in his reelection campaign. It might even turn attention away from the spotted-owl controversy. He and Derrie had tried their best to keep Clayton from getting involved in that debate. But perhaps this would smooth over the controversy.

Some days, Mark thought smugly, things just couldn't help going right. He picked up the telephone receiver and began to dial Clayton's house number. It was Friday night and Clayton Seymour was very predictable in one way: he was always home in Charleston by seven on a Friday evening.

He'd expected the candidate to sound tired, but Seymour actually snapped at him when he answered the telephone. "What is it that couldn't wait until Monday?" he added tersely.

Mark hesitated. "Perhaps this isn't a good time to talk about it," he said, faintly ruffled. "But I thought you'd like to know that Kane Lombard has contracted with a fly-by-night waste disposal company that's suspected of dumping toxic waste some-where in the coastal marshes."

"What?!"

That did it. Mark grinned. "Can you be-lieve it? He's been so careful in every other area not to antagonize anyone about con-servation issues. Now here he goes and hires a local man with a really bad reputa-tion to dump his toxic waste. And he fires a company with the best reputation in the business to do it!"

"Facts, Mark, facts."

"I've got them. Give me a few days and I'll prove it."

"Remind me to give you a raise. Several raises."

Mark laughed out loud. "In that case, you can have the videotapes in stereo with subtitles."

"Good man. I knew I made the best choice when I hired you. Don't cross the line, though," he cautioned. "Don't give him any ammunition to use against us."

"I'll make sure I don't."

"Thanks."

He hung up, his former bad humor gone in a flash of delight. Lombard had publicly announced his intention to fund the cam-paign of Clayton's Democratic opponent for his House seat and one of Lombard's brothers was Democratic candidate Sam Hewett's executive administrative aide. Not only that, Lombard had been making some nasty, snide comments about Seymour having the background but not the brains and know-how to do the job.

This might be a little on the shady side, to expose a potential adversary's chief supporter thwarting the environmental laws. But if it gave Clayton a wedge to use in the election, then he was going to use it. He'd been bested too many times by people without scruples.

At least he didn't take money under the table, he thought, rationalizing his use of what Nikki would call gutter tactics. No doubt Nikki would disapprove, if she knew. But then, he added, he would be doing the city a service, wouldn't he? And perhaps it would make people stop hounding him about that infernal owl!

In the meanwhile, there was no reason for Nikki to know anything yet. She needed her vacation. He wasn't going to spoil it by calling her up to tell her how he was gaining on his rival. There would be plenty of time for that later.

He couldn't help but wonder how young Mark had managed to dig up such a tasty scandal for him. He really would have to watch that eager young man. He was an asset.

Derrie unpacked her bags in her small apartment and lamented about the nice dinner and play she could have been enjoying if Clayton hadn't dragged her back to Charleston with him. He never worked on Saturday, but he'd convinced her that tomorrow was going to be the exception and he couldn't work without her.

Not that she cared much about the D.C. official she'd been going to share the dinner and play with. In fact, he was something of a bore. But it had been an opportunity to show Clayton that he wasn't the only fish swimming within hook range.

Who am I kidding, she asked her reflection in the mirror. She had two new gray hairs among the thick blonde ones. She also had wrinkles at the corners of her big dark blue eyes, and dark circles beneath them from lack of sleep. She'd worked for Clayton for three years in Washington and he never noticed her at all. He was too busy enjoying the companionship that his political standing gave him.

He was very discreet, but there were women in his life. Derrie stood on the sidelines handing him letters to sign and reminding him of appointments, and he never did more than tease her about her deprived social life. Which was his fault, of course, since she didn't want to go out with anyone except her stupid boss.

The newly-elected congressman who'd taken her with him to Washington three years ago was changing before her eyes, she asserted as she got ready for bed. He'd run for the office on a conservation platform, but it was eroding these days. His lack of defense for the spotted owl was just the latest in a line of uncharacteristic actions lately.

It was the first issue Derrie had braced him on, but not the first she'd opposed. He'd had angry letters from any number of constituents about his voting record during the present session of Congress. He'd voted against most environmental issues, ever since he'd been sleeping with Bett. He'd hired that investigative reporter right off the local news show, and was using him to find flaws in other people's characters that he could use for leverage to accrue votes for issues he championed. And he was suddenly associating a lot with his ex-brother-in-law, Senator Mosby Torrance, an active anticonservation and pro-liberal advocate. He was also voting the way

Torrance wanted him to on major bills. In fact, he'd introduced a couple of bills for Torrance.

Derrie wondered if Nikki had noticed these changes in Clayton's personality. Nikki hadn't been well, and Clayton had spent more time in Washington than ever during the past six months. It was well-known that Bett and Senator Torrance were occasional companions. Perhaps he was using Bett to entice Clayton. Or perhaps there was some other connection. No one knew why Nikki and Mosby had broken up. Knowing Nikki as she did, Derrie blamed Torrance. Anyone who couldn't live with Nikki had to be a basket case.

She climbed into bed and pulled up the covers, heartsick and demoralized. She'd never argued so much with Clayton before. Now it seemed she was fated never to do anything else. She really must have a long talk with Nikki about him . . .

Bett Watts was going over accounts on her computer when the telephone rang stridently. She reached out a hand distractedly to pick it up.

"Bett?"

She turned away from the computer.

"Yes. Hello, Mosby. What can I do for you?"

"You can tell me that you've convinced Clayton to let me handle this thing about Lombard."

"Don't worry," she said gently. "I can promise you that. I've got him right in my little fingers."

"My God, I hope so. Don't let him do anything on his own, do you understand? Nothing!"

She hesitated. "Well, certainly, I'll take care of it. But, why?"

"Never mind. I'll tell you what you need to know. Good night."

She hung up, curious, but not worried. Mosby was careful and discreet. But she did wonder what he had in mind.

Chapter Six

It had been so simple at first, Kane told himself as he piloted his sailboat out into the Atlantic. All he had to do was ignore Nikki and her influence would disappear like fog in the hot sun. But she hadn't. It had been three days and he was more consciously aware of his own loneliness than he could remember being since the death of his wife and son a year ago.

He lifted his dark face into the breeze and enjoyed the touch of it on his leonine features. One of his forebears had been Italian, another Spanish, and even another one Greek. He had the blood of the Mediterranean in his veins, so perhaps that explained why he loved sailing so much.

He glanced over his shoulder at his crew. They were working furiously to put up the spinnaker, and as it set, his heart skipped a beat. The wind slid in behind it, caressed it, then suddenly filled it like a passionate lover and the sailboat jerked and plowed ahead through the water.

The wind in his hair tore through it like mad fingers. Kane laughed at the sheer joy of being alive. It was always like this when he sailed. He loved the danger, the speed, the uncertainty of the winds and the channels. In colonial days, he was sure that he would have been a pirate. At the very least, he'd have been a sailing man. There was nothing else that gave him such a glorious high. Not even sex.

He spun the wheel and brought the sailboat about to avoid collision with a lunatic in a high-powered motorboat. He mumbled obscenities under his breath as he fought the wake of the other boat.

"Damned fools," he muttered.

Jake, his rigger, only laughed. "It's a big ocean. Plenty of room for all sorts of lunatics."

The older man was wiry and tough. He had red hair, going gray, and a weather-beaten sort of leathery skin. Jake had crewed for the yacht *Stars and Stripes* with Dennis Connor in the America's Cup trials the year she won the race. Like the other tough seamen who survived that grueling sport, Jake had a freeness of spirit that gave him a kinship with Kane. From the time Kane was a boy, he had looked to Jake for advice and support in hard times. The older man was in many ways more his father than the tabloid owner in New York who shared his name.

"You're troubled," Jake observed as they traveled seaward amid the creaking of the lines and the flap of the spinnaker as Kane tacked.

"Yes."

"Bad memories?" Jake probed.

Kane took a slow breath. "Complications. I seem to be acquiring them in bunches like bananas lately. Especially one slender brunette one."

"A woman. Not a professional woman . . . ?"

Kane chuckled. "No. She's the pipe and slippers sort, to be avoided at all costs."

"Not like Chris, in other words."

Kane gave him a narrow look. "No. Definitely not like Chris. She isn't an opportunist."

"What is she?"

"Intelligent and proud," he muttered. "Possessive. Independent." He didn't want to talk about her. "I don't want another hard fall. One in a lifetime is enough."

"Oh, by all means, avoid entanglements," the older man agreed easily. He glanced up at the ballooned sail and smiled as he admired the set of it. "We're making good time. We really ought to enter this baby in the Cup trials."

"I don't want to sail in the Cup."

"Why not?"

"For one reason — because I don't have the time."

Jake shrugged philosophically. "I can't argue with that. But you're missing the thrill of a lifetime."

"No, I'm not. Look out there," he said, gesturing toward the horizon. "This is the thrill of a lifetime, every minute I spend on this deck. I don't have to prove anything to the world, least of all that I'm the best sailor in the water."

"Nice to feel that way. Most of us feel we have to live up to some invisible, indefinable goal."

"Why bother? You can't please most people. Please yourself instead."

Jake leaned against the rail and stared at him, hard. "That's selfish."

"I'm a selfish man. I don't know how to give." He met Jake's eyes, and his own were cold, leaden. "Like the rest of the minnows in this icy pond we call life, I'm just trying to stay alive in a society that rewards mediocrity and punishes accomplishment and intelligence."

"Cynic."

"Who wouldn't be? My God, man, look around you! How many people do you know who wouldn't cut your throat to get ahead or make a profit?"

"One. Me."

Kane smiled. "Yeah. You."

"You're restless. Isn't it about time we went back to Charleston and you did what you do best?"

"What do I do best," he asked absently, "run the company or make waves for the local politicians?"

"Both. I don't run a major business, but I know one thing. It's damned risky to leave subordinates in charge, no matter how competent they are. Things go wrong."

Kane turned to study his friend. "Something you know from experience, right?"

Jake chuckled. "Yeah. I sat out half a race and we lost the Cup."

"Not your fault."

"Tell me that every day. I might believe it." He glanced out over the sea toward the horizon. "Storm blowing up. We're in for some weather. It might be a good idea to head back, before you get caught up in the joy of fighting the sea again," he added with a dark look.

Kane had cause to remember the last time he'd been in a battle with the ocean during a gale. He'd laughed and brought the boat in, but Jake hadn't enjoyed the ride. He'd been sick.

"Go ahead, laugh," Jake muttered.

"Sorry. I need a challenge now and again, that's all," he said apologetically. "Something to fight, someone to fight. I guess the world sits on me sometimes and I have to get it out of my system."

"The world sits on us all, and you've more reason to chafe than most. It's just a year today, isn't it?"

"A year." Kane didn't like remembering the anniversary of the car bomb that had killed his family. He scowled and turned the wheel, tacking suddenly and sharply, so that the sailboat leaned precariously.

"Watch it!" Jake cautioned. "We could capsize, even as big as we are."

"I hate anniversaries," Kane said heatedly, hurt in his deep voice. "I hate them!"

Jake laid a heavy, warm hand on the broad, husky shoulder of his friend. "Peace, compadre," he said gently. "Peace. Give it time. You'll get through it."

Kane felt sick inside. The wounds opened from time to time, but today was the worst. The sea spray hit him in the face, and the wind chilled it where it was wettest. He stared ahead and tried not to notice that there were warm tracks in the chilled skin.

Chris was waiting for him in the beach house when he returned. He didn't like her assumption that she could walk in and boss his people around whenever she felt like it. She was giving Todd Lawson hell because he was drinking up Kane's scotch whiskey. Ironically, she was sharing it with him.

What, he wondered, was Lawson doing here?

He walked in, interrupting the argument. They both turned toward him. Lawson was tall, just over six feet, very blond and craggy-faced. He was an ex-war correspondent and had the scars to prove it. He also had a real problem with career women, and his expression as he glowered at Chris punctuated it.

"I see you've met," Kane remarked. He went to the bar and poured himself two fingers of scotch, adding an ice cube to the mixture.

"Wouldn't collided be a better choice of words?" Chris asked testily. She glared back at Lawson. "Shall I leave, so that you *men* can discuss business?"

"Why?" Lawson asked innocently. "Don't you consider yourself one of us?"

Chris's face went an ugly color. From

the severely drawn back hair to the pin-striped suit and bralessness under it, she felt the words like a blood-letting whip. She whirled on her heel and departed, so uncharacteristically shaken that she did it without even a word to Kane. Normally, Kane might have taken up for her. But today was a bad day. His grief was almost tangible.

"No purse, either," Lawson drawled, watching her empty-handed departure. "Don't tell me. It's a sellout to carry some-thing traditionally female."

Kane lifted an eyebrow. "What do you want?" he asked, irritation in the look he bent on his family's star reporter.

"To tell you what I've uncovered."

Kane's hand stilled with the glass of scotch held gingerly in it. "Well?"

"You take your scotch neat," Lawson re-marked, moving closer. "I suppose you can take your bad news the same way. Seymour is after you. The rumor is that he's got something he can use to get you on envi-ronmental charges. Since that little inci-dent last month, he's confident that he can find something."

"That incident was an accidental spill into the river," Kane said curtly. "We weren't charged."

"Not for that, no. But evidently Seymour thinks where there's one accident there are bound to be others."

Kane ran his hand through his windblown hair. He knew there were problems with his plant manager being absent so much, and there was a new man in charge of waste control. The new man had been responsible for the sewage leak. He was just new, that was all. He told Lawson so.

"New or not, he's clumsy. You can't afford to let this go without looking into it."

"Why is Seymour on my tail?"

"Because your family's tabloid is crucifying him over his support for the loggers, because your brother Norman is Sam Hewett's new executive administrative assistant for his campaign, and because your whole family is endorsing Hewett, Seymour's major Democratic opponent. But I think Seymour's ex-brother-in-law is behind this campaign to smear you."

"What ex-brother-in-law?"

"Senator Mosby Torrance."

Kane frowned. "Why would he be after me? He's a business advocate — notoriously a jobs-over-environment man. The Sierra Club would furnish the firewood to burn him at the stake. Like Seymour," he continued, "he's supporting the opponents of the spotted owl in the northwest."

"The spotted owl won't hurt Torrance very much right now because he doesn't have to run for reelection this year. But Seymour does, and the spotted owl bill has hurt him at home," Lawson said cynically. "However, a few well-placed and well-timed blows at industrial pollution in his home district could kindle a lot of public opinion in his favor and put him back in Washington. I don't know what he's found, but he's got something. You can bet if John Haralson is helping him — and he is — he's got something."

"Haralson."

"Senator Torrance's district director. Mr. Sleaze," he added curtly. "The original dirty tricks man."

"Working for Seymour? That doesn't sound like Seymour. I'm a Democrat from the feet up, but even so, from what I've read about Seymour, he's never been a politician who tried to smear anybody for personal gain. He's an idealist."

"Perhaps he's learned that idealism is a euphemism for naïveté in politics. You can't change the world."

"That doesn't stop people from trying, does it?"

"Seymour is going to concentrate on you. Your family news tabloid has been his major embarrassment since this spotted owl thing began, and the press coverage he's been given has cost him points in the polls. If he can connect you with anything shady, the inference is that he can cost your family some credibility. That will also hurt Hewett — because your brother is his senior advisor. That's what your father thinks, anyway," he added.

"You're his star reporter," Kane said. "What do you think?"

Lawson put his empty glass down. "I think you'd better make sure there's nothing to connect your company with any more environmental damage."

"I told you, that sewage leak was purely accidental. I don't have anything shady to worry about."

"You sound very sure of yourself," Lawson said quietly. "But you've been away from work for a couple of weeks."

"I have competent managers," Kane said, getting more irritated by the minute.

"Do you?" Lawson straightened. He was almost Kane's own height. "Then why have you turned out a reputable company like CWC?"

"CWC." Kane nodded. "Oh, yes, I remember. I had a talk with the new solid waste manager. He said that CWC had done a sloppy job at enormous cost. He wanted permission to replace the company and get someone more efficient — and a little less expensive."

"That's very interesting. CWC has a very good reputation. One of the national news magazines recently did a piece on them. They're very efficient and high-tech."

Lombard pursed his lips and scowled. "Are they? Well, perhaps they've fallen down on the job. I'll look into it when I get back to Charleston. Meanwhile, what have you found out about Seymour?"

"Not much. But I've got a few rumors to check out about Seymour's connection with Mosby Torrance."

Kane laughed coldly. "Dig deep. I may need some leverage if he finds anything. Good God, I take a few days off and everything falls apart. I'd better telephone the plant and talk to that new man."

"I wouldn't," the other man advised. "Let me check around first."

"Why?"

"If there's any under-the-table dealing going on, the fewer people who know we suspect, the better."

"It won't do me any good to wait if Seymour's investigator finds anything illegal going on."

"That's what worries us," Lawson said. "Our sources think Seymour has found something. Worse, they think there may be some deliberate evidence." He stressed the words.

Kane rubbed the back of his neck, wincing as he touched a sunburned area. "When it rains, it pours," he said to himself.

Lawson put down his glass. "Well, all I have are suspicions right now, mainly because of Haralson's involvement. But I'll let you know if anything surfaces."

Kane nodded, his mind already away from the small problem of waste disposal and back on Nikki.

John Haralson was sitting in Mosby Torrance's office, grinning from ear to ear.

"What do you know? Lombard's company just kicked out CWC in favor of old fly-by-night Burke. Remember him? He was charged with dumping toxic waste in a swamp a year or more ago and he weaseled out of the charge."

"How do you know?" Mosby asked curiously.

Haralson pretended innocence. "Contacts. I have all sort of contacts."

Mosby studied the older man curiously. Haralson tended to work miracles, and usually Mosby didn't question how he accomplished them. But just lately, Haralson seemed to be getting a bit out of hand. He had to be more careful. His private life was precarious right now, he couldn't afford to have Haralson making anyone angry enough to start digging into Mosby's past.

"Go on."

"Well, Burke ordinarily charges about one-fifteenth of what Lombard was paying CWC for hauling off the waste. Now he gets what CWC used to get, and he doesn't have their overhead."

Mosby frowned. "That puts the onus on Lombard's hired man, not on Lombard himself. He's not getting anything out of it."

"We can make it look as if he is," Haralson said smugly. "We don't have to mention the kickbacks to his janitorial man. We can say that Lombard was cutting costs. It's a well-known fact that he's just recently laid off some employees because of the recession."

Mosby hesitated. "You're talking about concealing facts."

"Not permanently," Haralson said smoothly. "Just long enough for the news media to pick up the story and run it a few times. They love dealing with industrial polluters. Save the planet, you know."

"But . . ."

Haralson's eyes narrowed and he leaned forward intently. "If you don't get Lombard's neck in a noose and squeeze, his man is going to eventually uncover the truth about you and Nikki and your marriage. Can you think what that will do to you, if the press get wind of it?"

"Oh, my God," Mosby said, shaken. "It doesn't bear thinking about!"

"That's right. It could cost Seymour the election, and you your seat."

Mosby was sweating. It wasn't the first time he'd compromised his ideals to save his career. And this time he had no choice. "All right. Go ahead and do what you have to." He glanced up. "But make sure that Clayton doesn't know how you're doing it. Do you have an investigator in mind?"

"You bet I do. He works for the Justice Department. He's FBI."

"Hold it, what if we get charged with appropriating personnel . . ."

"It's all right. He's on vacation. They had to threaten to fire him to get him out of the office. He's been sitting around muttering for days about the inactivity. He jumped at the chance when I mentioned I had a small problem."

"Can he keep a confidence?"

"He's a Comanche Indian. You tell me."

"Does he have a name?"

"Sure. It's Cortez."

Mosby found himself grinning, the fear subsiding a little. Haralson always seemed to work magic. "You're kidding me."

"I'm not. One of his great-grandfathers was a Spaniard. He calls it the only bad blood in his family tree. His sense of irony is pretty keen, which is why he uses the anglicized name of the Spanish conqueror of Mexico. He spends his free time in Oklahoma with his parents. There, you couldn't pronounce his name."

"You say he's a good investigator."

"One of the best."

"There won't be a conflict of interest involved?"

"Only if we tell anyone he's helping us," Haralson said innocently.

He got a glare in return for his helpful comment.

"It was a joke! There's no problem," Haralson chuckled. "When he's on vacation, what he does with his free time is his own business. We're not asking him to do anything illegal, are we?"

Mosby wasn't so sure about that. "No. I suppose not. In essence, we're asking him to look for a violation of the Environmental Protection Agency codes."

"That's right. So just pretend I never said a word. I'll do what's necessary to save your bacon."

Mosby's light eyes narrowed. "Don't sweep anything under the carpet," he said.

"Not unless I have to," Haralson promised.

"You want me to save the hide of a *Texan?*"

"Not at all, Cortez . . ." Haralson said quickly, trying to pacify the darker man. Cortez was powerfully muscled, scar-faced, with deep set large black eyes and a rawboned face that seemed to be all sharp, dark angles.

Cortez wasn't handsome, although the tall lean man seemed to draw women just the same. Anyway, his record since he'd joined the FBI was impressive and far outdistanced that of some of the handsomer agents.

"You know I hate Texans," Cortez was saying. He didn't blink. It was one of the

140

more disconcerting things about him.

"If I remember my history, Texans weren't too fond of Comanches, either. But I'm not asking you to help a Texan. I'm asking you to help put one in front of a congressional subcommittee."

"Ah," Cortez said smoothly. "Is that so?"

"It is, indeed. I need a little help. A little detective work . . ."

"I'm on vacation. Do your own detective work."

"Cortez . . . ?" Haralson held out an object on his palm.

The other man hesitated, his brow furrowing. "What is that?"

"You know what it is. You've been trying to beg, borrow, buy or steal it for the past five years. Help me out on this," he added, "and I'll sell it to you at the price you first offered."

Cortez's face hardened. "I don't want it at that price."

"Yes, you do." Haralson flipped it, emphasizing his possession of it.

Cortez groaned. "That's right, hit me in my weakest spot!"

"Always know a man's weaknesses when you plan to trade with him," Haralson chuckled. "Well?"

Cortez pushed back his raven-wing hair,

141

his long fingers settling on the ponytail he wore it in when he was among whites. It seemed to draw more attention when he wore it down. "All right," he said bitterly. "But only because I'm a certifiable collector."

Haralson handed him the coin, a nineteenth-century two-and-a-half dollar gold piece.

"If you knew," Cortez murmured, handling the coin with something akin to reverence, "how many years I've been looking for one of these . . ."

"I do know. After all, I'm the one who bought it out from under you the day Harry in the code section put it on the market and I happened to be at FBI headquarters doing some research for Senator Torrance. I had a feeling it would come in handy one day."

Cortez gave him a skin-scorching glare. "So it did. All right, you'll get your pint of blood. I'll see if I can connect Lombard's larcenous employee to Burke's with something concrete. If I find anything illegal going on, I'll inform the appropriate people."

"Would I expect anything less from you?" Haralson asked with a wicked smile. "Trust me." He put his hand over his

142

heart. "I have a soul."

"If you do, you keep it in your wallet," the Native American agreed. "I know you too well, Haralson. Just don't forget that you may have something on me, but I've got something on you, too. You had knowledge of a crime and didn't report it."

Haralson stared at him uncomfortably. He hadn't thought things through that far. He and Cortez were acquaintances, not really friends, but they occasionally did each other some good.

Cortez didn't smile, he smirked. He didn't like Haralson, but the man could be useful at times. It wouldn't hurt to do him one small favor, so long as it didn't breach any legalities. Cortez followed the very letter of the law in most things. He turned away, coin in hand, and went to pick up his jacket. "I'll be in touch as soon as I've checked out a few people and places."

Nikki had waded out into the surf to watch the distant freighter sail out toward the horizon. She wondered how it had been during Charleston's early days as a port city, when great sailing ships came here, carrying their precious cargoes of spices and rum and, sadly, slaves.

Pirates had come from here, people like

143

female pirate Anne Bonney and her cohort Stede Bonett. Descriptions of those early days had fascinated Nikki in college, so much so that she'd done three courses in colonial history. The somber and dignified George Washington came to life as her professor lectured about the way the old warhorse had put on his old Continental uniform in 1794 and led 15,000 volunteers off to put down the Whiskey Rebellion — and how the rebellious Pennsylvania distillers had quickly dispersed at little more than Washington's threat of dire action. Far from the conventional image of George Washington with his little hatchet, the real man emerged from legend with stark clarity.

She wandered along with her toes catching in the damp sand and felt suddenly alone. Funny how a man she hadn't even known a week ago had made a place for him in her mind, in her heart. He didn't want Nikki in his, of course. He'd made that very plain. She supposed that, not knowing her, he'd classed her as a gold digger and decided to cut his losses before she found out who he was. How amusing that she did know, and had tried to subdue her own interest for equally good reasons.

She felt a chill and wrapped her arms

around herself. Just as well that it was over, she told herself. The chill grew worse. She laughed, because her chest felt cloggy and she'd been sure she was completely cured. She'd make herself a hot cup of soup and see if that wouldn't help. Then she'd have an early night, and soon enough Kane Lombard would become a sad memory.

She woke in the middle of the night coughing uncontrollably. Her throat was sore and her chest hurt. This was going to need the services of a doctor, she realized. She dialed, but Chad Holman wasn't at home. She lay back down. He'd be back soon, she was sure. She'd just close her eyes and phone him later.

But it didn't quite work out that way. She slept and didn't waken until morning. When she did wake, she couldn't talk at all and she was coughing up colored mucus. It didn't take a high IQ to realize that meant an infection. She had bronchitis or a recurrence of pneumonia, and a fever to boot. She was too nauseated even to sit up. She couldn't talk, so how could she call anyone? She could tap on the receiver, but Chad was a doctor, not a communications specialist. She couldn't get word to him to come and see her, although he certainly would, just as he'd come to see Kane. The same would be true of Clayton.

But sailors knew Morse Code, she thought foggily. Certainly, they did! So if she could remember just the distress signal and how to spell her name in Morse, she could get Kane to come. He didn't want her, but in an emergency, that didn't even matter. Thank God she'd taken an interest in Morse Code when Clayton's senior legislative counsel Mary Tanner's boyfriend had bought his first shortwave. He and Mary had broken up years ago, but Nikki still remembered the code.

She had Kane's number. He'd given it to her to telephone him that last morning they'd gone out together. She painstakingly pushed the buttons. There was a pause and then a ringing sound. She waited. Waited. Three rings. Four. Five. Her heart began to sink when the phone was suddenly jerked up and an impatient male voice demanded. "Who's there?"

He was in a hurry. It didn't dawn on her that his housekeeper would normally have been answering the telephone, which was a good thing or she might not even have tried to get him. She tapped on the receiver.

"What the hell . . . ?!"

She made a hoarse sound, afraid that he was going to slam the receiver down. She tried again. S . . . O . . . S . . .

The code caught his attention. "All right, I get the message, you're in trouble and you can't talk. Is it Chris?" he added, because he'd taught her Morse.

One tap. He frowned. "One for no, two for yes. Try again."

One tap.

He hesitated. Who could be doing this? Jake? "Can you give your name in Morse?" he asked.

There was a pause and a cough, and the cough made his breath catch. "*Nikki? Nikki, is it you?*"

Two taps. Two taps. "I'll be there in two minutes."

He put the receiver down and ran out the door.

Nikki lay back on the pillow, weak tears of gratitude rolling down her pale cheeks onto her dry, cracked lips. She hadn't thought he'd understand, but he had. And at least his voice had sounded concerned. That could have been an illusion. At the moment, she didn't care. She only wanted to sleep.

Chapter Seven

Nikki heard him at the door, but she was too weak and sick to know or care how he was going to get in. She only knew that he would. He was the sort who got things done even in an emergency. Nikki recognized that trait because she had it herself. She might go to pieces later, but she was always cool when it mattered most.

Kane discovered an unlocked window and went in through it. He found Nikki on the bed, feverish and sick, sounding as if she were breathing water in and out of her lungs.

"My God," he said quietly.

Her eyes opened, dark green with pain and illness in a face like rice paper. "Kane," she whispered, but her voice made no sound.

He didn't waste a minute. He wrapped her up in the cover and carried her out the door to his waiting car. Ten incredibly fast minutes later, he walked into the nearest emergency room carrying her in his arms.

Time seemed to blur after that. She remembered voices and needles and the coldness of metal against her bare skin. Then she slept, very deeply, and the pain mercifully went away.

When she woke, it was dark and she was lying in an unfamiliar bed. It was king-size, with a white and brown and green color scheme that was repeated in the curtains and the bedclothes. The furniture was dark Mediterranean and as sturdy-looking as the man who obviously lived here.

She stirred, trying to raise herself, but it was just too much of an effort.

Kane opened the door and came in, wearing a black-and-white-toweling robe and nothing else. His dark hair was damp, if neat. He smelled of soap.

"Need something?" he asked quietly.

"I need to get to the bathroom," she whispered hoarsely.

"No problem there." He pulled back the covers, revealing Nikki in a pale blue silk gown, and lifted her gently free. "Silk. Does he buy them for you?" he asked as he carried her toward the bathroom.

"I buy them . . . for myself. Why am I here?" she croaked.

"Because I didn't fancy trying to sleep on that damned bed in your guest room again," he said bluntly. "How can I reach your lover to tell him where you are?"

"He's abroad," she lied shakily. "And I don't know where he is exactly."

He sighed. "Well, that solves one problem, at least. Here." He put her down. "If you need help, don't stand on modesty."

"I won't."

Several minutes later, her face washed, she opened the door and he returned her to bed.

He sat down beside her, disturbing the tie of his robe to reveal a portion of his broad, hairy chest. "Here, swallow this," he said, producing a pill from a small vial. "Doctor's orders," he added when she hesitated.

She took it from his big hand and managed to swallow it past her sore, tight throat. She grimaced as she handed back the glass of water he'd given her. Her eyes lingered on what she could see of his bare skin and as she dragged them away, he glanced down and chuckled at his state of undress.

"Was I giving you a floor show?" he mused. "Does it matter? You know what I look like. You stood in the doorway and stared at me that first morning after I washed up on your beach."

She flushed uncomfortably. "I didn't

know you saw me."

"Oh, I was flattered," he remarked dryly, refastening the robe. "But I've already got a lover."

"Yes, so you've said."

He reached down and touched her skin at the collarbone, feeling the heat and dampness of her skin, her involuntary withdrawal from his fingertips.

"I said some harsh things," he said quietly. "You can't forget them. Probably it's a good thing. I have too many complications in my life right now."

"So do I," she whispered. "I only wanted to be friends. I never said I wanted to be your lover."

"That's true," he said lazily. "But your eyes say it all the time." He lifted his hand and softly traced around a taut nipple, watching her reaction to the blatant intimacy. Her body shivered and she caught her breath. "What a fierce reaction for such an innocent little caress, Nikki," he said, his voice deep and seductive. His big hand flattened over her breast, feeling its firm, hot contour while his thumb and forefinger worked tenderly at the hard nub that crowned it. She was gasping now, even if her hand did raise to catch his wrist in a token protest.

His eyes were steady and speculative on her face. She wasn't accustomed to this kind of intimacy. Like a rank innocent, she was torn between the need to protest and the longing to submit. The pleasure she was feeling was all too evident. So was an odd fear.

"Doesn't he make love to you at all?" he asked quietly. "You're starved for a man's touch."

"Please . . . don't," she said, shaken.

His dark eyes slid down to the clinging fabric. Only spaghetti straps held the bodice in place, and he'd already dislodged one. His hand moved, slowly tugging it the rest of the way down until he bared her breast to the mauve rise of her nipple. Her eyes widened on his face, as if she couldn't believe what was happening.

"You let me touch it. Now, are you going to let me see it?" he whispered deeply.

Her nails bit into his wrist. This couldn't be happening! She was sick, she was helpless, perhaps it was the medicine . . .

"Yes," he murmured, completing the slow descent of the silk, and his eyes found her, enjoyed her, took pleasure from the exquisite creamy firmness of her breast in the sudden silence of the room.

No one had ever made her feel that she

might die if he didn't do more than look. Not even in her younger days, before Mosby destroyed her confidence in her femininity, had she known such a primitive need.

"You have a little fever, still," he said, letting his fingertips touch her, trace her, worship her. "Your skin is hot to the touch. Especially here, Nikki, where it's hardest. It makes you tremble when I caress it, doesn't it? It makes you want to pull me down and wrap your legs around my hips and pull me into you, because you know that's the only thing that's going to make the aching stop."

"Damn . . . you!" she choked.

"You don't want it any less than I do," he whispered. "Look, Nikki. Let me show you."

He stood up, his body vibrating with the same fever that held her captive. His hands loosened the single knot that held his robe in place. He pushed it aside and dropped it, and stood before her with magnificent pride in his aroused masculinity, in the perfection of his tall, hard-muscled body without a single white line to mar the even tan that covered it.

Nikki's face colored, but she couldn't look away. He was beautiful. Her eyes traced him with the same rapt fascination an artist would bend on a work of art. He was a work of art.

"You are utter perfection," she whispered.

"So are you." His legs held a faint tremor as he looked and wanted her just short of the point of madness.

"Oh, Kane," she bit off, too weak and shaky to do anything at all about the anguish of her need.

"It's been a very long time since I've been this aroused," he said matter-of-factly. "But you're hardly in any condition to satisfy me."

With sheer force of will, he picked up his robe and shouldered back into it. Nikki lay watching him, helpless, submissive as she never would have been if she'd been completely well.

"That could become addictive," he mused, watching her pull up the loosened spaghetti strap to stay the confusion his dark eyes were causing.

"What?"

"Letting you look at me," he said, smiling faintly. "I can never remember wanting the lights on before, when I was aroused like this. Have you ever made love in the light, Nikki?"

She couldn't stop shaking. "I feel ill," she whispered.

"You are ill, little one," he said, contrite as he realized how ill she'd been. "And I'm a brute for behaving like this. The sight of you in that gown has made me mindless, I suppose. You need rest, not sexual innuendoes."

"Were they only that?" she asked unguardedly, watching his face close up at the question.

"I wish I could tell you that they were," he replied curtly. "But the fact remains that a relationship between you and me wouldn't work."

"Are you sure?" she asked hesitantly.

He sat down beside her, his expression one of reluctant resignation. "Nikki, a year ago my wife and son were killed in an explosion," he said bluntly. "I'm not coping very well, despite the lover I told you about. Sometimes nightmares keep me awake. I don't know how I feel, because I've tried so hard not to. It's too soon," he concluded roughly.

"I'm very sorry," she said gently. "You must miss them terribly."

"I do." He put his head in his hands and leaned his elbows on his knees. "I miss them every day of my life. God, I'm so tired."

"Am I contagious?" she asked after a minute.

"I don't know. Some types of pneumonia are. Some aren't."

"If you don't mind the risk, you might climb in here with me," she said, croaking with every word.

He looked down at her cold-eyed. "Why?"

She managed a weak smile. "Because you look very much as if you need someone to hold you." She pulled her arms free of the covers and held them up to him.

He was still wondering two hours later why he'd gone so eagerly into those out-stretched arms. It hadn't been sex, because what he'd felt in her embrace was nothing if it wasn't tenderness. He'd rolled over with her, cradling the length of her overwarm body to his, holding her as he tried to cope with the nightmare his life had become.

She'd smoothed his dark hair, whispering soft incoherences, and after a time, the edge of the pain had been dulled and he felt a sigh of peace ease out of his broad chest.

"It's all right to be alive, even if they can't be," she whispered at his ear. "They love you, too, and miss you, and know where you are. In some sense or other, they know."

His big hands flattened on her back, feeling the warmth of her seep into him, making him stronger. It was an incredible sensation, as if they were touching inside somehow, mind and heart and spirit. He wasn't sure he wanted to. On the other hand, the wonder of it overshadowed his doubts and fears, and suddenly all he could think about was how sweet it was to hold her. But it wasn't close enough.

"No," he whispered when she softly protested the sweep of his hands carrying away her gown. "No, let me. I want to be close to you all night. I won't take you. Let me hold you like this."

While he spoke, he shouldered out of his robe, and seconds later she was lying nude against his equally bare body. She shivered at the unfamiliar contact and tried to pull away, but he wouldn't permit it.

"You're afraid," he whispered, and his voice was both surprised and tender. "There's no reason to be. You're an invalid and I have too much conscience to take advantage of it."

"Are you sure?" she asked nervously.

His hands swept down her spine and he groaned pleasurably as he felt her silky skin in exquisite detail, her breasts on his chest, her belly against the helpless thrust of his body.

"No, I'm not sure, but I can't let you go," he murmured roughly. His hands pressed gently at the base of her spine and moved her, his long leg trespassing between her thighs.

"No," she said quickly, staying his hip. "No, don't."

He lifted his head and looked into her frightened eyes. None of this made sense. He moved back, but his hand slowly eased down and, containing her shocked jerk, he whispered her name softly and kissed her frightened eyes closed. The caresses weakened her resolve. He was touching her . . . !

She caught his arm, but it didn't stop him. He was slow and tender, but relentless. When she felt the sudden twinge of pain, she was unprepared for his shocked roar.

"My God!"

She swallowed. Her legs were trembling from the pleasure of his intimate testing of her, but her hand pulled at his invading one.

"You can't know," she said weakly. "A man can't know . . ."

He threw himself over onto his back, his

eyes wide-open on the shadows that played against the ceiling. His body throbbed, his mind throbbed. He lay on top of the covers with moonlight streaming in the window and outlining him. He couldn't believe what he'd just found out.

"Kane?" she murmured. Her voice sounded rusty.

"Is he gay?"

She swallowed. "He doesn't want to sleep with me," she said, avoiding the implication.

"Why?" he persisted.

"It . . . isn't what you think."

He felt her move and his head turned. She was reaching for the cover, but he stayed her hand.

His eyes looked at her in a new way. The same boldness was there, but now there was curiosity and wonder.

"Haven't you ever wanted to, with someone?" he asked.

"Oh, yes," she replied honestly, remembering her unbearable pleasure when Mosby had asked her to marry him and she'd thought he felt the same raging desire she did.

"But you didn't?"

She met his eyes levelly. "He couldn't, Kane," she whispered. "He really wanted

159

to, I think. But he . . . couldn't."

His breath felt suspended. "And you didn't want anyone else?"

She smiled sadly. "I'm afraid not."

He stared down at her without smiling back, without speaking. "I see."

"Your lover," she began. "You said she'd managed to make you impotent."

He lifted an eyebrow and faint humor stole into his eyes. "Yes. Well, obviously, you don't produce the same reaction."

She laughed through the weakness and pain. "No, I don't, do I?"

His eyes slid over her nudity with gentle appreciation. "You aren't in any condition now. But later, when you are . . ."

Her eyes fell to his chest. She couldn't tell him about her past, or her present. She'd lied to him all around. He would have to know eventually who she was.

"It isn't that easy," she said.

"I remember. You don't want to get pregnant." He let his eyes drift down to her flat stomach and he felt a jolt of pleasure at the thought of it growing large, round, as his wife's had years ago. His wife hadn't really wanted a child until Teddy was born, he recalled. She'd been viciously accusing and horrible, until they laid the tiny infant in her arms and she learned to love him.

"A baby is . . . a terrible responsibility," Nikki managed, without realizing what she was saying.

He wasn't listening. His big hand suddenly flattened on her stomach, so large that it covered most of her to the navel.

"Babies can be prevented," he said. "So can most diseases, with a very simple device." His eyes lifted back to hers. "I'll use one. There won't be a risk, of any kind, and you won't catch anything from me."

"You talk as if it's only the risk I don't want," she said. She was too weak to fight, and her illness had confused her. Surely that was the only reason she was lying here naked in a man's arms. "Kane, sex is more than a casual pastime to me," she added gently. "I want to be loved, not had."

"Do you think I won't know how to love you?" he asked quietly. His hand began to move, very tenderly. "How to please you? How to give you pleasure beyond your wildest dreams of intimacy?"

She pulled his hand away from her body with a shaky sigh. "What you want is a body to ease your physical need for sex," she whispered. "Presumably, you already have someone you can do that with. I want much, much more. I want total commu-

161

nion and total commitment. I want forever."

His face hardened and his eyes grew mocking. "Forever is an illusion. No one has forever."

"I will," she said stubbornly.

"You won't. You're living in dreams."

"Then I'll live in them. But I won't be taken in a fit of screaming passion and then discarded like a morning paper that's just been read."

His dark brows arched in surprise.

"You know what I mean," she said stubbornly. "I won't be a sexual object to any man."

"You're naked," he pointed out. "So am I."

She dragged up the covers to her chin. "I'm sick," she said accusingly.

"So you are." He smiled at his own fallibility. "Do you want me to leave?"

She did. She didn't. Her eyes sought his and she vacillated.

He jerked the covers back, slid under them, pulled her close and replaced them. "Lay your cheek on my chest and go to sleep," he murmured.

There was no more argument left in her. She closed her eyes and her body seemed to melt into his. Only seconds passed before she was asleep.

In the morning, she woke in her gown and alone. She must have dreamed the whole thing, she thought dazedly. But it had seemed so real. She laughed at her own folly. She really did have to get her life back together.

When Kane stopped in the doorway later to check on her, she smiled warmly but without embarrassment and said that she was fine.

"I have to make a few telephone calls, but I'll come back in time to have lunch with you. Can I have Mrs. Beale bring you anything?"

"No, thanks. I still have some of the juice she brought me at breakfast."

"Okay."

He smiled, letting his dark eyes slide over her pretty face. Even sick, she was lovely to look at.

"You've got a little more color than you had yesterday. How's the chest?"

"It's better," she assured him. "Kane, thank you for bringing me here and taking care of me."

"How could I let them put you in the hospital, when you have no one else to look out for you?" he said quietly.

That wasn't true. She had a brother who

loved her. But she couldn't admit it. "Thank you anyway," she murmured while she wondered in a panic what would happen if Clayton should telephone late at night and not find her at the beach house. Would he rush up here looking for her, involve the police? She had to find a way to contact him.

Meanwhile, she looked at Kane with faint puzzlement and involuntarily, her eyes drifted to the pristine pillow beside her head.

He moved into the room and came to a stop beside the bed. "Nikki, it wasn't a dream," he said soberly.

Her eyes dropped suddenly. On the covers, her nails looked like pink ice. "Then you know . . ."

"Yes. And so do you," he replied with a quizzical smile. "Everything there is to know about me, physically. Does it matter? I didn't seduce you, even if it was touch and go for a few minutes."

"I suppose not."

"Don't look so stricken. A few intimacies aren't going to stain that snow-white conscience too much. You're old enough to play with fire, aren't you?"

He was fire, she thought, studying him. He was a wildfire, and he caught her up

164

every time he touched her. She'd never known what it was to be so helpless.

"You don't know anything about me, really," she said. "You might not like what you find out one day."

"What sort of dark secrets can a virgin have?" he asked, his voice soft as velvet.

"You might be surprised."

"And I might not." He reached down and brushed the unruly hair away from her oval face, his touch as tender as his voice. "I'm not going to love you, you know."

"I'm not going to love you, either," she whispered.

He bent and brushed his lips softly over her forehead, her closed eyes, her cheeks. He paused at her mouth, barely touching it.

"I'm contagious," she whispered, a plea in her voice.

"You won't be forever," he whispered back. He hesitated but after a heartbeat, he lifted his head.

He looked vibrantly alive, big and dark and dear. Nikki's eyes adored him hopelessly.

"Don't push your luck," he teased with black humor. "Last night is all too vivid in my mind."

"Don't you sleep with her like that?" she asked suddenly.

He chuckled at her fierce glare. "Not naked," he returned easily. "Usually it's in a feverish rush and then I get up and go home. Neither of us has much inclination toward tenderness. In fact, she doesn't really like sex. She likes controlling men. I tolerate the relationship because I don't want commitment and neither does she. I like it quick from time to time."

She was curious. She shifted a little against the pillow and studied him. "Was it like that with your wife, if you don't mind my asking . . . ?"

"I felt very tender with my wife when we first married," he said, reading the question. "I was in love with her, and she with me. We reached heights that I've never found with anyone else. But it all went wrong when she got pregnant with Teddy. After he was born, she lived for him, I suppose I did, too. We lost each other in the act of becoming parents." At the mention of the little boy's name, something terrible flared in his eyes, in his face. The nightmare exploded, like the bomb that had wiped out the young life and all his hopes and dreams . . .

"Kane!"

She dragged herself up from the bed, shaky on her feet, but anguished at what

166

she saw on his face. He was sweating and his eyes were wide, wild, dangerous.

"Darling, it's all right," she whispered, hugging him fiercely. "It's all right, it's all right!"

He swallowed and his body jerked. His hands found her shoulders, resting heavily there while he fought the terror. He'd shut it out for a whole year. Now, with her, it was all coming back. The comfort she offered was making him vulnerable. He realized, shocked, that he felt safe to talk about it because Nikki was there to hold him when the nightmares came.

"Kane, don't look back," she said, nuzzling his chest with her cheek. "You have to stop tormenting yourself."

"They died," he said in a ghostly whisper. "They were torn to pieces, lying there in the metal shards that had been a car."

Her arms contracted. She could barely stand, but she couldn't leave him now. She smoothed her hands over his broad back through the soft knit shirt and heard his voice drone on, the painful memories spilling over from his mind to his tongue. Almost incoherently, he told her all of it, and his voice shook when he reached the end.

"I'm sorry," she whispered. "I'm so sorry, Kane."

The words were barely audible now as his voice and his strength gave out. He hadn't talked about it until now. He couldn't seem to stop. The fears and pain were dragged from him until he felt helpless.

"They never knew," she assured him. "It was quick. At least be grateful for that small mercy, that they didn't suffer."

"He was my son," he choked. "And what was left of him . . . God! God, I can't . . . think . . . can't bear to think of it . . . !"

She reached up and kissed his wet eyes, his face, gently comforting him while he relived the nightmare. Except that this time, he wasn't alone. He didn't have to face it by himself. His big arms pulled Nikki closer and for the first time in his life, he clung willingly to a woman for strength.

Nikki felt the moment when he came out of it, when his own will began to reassert itself.

His big hands contracted roughly on her shoulders. "I haven't spoken of it to anyone. Not even to my friend Jake."

"It's good to talk about the things that hurt most," she said quietly.

"So they say. So Chris says, constantly. She's a psychologist, she psychoanalyzes me when we aren't making love," he said, angry at himself for pouring out his pain and angry at Nikki for being here, for listening. He felt her stiffen as he continued, "She's very inventive in bed. She likes to get on top and . . ."

She jerked back out of his arms, savaged by the deliberate revelations as he'd known she would be.

"There's no need for this," she told him with cold pride. "I wanted to help, that's all. I wasn't asking for promises of forever or commitment."

He glared at her. "You wouldn't get them. Once was enough."

"You won't believe me, but I know exactly how that feels."

"Yes, I remember," he said with a mocking laugh. "He couldn't, could he?"

Her face paled. She turned and got shakily back into bed, pulling the covers up.

He hated himself for the look on her face. She'd been trying to help, but he couldn't accept his own vulnerability. He'd always thought he was invincible until Nikki came along.

"That was low," he said heavily. "I'm sorry."

She lifted her eyes but didn't say a word.

He jammed his hands in his pockets. It disturbed him to see her in bed. "If you need anything, just sing out."

"I'm fine," she replied with involuntary formality. "Thank you for taking care of me."

"Who else did you have?" he asked. He started out and then hesitated. "Where did you learn Morse?" he asked suddenly.

"I had a friend with a ham radio."

He smiled. "You thought I'd know the code. Why?"

"You're a sailor."

Something changed slightly in his features. "Because I can drive a motorboat?" he asked.

She realized suddenly what she'd given away. A yachtsman could be expected to know Morse Code. But would an ordinary boater know it? Perhaps. Probably. She had to bluff.

"Well, you did, didn't you?" she asked innocently. "I thought anybody who was around boats would have to know the code. I mean, what if you had a communications breakdown or something and a lot of static?"

The suspicion slowly faded. "I guess so," he said, and laughed dryly at his own sudden stupidity.

He shook his head as he turned and left the room. Nikki stared at the closed door for a long time. He wasn't the only one with unpleasant memories, and he'd brought some of her own back. She had to get well quickly and get out of here. Charleston seemed very far away, and there was Clayton to inform about her illness. She only hoped that he didn't decide to telephone the beach house in her absence. Things could get very, very complicated if he did.

Chapter Eight

Cortez hated being stared at. In many big cities, he went unnoticed, but Charleston had a small town atmosphere and he looked alien with his dark bronze skin and long hair in its neat ponytail. Even the sunglasses he wore with his gray suit set him apart. The suit probably added to his uniqueness, he thought ruefully, he seemed to be the only person on the streets wearing one.

All the same, he was on the track of some interesting news for Clayton Seymour. It seemed that Kane Lombard had gone missing for a few days, and at the same time his plant manager had been out sick. It was during both absences that Burke's had been contracted to replace CWC. But the really damning thing was that Lombard had been contacted about the replacement. He'd given his approval, two of his employees had said so when they were questioned about it by Cortez, who had telephoned a state official to ask the questions.

He'd followed up that visit with one to Burke's, posing as a small businessman who might need to hire Burke. In the process he got an earful about Burke's latest deal with Lombard.

"Cherokee, aren't you?" his informant had asked. "I been up to Cherokee myself. Pretty impressive, seeing them chiefs stand out there in them pretty warbonnets. Must have had to kill a lot of eagles to get all them eagle feathers."

Cortez had almost bitten through his tongue while he tried to smile nonchalantly. He wanted to tell the man that Eastern Cherokees never wore warbonnets except for the tourists, that warbonnets were limited to the Plains Indians. He wanted to add that the Cherokees had been a very civilized people who had their own newspaper in their own language in the 1820s and that their capital of New Echota was in no way dissimilar to a white town of the same period. He could also have told the man that killing eagles was an offense for which a man could go to prison these days.

But he didn't. Over the years he'd learned that whites grouped Indians under one heading and stereotyped them, and that those old attitudes were as constant as the summer sun. It took more time than he was willing to spend to start spouting facts at a man who was already looking him over for a hidden tomahawk. It wasn't the first time he'd had to cope with the situation.

Laden with information that he could use, he was having a quick sandwich and coffee in a small café, and getting a frank appraisal from a pair of pale blue eyes. He turned his head and stared back. Usually that was intimidation enough to stop a curious person. It didn't stop this one. Her head tilted a little and the light caught her platinum-blond hair, making lights in it that held his attention. She couldn't be much more than a teen, he thought. She was slight and not especially pretty except for that hair. She was wrapped up in a huge denim jacket, odd because it was a hot day. Dirt stained it in random smudges. He frowned slightly. She looked like the fastidious sort. His eyes dropped. She was wearing Western boots, but not pretty city ones. Those were hard-used boots, with caked mud and scratches. She gained points.

His black eyes lifted back to hers. She smiled almost apologetically, as if she realized that he didn't want her attention, and went back to sipping her coffee.

His eyebrow jerked. She'd seen enough, had she? He laughed silently and finished his small meal, leaving a tip for the waitress before he went to the counter to pay his check. He had to find a local marsh. Burke's idiot employee had let something slip that he shouldn't have, and Cortez was going to take a quick look around the area. He'd have to buy a map and find out where to go.

He started to leave the café. On impulse, he walked to the young blond girl's table and stood next to her, his sunglasses dangling from one lean, dark hand.

She looked up and grinned. "I know. I was staring. I'm sorry if I made you uncomfortable."

Both eyebrows lifted. That was forthright enough. "Why were you staring?" he asked bluntly.

"You're a Native American, aren't you?" she asked, tilting her head a little more. He didn't reply. "There's something I've been dying to ask you, but I thought I'd already irritated you enough."

"What?" he asked curtly.

She hesitated. "Do you have shovel-shaped incisors?"

He let out a loud breath and one corner of his thin mouth drew up. Now it made sense. The mud-caked boots, the dirt-stained clothing. She'd been on a dig.

"Good God, an archaeology student," he muttered.

"An anthropology major, doing my minor in archaeology," she corrected, and laughed. "How did you know?"

"You look as if you've been digging."

"Indeed we have," she said enthusiastically. "We found part of a Woodland period pot with charred acorns in it. My professor says that it's over two thousand years old."

"Along a river bottom, no doubt?"

She grinned. "Why, yes!"

"Find anything else?"

"No. It wasn't a burial site, thank God," she said heavily. "I wouldn't like to dig up somebody's great-grandfather. I think you get haunted for things like that."

He smiled approvingly and checked his watch. He was running out of time. "To answer your original question, yes, like all Native Americans and Asians and other members of the Mongoloid classification, my incisors are shovel-shaped," he said, surprising her. "Now," he added, leaning down menacingly, "are you going to ask how many scalps I carry on my war lance?"

Her eyes twinkled. "Oh, that would be much too personal a question," she said with mock somberness.

He couldn't contain a chuckle. He turned and walked out of the café, shaking his head. If she'd been a little older, who knew what might have developed. As it was, he was a man on holiday doing a friend a favor. He had no time for cute college girls.

Armed with names and backgrounds, when he reached his hotel room he removed his laptop computer from its padded briefcase, hooked it into the modem, and plugged it in. He accessed the mainframe in Washington, D.C., at FBI headquarters with his password and called up the information he needed.

The unit was attached to a small printer. He printed out hard copy of the data and disengaged the modem. How interesting, he thought. Burke had a record. Not only had he violated EPD regulations, he'd actually been charged twice already. The witnesses had never shown up to testify and he'd gotten off. But this time, Burke and his brother-in-law had left a trail. Who better to follow it than me, Cortez reasoned dryly.

He changed into jeans and boots and a blue checked shirt and let his hair down. He was going tracking. If people wanted to stare, let them.

The rental car he was driving was nice without being flashy. He enjoyed driving. Back at his home he had a banged-up pickup with a straight shift. He thought of it longingly.

As he started out of the city, he deliberately drove back by the café where he'd had lunch. He hated himself for the weakness of this impulse. Sure enough, it had paid off.

There was the young blonde, standing beside a muddied old Bronco. Her face was red and her hair was askew. She was kicking the flat rear tire repeatedly while asking God to do some pretty strange things to her vehicle.

Cortez pulled in behind her and cut off the engine. She hadn't even slowed down when he reached her.

"Flat tire, huh?" he asked, nodding. "I saw one of those once."

She pushed back her tangled, windblown hair and looked up at him in disbelief. He looked so different with his hair down and wearing jeans that she didn't even recognize him at first.

He took off his sunglasses. "You busy?" he asked.

She was catching her breath from the exertion. "Why? Are you going to offer to kick it —" she indicated the flat tire "— while I rest?"

"No. I thought you might come with me and help me track a truck."

He caught her by the hand. Nice, he thought as he led her toward his car. She had good hands, strong and soft all at once. He opened the passenger door, but she hesitated.

With exaggerated patience, he pulled out his wallet and flipped it open, holding it under her eyes. He watched her expression change. That was another familiar sight. His credentials seemed to intimidate most people, who blurted out terrible secrets like unpaid parking tickets and promised immediate restitution.

"FBI," she stammered. Her face paled. "You can't be serious. You're going to arrest me for assaulting a Bronco?"

"Unprovoked assault on a horse," he agreed.

Her lower jaw fell.

He pursed his lips. "Okay. I'm deputizing you to assist me in an investigation. Better?"

"Me?"

"You."

She shrugged. "All right, but I'm not shooting anybody."

"Deal." He put up his wallet and inserted her into the passenger seat. Minutes later, they were on the way out of town.

"I have to find a place called Pirate's Marsh. Do you know it?"

As he'd guessed, she did. "Why, yes, it's just a few miles down the road. Turn right at the next intersection."

He grinned, glad that he'd followed his intuition. An archaeology student would know all the isolated spots. Or, most of them.

He followed her directions easily to a large area near the sea with huge live oaks dripping moss dotted around the shore. Two or three were uprooted.

"That's from Hurricane Hugo," she told him when they got out of the car and he stared at the felled giants. "Amazing how powerful wind can be."

"Wind, rain, all of nature," he murmured.

He started walking, his eyes on the ground. His little sojourn at Burke's had given him a good look at the sort of tires the man used on his dilapidated vehicles. They had an odd tread that he'd memorized. Plaster casts would be better, but he could do that later. He had some plaster in the car, and a jug of water. All he had to do now was find something in this bog and a tire track that he could link to Burke.

It was a link that he needed for the chain of evidence. He wasn't going to ignore blatant evidence of a federal infraction. It might not be his jurisdiction, but he knew a couple of the EPA boys. He'd had quite enough of white people polluting the earth with their industrial waste.

"What are you looking for?" she asked. "Maybe I could help."

He glanced at her. "Tire tracks. Something nasty in the water."

"Okay." She started walking alongside him.

"Do you have a name?" he asked suddenly.

She looked up. "Of course I do," she said, and kept walking.

His lips tugged up. "What is it?"

"Phoebe."

He sighed audibly.

"Well, it is," she muttered, glaring at him. "What's wrong with being called Phoebe?"

"It's unusual, that's all."

"What are you called?"

"Wouldn't you like to know?" he challenged. He knelt and his eyes narrowed on a tire tread. Close, he thought, but not the

181

right one. Not by a long shot.

"What are you called?" she persisted.

He got up, his eyes still on the ground. He pronounced a set of syllables with odd stops and a high tone. He glanced at her perplexed expression and smiled.

"It doesn't translate very well," he told her. "My mother saw a red-tailed hawk the morning I was born. If you translate it, it means something like 'He who came on the wings of the red-tailed hawk.' "

"That's beautiful."

"Sure." He knelt again to examine a print. This one was right on the money. "Bingo," he murmured to himself. He got up, ignoring the girl, and followed the tracks. When he came to a boggy place, he stopped and his keen eyes swept the expanse until he found what he was looking for: just the rusty edge of a barrel.

"Well, well," he said to himself. "Some days it all comes together."

"Did you find what you were looking for?" she asked, joining him.

"Yes. Thanks for your help."

She grinned. "Do I get a badge now?"

He laughed out loud. "No."

She sighed. "It was fun while it lasted."

He reached out and caught a strand of

her hair, fingering it gently. "Is it naturally this color?"

"Yes. Both my parents are very dark. They say that I'm a throwback to a Norwegian ancestor."

He let the hair go reluctantly. It was very soft, and he looked at her for a long moment, aware of some regrets. "How old are you?" he asked.

"Twenty-two. I was a late starter in college," she confessed.

"Not that late." His dark eyes slid over her body in the concealing thick coat and he wished that he had time to get to know her properly. "I'm almost thirty-six," he said. "The name I use with whites is Cortez."

She held out her hand. "It was nice to meet you."

"Same here. Thanks for the help."

Her fingers contracted briefly around his and he smiled down at her. "Two different worlds," he remarked quietly. "And too much age difference, not to mention the kind of life I lead."

"I was thinking the same thing," she confessed shyly.

His fingers gently caressed hers. "Where do you go to school?"

"University of Tennessee at Knoxville,"

she said. "But I'm off this summer, so I've been hanging around with some friends who study archaeology locally. I'm a senior at the university. I graduate next spring."

"Then maybe I'll see you at graduation, college girl," he said unexpectedly.

Her expression was very still, and he dropped her hand.

"I'd stand out too much, wouldn't I?" he asked curtly, turning on his heel.

"You bigot!" she exclaimed, picking up a small dead limb and heaving it at his back. "You take offense without any provocation whatsoever, you bristle before you even ask questions, you . . . you . . . !" She found another limb.

He moved suddenly with the kind of speed that usually caught people off guard because his normal movements were so calculatedly slow. He gripped her wrist before she could throw the limb. "Not nice," he chided. "Don't throw things."

"It isn't a thing, it's a tree limb," she pointed out, struggling against his strength. "Let go my wrist!"

"Not on your life." He took the limb away effortlessly, but he didn't release her arm.

She stared up into his eyes with resignation and faint excitement. He was very strong. "I would be honored if you came to my graduation, even if you came just as you are now," she said curtly. "I have friends of all colors and cultures, and it doesn't embarrass either me or my family to be seen with them!"

"I beg your pardon," he said genuinely.

"So you should!" she muttered.

"You kick vehicles with flat tires, you throw things at men . . . what other bad habits do you have, besides that nasty mouth?"

"It takes a few bad words to show a flat tire you mean business!"

He smiled. "Does it, really?"

"You don't curse. Not in your own tongue," she said smugly, surprising him. "I haven't come across a Native American language yet that contains nasty words."

"We don't need them to express ourselves," he said with a superior smile.

"Well, stand me in the rain and call me an umbrella!" she said, tongue in cheek.

"No time," he returned. He let go of her wrist and turned. "I'll drop you off at a garage. You'll need help changing that tire."

"You aren't going to offer to help?"

"I can't change a tire," he said matter-of-factly. "I was one of the last guys to serve in Vietnam, when they were evacuating refugees. I caught a burst of shrapnel in the shoulder. It did some damage. It doesn't slow me down, but I can't lift much."

She winced. "Oh, I'm sorry, I didn't mean to sound that way," she said miserably. "I keep putting my foot in my mouth."

"Pretty little feet," he mused, staring down at them. "Boots suit them."

She smiled. "You aren't angry?"

He shook his head. "Come on."

He drove her to the garage nearest her Bronco and waited until she came around to his side of the car to tell him she was going back out with the mechanic.

"Thanks a lot," she told him.

He shrugged. "My pleasure."

She hesitated, but there wasn't really anything else to say. With a funny little smile, she waved and ran back to the waiting mechanic. Cortez forced his eyes away from her and drove on without a backward glance. He was already working on the proof he'd need to have Lombard and his company cited for violation of the environmental laws.

Nikki was sitting in the living room when Kane's friend Jake came to see him. Jake's eyebrows lifted, but he smiled when Kane introduced her only as "Nikki."

"Nice to meet you," he said politely. "Uh, Kane, I need to see you for a minute outside."

"Sure. Excuse me, Nikki." He left her on the sofa, wrapped up in her white chenille robe, and followed Jake out. It was hot today. Both men were in shorts, although Kane's legs were much better suited to them than his friend.

"Well, what is it?" Kane asked.

"I've got to replace the radio," he told the older man. "It's almost gone. I had an estimate on repairing it, but it's going to be less expensive in the long run just to replace it. Is it all right if I order that one we looked at and have it expressed down here?"

"Go ahead," Kane invited. "I have plans for her weekend after next." He glanced back toward the house, his face happier than Jake had seen it in months. "I thought I might take Nikki out on her."

Jake cleared his throat. "I guess you know your own mind, and I'm not one to interfere. But is it wise?"

Kane scowled. "What do you mean?"

"Well, she is your worst enemy's sister, isn't she? I would have thought that you wouldn't want to give Seymour any intimate glimpses into your life."

A big hand shot out and caught Jake's upper arm with bruising strength. "Seymour's sister?"

Jake nodded. "That's who she is, Nicole Seymour. My daughter is married to a senator from Virginia, remember. She and Nikki are casual friends and she's got photos of her. She's a dish, isn't she?"

Kane was feeling betrayed. He honestly hadn't had a clue who Nikki was. But if he knew her identity now . . . did she know his? He needed to find out. Afterward, whether she did or not, he had to get her out of his life and fast. He couldn't afford any connection whatsoever to his worst enemy.

"And to top it all off, she's a Republican," he said aloud.

"You win a few, you lose a few," Jake said philosophically. "Sorry to tell you about her, but you had to know sometime."

"Yes. I did." A hollow feeling claimed Kane as he dismissed Jake and walked back into the house. Nikki sat watching him with wide, curious eyes. Had she ever planned to tell him, he wondered. Or did she really not know who he was?

"We need a new radio on the boat," he told her, wary and curious now.

"Oh, I see." She smiled at him. "I really need to get back to my own cottage. I'm much better now, and I need to make a telephone call," she said. "I . . . my friend might come looking for me if he tries to phone me and I'm not there."

Kane's dark eyes narrowed. "What is your friend, a mob hit man?" he asked slowly, trying to draw her out.

"Oh, nothing like that," she said.

"You never did tell me. Is he impotent or gay?"

Her eyes fell. "Neither," she said, and clammed up.

His eyes narrowed as he stirred his coffee. It was beginning to make sense, like puzzle pieces suddenly fitting. "The man who owns that house, are you related to him by any chance?"

Her expression told him what he wanted to know. Her brother. Her brother Clayton Seymour owned it. He wanted to curse her for making him vulnerable, when she had to know there was no possible chance for them.

"You're very curious about him," she managed.

"Suppose you call him from here and have him come up?" he asked. "I'd like to meet him."

189

"I couldn't possibly do that!" she said, flushing. "He's . . . I mean, he's very busy!"

Of course he was, Kane thought with venom. He was busy trying to take Kane down so that he wouldn't have to lose the election to their candidate. He was so angry that he only just controlled it. Nikki knew who he was. She'd probably known ever since he washed up on her beach.

"Is there anything you want to tell me?" he asked coolly.

She lifted her gaze to meet his. "I do," she replied honestly. "But I can't."

He made an angry sound. She was getting under his skin. The longer he was around her, the more he wanted her. But his need was choked by the knowledge of her identity. It had to end here and now.

"You're very quiet," she pointed out.

He finished his coffee. "I have to get back to work," he said, averting his eyes. "I've been on holiday long enough."

Besides, he didn't dare tell her the real reason he had to get home. Not when her brother was going over his waste control methods with a magnifying glass. He faced a real challenge now. He had to get to the bottom of what could become a scandal if his idiot employee had engaged some guy with a pickup truck to haul off his indus-

trial waste and dump it in a river somewhere. Once he hadn't believed that
people could be so naive as to think they
wouldn't be caught. Now he knew better.
Wouldn't Seymour just love catching
Lombard International with its hand in the
toxic waste?

Nikki was thinking that she needed to go
back to Charleston herself. She wasn't really feeling well enough to stay here by
herself and she couldn't expect Kane to
take care of her indefinitely.

"If you could drop me back by the beach
house," she asked again.

His eyes lifted. "Certainly," he said formally. "Will he come and take care of you
if I do?"

"He'll be there in a minute, as soon as
he knows," she replied, wondering at his
sudden, stark change of attitude toward
her.

"In that case, I'll have my housekeeper
get your things together," he said abruptly,
and left her sitting there alone. She didn't
move for several minutes, too shocked and
hurt by his coolness to think rationally.

Half an hour later, she was back in the
beach house, sitting on the sofa and
gasping for breath. Pneumonia made the

smallest walk feel like mountain-climbing, although she was no longer feverish and her chest was slowly clearing.

"If he doesn't come, telephone the house," Kane said, sounding as if the words were being dragged out of him.

"I won't need to, but thanks for the offer."

He stood over her in white linen slacks and a yellow knit shirt, looking very handsome. "It wouldn't work out," he told her.

She smiled sadly. "I knew that from the beginning," she confided. "But some things are very difficult to resist. You must know that you're devastating at close range."

"So I've been told." His eyes narrowed. She was full of secrets and he couldn't find out even one. "The man who couldn't — did you love him?" he asked bluntly.

"Yes," she said, her voice faintly husky. She looked up unguardedly, and the pain in her eyes was briefly visible. "I loved him more than my own life."

"Didn't he even offer to have therapy?" he persisted.

She laughed coldly. "What good would that have done? You don't need therapy just because you can't feel desire for someone who loves you."

Her pain disturbed him. He wanted to take her in his arms and comfort her, but that was out of the question now. She hadn't trusted him. He couldn't get past that.

"How long ago was it?" he asked.

"Years and years. I've mostly avoided men until now." She glanced at him. "Don't worry, I'm not fixated on you," she added when she saw his expression. "I'm not going to dive off the roof or anything when you leave. I hope I didn't shock you. It's always best to be honest," she said, and felt a twinge of guilt because she hadn't been. But he was hardly likely to ever find that out.

"Yes, it is best to be honest," he said with involuntary anger as he studied her. "But most people don't know how to tell the truth." He averted his angry eyes from her flushed face and looked around the room. "Can I get you anything before I go?"

"No, I'm fine. Thanks again for taking care of me, Kane. I won't forget you."

"I won't forget you, either. Get well, Nikki," he said pleasantly. "I'm glad I met you."

"The same goes for me. Goodbye, Kane."

He searched her face as if he wanted to

memorize it. Then he smiled mockingly, and left. Nikki stared after him for a long time. She knew she'd done the right thing, especially for Clayton, but it didn't feel noble. It hurt. So did Kane's very cold attitude toward her. He didn't know who she was; it couldn't be that. Perhaps it was just that he didn't want to feel anything for her beyond physical attraction. Whatever his reasoning, he'd just killed any possibility of a future for them.

She lifted the receiver on the telephone by the sofa and dialed Clayton's number. It would be good to get back to Charleston, she told herself. And she could hardly stay here in her present condition.

Chapter Nine

Senator Mosby Torrance's aide John Haralson drove out to Pirate's Marsh the following day in his gray BMW. He was at the tail end of a convoy that combined local media with a team of EPA investigators, Cortez, and a shocked public health official.

"This marsh is practically in the Edisto River," the public health official gasped. "What is that?" he persisted as the investigators got the barrel out of the marsh and began to inspect it.

"Paint solvent," one said curtly, rubbing his gloved hand over the muck to read the stenciled legend on it. "Lombard International," he added shortly. "Here's another one — antifreeze. And another, full of motor oil. Of all the cheap . . . there are provisions for disposal of substances like this. Why, why, would he pay someone to dump it here instead?"

"To cut costs, of course. A man with a truck is plenty cheaper than an outfit qualified to handle toxic waste."

"Hold it right there and let me get a shot of it," one of the print media reporters called. He snapped the picture, including two dead water birds floating on the surface, waited for the film to advance automatically and took three more. The broadcast journalists were rolling their own videocameras furiously. "That should do it. Do you think this will make a case?" he asked the environmental people.

"Indeed it will," one of them commented.

Haralson dragged Cortez aside. He was wiping away sweat as he glared at the Comanche. "Busybody," he told his friend. "I didn't want to release this to EPD and the local newspapers and TV people until I had time to write a statement giving Seymour the credit!"

"Go to it. There's still time. And you'll never get a better opportunity than this," Cortez pointed out. "As to reporting what I found, I work for the federal government," Cortez reminded him. He produced his wallet. "See? I have a badge."

Haralson was thinking ahead. "This will be all over the state by morning."

"I do hope so," Cortez said easily. "A man who dumps this sort of garbage in a wildlife area should be drawn and quartered by the media, along with the people who hired him to do it!"

Haralson whipped out his pad and began to take down what he was going to say. This was a heaven-sent opportunity, and it was going to stand Clayton Seymour in excellent stead with local voters. He began to smile.

"You must have proof of a connection," he mumbled jubilantly to Cortez. There was something in Haralson's eyes. Something Cortez almost questioned.

"I wouldn't have called all these people if I hadn't," Cortez said, gesturing as the EPD people pulled yet another drum out of the marsh. "I can tie these tire treads to one of Burke's trucks, and one of Burke's own employees told me about the site."

"This is one excellent piece of investigation."

"Of course it is. I work for the . . ."

". . . government!" Haralson chuckled. "Yes, I know. You eat, drink and sleep the job. How could I have forgotten?!"

"Think how well this is going to work out. Sam Hewett will lose the attention of his senior aide, Norman Lombard, with Kane Lombard fighting the environmental people. Seymour will win the election, Lombard will be prosecuted for environmental homicide, and Burke will be spending years as someone's girlfriend at Leavenworth."

"You're right. It's going to work out very well indeed. I'll just get this release over to the press and wait for results. Now that we've got Lombard on the run, maybe we're safe."

"What was that?" Cortez asked curiously.

"Nothing," Haralson said. "Nothing at all. Thanks for your help."

"Thanks for selling me the gold piece. See you back in D.C."

"Yeah. Sure. Think nothing of it." Haralson was already walking away, grinning like a Cheshire cat as he bent his head to light a cigar. Cortez, watching him, wondered if the man had scruples. Maybe he thought keeping Seymour in office was worth sacrificing any he had left after years as a political insider. This had been so easy. Maybe too easy. His mind locked on it like a dog's jaw on a bone as he watched Haralson. He felt used suddenly, and he didn't like it.

Todd Lawson gleaned the situation when he heard the traffic on the CB radio receiver he always carried with him. Something big was going on out at Pirate's Marsh, one CB'er said, and proceeded to elaborate on what had been found. Industrial pollution, and linked to the newest industry in Charleston, Lombard's automobile manufacturing company.

Lawson felt his job passing before his eyes. He'd tried to warn Kane, but apparently the other man hadn't thought there would be any rush. It was going to be hard to tell him what was going on. Seymour had all the aces this time.

Telling Kane wasn't as bad as Lawson had expected; it was worse. Kane ran out of foul language after the first five minutes of yelling down the telephone receiver at him. Then he got really nasty.

"My God, why didn't you know until now? How did you ever get to be an investigative reporter in the first place?" Kane snarled.

"I tried. I just couldn't get any doors to open for me," Lawson said quietly. "It was really bad out there," he added involuntarily. "They ran some footage here a few minutes ago. There are dozens of dead birds strewn around the marsh, and Congressman Seymour called a press conference to denounce you and promise retribution. Senator Mosby Torrance has started forming a committee to investigate . . ."

"Sweet Jesus," Kane exploded with

something akin to reverence. "I'll kill Burke with my bare hands!"

"Get in line. Yours isn't the only company logo they found out there, although it was the most prominent. Listen, call a press conference of your own while there's still time. Give a statement. Tell people where you were those two days when you went missing and the solid waste manager changed waste disposal companies."

Kane hesitated. He suddenly realized that if he did that he would have to tell the world that he'd let himself be knocked out and that a woman had nursed him alone for almost two days. Not only that, he'd have to admit that Nikki had stayed with him alone for three days. He pursed his lips and considered that it would give him some leverage later with Seymour if he needed it. He'd keep Nikki's dark secret, for now. Not that she deserved it, damn her. He could almost hate her for making a fool of him with her deception.

"I won't do that," Kane told Lawson.

"Why not?"

"Because there's a woman involved," Kane mused. "And I might need that little tidbit later on. So I won't mention it now."

"Seymour is going to hound you to death over that marsh," Lawson pointed out. "You can't sit down and let him crucify you! You could go to jail, for God's sake!"

Kane stared blankly at the other man. "Don't be absurd. I'll have to pay a fine, but it won't amount to more than that."

"When Senator Torrance gets you in front of a microphone, it sure as hell will," Lawson said doggedly. He stared at the floor. "Look, let me poke around and see if I can turn up anything fast. I know there's a link between Torrance and Seymour that we can use. I just have to find it before Seymour gets you to Washington!"

"Go for it," Kane said heavily. "Lawson . . . I shouldn't have flown off the handle like that. It's been a hard week."

"Things will get better. I'll phone you in a couple of days. Sorry to be the bearer of such bad news."

He hung up and Kane stared down at the telephone, barely seeing it at all. Amazing how much had happened in these few days. He was surprised by the protective instincts that Nikki provoked in him. He could save himself so easily by just mentioning where he was, and the circumstances of his two-day absence. But if he did that, not only would he sacrifice his ace-in-the-hole, he had to consider what it would do to Nikki. She was ill. He couldn't land her in a scandal until she was in fighting shape. Then, though. Yes, by God, she was going to pay for ingratiating herself to him and pumping him for information. God knew what she'd managed to find out from his housekeeper and Jake during her residence. He'd have to grill both of them and make sure. Damn his own blindness! He'd been so attracted to her that he hadn't even considered that she might have ulterior motives.

He forced his mind back onto the problem at hand. Indiscriminate dumping was a long-standing problem. Many people had been charged with it. He hoped Lawson would turn up something else on Seymour. He didn't relish the thought of having to use Nikki's presence in his life as a weapon against her brother.

Derrie was cheerful in the office the next morning, having just heard the news.

"Nice going, boss," she chuckled.

"Don't thank me, thank Haralson and his friend, Cortez," Clayton returned, smiling at her as he put down his briefcase in the small office he kept for constituents in Charleston. It was part of a suite of law offices, but he rented a room. It was nicely furnished and very sedate. Everything a congressman's office should be, he thought approvingly. He had another in the state capital. A man couldn't gather too much support, and he had to be accessible everywhere.

"Was he personally responsible, do you think?" Derrie asked. "Mr. Lombard, I mean."

"What does that matter?" he asked, puzzled.

She frowned. "That doesn't sound like you."

Clayton sat down and stared at her. "I'm fighting for my political life," he said slowly, as if he were talking to an idiot. "If I don't get Lombard's back to the wall, his family may discover something about Nikki and Mosby and print it. Can you imagine in your wildest dreams what that would do to Nikki?"

"Yes, I can," Derrie said sadly. "But it hardly seems fair to destroy a man's whole life to spare your sister. Mr. Lombard's wife and little boy were killed in a car bombing in Lebanon just last year. He doesn't deserve to be crucified if he's not personally responsible."

"Of course he's personally responsible. I feel . . ." He stopped as the telephone rang,

203

picking it up. "Seymour," he said. "What's that? You've had them blow up some photographs of those dead birds and put them on the placards they carry? Are you sure . . . okay. Well, listen, don't pay them any more than you have to, we're on a tight budget right now. Okay. You do that. Thanks, Haralson."

He hung up, a little hesitant about feeling triumphant. Haralson sounded very happy, but Clayton felt a sense of guilt. How absurd. He had to keep Lombard off his back and protect Nikki. This was the best way.

"Well, that should heat things up at Lombard's plant," he said thoughtfully. He glanced at Derrie. "You might call the local television stations," he told her. "Tell them we've heard that a group of environmentalists are about to start a picket line at Lombard's plant."

Derrie was just staring at him, her blue eyes incredulous. "You've paid people to picket him!"

"I haven't. Haralson's taking care of it," he said stiffly. "He says that by putting Lombard on the defensive, we can protect Nikki and Mosby from any tabloid threat."

"And you believe him? Clay, this isn't

204

the way!" she cried. "For heaven's sake, this is dirty!"

"And you don't want to soil your lily-white hands?" he chided coldly. She pricked his conscience, brought out his own doubts and fears. He didn't like it.

"What you're doing is against everything I've ever believed in," she said quietly.

"Do you think you're irreplaceable?" he asked, furious with her scruples, her refusal to obey instructions. "Do you think I keep you on the payroll out of undying love? My God, the only reason you're still working here is because of your typing skills. You're so starchy that you rustle when you walk, Miss Prim! No wonder you can't get dates except with nearsighted acne lepers!"

She felt her chest expanding with incredulous temper. "How dare you!"

"You moralistic little prude, you belong in a convent somewhere," he continued hotly. "Always defending animals and plants, street people, and the like . . . Bett said that you're pathetic and she was right. I need someone in this office who can help me politically, not a far left conservative trying to undermine everything I do!"

"I won't support dishonesty and corruption, thank you very much," she fired back.

"You've changed since you got thick with Mosby Torrance and that Haralson plague of his and Bett Watts. You've convinced yourself that your position is worth anyone else's sacrifice, haven't you, that a little lessening of principles is worth all the prestige and money?"

"I'm protecting my sister, and you know it," he said angrily.

"No, you aren't. You're protecting yourself against the Democratic challenger and trying to regain the points you lost by sacrificing the spotted owl on the altar of profit."

"Don't judge me!"

"Oh, I wouldn't dream of it," she agreed. "Your own conscience will hang you out to dry one day, if Ms. Watts doesn't pin it on the line right next to your manhood!"

He stood up abruptly, almost shaking with rage. "Get out!" he yelled.

"I'd be delighted!" she said fiercely, her small hands making fists beside her slender hips. "I was offered another job just a week or more ago, with a politician who has a conscience and a little moral fiber. I daresay he'd hire me in a minute!"

"Then feel free to join him!" Clayton growled. She made him hate himself. He wanted her gone, now! "If you want to go, go. And damn you and your pristine little conscience!"

She couldn't remember a time when he'd ever cursed her. She stood glaring at him with the blood draining out of her soft complexion. As her burst of temper dissipated, it dawned on her that he'd just fired her. After three years of hard work and hero worship, he'd admitted that he loathed her. She'd been fired, and he'd made it sound as if she were quitting. It didn't quite all register at once.

The ringing of the telephone startled them both. Automatically Derrie reached for it. She listened for a minute and in a taut voice announced, "It's Nikki." She handed him the receiver and walked out, closing the door quietly behind her.

"Hello, Nikki, what do you want?" he asked irritably.

There was a pause. "I need you to come after me," she said, her voice hoarse and strained.

He was immediately concerned. "What's wrong?"

"I had a relapse. It's pneumonia," she said heavily. "I've seen a doctor and I have antibiotics," she added quickly, "but I really can't stay here alone."

"When was it diagnosed?"

"Three days ago . . ."

"And you haven't called me until now?" he raged. "Nikki, in the name of God . . . I'll be there in two hours."

He put down the receiver, worrying his thick hair as he stormed into the outer office. The path had been very clear in his mind — he'd tell Derrie to take over the office and he'd fly up and get Nikki. His plan altered immediately when he saw his aide.

Furious tears were streaming down Derrie's face. She'd already cleaned out her desk drawers and was picking up the small box that held the meager contents of her three years as his aide. All at once, he came to his senses.

"Derrie, no," Clayton said in shock. "Listen, I didn't mean it," he added quickly, realizing that he'd said too much. "I've had a bad morning . . ."

"I've had a worse one," she said icily, her blue eyes glaring at him. "You can call the temporary agency. They'll replace me. I'll come back to retrain someone, but it's Friday and you have no pressing appointments today." She nodded toward the appointment book. "The names and telephone numbers of your appointments are right there. I guess you can make a pot

208

of coffee all by yourself if you have to," she added with bitter sarcasm.

"You can't leave," he groaned.

"No? Watch me. I'm sorry if it's inconvenient. You did invite me to leave," she reminded him with cold pleasure when he grimaced. "But even if you hadn't, I can't work for a man who puts his political career above honor." Her soft eyes had gone hard, glaring at him. "You've been around Ms. Watts and Senator Torrance too long, haven't you? Whatever they've got is contagious and you've caught it."

"You can't leave!" he ground out. Then he dashed all her illusions by adding, "Damn it, Nikki's got pneumonia. I need you to stay here and hold down the office. I have to go up and get her at the beach house."

He needed her to work. That was all it had ever been, all it would ever be. She'd loved him, and he had nothing to give her. Why had it taken so long for her to realize it? She sighed heavily. "I'll go up and get her," she offered. "I like Nikki."

"What am I supposed to do in the meanwhile, type letters?" he raged. "That's what I pay you for!"

"Not any more," she said with quiet dignity. She shifted the box in her arms. "If you'll have the pilot stand by, I'll go to the airport and then I'll bring Nikki home."

He was furious. He couldn't hide it. Logic told him that he couldn't get a temporary girl in here and train her in the next thirty minutes. Derrie wasn't going to stay, but she would go and retrieve Nikki. She had him over a barrel.

"All right," he said gruffly. "I'll phone the pilot." He indicated the box. "Don't you want to leave that here?"

Her eyebrow lifted. "Why? I'm not coming back."

She turned and walked out the door, leaving it ajar because she had her hands full.

Clayton stood by the desk and stared after her with a mind that absolutely refused to register what had happened. He'd never had to worry about leaving the office before, because Derrie was so competent and capable. She could handle anything. Now she was gone. He'd fired her. He would have to replace her. He wondered if he could. His delight over Seymour's downfall was overshadowed by his emptiness at losing the best assistant he'd ever had. Bett would be delighted, he realized, because she'd never liked Derrie. But Clayton felt a growing sense of great loss.

And not only that, now he was faced with the unpleasant task of learning how to make his own coffee.

Nikki was surprised to see Derrie at the door when she answered it.

"Clayton didn't come with you?" Nikki asked weakly.

"He has to answer the telephone and make coffee," Derrie said with forced carelessness. "You see, this is my last official act as his secretary. I quit."

Nikki stared at her, seeing the faint swelling around her eyes and the visible pain of her decision.

"Why?"

"Because your brother is letting Torrance and Bett Watts mold him in their image," the younger woman said quietly. "He's helping to dispossess the spotted owl out west, and now he's using some underhanded methods to crucify Kane Lombard for something he may not even be guilty of."

Nikki's heart jumped wildly in her chest. "Lombard . . . what did he do?"

"You don't have television here, do you?" Derrie asked. "Well, it's all over the news. Mr. Lombard has been charged with several counts of industrial pollution of a major tributary. They say he cut costs by throwing out a reputable waste disposal company and replacing it with some local who was notorious for dumping vats of pollutants in deserted fields and marshes. There's been terrible damage to wildlife. Dead birds everywhere. The Resource Conservation and Recovery Act and the Toxic Substance Control Act of 1976 make it a felony to dump toxic wastes illegally."

"Oh, my God," Nikki said shakily.

Without registering Derrie's curiosity, she wobbled to the phone, picked it up and blindly dialed Kane's number without considering the consequences.

His housekeeper answered, and all she would tell Nikki was that Mr. Lombard had been called urgently back to Charleston.

Nikki put down the receiver. She'd never felt quite so bad. "He wouldn't do such a thing," she said.

"I know that," Derrie said. "The poor man's had so much . . . Wait a minute, how do you know he wouldn't?"

Nikki started. "I've read about him," she began.

"Of course," Derrie said with an apologetic laugh. "So have I. He seems like a decent sort of man." Her smile vanished. "Your brother is losing all his values, you know. I said I'd come and get you, but I'm through entertaining Ms. Watts and making coffee and I'm not sacrificing my conscience for the sake of any job. I have a good brain and it's going to waste."

Nikki managed a wan smile. "Indeed you have, but I fear for my brother's future if you aren't in it. You were a moderating force. Now, Bett will be telling him how to tie his ties."

"I know." Derrie's eyes were sad as she recalled the things Clayton had said to her, but she forced the misery away. "We have to get you back to Charleston. What can I do?"

"Help me pack," Nikki said. "Then I'll dress and we'll get underway. Are we flying?"

"Afraid not. You know you can't fly in a pressurized cabin with pneumonia, you'd have to be taken off by an ambulance when we got to Charleston. I hired a limo."

"Extravagant . . ."

"Very." Derrie smiled. "I hope your brother has a migraine when he sees the bill."

Nikki was too sick to argue, but she couldn't help but wonder what Clayton had done to make loyal Derrie quit.

Kane Lombard met the vicious publicity head-on. He knew what was going to happen from the minute Lawson had called to tell him the news. He wasn't guilty, but by the time the media got through with him, he'd look it.

It wouldn't be a nine-day wonder, either, he realized when he saw the headlines. Seymour had jumped in feetfirst with charges that Lombard was a prime example of the capitalist who put profit before conservation. He was going to make an example of Kane. He had strong support, too, from every local environmental group and a few national ones. When Kane got to his plant, he had to get through placard-carrying mobs of people who had probably been hired by some of Torrance's crowd for the benefit of the TV cameras that were strategically placed.

Many of the same public officials who had paved his way when he opened the automobile plant were now lined up visibly with the opposition.

"It's going to be a circus," Kane remarked, looking down on the mob at the gates of the plant from his sixth-story window.

Gert Yardley, his elderly executive secretary nodded. "I'm afraid so. And the news people are clamoring for interviews. You'll have to give a statement, sir."

"I know that. What kind of statement do you recommend? How about, 'I'm innocent'?" he asked, turning to face her.

"I have no doubt whatsoever about your innocence," Mrs. Yardley said, and smiled sympathetically. "Neither does Jenny," she added, naming the junior secretary who shared an office with her. "Convincing yon ravenous wolves outside is going to be the problem."

He stuck his hands in his slacks pockets and turned away from the furor below. "Get my father on the line, will you?"

"I can't, sir," she said. "He telephoned two hours ago and said to tell you that he's on the way down here."

"Great." He lifted his eyes skyward. "My father is just what I need to make a bad day worse. I can handle my own problems."

"I'm sure he knows that. He said you might need a little moral support," she added with a smile. "A man who's being publicly hanged shouldn't turn away a friend. Even a related one."

"I guess you're right." His dark eyes narrowed. "I want to see that new waste disposal man, what's his name, Jurkins. Get him up here."

"He's out sick," she returned grimly. "And Ed Nelson is still recuperating from his kidney stone operation. He and Mr. Jurkins both called in, both also protesting their ignorance of Burke's true operation."

"They would, wouldn't they? God forbid they should try to cross the picket line. All right, call Bob Wilson and get him over here," he said, naming the head of the legal firm that represented Lombard, International.

"I anticipated that," she said. "He should be here momentarily."

"Thanks, Gert," he replied.

She smiled. "What's a good secretary for, if not to help the boss? I'll buzz you when Mr. Wilson arrives."

She left him, and he turned back to the window. It was threatening rain. Maybe it would dissuade some of the lesser-paid protesters, he mused. He thought about Nikki and allowed himself to wish that she was here. He'd cut her out of his life, and he couldn't sacrifice her even to save his reputation. He wondered how badly he was going to regret that decision, even as he firmed it in his mind.

"As far as the company goes, you haven't got a legal leg to stand on," Bob Wilson told him regretfully a few minutes later. "I'm sorry, but they've got ironclad evidence linking Lombard, International, with Burke's and the illegal dumping site. The fact that you didn't personally make the decision to hire him doesn't negate the fact that you approved your subordinate's hiring of him. The buck stops at you. The company is in violation of several environmental laws, federal, local and state, and it will be prosecuted for at least one felony count, probably more as the investigation continues and they find more of Burke's handiwork. A fine is the least of your worries right now."

"In other words, even if I was willing to prove that I was incapacitated at the time of the hiring, it wouldn't lessen my responsibility in the eyes of the law."

"That's exactly right." Wilson frowned. "Of course, Burke will be prosecuted along with you. He's an accessory."

"Good. I hope they hang him out to dry. His brother-in-law Jurkins is my new solid waste manager, but I didn't know about any relationship between the two of them until this came up. How am I supposed to know things like that?" He glanced at Wilson. "Can I prosecute Jurkins for making that decision without my preliminary approval?"

"You did approve it," Wilson said with forced patience. "Jurkins denies any wrongdoing. He said that he told you what he'd done and you said it was all right."

"But, my God, I had no idea who Burke was or that CWC's record had been misrepresented to me!"

"Jurkins swears that he can show you on paper what CWC did to discredit them. He also swears that he didn't know Burke had been in any trouble, whether or not that's true. You're still culpable, regardless of that," Wilson informed him. "I'm sorry. I can't see any legal way out of this. You'll have to plead guilty and hope that we can negotiate a reasonable settlement."

"While that SOB gets away scot-free?"

"Which one?"

"Burke."

"We're investigating," Wilson assured him.

"Could kickbacks be involved here?" he asked suddenly, staring at his legal counsel. "If they were, there'll be proof, won't there?" Kane persisted.

"Well . . ." He grimaced, sticking his

hands deep in his pockets. "We can't find any evidence that anyone who works for you has had any drastic change in lifestyles. We're checking into employee backgrounds right now, though. If there is anything, we'll turn it up."

Kane leaned back against his desk. "You mean that this whole situation was innocently arrived at?" he asked.

"I can't prove that it wasn't at this point."

"Suppose I fire Jurkins?"

"What for?" Wilson replied. "He's done nothing except make a mistake in judgment, allegedly trying to save you money on operating expense. He's full of apologies and explanations and excuses."

"We could take the case to the newspapers. My father's, in fact."

"You aren't thinking," the other man said patiently. "Burke may be a scalawag, but he's a working man with a family to support. If you start persecuting him, despite what he's done, it's only going to reinforce the negative image of your company as a money-hungry exploiter of working people. People will overlook his illegal dumping because you're picking on him. In fact, the press will turn it around and make a hero of him — the little guy trying to make a buck, being persecuted by big business."

"I don't believe this!"

"I've seen it done. Being rich is its own punishment sometimes."

"I've provided hundreds of new jobs here," Kane thundered. "I've employed minorities without government pressure and put them in top executive positions. I've donated to civic projects, I've helped renovate depressed areas . . . doesn't any of that work in my favor?"

"When the hanging fever dies down, it probably will. You only have to live through the interim."

"You're just full of optimism, aren't you?"

Wilson got to his feet and went to shake hands with Kane. "I know it must look as if we're all against you. Don't give up. It's early days yet."

Kane glowered at him. "And when it rains, it pours. Get out there and save my neck."

"I'll do my best," he promised.

Nikki was exhausted when she and Derrie reached the old Victorian family home in the Battery.

"You'd better sack out in the downstairs

bedroom until you're more fit to climb those stairs," Derrie pointed out.

"I guess so," Nikki returned, with a wistful look at the gracefully curving staircase with its sedate gray carpet.

Derrie helped Nikki into the bedroom and then unpacked for her while Nikki got into her pajamas and climbed in bed. "Good thing Mrs. B. has been here."

"If it wasn't for Mrs. B. three times a week, I couldn't keep this place," Nikki pointed out. "She was a young girl when she kept house for Dad, but even middle age hasn't slowed her down. Doesn't she do a good job?"

"Wonderful." Derrie put the last of the dirty clothes in the laundry hamper. "You said that you'd had pneumonia for four days. However did you manage alone?"

Nikki averted her eyes. "I didn't eat much," she said, "and I had a jug of bottled water by the bed. The antibiotics worked very fast."

"Oh, that's right, you have a doctor for a neighbor up there, how silly of me to have forgotten," Derrie said.

"That's right, Chad Holman lives just down the road," Nikki assured her, relieved. It was highly unlikely that Derrie would run into Dr. Chad Holman to ask about Nikki's return bout of pneumonia. Kane's intervention would never have to be mentioned.

"I told you that you were doing too much at Spoleto," Derrie chided, glancing at the other woman as she lounged in the bed. "Summer pneumonia can be the very devil."

"I'm on the mend. I got chilled, that's all. I'll be more careful."

"You need to take better care of yourself," Derrie chided.

"Yes, ma'am," Nikki said. "Stop brooding. You've stopped working for my stupid brother, so you're hardly required to worry about me."

"I'll miss your stupid brother," Derrie said sadly, as she looked at Nikki and smiled. "But it wasn't because of him that I've been your friend."

"I know that. I'm sorry Clayton ever let himself get mixed up with Mosby," Nikki said quietly. "My ex-husband is a desperate man, and Bett Watts makes a vicious coconspirator. They're going to take my brother down if he isn't very careful. This fight with Kane Lombard could be just the thing to do it, too. Mr. Lombard doesn't strike me as the kind of man who takes anything lying down, and his family owns one vicious tabloid in New York."

"Mr. Lombard is very much on the defensive right now," Derrie observed. "They say his plant is surrounded by rabid environmentalists with blown-up photos of the dead birds in that marsh."

Nikki winced. She could imagine how Kane would feel. She'd learned enough about him during their acquaintance to tell that he was a man who loved wildlife. He'd been against the lumbering bill when her own brother wasn't. If he wanted to preserve the owl, certainly he wouldn't do anything deliberately to kill birds.

"I think you should know," Derrie began slowly, "that some of those protestors who are picketing Mr. Lombard's plant were hired to do it."

Nikki's lips parted as she let out a sudden breath. "Does Clayton know?"

Derrie turned, uncomfortable and uneasy. "Well, you see, that's why I quit. It was your brother who hired them."

Chapter Ten

Nikki couldn't believe what she was hearing. But she knew that Derrie wouldn't lie.

"But Clayton has always been so concerned for the environment, especially here at home," she said. "It's Haralson, isn't it?" she asked quietly. "He's fighting in the way he knows best. But meanwhile, Clay is allowing himself to be used for what he thinks is political power."

"He thinks he's doing it to protect you from a scandal," Derrie replied, frowning. "Nikki, do you have a skeleton that Kane could rattle?"

"Doesn't everyone?" Nikki asked uncertainly. She chewed on a fingernail. "What are we going to do?"

"Talk to Clay," Derrie invited. "Perhaps he'll listen to you. He's gone deaf with me."

"I'm sorry you won't stay," Nikki murmured.

"I can't. He wanted me to call the television stations and get them over to Mr. Lombard's plant." She grimaced. "That was Haralson's suggestion, too, I'm pretty sure, but Clayton was willing to do it."

"I see." Nikki didn't recognize these tactics. Not only were they not like Clayton, they weren't like Mosby, either. Mosby wasn't a malicious man. Even in his antienvironment stance, his goal was to save jobs, to put people to work. He wasn't working for personal gain. He never had. But he'd sent Haralson to help Clayton's campaign. Why?

"I would have refused to call the TV stations, too," she said when Derrie appeared to be waiting for reassurance.

Derrie forced herself to smile. "It feels funny to be without a job," she said slowly.

"What will you do?"

"Something I may regret. I'm going to work for the competition. Sam Hewett asked me to work for him when the race started. He's very pro-women's rights and I know his family," she said, grimacing at Nikki's pained look. "He's a good man and he won't fight dirty. He has integrity — the sort of integrity that your brother always had until that Haralson man came along and started helping him." She lowered her eyes. "I'm very sorry. I wish it hadn't come to this."

"So do I. Let me talk to Clayton before you rush into anything," Nikki pleaded.

Derrie moved closer, a hand going to her tangle of blond hair. "You don't understand, Nikki," she began. "He told me what he really thought of me. I guess because we joked so much I never took him seriously when he teased me about being a prude. But he was really mad this morning. He said the only reason he kept me around was because I was efficient." She shook her head. "I didn't realize how much I cared until then. It's hopeless, you see," she said with a sad smile. "I can't make him love me."

Nikki knew how that felt. Her own heart was still raw from Kane's unexpected rejection. "Oh, Derrie," Nikki said miserably. "Whoever he gets as a replacement won't come close to you. You're the only long-term staff member he's kept from the old days in the state house of representatives."

"I know. Well, I hope you and I will still be friends."

"Don't be absurd, of course we will. Thank you for helping me get home, Derrie."

"Any time." She picked up her purse and moved to the door. It was all beginning to hit her now. "I'll call Mr. Hewett and then have a nice lazy weekend before I start back to work, if he still wants me, that is."

"I have no doubt that he will."

Nikki looked concerned and Derrie instantly knew why. "I'm not going to sell out Clayton, even if he is a rat."

Nikki flushed. "Derrie, I wasn't thinking . . ."

"Yes, you were, it's quite natural to. But I'm not that mad. Mostly, I'm hurt." She breathed heavily. "I'll get over it. Life happens."

"Doesn't it just?" Nikki said sadly, remembering Kane and what she'd had to sacrifice. "I want to know how things work out for you."

Derrie smiled at her. "You will, I promise."

Clayton came that night to see about Nikki. He looked drawn and preoccupied.

"Worn out from learning to make coffee?" Nikki asked mockingly when he walked into the living room, curled up on the couch waiting for him.

"So she told you," he said. He dropped heavily into his armchair and stared at her. "You look awful."

"I feel better than I did," she replied. "I caught a chill. Stupid of me, under the circumstances, but I'm better now."

"I'm glad. I would have come, but Derrie

made it impossible," he said angrily.

She laughed in spite of herself. He looked as he had when they were children and someone took something he treasured away from him. The two of them looked very much alike except for the darkness of Nikki's skin. He shared her dark hair but he had blue eyes, and she had green ones, a legacy from both sides of the family.

"She quit," he muttered. "Can you imagine? I asked her to do one little thing beyond her regular duties, and she walked out!"

"I know why she walked out," Nikki returned. "I'd have walked out, too. Haralson is destroying you, Clay. You've changed more than you realize."

He glared at her. "If the Lombards get hold of your marriage, do you have any idea what they'll do to you and Mosby in that supermarket sleaze sheet they've made millions on?"

"Yes, I know," she agreed quietly. "And I'd rather face that than watch you use the same tactics to get reelected."

"You have to play hardball sometimes. Haralson knows what he's doing. Maybe his methods are a little ruthless, but Lombard is ruthless, too."

"Not like this," she said. "If he hit you,

you'd see him coming."

His face cleared. He stared at her for a long moment. "How do you know?" he asked quietly.

She hesitated. "I've read some very interesting things about him," she said. She couldn't tell her brother that she'd spent several days alone with Kane Lombard, or that she'd been falling in love with him. In Clayton's current frame of mind, that would have been foolish.

"No more Derrie," Clayton was mumbling dully. "I can't even believe it! She's been with me for years, from when I was first elected to the state legislature until I was elected to Congress, she was always there. And now she walks out over a triviality."

"It isn't a triviality," she said.

He glanced at her curiously. "Wake up, Nikki. You know what politics is like. Neither of us has ever been blind to what went on behind the curtains."

"Yes, but Clay, you've never been part of that before. You were an idealist."

"I can't change anything until I garner some political clout, and I can't do that until I'm reelected. Two year terms for Congressmen are outrageous, we aren't even settled in office before we have to run for reelection. I want back in. I have plans, an itinerary," he said, talking to himself. "How I win isn't that important. Once I'm reelected, I've learned that nothing changes, no matter how hard you work," he said dully.

"Unemployment is growing by the day." His face hardened. "Derrie's worried about an owl and I'm trying to save jobs. Well, I can recoup my support right here in my own state. All I have to do is throw Lombard to the wolves. He's been dumping chemicals in a marsh. The media is having a field day at his expense," he added, brightening. "This is the first break I've had since the campaign began. I got full credit for helping catch him."

"Do you know what Mr. Lombard's been through in the past year?"

"Who doesn't?" he said shortly, rising. He held up his hand when she threatened to continue. "Enough, Nikki. It doesn't change facts. He's guilty and I'm going to nail him to the wall."

"Mosby is behind you, I gather," she said coldly.

"He loaned me Haralson. He always liked me."

Nikki averted her eyes. Yes, he had. Mosby even liked Nikki, but that was all.

She couldn't forget the revulsion in Mosby's eyes the one time she'd tried desperately to arouse him by stripping in front of him. The damage he'd done, without any malice at all, to her image as a woman was never going to be fully erased. Kane might have helped, but he had his own emotional barriers.

"You've forgiven Mosby," Clayton said slowly.

"Yes," Nikki replied softly. "He couldn't help it."

Clayton winced. "If it got out, he'd kill himself," he told her. "He's a decent man, a very private man. He supports job programs and minorities, even if sometimes he only does it for political gain. The environmentalists may hate him, but they're the only ones. He's kind, in his way."

"Yes, I remember," she said. Her heart was still bruised, and it didn't help to recall Mosby with an injured bird on his lap driving wildly to the nearest veterinarian's office to have it treated.

"You never even suspected, did you?" Clayton said sadly. "Dad did, I think, but he wouldn't admit it even to himself. He was too bent on saving his own skin. Mosby needed a wife, and Dad needed Mosby."

"And the only one who suffered was me," Nikki said miserably.

"That's not quite true," Clayton told her. "Mosby was devastated when he realized exactly how you felt. It took him a long time to get over it. He's more sensitive than most, and he doesn't like hurting anyone."

"I know that," she said. She looked at Clay. "But Bett doesn't mind hurting people. She's trained you so that you're the same way lately."

He glared at her. "Bett is my business. And she doesn't like you, either."

"Heavens, should that surprise me?" Nikki laughed. "I don't think she owns anything except pin-striped suits and ties. I'll bet you've never seen her in a dress."

Clayton scowled. "What does that have to do with anything?"

"I like dresses," she replied, her green eyes sparkling. "I don't have to prove that I'm better than a man. I already know that I am," she added wickedly.

He sighed, shaking his head. "Nikki, you're hopeless."

"Probably. Don't lose yourself in the political maze," she pleaded. "Don't lose sight of why you ran for the office in the first place. You're on the Energy and National Resources Subcommittee and the energy committee. You've made suggestions that won you more support on the hill. I'm very proud of you. Don't blow all that to keep Mosby and Bett on the good side of the timber lobby."

"I'll reconsider my position," he told her. "Now. When you get back on your feet, I thought we'd throw a few gala parties."

"I know, beginning with one in Washington, D.C., in September," she added, feeling brighter and happier as she considered the motif for the first party.

"The primary election will be over by then," he said uncomfortably.

"And we'll win," she assured him, smiling. "And the party will be a celebration."

He hoped so, but didn't put it into words.

"I do love politics, Clay."

"So do I," he seconded. "And I'll try not to disillusion you too much with my campaign. Just remember, Nikki, we both have a lot to fear from Lombard. If he's occupied with defending himself against the EPA rules, his family will be too busy trying to help him to pay much attention to you and Mosby before the primary. It's only a delaying tactic, and he's filthy rich.

They won't hang him too high."

Nikki didn't like agreeing with him, but he was probably right. All the same, she wondered at what it was already costing him to adhere to his new policy. The first casualty was Derrie. She wondered how many would follow.

Mosby Torrance sipped wine as he stood in front of his lofty window overlooking the traffic of nighttime Washington. He was barefooted, wearing a silver and gold robe that emphasized his blond good looks.

He felt triumphant over Haralson's victory against Lombard in Charleston. Now Lombard had his hands full trying to defend himself. The very action of keeping Lombard's family occupied would keep Mosby off the line of fire as the campaign escalated.

He couldn't afford to let Clayton lose the election. The Democratic contender was mild-mannered, but still a liberal who had no sympathy with Mosby's position on the real major issues like tax incentives for industry and a bigger military budget and supporting the lumbering industry. He needed all the support he could get from the House, and Clayton was shaping up very well as an environmental candidate and a strong national defense ally.

Mosby needed that wedge on his team, because he didn't support environmental programs; he supported industry and expansion and growth to provide much-needed jobs for the unemployed. Privately, he thought that Clayton did, too, but it was politically correct at the moment to be an environmental candidate. And until Mosby had coaxed Clayton into helping him with the timber bill, the congressman had a spotless record of environmental championship. It had been a shame to blot that record, but Mosby had needed Clayton's support. Besides, the Lombard scandal was going to make everyone forget that Clayton hadn't helped the spotted owl.

Mosby leaned his head wearily against the cool glass. It was good not to have the Lombards after him. He was older than Clayton, raised in a generation with stifling attitudes toward anyone different from the norm. His parents had hidden his flaw from other relatives. They had made Mosby ashamed of it. Because of his upbringing, he'd always had to hide what he was. No one would have understood. At least, that's what his parents had said. Often he'd wondered what Nikki would have said, if she'd known. He'd had to steel himself not to show desire for her, not to let her know, ever, how attractive he found her. All he could have given her was a travesty of the real thing and, inevitably, she'd have wondered why he couldn't function as a man. It was better this way, he told himself. Much better.

He was dignified and very conservative on the outside, and that won him votes. But inside, he was a frightened, insecure man who dreaded the new climate that threatened to expose any politician who kept a secret. Mosby had exacted many sacrifices. He would do anything to keep his private life secret, and he had; he'd married Nikki. He winced, remembering. It had been hopeless from the very beginning.

His fist clenched on the glass. Poor Nikki. Poor, poor Nikki, to be so much in love and have all her dreams shattered. He'd engineered that sight she had of his private life, that fiction of himself as a gay man. He'd known that it would drive her away, and it had. But he also knew that she'd never become serious about anyone since their divorce, and he knew why. He regretted hurting Nikki most of all.

It was all over long ago, he told himself. He just had to live with it, and with the fear of exposure. The thing now was to get Clayton ahead in the polls while keeping the pressure on Lombard. That last part was Haralson's idea, just as it had been Haralson's idea to go to South Carolina and help with Clayton's campaign. In fact, Haralson said that he knew the truth about Mosby and wouldn't hesitate to give it to the media if Mosby didn't send him to Charleston to help Clayton.

He scowled. Haralson was a wild man just lately, into all sorts of shady things that Mosby had tried not to notice. But the man was like a loose cannon. Mosby had a bad feeling about his obsession with getting something on Lombard. He didn't know why he should. After all, Lombard was no friend of Mosby's, with his family sticking its nose into his past. But just the same, Mosby didn't like the idea of doing anything illegal. Perhaps he should take a closer look at Haralson's methods. If worse came to worse, there might be a way to nudge Haralson into a corner and keep him quiet about what he knew of Mosby's worst secret.

He picked up the telephone and dialed a number.

While he waited for the connection, he remembered his first year in the Senate, a young idealist with so many hopes and dreams that an unfortunate bit of publicity — a hint about his sexual preferences — had almost ended. His marriage had saved him, at Nikki's expense. But even marriage would no longer protect him, not if Lombard got wind of his past. The dreams and ideals had gotten lost in the shuffle to protect his secret, until now it was almost second nature to him. Perhaps his three terms in the Senate had jaded him, he thought miserably. He lived in a closed society, despite his frequent trips to his home state to keep in touch with his constituents. But the longer he lived in the Capitol, the more distasteful the outside world became to him. He was safe here. For the time being, at least. As long as he had Haralson out of his hair for a few weeks while the campaign picked up steam. He'd have to find some leverage to use against Haralson if it became necessary. If he dared, he'd warn Clayton about him as well, but that wouldn't be wise at this point.

"Hello," came a quiet voice on the other line.

"I need a favor," Mosby said. "I want you to do a little digging for me, strictly on the QT."

There was a pause. "Okay. Shoot."

He gave the man Haralson's name and background.

"Isn't this the one who's working for Seymour down in Charleston, the one who just exposed some nasty mess concerning Kane Lombard?" the man asked.

"The same."

"Well, well. Now isn't this interesting?"

"What is?"

There was a low chuckle. "I'll tell you all about it in a few weeks. Haralson got careless. That's all you need to know right now."

"This . . . carelessness. Is it to my advantage?"

"Yes, indeed. And as you say, that message is on the QT. I'll be in touch." The receiver went dead with a gentle click.

That sounded as if Haralson could find himself in water over his head very soon. As he'd said about the Lombards, if pressure was put on a man he was less likely to find time to smear anyone else. The best defense, in other words, was a good offense. Try that on for size, Haralson, he mused. Mosby put down his wineglass, relief draining away the fear. He slid the robe away from his body and walked, smiling, back to bed.

★ ★ ★

The wheels of justice were slow, but relentless. Kane Lombard spent a lot of time with his attorneys and his production people and managers, trying to sort out the nightmarish complications of his own negligence. Both Will Jurkins and Ed Nelson came back to work. Nelson was feeble, but involved himself in the defense of his company. Jurkins provided the paperwork that showed CWC's lack of efficiency and showed a reason for firing them. However, Kane couldn't help notice that Jurkins had dark circles under his eyes and asked if the man wasn't sleeping well. Jurkins had mentioned something about a sick child and had gone back to his office, looking haggard. Like the rest of the staff, Kane decided, Jurkins was feeling the pressure of public animosity. All of them had to pass through the picket lines daily, and only the security force kept them safe at all.

The day of the primary came, and Nikki went with Clay to their local precinct to vote. Crowds were already standing in line at eight in the morning, and Nikki's heart lifted. It did look as if he had the Republican seat firmly in hand.

She had collaborated with one of Washington's leading hostesses to concoct some sort of party that people would be talking about years from now. Assuming that Clay won the primary, there were other parties planned for Charleston, fund-raisers and banquets and social evenings to garner more support. Nikki expected to be worn to a frazzle, but it would be worth it. If only he would win the primary!

"This looks encouraging," she said.

Clayton didn't agree. The turnout frightened him. He'd made a major blunder by supporting the timber bill, and he prayed that people were going to remember that he'd helped nab a local industrial polluter. Usually when so many people went to vote, it was because they were angry and wanted to get someone out of office. He'd actually known some old-timers who only ever voted against — not for — candidates.

"Don't look so nervous," she chided.

An African American lady next to them grinned. "That's right, it's not against the law to vote for the candidate of your choice."

Clay grinned. "Picked the best man, have you?" he teased.

"Oh, yes, sir," she said. "Going to have a new president this fall, so I figure we may as well get those other rascals out of there and put in some people who can get something done. I have no insurance. I can't make my house payment this month. I can't even afford to buy a new pair of shoes."

The woman looked down at them, worn on both sides and scuffed. "The plant I worked for moved down into the Caribbean so it could get cheap labor and make more money. It don't bother the government that I wouldn't have a job," she added. "What a pity that we pay those people so much to represent us and they just forget how hard life is outside the capitol."

She nodded politely and moved on as her line shortened. Clayton had gone pale. Nikki touched his arm and tried to encourage him, but he felt bad. Why hadn't he realized what was happening? These people wanted change because their economic situation was a nightmare. They weren't going in that polling place to vote for him, they were going to vote him out of office!

All those plants that had closed down their domestic operations and moved to other countries, all those jobs lost, all those unemployed people hadn't seemed to register with him before. He saw the homeless people and he slipped them a dollar from time to time, but he never noticed that they had no house to go to. Where had his mind been? On the spotted owl, he thought, and on keeping Kane Lombard's family off Mosby Torrance's neck. He'd spent almost two years feathering his own nest and thinking of his own political future and satisfying his own ambitions. He'd forgotten that most important thing of all; that these people had elected him to represent their interests in Washington. How could he have been so blind?

"Derrie tried to tell me," he began.

Nikki looked at him and her eyes asked a question.

"I hope it's not too late," he said quietly.

"What do you mean?"

But the line moved, and so did they, and the question was drowned out by the low buzz of conversation.

The polls closed at seven, but there were still lines of people waiting to get into the polling booths. Early returns gave Sam Hewett a tremendous lead in the Democratic primary, but on the Republican side, Clayton was running neck and neck with a well-known Charleston attorney. It was much too tight a race for comfort. It meant that voters were unsatisfied.

"Will you stop pacing and worrying?" Nikki chided, sweeping into the hotel room in his headquarters in a blue-and-green-silk pantsuit that suited her dark complexion.

Clayton, with his hands in his slacks pockets, standing flanked by Haralson and Bett, glowered at her. "Do you see these figures?" he asked.

She handed him a cup of coffee in a foam cup. "You're not going to lose."

Bett glanced at her. "You sound very sure."

Nikki smiled. "He's the best man, isn't he?"

"Of course," Bett agreed.

"Then he'll win." Nikki moved her eyes back to the television screen. "It's early yet, and these are small typically Democratic precincts they're reporting. Wait until we get the urban vote. That's where Clay's strength is."

Bett was surprised. "How do you know so much about politics?"

"I have three and a half years of college," Nikki said. "I'm only a semester short of having my degree."

"I didn't realize that."

"No, you were much too busy resenting my — how did you put it? — empty-headed hostessing."

It was a challenge from a face dominated by sparkling green eyes. Bett had character enough to admit when she was wrong. She smiled ruefully.

"Sorry about that."

"Oh, we're all guilty of making snap judgments," Nikki said mischievously. "I won't mention what I asked Clay about you when I first met you."

"Thank you," Bett murmured sheepishly.

"Clay!" Haralson called suddenly. "Look!"

They all turned their attention to the television screen where new figures were being posted. The urban precincts were just beginning to be reported and Clay's two-percent lead had just turned into a twenty-percent lead.

"Hallelujah!" Clayton shouted.

"See?" Nikki asked, smiling, "I told you so."

Chapter Eleven

The celebrating went on all night. The Republican opposition conceded early on, and Clayton and Bett and Nikki bathed in the adulation from his supporters.

At midnight, Clayton went on television to make his acceptance speech for the Republican nomination.

"I want you to know that I'm going to fight hard to win this time," he told the camera. "And I'm not going to sit on my record. I've had my eyes opened today about issues I haven't confronted. People are out of work because of jobs going to other countries. We have such people, right here in our city. It's time we did something about the economy and learned to balance the budget. I've seen the light. I'm going to blind you with it until I get back into Washington, and then I'm going to tackle a new agenda. The environment is still an important issue to me, but the thing is to get our people back to work. That's going to be my number one priority. Thank you all for your support. Let's go on and win in November!"

The supporters cheered wildly. Clayton smiled, but there was a new fire in his eyes that everyone around him noticed. Bett saw it with trepidation, because she also represented a lobby that supported foreign expansion of American businesses. Her smile was a little strained as she contemplated the future.

Nikki was oblivious to the other woman's thoughts. Her eyes were on her brother, and she was bursting with pride. Her only sadness was what was happening to Kane Lombard. She knew that he wasn't responsible for that dumping. But how to convince everyone else was the problem. It had to have happened while he was lying injured in her beach house. She wondered if he'd kept that quiet because he was trying to protect her reputation. After all, he didn't know who she was. He'd think she was just a beachcomber.

She often thought of him and remembered the joy of being with him. It had ended all too soon. He haunted her dreams, and made her sad. Not since Mosby had she felt quite so valueless. Apparently her only worth to men was as a decoration, and that attraction soon paled. Mosby had wanted a storefront. Kane had wanted a careless lover. She was suited to be neither.

She'd seen Kane on television several times, and she'd felt sickened by the trials he was facing because of her brother's supporters. She knew that Clay hadn't engineered the incident, but he was certainly using it to his advantage. She wondered if it had made Kane hate him even more, and what form of retribution he might select in reprisal. It worried her so much that she almost telephoned Kane once to discuss it with him. But he didn't know who she was, and she didn't want him to. He'd surely hate her if he knew the truth, especially after what had happened. So many secrets lay behind all this sparkling hoopla of politics. Everyone had a skeleton in the closet. Some skeletons were even able to speak.

The elder Lombard puffed angrily on his big cigar as he paced around his son Kane's office.

"Damned stupidity," he muttered, glancing at his eldest son to make sure he was being listened to. "You know better than to run off on vacation and leave the business unattended. Think I've ever done that?"

Kane didn't answer. This speech was familiar. His father always asked the same question. The elder Lombard didn't make mistakes, always knew what to do, and was there on the spot with an I-told-you-so whenever he deemed it necessary.

"In my day, we'd have had that employee drawn and quartered," he continued hotly. "No questions asked, either, mind you. And the press would have been muzzled!"

"You're the press," his son pointed out.

The old man made a dismissive gesture with a big, wrinkled hand. His hands were almost out of proportion to his tall, spare frame. "I'm not that kind of press, I'm not easily led and fed lies. I print the truth!"

"No, you don't."

Fred Lombard glared down his thin nose at Kane. "I print it sometimes," he clarified, "when I think it needs printing. The rest of the time people expect to be entertained, and they pay through the nose for it. Don't you appreciate how to sell news?"

"Sure. Put two heads on the victim and draw in a flying saucer on a photograph, blow it up, and cover the front page with it," Kane returned.

Fred chuckled. "Sure, that's how you do it."

"You won't win a Pulitzer."

"I'm crying all the way to the Swiss bank

where I keep my money," Fred returned. "No interest, but total confidentiality, and I like that. Don't expect to inherit everything," he added. "You have two brothers."

"I don't need to inherit anything," came the cynical reply. "I'm set for life already. I'll have free room and board and three meals a day at Leavenworth."

"Bosh." Fred waved the cigar at him. "They can't put you in prison for something an employee did in all innocence."

"Illegal dumping is a felony, didn't you hear the attorney?"

"Sure I did, but I'm telling you that the current administration is so slow about investigations that you'll be my age before any charges are brought."

"That could be true. But what if this administration loses in November?"

"Then we're all in a lot of trouble. Especially you, because that young fellow not only has some bright ideas about the economy and the jobless, he's keen on keeping the earth unpolluted."

"More power to him," Kane replied. "I feel the same way. But even if I didn't do the dumping, I allowed it. It's my responsibility to make sure my employees hire disposal people who obey the law. I didn't."

"You weren't here," Fred returned. "I

keep reminding you, you weren't here! If you want to take long vacations, sell the business!"

Kane sat down on the edge of his desk with a heavy breath. "I've got the company attorneys working night and day on a defense, but my heart isn't in it. Did you see the photographs?" he asked, anger and sadness in his dark eyes. "My God, all that destruction. I hope they lock that idiot up in one of his own trucks and push him into a swamp."

"He'd pollute the environment," came the dry reply.

"I suppose so," Kane agreed reluctantly.

"Cheer up. I'm working on a way to save you."

Kane's head cocked. "If you dare put a picture of a flying saucer over a photograph of that marsh and print it . . ."

"Son, would I do that?"

"Hell, yes."

"Not this time," Fred promised. "I've got that fellow Lawson investigating some ties of Seymour's to Senator Torrance."

Kane scowled. "What sort of ties?"

"It's very interesting. Did you know that seven years ago, Seymour's only sister married Mosby Torrance?"

Kane felt his heart turn over. *"What?"*

"The marriage lasted six months. After a quiet divorce, there was talk that Torrance had only married to stop some gossip about his continuing bachelor status."

Kane's mind was spinning as he connected what he was being told. Nikki had been married. She hadn't told him that, but she'd said that she was involved with a man who couldn't touch her. Torrance? Could it have been Torrance?

Fred stopped pacing and stared at him. "What are you brooding about?"

"What do we know about Torrance?"

"Not much. He's a secretive devil. I've got Lawson doing some discreet back-tracking. We know that Torrance grew up in a little community near Aiken. Lawson has gone up there to talk to some people. If Torrance is hiding anything, that's where we'll find it."

"And if you do find something, what are you going to do?" Kane asked suspiciously.

"Use it as leverage," came the terse reply. "You and I both know that it's Torrance more than Seymour who's after you. I suspect it's to keep your back to the wall so that you won't have time to do any digging and point any fingers in his direction. He needs Seymour, but he'd jettison him in a minute to get us off his back.

That's what I'm counting on. I want leverage."

"You're an underhanded man," Kane said after a minute.

"Luckily for you," his father replied. "Your lofty principles would land you in the hoosegow for sure if I wasn't!"

Kane wasn't so certain that his father's lack of them wouldn't land him there, but he kept quiet. His mind was on Nikki and the time they'd been together, when he'd felt safe for the first time in his adult life. It seemed very far away right now, with his business in turmoil. He should have been honest with her from the beginning, and let her be honest with him. If he hadn't been so wary of commitment, anything could have happened. Now, there were too many barriers. His eyes narrowed and his temper flared. What had Torrance done to her?

When Clayton went back to Washington, Nikki went along and moved into the small cottage at the Royce Blair estate which Madge Blair had made available to her. Madge was contributing the setting for a gala evening to celebrate Clayton's party nomination and also to garner support for his campaign. Nikki's genius for organization was being put to good use as she hired caterers, made arrangements for entertainment, and played overseer for the immaculate theme decorations that were being installed in the mansion's great ballroom.

"You never cease to amaze me, Nikki," Madge confessed while she helped hang delicate silver filigree musical notes against a background of golden staffs on white satin. "A theme party built around opera, with all the guests to come dressed as their favorite singer or operatic character. I expect we'll have twenty Pavarottis," she confessed, laughing.

"Where's Claude?" Nikki asked, looking around the room.

"In hiding with the cats," Madge said, laughing. "He does so detest parties, my poor darling. He's shut himself in the library with the Siamese twins and he's furiously reading Greek tragedies. It inspires him, he says."

"Madge, he writes sexy murder mysteries," she commented. "He's world-famous. Everything he writes is made into a major motion picture. There's one debuting next month."

"I know, dear, I'm married to him," Madge returned, tongue in cheek.

Nikki laughed. "Is he going to come to

the party, at least? He does live here."

"He might. But rest assured that he'll roll himself in flour and come as something disgusting like the ghost in that Mozart opera I hate." She tacked a note into place. "Who are you coming as? I know — Madama Butterfly! With that jet-black hair, you'd be a natural."

"Actually, I'm going to wear a gauzy gown and come as Camille. I feel tragic."

"Oh, Nikki, not you. You always sparkle so."

"I've had my share of sadness."

Madge glanced at her. "Indeed you have. But your face doesn't show it. You look almost untouched."

Nikki could have howled. She was, but Madge didn't know why; she only knew that Nikki had a failed marriage behind her.

"Hand me that stapler, could you?" Nikki asked.

"Here, dear. The invitations have all gone out, and we're very nearly through here. Only a few more hours. Clayton and Bett will be on time, won't they?" she added worriedly.

"They promised."

"Nikki, Claude insisted that we add a couple of names to the list, so I sent out a few extra invitations. I hope you don't mind?"

"How silly. It's your house and you're our friends. You're even loaning us your home for this oh-so-discreet fund-raiser. How could I possibly mind?"

"It's just that Clayton is at odds with Kane right now. But, Kane and Claude belonged to the same yacht club at one time, and they're still very good friends. I hope you won't hate him . . ." Madge said worriedly. "Why, Nikki, are you all right?"

Nikki had dropped the stapler and almost fell off the ladder where she was perched. "Kane Lombard? Claude invited Kane Lombard?" she asked, shaken.

"They're friends, you see. Oh, dear, I did try to stop him. He invited Kane's woman friend, too. They're almost inseparable these past few weeks since he's had such terrible problems — not that Clayton should be blamed for them, of course." She sighed. "Oh, Nikki, Claude doesn't think. He means well. It's those four cats," she added darkly. "Two Siamese and two Persians, and they drive me mad! How he can write with those furry assassins all over his desk is beyond me!"

Nikki's heart was beating madly. Kane was coming here. He'd see her. He'd find out who she really was. She'd have to watch him with the lover he'd told her about, the faceless woman who had part of him that Nikki would never know.

"Perhaps you should go and lie down," Madge suggested.

Nikki's wide eyes met the green ones of her blond friend. "No. Really. I'm fine. I just got a little dizzy. I haven't eaten anything."

"Then you must have a sandwich. Come with me. I'll have Lucie make you one of her famous Philly steak sandwiches and cottage fries."

"Thanks just the same, but I really don't want to die of cholesterol poisoning," Nikki chuckled. "Make that a small salad and some bread sticks instead, if you could."

"You sparrow, you." Madge smoothed her hands over her ample hips with a grimace. "If I liked lettuce leaves, I could look like you in places, at least."

"You're very nice as you are, as I'm sure Claude tells you constantly." She linked her arm with Madge's. "Now, let's go over these catered items just once more."

The day's activity, frantic though it was, didn't take her mind off the coming confrontation with Kane. She nibbled at her fingernails until she almost gnawed one into the quick. She looked around the room at the arrangements, satisfied, and went toward the staircase. It was nearing time for people to start arriving. If only it would go smoothly. She always worried about the food and musicians arriving on time.

"I can see the wheels turning in your head," Claude observed, coming into the hall with a cat under one arm. One of the felines was a big, chocolate-point Siamese with blue eyes that appraised Nikki and found her uninteresting. He closed his big eyes and curled closer into Claude's jacket.

"Mudd is hopeless," he remarked, nodding toward the sleeping cat. "He only wakes up to eat. He's so lazy that he even lets the others bathe him. His psychologist says it's because he's depressed. He isn't let outside you know, and it's frustrating him."

Nikki didn't dare grin. Claude took Mudd's therapy sessions very seriously indeed.

"How is he progressing?" she asked cautiously.

"Well, I don't notice much change, but at least he's stopped chewing on my computer keyboard. Damnedest thing, all those toothmarks. Jealousy, you know. Yes, that's right, he's jealous of the computer when I'm writing."

It was impossible to be mad at Claude for long. Nikki, like everyone who knew him, adored him. She'd manage to stay out of Kane's way. He didn't know who she was, really, and in costume, perhaps she could go unrecognized. "Are you coming to the party?" Nikki asked her host.

"I might. I think I'll come as Ravel, with a cat under each arm," he added. "Ravel kept cats, you know. Dozens of cats. He even spoke to them."

"I used to speak to my cat," Nikki pointed out.

"Not in its own language," he returned with a wicked grin.

"Puff understood me well enough. He could hear the sound of a can being opened from the balcony upstairs," Nikki recalled wistfully. Puff had died of old age a few weeks back, and she was still sad about it.

"You need a new cat," he said gently.

She shrugged. "I'm too busy for cats," she lied. It was unthinkable to replace Puff so soon.

"Why do you look so sad?" he remarked.

"Clayton won the nomination."

"That isn't what I feel sad about."

"He'll discover that Bett isn't right for him and marry that Derrie of his one day," Claude chuckled.

"Derrie quit, and Bett's already announced their engagement. She isn't so bad."

"She's a lobbyist. If she marries Clayton there will be a major conflict of interest and she'll lose her job. She's an ambitious lady. When she has to make the final choice, she'll leave him."

"How do you know so much about people?" Nikki asked, aghast.

"My dear girl, I'm a writer. Who knows more about people than we do?"

"Good point."

"Didn't Camille have a cat?" he asked, frowning. "Madge told me that's who you're going dressed as. You could carry a cat, too."

"I think having a woman with tuberculosis carry a cat would be a bit . . . how shall I put it . . . unexpected?"

"Oh, yes. I see." He chuckled. "Bad suggestion. I know! I'll see if I can get Madge to dress as something Egyptian or even Babylonian — from the Rossini opera *Semiramide*, you know — and *she* can carry a cat under each arm."

"Why does someone besides you have to carry a cat?"

"Two cats," he corrected. "I have four. They get in my box of fanfold paper and eat it if I leave them alone. Or they chew up manuscripts. Mudd can open the cabinet under the desk, remember."

"You need a filing cabinet."

He frowned. "That's cruel."

"What is?"

"Suggesting that I lock my cats up in a filing cabinet!"

Nikki gave him an exasperated look and dashed upstairs to the sound of mischievous laughter. Poor Madge, she had to live with him!

The gauzy white costume suited Nikki. She felt as if she were a floating island of sand among all the brightly colored costumes of the guests. Clayton and Bett had arrived, dressed as Carmen and her soldier. Clayton looked uncomfortable in the high-collared uniform while Bett was unconvincing as a peasant girl in the revealing blouse that showed little more than her extreme emaciation.

There was no sign of Kane as yet, and Nikki entertained a faint hope that he might not come. He didn't like Clayton, after all, and he must know that the party was being given in Clayton's honor. Nikki hadn't told Clayton that his archenemy was expected. She might not have to, she thought, as time passed and still Kane didn't make an appearance. She began to relax a little.

Claude and Madge were exceptionally colorful as Maurice Ravel and Madama Butterfly. Claude had Mudd under one arm. A quick scrutiny of the other guests revealed three more carrying cats. She smiled to herself. Claude was exceptionally persuasive, and the cats were like children — they loved being held.

"It's the odd couple," Nikki quipped when they joined her.

"Look who's insulting whom, the coughing courtesan," Claude returned, clutching Mudd under an arm. Mudd was wide-awake and very obviously irritated at the company he was having to keep. He gave his human friend a pie-eyed glare and suddenly sank his teeth into Claude's arm.

"Ouch!" Claude cried.

"Repressed hostility can stunt mental growth," Nikki said, nodding. "Better allow him freedom of expression. We wouldn't want to inhibit him."

"I'll inhibit him into a *boeuf bourbonnais* if he does that again," Claude said, glaring at the cat.

"Don't be absurd, dear, you can't cook a cat with red wine, it's so bourgeoisie," Madge told him.

Nikki laughed. These two were the closest friends she'd ever had, and the most loyal. They didn't know of her background, but it wouldn't have mattered if they had. They were the least judgmental people she'd ever known.

"What a crowd," Clayton murmured, joining them. He scowled at his sister with her stark white complexion and painted cheeks. "What are you supposed to be, Vampira?"

"I'm dying of tuberculosis, can't you tell?" she muttered at him. "I'm Camille."

"I hate opera," Clayton remarked to no one in particular.

"You'll learn to like it when we're married," Bett said carelessly. "I love opera, so we'll be going quite often."

Nikki didn't say a word, but she raised an eloquent eyebrow for her brother's benefit. He gave her a hard glare.

"Why isn't Derrie with the two of you tonight?" Claude asked suddenly. "Did she have other plans?"

Bett looked murderous. Clayton cleared his throat.

"Derrie quit and went to work for the competition," Nikki replied. "She found that her job description didn't quite cover what the boss expected her to do."

"She wouldn't follow orders so I fired her," Clayton said, daring Nikki to argue. "She was a turncoat."

"Indeed she was," Bett agreed eagerly. "I never trusted her."

"I did," Nikki replied, staring at them both levelly. "She was the most loyal employee Clay ever had. She stayed with him through thick and thin, even when his office was attacked because of some unfavorable legislation he introduced in the state house of representatives, before he even dreamed of going to Washington. Derrie was threatened, but she still wouldn't quit." Her tone became fierce as she stood up for her friend. "She worked twelve-hour days without complaint, gave up her home to move to Washington with Clay to oversee his personal and constituent staff. She even sacrificed her personal life to do it. Untrustworthy? Well, if that's how you define it, I think we need more people like her."

Clayton fidgeted uncomfortably under

his sister's hot glare. "You're very loyal to your friends, Nikki, but you don't understand the situation at all."

"Do explain it to me," she challenged.

"Please," he laughed. "Don't rock the boat, sis. A lot is riding on this. I need more support if I'm going to get back in the saddle come January."

"Mosby and I are drumming up all sorts of support for you," Bett told him.

"Where is Mosby?" Madge asked.

"He had other plans and sent his regrets," Clayton said quickly. "He's not much of a mixer. Parties make him nervous."

"It's because all the women throw themselves at his feet," Madge said with a wicked smile. "He's so handsome, isn't he? Oh, my, even my knees go weak when I look at him."

Nikki's had once, too. But now she thought of Mosby with sadness and pain. She didn't reply. Bett knew about the marriage, but only that it had existed. Apparently Clayton didn't trust her very much, either.

"Look, more guests are arriving," Claude said enthusiastically. "I must mingle, my dears. Here. Have a cat."

He handed Mudd to a protesting

Clayton, who promptly dumped him into Nikki's arms with a grin.

"You know you love cats," he reminded her. "You have Puff."

"I *had* Puff," she amended. "I do miss him." She petted Mudd, who narrowed his eyes and began to growl.

"He's expressing his buried hostility," Clayton pointed out.

"He's asking to be put down. I wonder if I dare?" she mused, looking around for Claude.

"If you do, and he gets into Claude's manuscript, you'd better have an escape plan," her brother said.

"Why can't you hold him?" she muttered.

"He doesn't like me."

He was growling louder now, and Nikki held him out from her dress. His gleaming claws began to flex.

"Take him, Clay," she pleaded.

"He matches your costume better than he matches mine," he protested. "Spanish officers hated cats, didn't you know?"

"They did?"

"How many paintings of Spanish officers holding cats have you ever seen?" he queried.

Nikki had to admit that she hadn't seen

any. She was about to protest his sly escape when she heard a voice she'd never expected to hear again.

Catching Mudd from behind so that he couldn't bite or claw, she turned and looked straight into a pair of black eyes that held no shock or surprise whatsoever.

Chapter Twelve

Nikki felt her knees go rubbery underneath her. It was Kane. He wasn't paying much attention to the elegant woman standing close at hand that he was with. His whole attention was focused on Nikki, and there was accusation and anger and pain in his dark eyes.

She didn't understand the anger. He couldn't know she was Clayton's sister. Her own heart was turning over. She'd hoped to avoid him, although that was absurd. There weren't so many guests that she could have gone unrecognized.

"Hello, Kane," Claude greeted, clapping the other man on the shoulder. "No costume, I see."

"He wouldn't put one on," Chris said carelessly. "I see that I don't have dibs on *Semiramide*," she added with a raised eyebrow at Madge's costume. They were both wearing the same colors, but Chris's smug smile was justified. Madge looked too chunky in her gear, while Chris's showed off her slender figure to advantage.

"Ah, but you don't have a cat, my dear," Claude purred.

She gave the cat in his arms an unpleasant look. "I hate cats," she said. "Nasty, sneaky things."

Claude was affronted. He clutched Mudd closer and started to speak.

"Why, there's Ronald!" Chris said suddenly, brightening as she waved to a dark young man across the room. "Kane, do come and meet him. His father is chairman of an oil company."

"I'll be along," Kane said, refusing to be led.

Chris shrugged and went off by herself, her whole expression seductive as she wrapped herself around the younger man and then spoiled the effect by looking back to see if Kane noticed.

He didn't. His eyes were on Nikki.

"Expensive company for a beachcomber," he remarked.

She flushed. "Well, you see . . ."

"Don't bother thinking up lies," he continued curtly. "I know who you are. I knew before you left the beach house."

"You never said a word," she accused.

He stuck his hands in his slacks pockets. "I was waiting to see why you were playing games," he said.

"It wasn't a game. I didn't know how to tell you," she replied quietly. Her green eyes searched his face, learning it all over again as the silence stretched between them. "You look so tired. It's been terrible, hasn't it?"

He lifted one thick eyebrow and smiled cynically. "Gathering tidbits to feed your brother?"

She drew herself up to her full height. "No. I was asking about the health of a friend," she returned. "You were that, for a brief time."

"And you weren't playing me for a sucker," he agreed mockingly.

"Would that be possible, even if I'd wanted to?" she asked. She smiled wistfully. "You'd have seen right through me."

He felt the ground going out from under him as he looked at her. He'd missed her. Being with Chris, even in the beginning, was nothing compared to the high he felt with Nikki. "Are you completely well this time?" he asked.

The concern thrilled her. "I think so. I've been taking it easy."

He looked around. "So I see. Everyone knows that Madge can't organize. If she could, Claude's desk wouldn't be in such a deplorable mess. You did all this, I presume?"

"Madge helped," she said in defense of her friend.

"And Claude reads Greek tragedies and listens to opera and pets cats when he isn't murdering people to entertain the public."

"Shame on you. Claude's your friend."

"Indeed." His eyes scanned the room until he saw Clayton, and then they narrowed angrily. "Your brother plays dirty pool. He's going to discover that the mud sticks when it's thrown. Remind him what my people do for a living," he added, glancing back down at her so quickly that she started. "And tell him that I said not to get overconfident. I'm on the firing line because one of my employees made an error in judgment. Your brother could be there for another reason entirely, along with his major cohort."

Nikki felt the blood draining out of her face. Major cohort. Mosby!

"Whatever Clayton's done — and I'm not defending him blindly — you have no right to hurt Mosby."

Her defense of her ex-husband irritated him. "Why not? He's behind this effort to discredit me, and don't think I don't know why. He's got a secret, hasn't he, Miss Seymour? And he thinks keeping my neck under his foot will keep us from digging for it while he uses every gutter tactic in the book to put Clayton Seymour back in office!"

"Mosby isn't underhanded," she began.

"One member of his staff is. And the honorable senator is putting pressure on me from a new angle," he said suddenly. "He has powerful contacts, you see, and he's using them all. Now it seems that I'm about to be investigated for income tax evasion. And guess who's heading the IRS in my direction?"

She just stared at him. It was inconceivable that Mosby would go so far unless he was really afraid. What did Kane know?

She moved closer to him, looking up with a plea in her eyes. "Don't hurt him," she said softly. "He isn't what you think. He's not like that."

"What is he like?" he demanded. "You ought to know, you married him, didn't you?" He caught her arm tightly and his dark eyes glittered down into hers. "Was he the one who didn't want you, Nikki? Did he only marry you to keep the gossip columnists from finding out that he was involved with some married member's wife, was that it?"

She gasped.

"I thought so," he said coldly. He dropped her arm as if it offended him to touch her. "And you went along like a lamb. Did you love him?"

She bit her lower lip until she tasted blood. Her eyes were huge, tragic.

"Well, did you?" he demanded.

"Yes!"

"But he didn't love you, did he? Or want you." His eyes ran over her with involuntary appreciation, almost hunger. "But you still want him. You can't let go, can you? There hasn't been another man in your life since the divorce. Oh, yes," he said smugly, "we checked."

"We?"

"My father owns a tabloid," he reminded her. He smiled slowly. "There's nothing he can't find out. In fact," he added, "he's on the trail of something very big. If he finds it, your brother may be very sorry indeed that he took advantage of my unfortunate circumstances to feather his own political nest."

"Clayton wasn't thinking beyond winning the race," she said, defending Clayton, as she always had. "Sometimes he gets tunnel vision. But he's a good man, and he does care about his constituents."

"I'm one of his constituents," he reminded her. "He didn't show me any of that concern."

"You're supporting his major opponent, a Democrat," she pointed out.

"And I'll support him even more, now," he returned. His face went even harder. "I'm going to see your brother thrown out of office in November. I promise you I am, no matter what it takes."

She felt chills run down her arms. "Revenge, Kane?" she asked.

"Call it what you like." He studied her beauty in the costume and felt regret like a wound. "Why didn't you tell me the truth?" he asked raggedly.

"It wouldn't have mattered," she replied. Her eyes were haunted. "All you had to offer was an affair, and I'm not heart-whole anymore. It was never meant to be."

One big, lean hand came out of his pocket. He reached out and touched her cheek, as lightly as a breath. She flinched, but she didn't pull back from it. Her soft, misty eyes sought his and gloried in their admiration of her beauty.

"Did you know what he planned to do?" he asked.

Her mouth pulled into a sad smile. "What do you think?"

"You're too honest for your own good in some ways, and a little liar in others. It hurt me to let you go, Nikki."

The pain she felt was naked on her face. "It hurt me more," she whispered unsteadily. "I don't have a lover hidden away to console me."

His jaw tightened and he dropped his hand. "She's convenient and she doesn't make demands," he said.

"I thought she made you impotent," she shot back, green eyes sparking with jealous rage.

He smiled in spite of himself. "You hope," he taunted.

"I loathe you," she spat under her breath.

"Go ahead," he challenged. His eyes were black, bright with wicked delight. "Hit me, Nikki. Come on." He stepped closer. "Throw a punch. You want to."

"If I hit you, it will be with a lamp!"

"You won't get that far. Know why?" He bent down, so that only she could hear him. "Because the minute you lift your hand to me, I'll back you up against a wall and kiss you blind."

"Is that how you manage women, Mr. Lombard?" she choked.

"It's how I'd manage you," he replied, so arrogant that her leg positively ached to kick him where it hurt most. "I haven't forgotten the way you looked at me that first morning," he added, his eyes narrow with masculine glee. "You lusted after me,

Nikki. And the one time I kissed you, do you remember who pulled my mouth down to your . . ."

"Isn't it warm in here?!" she croaked, fanning herself with the feather boa around her neck.

"Come out onto the balcony," he invited. "We'll . . . reminisce."

She could imagine how he'd do it. She had visions of being crushed between his powerful body and the stone wall, and her knees went rubbery. It wasn't fair. She was an independent, grown woman. He was making the sort of sexist remarks that required her to pick up the nearest blunt object and lay his head open. If only her body would cooperate with her dizzy hormones.

"The ambitious senator obviously can't or won't do you any good," he said huskily. His dark eyes slid down to the low neckline of her dress. "But I could. I know how to make love, Nikki."

"I'll bet you do!" she said fiercely. "How many women did it take?"

"Not as many as you're thinking," he mused. "And I'm not promiscuous, either. There'll be no accidents and no risk."

"There'll be nothing, period," she said shortly. "I'm not about to replace Miss Ribs in your bed."

"Does your brother know about us?" he asked with pure honey in his deep voice.

Her face gave her away. That was an unexpected riposte.

"I didn't think so. Why didn't you tell him, Nikki?"

"Because I knew he'd have a screaming fit, that's why," she said. Her eyes searched his and she felt the hunger for him all over again. It was an odd hunger; something gnawing and deep that was more than glands and hormones. "Why didn't you tell the reporters?" she asked. "It would have hurt Clayton in the polls."

"It would have hurt you more. I don't have to stoop that low to win fights." He traced her cheek down to the small, pointed chin, and he smiled as he touched the faint hollow in her long, graceful neck. "I won't sacrifice you. Not even to save myself."

The shock of what he was saying went all the way down to her toes. She stared at him with aching need, with a terrible sense of loss. She could have loved this man more than she ever dreamed. But her brother stood between them.

"Clayton won't stop. Neither will Mosby," she said miserably. "They'll carry the pollution charges all the way to the court of last resort if they have to."

"It was a nasty piece of work, wasn't it, Nikki?" he asked quietly. "I hated the photographs, the damage it did. It wasn't my fault, but I can't prove that."

"If you told about the accident, on the beach . . ."

He shook his head, smiling. "Even that wouldn't exonerate me. I told you. I won't sacrifice you."

"Why not? Everyone else has, at one time or another," she said bitterly. First her father, then Mosby.

"I'm saving you for a special occasion," he replied. "I miss you, Nikki."

"I miss you, too," she said sadly.

His dark eyes slid over her with a kind of possession. "You look lovely. Your brother is glaring at us."

"My brother is glaring at you," she corrected. "He likes me."

He smiled. "So do I. I'm sorry it didn't work out."

"We never had a chance," she replied.

The band was playing, and out of the corner of his eye, he could see Chris draping herself against the oil millionaire's son on the dance floor.

He caught Nikki's hand. "We're going to be burned at the stake before the evening's over," he said. "We might as well enjoy it. Come here."

He drew her into his arms, into his body, and wrapped her up tight as he began to move to the lazy two-step. Nikki shivered and tried to stop.

"Why?" he whispered at her ear.

"I can't," she ground out, clutching his lapel.

His big arm contracted, bringing her breasts right into his shirtfront. "Relax," he said huskily, his voice deep and sultry in the space between them. "It's all right to let me see that you want me. I want you, too."

Her legs trembled as they brushed his. She couldn't remember feeling anything so explosive since Mosby had first come into her life. But Mosby hadn't wanted her close like this. Mosby hadn't made her feel like this. She shivered as she let it happen, and her body melted into the warm strength and power of Kane's.

"Chemistry," he said deeply, feeling her tremble. "We mix like oxygen and hydrogen, bubbling where we touch. Blood rushing into empty spaces, churning, making heat and magic. Feel it, Nikki?" he asked, and his arm dropped just a fraction, rubbing her against the suddenly changed contours of him.

She gasped and instinctively started to step back, but he laughed deep in his throat and held her firmly in place.

"Now you know, don't you?" he whispered. "There's only one secret left. And if we go outside in the shadows, I can ease up that voluminous skirt and we can have each other against the wall I mentioned earlier."

Her fingers curled into his chest under the dark evening jacket, against his spotless white silk shirt. She could feel the thick hair under it, the warmth. "No."

"No," he repeated. "It's unrealistic, isn't it? But I know how it would feel. So do you." He moved, deliberately letting her feel the power of his body as his cheek lay against hers and his breath feathered the hair at her ear. The music, the people, the world vanished in the heat of what they were sharing. Her eyes closed. She felt him in every cell of her aching body.

"Come closer," he said, his voice harsh.

She pressed into him, shivering.

"Move, Nikki," he challenged. His hand slid to her lower back, pulling, pressing.

"Kane," she protested once, the fragile sound lost in a gasp as she felt herself going helplessly on tiptoe to search for a more intimate contact.

His other hand clenched in the thick hair at her nape and he made a muted, hoarse sound at her ear.

"Oh, God," he groaned, shivering.

She couldn't stop. She hoped they weren't being watched, because she couldn't stop what was happening. The sheer heat they were generating was becoming a throbbing pleasure that outweighed every single thought of modesty.

The sudden change of tempo in the music was a shock like ice on fire, and Kane's head lifted to see that people around them were beginning to shift gears into a complicated disco pattern.

"I can't dance anymore." Nikki's voice sounded choked, as she looked up at Kane.

His face was faintly flushed, high on his cheekbones. His dark eyes were fierce as they searched her face. "We'll have to," he said huskily. "Would you like to look down and see why?"

She felt her cheeks color. "No need, thanks," she said huskily, and forced a smile. "I won't ever dance with you again, you know."

"I would very much like to take you into a closet or a bathroom or even a recess in the wall and make love to you until you fainted," he said roughly.

"You have someone to do that with," she pointed out, fighting for control.

"I don't want her," he said passionately. "My God, I don't want anybody else. You. Only you."

"My brother, your father, Mosby, the other candidate," she moaned. "It's too complicated."

He felt his body begin to unclench as he concentrated on the music to the exclusion of everything else. "What do you want to do, then?" he demanded. "Forget it?"

"We have to." She looked up into his eyes. "We have to, Kane. I can't hurt my brother."

"But you can hurt me?"

"It isn't that way." She dropped her eyes to the swift, hard rise and fall of his chest. "You just want me. It will pass. I'm sure you felt that for Miss Ribs at the beginning."

"Not like this," he confessed curtly. "I'm on fire for you."

"I'm an unknown quantity, that's all. That's all it is!"

"Oh, I see," he said mockingly. "You're a virgin, so I can't wait to get you into bed, hurt you, force your body to accept me, and enjoy the suffering I'm going to see in your face. Is that what you think I need?"

Her eyes widened. "No!"

"I'm glad. I don't see virginity as a sacred quest," he said shortly. "It intimidates me. I'd prefer you with enough experience at least to welcome me." His eyes slid over her narrowly. "You were married. Didn't he even . . . ?"

She stopped dancing. The memories were painful. "Let's sit down."

He restrained her. "Tell me."

"He didn't want any part of me, Kane," she said wearily. "He found me totally undesirable. So undesirable that I never had the nerve or the confidence to let another man that close. Until you came along," she added bitterly, her green eyes accusing. "And look what happened."

"Yes," he mused. "Look what happened," he agreed, glancing back toward the dance floor. "You're very sexy."

"You're just looking for a good time."

"It wouldn't be, for you," he remarked.

"I believe some women actually have a very easy time of it," she countered.

He thought about that and began to nod. "Yes, if you wanted me enough, you might." He smiled slowly. "And you did. My God, you did, Nikki."

She dragged her eyes away. "I need to sit down."

"Thank your lucky stars that what you feel isn't noticeable," he said with dry humor.

She cleared her throat, refusing to look at him as he escorted her off the floor and toward the refreshment table.

Clayton and Bett were glaring at them. Kane didn't even acknowledge Clayton. He lifted Nikki's hand to his mouth and kissed the back of it with flair and seductive grace. He left her, striding back toward a livid Chris.

"Did you have to embarrass me on the dance floor?" Clayton demanded petulantly. "You were practically devouring each other."

"We most certainly were not!" Nikki said. "We were talking."

"That's a new name for it," Bett mused. "He's very attractive, but he does have a mistress, Nikki. I hardly think you'll displace her. An acquaintance of mine says that she's been with him since even before his wife was killed."

Nikki searched the other woman's face. "He isn't that sort of man."

Clayton was very still. "How do you know?"

"I just do. I'm going to circulate, Clay. You'd better, too."

"Could you manage not to make love to my worst enemy on the dance floor for the rest of the evening?" he asked sarcastically.

"It doesn't help the campaign, you know, Nikki," Bett added her piece.

"Neither does slinging mud," Nikki said flatly.

She avoided Clayton and Bett for the rest of the evening, which was just as well. She'd made an enemy there, she thought, watching Bett cling to Clayton. And now Bett would have the inside track. She'd be able to influence Clayton all over again, just when Nikki had almost made him see the error of his ways. She regretted that Derrie had left. The younger woman had always been able to reason with him before Bett came along. But it was too late for that now. Mosby and Bett had spun a nice web around Clayton.

Derrie was enjoying her new job, but she missed Clayton terribly. It had been like cutting out her heart to leave him. Every time he appeared on television, he had Bett with him. Her place in his life was obvious now. Not that Derrie could have competed, even so. She was a repressed prude, after all.

She was leaving the office, on her way to catch the bus, just behind a junior aide to the candidate for whom she now worked. She watched him cross the next street over, and suddenly she spotted Senator Torrance's man, Haralson, standing on the curb talking to a dark man in an even darker suit, wearing sunglasses. Haralson didn't see Derrie, who'd come out the side door. He was watching Curt Morgan, Sam Hewett's junior legislative counsel, and when the aide got past him, Haralson said something to his companion and gestured toward Curt's retreating back. The man nodded and began walking. There was a stealth in what they were doing that disturbed Derrie.

Haralson knew her on sight, but the other man wouldn't. She waited for Haralson to get into a cab and for it to drive away. Then she dashed down the street after the mysterious man.

He was trailing someone. She knew it instinctively. Clutching her purse close, she tried to remember all the things she'd heard and read about following people. Don't be seen was number one. Get lost if you're discovered was number two. Somewhere after that, there were other rules of thumb that she'd already forgotten.

She pushed back her blond hair and moved a little closer, pretending to be looking for an address. She held an old grocery list from her coat pocket in her hand and pretended to compare it with street numbers. Meanwhile, she was moving right along with the crowd, behind the strange man who went from one street to another, waiting for traffic lights to change.

He had an odd walk. He seemed to glide as he went along, as if he were used to long distances and knew how to navigate them with the least effort. He looked foreign. She wondered if he was.

At the next corner, just when she thought she was getting close, she lost him.

She stopped looking at the paper in her hand and began looking all around, her blue eyes curious and wary. The wind blew her soft blond hair from its bun in wisps around her oval face, and she felt exposed, standing there in her close-fitting pale gray suit and white blouse.

She was attracting attention, too, worse luck. Well, she'd lost him. But it was very curious. Why would Haralson have someone following a man who worked for her new boss?

Chapter Thirteen

Derrie made a mental note that she'd have to tell Sam Hewett about the strange occurrence. She wondered if Clayton was behind the snooping. She'd seen him stoop pretty low lately. But why would he be interested in the comings and goings of Sam's staff?

She walked back the way she'd come, toward the bus stop. As she got on the bus, she felt a strange tingling at the back of her neck. She laughed at her own suspicious nature. She'd been watching too many detective shows.

But when she got off at her apartment house, she had the same odd feeling. She couldn't shake it. As she started to use her key in the apartment building door, she suddenly turned and came face-to-face with the dark man in the suit. At close range, he was very tall and fit, and there was something quite intimidating in the untamed look of him. Her first thought, uncoordinated, was that he might be a mugger. She dropped the key and fell back against the door, ready to defend herself if she had to.

"Don't scream," he cautioned.

He sounded whimsical. She stilled. "Why not?" she asked.

"Because I don't want to have to show my credentials to a police officer. I'm supposed to be on vacation." He bent and picked up the key, handing it to her. "Here. I need to talk to you."

"You were with Haralson," she said, accusingly. "I won't tell you anything. I don't work for Clayton Seymour anymore."

"Neither do I, in the sense you mean." He lifted his hand and took off the dark glasses. His eyes were large and very black, like coal. The shape of his face up close was clearly American Indian. She stared at him, fascinated and realized he must be the mysterious stranger her niece Phoebe had encountered recently.

"Yes, I'm a Native American," he said with exaggerated patience, as if he'd grown weary of repeating it. "I don't have a tomahawk. I don't speak Sioux. I never hunted buffalo in my life. I don't take scalps except on Saturday. This is Friday."

She smiled. She liked him. "Okay. Do you drink coffee?"

"Only if I can't get firewater or peyote . . ."

"Will you stop?" she muttered. "Honest to goodness, you'd think I didn't even know what an Indian was."

"Native American. Indigenous aborigine, if you prefer," he said smoothly. "Do you have many in South Carolina?"

"I don't think we have any. North Carolina has some Cherokee people." She glanced back at him. "I really don't want to do the laundry and wash dishes. Do you take prisoners?" she asked hopefully.

"Sorry."

She sighed with resignation. "You win some, you lose some," she said.

She led him into the small apartment. There was a framed photo of Clayton, in color, smiling at her from the mantel. She turned it facedown. "Traitor," she muttered at it, and went to make coffee. She felt proud of herself for doing that until she realized that she'd only put it back up later. She was such a wimp.

"Still mad at your ex-boss?" he asked, leaning against the door to watch her.

"Yes," she said, glancing back at him. He seemed to know all about the reason Clayton was her ex-boss. But then Phoebe had told her that he was a government agent. She had to hide a smile, remembering the odd light in her usually calm niece's eyes.

"Make yourself at home while I fix the

coffee," she invited.

He smiled, taking her at her word. He slid off his jacket, tossed it on the sofa, loosened his tie, rolled up his sleeves, and took the rawhide tie out of his ponytail. His thick, jet-black hair fell into clean, graceful strands all around his shoulders.

"You said to make myself at home," he pointed out. "This is how I relax at home."

Derrie paused with the coffeepot in one hand, laughing. "Fair enough. I've never seen hair like yours," she said. "It's very thick, isn't it? Why do you wear it in a ponytail?"

"Because people stare less," he said simply.

"Sorry," she said with a rueful smile. "But it suits you." She averted her eyes away from his handsome face and the powerful lines of his tall, muscular body. She could see why Phoebe was attracted to him. If Derrie hadn't been crazy about her ex-boss, who knew how she might have felt?

"Flattery will get you nowhere," he said. "I'm used to women throwing themselves at me because of my hair."

She laughed. "Do they?" She spooned coffee into the crinkly paper lining of the filter cup and inserted it in the coffeemaker. She missed it the first time, muttered, and finally maneuvered it into the slots. She glanced back at him. "It must be terrible for you sometimes, though, all kidding aside," she said.

"What, trying to act white?" he asked bluntly.

"Yes." She started the coffeemaker and busied herself getting down cups and saucers and put them neatly beside the coffeemaker. "What do you do, when you aren't tracking down people?" she asked, just to see how much he'd tell her.

"I belong to the Justice Department."

She whistled, glancing back at him. "Weren't you just in a movie with Val Kilmer?" she teased.

"Nope, I'm not FBI."

That was interesting, she thought, because he'd told Phoebe he was. "You look like a younger version of him. He's very handsome."

"I look like a younger version of Val Kilmer?" he asked, aghast.

"You look like a younger version of Graham Greene, who is one of my favorite actors," she replied.

He liked the face and the sense of humor. She reminded him of the archaeology student he'd met, but she was older and more mature. He'd always been drawn to blondes, although he fought the attraction these days; fiercely when he'd caught himself staring at the archaeology student. Besides, he was here on business.

He pursed his lips. "I don't know if I like smart-mouthed blondes or not," he said, thinking aloud.

She poured coffee into cups. "We're even. I'm not at all sure that I like indigenous aborigines." She sat down and motioned him into a chair. He turned it around and straddled it, his hand idly smoothing over the coffee cup. It was hot.

"Why were you watching Sam's aide?" she asked.

He traced around the rim of the coffee cup. He had long fingers, flat-nailed, very dark and quite immaculate. Her eyes followed the movement. "Haralson asked me to. He's a casual friend of mine."

"That isn't a reason, really."

He lifted his dark eyes to hers. The humor was gone. He was serious. "Can you keep a secret, or are you too much in love with Clayton Seymour to keep things from him?"

She felt her breath catch "What do you know about me?"

"I did a check on Seymour. You're one

of his executive administrative people, so naturally you came under scrutiny. Your name is Deirdre Alexandra Marie Keller, but you're called Derrie. You have a degree in political science with a minor in sociology. You worked for Seymour from the time you graduated high school all the way through college, attending classes at odd times and different colleges when you could until you got your degree, a little later than your old classmates. You lived in Washington until just recently, and now you've been named executive administrative assistant to Sam Hewett. Not only that," he added with a curious smile, "but for the first time your intellectual capability is actually being fully utilized."

She flushed and averted her eyes to her coffee cup. She didn't like being reminded that Clayton had never thought her capable of much besides designating tasks to secretarial staff.

"My, what one can learn about people."

"My, yes," he mocked. "Come on. Can I trust you or not?"

She met his eyes. "I don't carry tales. Not even for men I've been in . . . been fond of," she amended.

"Which says a lot. Okay, here's the lowdown. Haralson thinks he has me in his pocket. He's letting a lot of things slip that he's going to regret. One of them is that Curt Morgan is directly connected to Senator Mosby Torrance, and is feeding him secret information about Hewett's campaign to be passed on to Haralson."

"Oh, my God!" She was aghast.

"What do you know about the boy?"

"Nothing," she stammered. She pushed back her blond hair. "Well, not much," she amended. "He's very handsome, and rather nice. He left a paid position as a senate intern to work for Sam's campaign. He came highly recommended . . ."

"By whom?"

She stared at him. "I don't know by whom. Mr. Hewett said he was. I didn't double-check because I didn't have a reason to." She frowned. "Listen, if Haralson's a friend of yours, then you're no friend of ours. That man is dirty. Really dirty."

"No kidding?"

She glowered at his exaggerated surprise. "Come on, what are you really trying to do, get us to throw out an essential staff member on the word of somebody from the enemy camp?"

"That's the problem. That's what it sounds like, doesn't it?" He leaned back in his chair and his dark eyes studied her with a rather unnerving, unblinking scrutiny. "I can't help noticing that you very much resemble a young woman I met in Charleston recently . . . an archaeology student named . . ."

". . . Phoebe?" She laughed at his look of surprise. "Yes, she told me. It's very natural that she'd have made a beeline for you. She's fascinated by Native Americans."

"So I noticed."

"I hope she didn't embarrass you. She doesn't mean to insult people. She's only eager and enthusiastic about her studies."

"How do you know her?"

"She's my niece," she said, smiling.

He snapped his fingers. "You're the aunt!" He shook his head. "I must not have been listening. She said her aunt worked for a politician, but I never made the connection."

"She told me all about you," she returned. "She's my brother's only child. He was killed in Lebanon a few years ago. Remember the Marine barracks that was bombed during the Reagan administration?"

"Yes. I'm sorry."

"So were we. My parents are still alive.

They live in Georgetown. My sister-in-law remarried, so Phoebe comes to see me fairly often. We do resemble each other, don't we? But she's very pretty . . ."

"She's very young," he said, smiling back.

"She'll mature."

He didn't want to think about the college girl. He crossed one long leg over the other. "If you know anything about Haralson, you'd better tell me."

"Said the fox to the chicken."

"I'm not directly involved in this," he said. "And I don't want to be. But if Haralson's mixed up in something illegal, I'm not going to be caught holding any bags. I did him what I thought was a simple favor. I found a toxic waste dump. But I didn't know he was going to use it to destroy a local businessman. That wasn't a civic duty, it was an assassination attempt. Lombard isn't a polluter, for God's sake, he's a card-carrying environmentalist."

"I didn't know that, but I never approved of what Clayton did. In fact, that's why I'm working for Mr. Hewett."

"I know," he returned. "I work for the government."

"The Justice Department, you said. What part of the Justice Department?"

"I'm a spy."

"Right."

"No, I am."

"Go on," she said, turning her head slightly away from him. "Spies aren't real. They're figments of Ian Fleming's imagination."

A corner of his mouth tugged up. "Sorry to disillusion you. They're not." He took out his wallet, opened it, and tossed it across the table to her.

She read the credentials, her eyes softening as they lifted back to his. "Jeremiah Cortez."

He shrugged. "My mother was studying biblical history when I was born. I have a brother named Isaac."

She handed the wallet back. "If Haralson is your friend, why are you checking up on him?"

"Force of habit. Even friends aren't exempt. I think Haralson set the thing up. I can't prove it, but that's what I think."

"Wouldn't it make more sense to tell Kane Lombard?"

He made a disgusted sound, deep in his throat. "Right. I tell him and he tells his father and the next day I read in the tabloid, Comanche Spy Accuses Senate Aide Of Desecrating Ancestral Burial Ground."

Derrie almost fell out of the chair laughing.

He glared at her. "That's right, chuckle, but that's what they'd say. I'm not going to be a human interest story. Don't you know anything about spies? We're supposed to keep a low profile."

"That's why you wear your hair long and dress in a suit in Charleston in mid-summer."

He pursed his lips and one eye narrowed. "If I cut my hair and wore jeans, do you really think I'd fit in any better here?"

"No, you'd just look as if you were trying to be something you're not," she replied honestly. "I like the way you look," she added, smiling.

"You and your niece are unusual," he said thoughtfully. "You're very honest."

"So are you, and I think that's going to be a real problem when you start pointing fingers at Haralson, because he's not. That picket mob at Lombard's was his idea."

He was suddenly intent, every trace of amusement wiped from his face. "Can you prove that?" he asked.

She shook her head. "He talked to Clayton. All I heard was what Clayton said to him, and my ex-boss wouldn't admit that in public in a million years. Haralson has him well-trained," she added bitterly.

"Apparently he has Senator Torrance well-trained, too," he said. "Because what I'm finding out about Haralson is that he's been given a more or less free hand to do what he likes. Until the past year or so, he was on the borderline of legality in his methods, but in this campaign he's crossed the line."

"What do you think he's up to?" she asked.

"I don't know. I'm going to find out."

"Do you think Senator Torrance has put him up to it," she persisted.

He scowled. "Torrance has a nasty tongue and he's probusiness all the way, but he's as honest a man as I've ever heard of. No, he wouldn't use that sort of under-handed method to win his own election, much less to help Seymour win his."

She hesitated. "Seymour's sister Nikki didn't seem to think so. She didn't seem surprised at the tactics."

"She doesn't know everything that's going on," he returned.

Plots. Plots within plots. There was something in this man's face that was se-cretive, careful. "Are you really just on va-cation?" she asked slowly.

He answered her with a question of his

own. "What do you know about Torrance's marriage to Seymour's sister?"

She hesitated.

"Derrie," he said, using her name for the first time, "I understand loyalty. If we're going to do anybody any good, you're going to have to trust me."

"That's hard."

"I know."

His eyes were without guile, without secrets. He didn't look away or fidget, and she read his body language very well.

"It's something to do with his marriage to Nikki," she said finally. "I never knew what, because nobody ever talked about it. All I know is that Nikki doesn't date or get serious about men since then." She paused, searching his face. "Don't hurt Nikki. She's an independent woman, but she's so fragile."

"That won't be necessary. Haralson is who I'm after." Dark lights flashed in his eyes and she got a glimpse of what it would be to have him for an enemy. The look made her nervous, even though it was meant for someone else. "He's up to his neck in this, but what I don't know is how and why. It has to be more than just making sure Seymour wins the election."

"Does Senator Torrance know more than you do?"

His dark eyes narrowed. "I'm not sure that he does. The senator doesn't follow Haralson's movements too closely. That's an error in judgment, surely, but I don't think he's malicious enough to deliberately discredit someone. Haralson, now, he is."

"You're his friend, aren't you?" she asked.

"I was a casual friend," he corrected. "I collect old coins. Haralson found out and we traded a time or two. He offered to sell me a piece I've been coveting for my collection in return for finding an illegal dumping site for him." He leaned back again. "I didn't know what he was up to at the time. When I realized it, it was too late. Now I'm plenty sore and out to settle the score."

"What can you do?"

"What can *we* do," he corrected.

She gaped at him. "Oh, no! I'm not getting mixed up in this," she said abruptly, standing up.

He got up, too. He was tall, muscular, powerful-looking. "You're already involved. Your boss stands to lose the election if that double-dealer gets his way. Seymour should stand or fall by his platform and its relevance to the voters, not by dirty tricks."

She grimaced. "The Seymours are still my friends."

"That won't change."

"Yes, it will. Haralson is helping Clayton. If I go against him, I'll hurt Clay," she said, wincing involuntarily.

"Are you in love with him?" he said quietly. "Or is he just a habit you can't quite break? Of course, love erases all faults, doesn't it?"

She lifted her eyes and found a sudden stark bitterness in his face. "You aren't quite as carefree as you pretend, are you?" she asked bluntly.

His thick eyebrows shot up. "My life is none of your business."

The curt, short remark made her smile. Poor Phoebe, if she got mixed up with this man. "Fair enough."

He picked up his jacket and shouldered into it. Then he straightened his tie, pausing to loop the rawhide around his hair again.

"Are you going to help me?" he asked.

"What do you want me to do?" she asked with resignation.

"Watch Curt. That's all. Nothing heavy."

"For how long?"

"A few days. I've only got another week of vacation."

She didn't want to do it. It seemed so disloyal to Nikki and Clay. But if Haralson was up to no good, it was just as well to find out the extent of it.

"All right." She looked up at him curiously. "You aren't going to get in trouble for doing this, are you?" she asked.

He seemed to withdraw, although he hadn't moved. He turned away. "I told you, I'm on vacation. If I want to watch people, so what? I'll be in touch."

She watched him walk to the door, intrigued by that somber remoteness when he seemed at first acquaintance like a clown.

"You're a very complex man, Mr. Cortez," she said quietly.

He opened the door and turned, his dark eyes meeting hers. "I think you ought to know that the rumors are flying about Seymour and Bett Watts. Gossip has it that she's setting a wedding date."

Her pain was almost tangible. Her eyes glittered with it, but she smiled nevertheless. "Thank you. I needed that."

He scowled. "Yes," he agreed, "you did. Bett is a lady with her eye to the main chance. She's no goldfish, she's a barracuda. If you care about Seymour, why don't you do something about breaking up that relationship?"

"You're very personal for a man I've only just met," she pointed out.

"You're the kind of person I feel comfortable with — you and Phoebe," he said. "A man can't have too many friends."

She relaxed her outraged stance and smiled sheepishly. "Well, no one can," she agreed. "Maybe you're right. But Bett's got a lot going for her."

"So have you," he said, and smiled.

She smiled back. "Thanks, pal."

He shrugged. *"De nada,"* he murmured in Spanish. "Don't let Morgan know you're watching him, will you?"

"I'll be very careful." She cocked her head. "You're very intelligent for a spy."

He smiled amusedly. "Am I? Good night, Derrie."

"Good night."

He was a curious man, she thought as she went to pour herself a cup of coffee. He'd shown her some credentials, but Phoebe had said he was FBI, and the identification Derrie had seen simply said Justice Department. What if he was neither? What if he was mixed up with Haralson and trying to get something on Sam

Hewett? Or what if he was really after Clayton?

She picked up the telephone and dialed Phoebe.

"Hi, Aunt Derrie! What's up?" Phoebe asked.

"Cortez was just here," she said bluntly. "Listen, didn't you say that he showed you FBI credentials?"

Phoebe brushed back her long hair and felt a faint twinge of jealousy that surprised her. Why had Cortez gone to see Derrie? "Yes, I did," she said.

"Tell me what the two of you did."

"He pushed me down in the long grass and ripped off my blouse . . ." Phoebe began wickedly.

"Phoebe! This is serious," she added. "And strictly business, if that's what's unsettled you. You know how I feel about Clayton."

"Yes, I do. I'm sorry. Isn't it silly to feel possessive about a man you've only seen two times in your life? And he's too old and too different, I know all that," she added before Derrie could.

Derrie, oddly, didn't agree with her. "I know he was looking for the waste dumping site. Think hard, dear, when you saw those drums, do you remember seeing a logo on them?"

Phoebe hesitated, trying to force her mind back. "Well, yes, I do," she said. "It was faint, though. Very faint . . ."

"That's all I wanted to know. Thank you." There was a pause. "Why are you sitting at home?"

"I'm not, really. I'm going out with some of the gang. We have to pick up Dale. He lives next door to the Seymours."

"I don't suppose you'd stop by there and tell Nikki to call me?"

"Why can't you telephone her?"

"Mainly because they've changed the unlisted number," Derrie said, hating to admit it. "I guess Clayton was afraid I might pester him on the phone or something! I can't get the new number from the operator, you know, and I certainly can't call Clay and ask for it."

"I see your point," Phoebe mused. "Okay. I'll do it. Uh . . . Cortez didn't mention me, did he?" she added offhandedly.

"In fact, he did," she returned. "He thinks you're very attractive."

"Oh." Phoebe's heart lifted. She smiled to herself. "Good night, Aunt Derrie."

There was a smile in the voice that replied, "Good night, my dear."

Chapter Fourteen

Nikki was deeply worried about the way Clayton was acting. He hadn't been the same since the party at the Blairs, and he was increasingly preoccupied.

They were back in Charleston the next weekend, and the campaign was escalating. There were new headlines in the paper about the legal battles Kane Lombard was facing with the South Carolina environmental people. He was probably not going to face criminal charges, but his company was in violation of several statutes of the Hazardous Waste Management Act, not to mention the Pollution Control Act overseen by the people at the Department of Health and Environmental Control. She couldn't help feeling sorry for him, and faintly irritated with her brother for making a campaign issue of it.

"Quite a dish Lombard had in tow that night," Clayton remarked over a small supper that night.

"Yes, wasn't she?"

He was watching her, waiting for a show of jealousy. "Her name is Christine Walker.

She's a clinical psychologist. Incredible, isn't it, with a figure and face like that? She could have made a fortune modeling."

"I didn't notice."

"Of course you noticed, Nikki!" he said angrily, slamming down his fork. "You were practically making love on the dance floor, you and Lombard. You've got to tell me what's going on!"

She stared at him coolly. "If you must know, he was injured and washed up on the beach. Chad and I looked after him."

"Chad Holman?"

"That's right."

He studied her. "Chad stayed at the beach house with both of you?"

Her eyes met his levelly. "No."

"Oh. My God, you didn't stay there alone with him?"

"He had concussion," she said stiffly. "I had no choice."

"Of course you had a choice, damn it! You could have put him in the hospital and left him there!"

She slammed down her own fork. "No, I couldn't! I wouldn't leave a man I hated in that condition."

"My sister. My sister slept with my worst enemy . . . !"

"You hold it right there!" She stood up.

Her green eyes flashed angrily at him. "I did not, ever, sleep with him. You know it, and you know why!"

He moved away uneasily, eyeing her. "All right," he said. "I know it. But nobody else would believe it, not with Lombard's reputation."

"I don't care what people think."

"I have to. Nikki, I'm running for re-election. This isn't some great cosmopolitan city, it's Charleston, where reputations and family honor still mean something! If news of that got out, it could ruin me!"

"It's not going to get out," she said stiffly.

"No? What if Lombard is faced with a jail sentence for that dumping?"

She gasped. "No. They'll fine him, but they wouldn't . . . !"

"Illegal dumping of toxic waste is a felony. CEOs and presidents of companies have gone to jail for it. Lombard could, too. Faced with years in prison, he'd throw you to the wolves without a second thought. He and his family would use any wedge they had to prevent that!"

"It wouldn't help him," she pointed out. "Even if I'd slept in the same bed with him on Seabrook Island, it wouldn't do him any good to tell it!"

"It would if he could claim that his accident prevented him from finding out the truth about what was going on back in Charleston."

"Nothing was going on," she said. "That employee of Lombard International's who hired Burke's swore he didn't know about Burke's bad environment record. They interviewed him on television, don't you remember?"

"Nevertheless, he can be charged for that," Clayton said with an attorney's knowledge of penalties. He'd studied environmental law. "The fact that he didn't check out Burke's is enough to make him liable under the environmental statutes. He's guilty of negligence, if nothing more criminal. The environmental people are very militant these days, and they should be. Pollution is easy to cause, hard to correct. Prevention is the only way we can insure future supplies of clean water and air."

"But it's okay if we wipe out a species of owl to temporarily save loggers' jobs," she said deliberately.

"You and Derrie! Damn Derrie!"

"You miss her, do you?" Nikki asked mischievously.

He didn't want to think about Derrie.

He hated his office since she'd left it, he was more alone now than ever. He stuck his hands in his slacks pockets and wandered around the room, his eyes lingering on familiar things, family heirlooms like the Early American furniture and the antique coffee mill and the grandfather clock that had been left behind when their parents died. He touched the clock, noticed that it wasn't running at proper tempo. He opened the case, picked up the key, and wound it.

"I remember the sound of that clock chiming when I was very small," Nikki recalled, smiling. "I always thought a little man lived inside."

"So did I." He put the key down and closed the case. His fingers lingered on it. "I feel alone sometimes. Do you?"

"Yes." She joined him, her arms wrapped around her chest. "It's different when you don't have parents. It's hard to talk to people who do."

"Have you . . . heard from Derrie?" he asked without looking at her.

She averted her amused eyes. "Not since just after the primary election. I guess she's getting settled." She glanced at him. "Mr. Hewett is well-liked," she said. "Don't get overconfident, or do anything illegal, will you?"

"I haven't." He sounded insulted.

She sighed. "Clay, you're walking right on the edge. Don't you know it?"

"I have to win."

"Why?" she asked bluntly. "Why do you *have* to win?"

He hesitated. Now that she was putting it in those terms, into words, he wasn't really sure. The campaign had been important to him, of course, but only in the past two or three months had it become the most important thing in his life. He stared at her.

"Well, because I want to go back to Washington, I suppose," he began. "I have programs I haven't been able to implement, unfinished projects to work on . . ."

"You weren't like this until John Haralson came down and started working for you."

"Mosby suggested it. Haralson has always worked well for him."

"Mosby walks around in a fog," she said. "He doesn't want to know how things are done, just that they get done. He's very naive in some ways, and altogether too trusting."

"You aren't still . . . ?"

She laughed gently. "Still grieving for him? Oh, no. I have scars, but I gave up hope long ago. Mosby can't help it, can he?"

"No." He looked at his shoes. "He's never been found out. That's the most amazing thing of all. He pretends to like women, then he pretends to like men. He's managed to keep anyone from finding out."

"How, do you suppose?" she asked quietly. "I mean, how would he keep someone from noticing, in bed . . ."

"He kept you from noticing, didn't he? You're a babe in the woods, sis," he said without malice. "It's just as well that you are. How about a movie?"

She shook her head. "I'm tired. Washington wrung me out."

He dug in his pocket for his keys. "Bett's still there, on business again." He hesitated. "I might go and see Derrie."

"That would be interesting."

He laughed unamusedly. "Yes. I guess it will." He started out, then paused and looked back at Nikki. She looked fragile these days. "When you had pneumonia, was it really Chad who looked after you?"

She hesitated.

"You'd better tell me. I see him occasionally."

"No," she confessed quietly. "It was

Kane. It was so far gone that I could barely remember Morse Code. He knew immediately that it must be me. He came and got me. I don't remember much except that I came to in an oxygen tent."

He stared at her, realizing how dangerously ill she must have been. Kane had saved her life. She hadn't said anything, but she must have bitterly resented the way Clayton had treated Lombard in the press. She owed her life to him.

Clayton felt guilty, and that made him angry. He didn't want to be beholden to his worst enemy. That reporter from the Lombard tabloid was still in Charleston and snooping around, and Haralson was getting pretty nervous. Too many undercurrents were at work here, he thought.

"I need to win the election. I can't have the Lombards digging into our pasts."

"Clay, if they published everything they know, they still wouldn't have a story," she said quietly. "It's Haralson's head that would roll. Mosby is a victim. It would hurt him if things came out, but perhaps not as much as you think. He's hardly a drinking, lecherous playboy."

"Not at all."

"Haralson is keeping you on a very short fuse," she said bluntly. "He's the one who's obsessed with winning the election. Why don't you find out why?"

He frowned. "I know why. He's trying to help me."

"Clay . . ."

"I'll be in later," he said, smiling easily. "Don't worry. It will be all right. So long as you keep away from Lombard," he said firmly. "Don't let me down, Nikki, please? No fraternizing with the enemy, regardless of what you owe him."

"All right."

She sounded subdued, but he trusted her. He winked lazily and left the house. Paying Derrie a visit had been on his mind for a long time. It wouldn't hurt to see how she was faring. Besides, he thought, Haralson had mentioned something about Curt Morgan and having him followed. If Morgan was doing anything suspicious, perhaps he could get Derrie to let it slip.

Nikki was more worried than ever as she sat watching the evening news. The environmental people had found another toxic waste dump on a deserted piece of farmland. Burke wasn't implicated in this one, and there were no logos on the old oil drums full of toxic waste they found there.

The cleanup crew was putting the drums

in overpacks — metal envelopes the purpose of which was to prevent further leaking. Hundreds of gallons of the unidentified toxic substances had already leaked out, however, and leached into the soil. The extent of the damage would be found over time, but first the waste had to be analyzed and identified, and then cleanup operations would begin. The onsite EPA coordinator was hopping mad, promising retribution for this latest "midnight dump" and prosecution to the fullest extent of the law.

Along with the new report was a rehash of the site that Burke's disposal operation and Lombard International were accused of creating. Charges were pending, and there had already been a red flag beside the company on the EPA list because of an earlier sewage leak. The news report made that one sound deliberate now, which was, Nikki thought, sure to make Kane's defense even harder. Her eyes narrowed. How strange that the company should change waste handlers on the heels of the leak, and that Burke's should be so easily traced to the site; how fortunate for the environmental people that the dumping site had been so quickly and easily located. And that the logos from Lombard International had been very readable, indeed. And painted on in orange . . .

She got up from her chair and moved to the telephone without a single thought in her mind except that it had to be a frame. Why hadn't anybody else thought of it? Why hadn't Kane?

She knew the number of his beach house on Seabrook Island. He probably wouldn't be there, but perhaps she could coax his housekeeper into giving her the number.

What if his lover answered? She panicked and almost put down the receiver. It was too dangerous. What if she hurt Clayton by doing this, what if Kane decided to use their time together against her, what if . . .

"Lombard."

It was Kane himself. The shock of his deep voice, unexpected, almost caused her to drop the receiver. She fumbled it back to her ear.

"Who is it?" came a curt demand.

"It's . . . Nikki."

There was a pause. "Are you all right?" he asked, and his voice was soft as velvet.

Tears stung her eyes. She blinked them away. The concern was awesome.

"I'm fine," she said. "How are you?"

"Notorious," he returned dryly. "I trust

your brother is enjoying the public enumeration of my alleged sins in connection with this latest dumping scandal?"

"He isn't here."

There was another pause. "Dangerous, isn't it? Calling the enemy just to talk?"

"Could I see you?" she asked.

"Sure. They're showing a file photo of my back on TV right now. Turn on channel . . ."

"Kane, don't joke. I've . . . found out something. Thought out something," she corrected. "I have to talk to you."

"I don't trust you, Nikki," he said flatly. "And you shouldn't trust me."

"You saved my life," she said simply. "Think of it as the repayment of a debt. I don't have anything to say that could compromise you any more than you've already been compromised. But I think you should listen to me."

"Go ahead," he invited.

She started to speak and then thought about possibilities. The telephone could be bugged. It would be a simple thing for someone with Haralson's contacts to do. In fact, he had connections in the Justice Department, Clayton had said . . .

"Suppose I meet you somewhere?" she asked.

"Risky."

"It's more risky to talk on the telephone. Someone might be listening."

"That's true," Kane said. "Okay. Where?"

"Where I found you."

"When?"

She was getting the hang of this. It was almost fun. "At the same time you got to the party in Washington."

"I'll be there."

Nikki put on a pair of dark jeans and a white sweatshirt with a jeweled rose on the front. This was going to take a little stealth. She'd looked out and the service truck she'd noticed earlier was still sitting there. It could be legitimate, of course, but she didn't think it was. There was some cloak-and-dagger stuff going on here. If someone was trying to follow her, for any reason, she was going to make it very difficult.

She went out through the basement. The back lot had two big live oaks in it, with the sidewalk just beyond, on the narrow street by the bay. There were some young people in a crowd going along it. In fact they were headed toward her house. She intercepted them, finding Phoebe Keller and a handsome young man and another couple in her path.

"Nikki!" Phoebe said, grinning. "I was just coming to see you. I couldn't get Derrie on the phone and I thought she might be over here. It was just a whim, we were out walking . . ."

"Come along with me for a minute, will you?" Nikki asked, glancing beyond them. A man was leaning out of the truck window watching another man steal toward her house.

"What's going on?" Phoebe asked.

"I'm not sure. But I need to get away from the house without being seen."

"Hey, no problem," Phoebe's companion said. "Where do you want to go?"

"To Seabrook Island. I have to get a cab . . ."

"We'll take you down," Phoebe said gaily. "I love the island!"

"Will they let us on it?" the boy asked.

"I have my pass," Nikki assured them. "And the refrigerator's full . . ."

"Say no more," Phoebe said, clutching the boy's hand tightly. "Nikki, you angel, we haven't even had supper!"

"Don't expect haute cuisine," she teased. This was an unexpected bonus. For all intents and purposes, she'd be out with her friend's niece and the young crowd on the

321

island. There was nothing to connect her with Kane, so far.

"Hamburgers are cuisine to us," Phoebe's male companion said, chuckling.

The beach house was all alight an hour later. Nikki took Phoebe to one side and turned up the radio. She couldn't take a chance that the beach house might be bugged, too. They weren't followed, she knew that. She'd watched all the way down here.

"Listen," she told Phoebe. "I've got to go down to the beach for a few minutes. Make a lot of noise, and if anyone comes asking for me, I'm lying down with a headache."

"Are you in trouble? Can I help?" Phoebe asked gently. "I know someone in law enforcement — well, sort of," she amended, remembering the new friend she'd made. She didn't know where to find him, but her aunt had mentioned talking to him. That had surprised — and disturbed — Phoebe. She knew her aunt Derrie was still in love with Clayton Seymour. But it bothered her that Cortez had gone to see Derrie, despite the fact that Derrie said it was just business talk. She felt rather proprietorial about Cortez, despite the age difference. She shouldn't, but knowing it didn't help. She'd gone out with this young crowd tonight for no other reason than to force Cortez out of her mind.

Nikki cleared her throat impatiently.

"I'm sorry," Phoebe said. "I tend to drift off. Nikki, you're not in any trouble, are you?"

"Not yet. I may be soon, though," came the rueful reply. "Never mind. I'll be back in a little while."

"It's not too safe alone on that beach."

"I won't be alone." Nikki smiled and darted out the door.

Kane was leaning against a moss-dripping live oak, smoking a cigarette. It was his second.

"I didn't know that you smoked," Nikki said.

He turned and moved to meet her. They were in the shelter of the tree at the water's edge and couldn't be seen from the beach house or the neighbor's houses.

"I stopped smoking," he said. "Until a few weeks ago."

She wrapped her arms around herself. She couldn't see him very well in the moonlit darkness, but she felt the warmth and size of him and felt secure despite the hostility between them.

"There was a truck parked outside my house when I started to leave. I think the phone is bugged and I think I'm being watched."

"Were you followed?"

She shook her head. "I made sure." She looked up at him. "Something is going on. I seem to be in the middle of it, and so are you."

"Explain."

She leaned against the tree beside him, her eyes soft on what she could see of his face. She wanted so badly to go up close to him and slide her arms around him and let him hold her. It had been a long time since he'd held her so intimately at the party.

"Someone is framing you."

"What?"

"Haven't you figured it out?" she asked. "The leak may have been accidental. But the dumping came right on its heels, as if somebody knew you'd be on the EPA's hit list for a prior offense. The dumping site was found with ridiculous ease. The logo of your company was stenciled on those containers in bright orange fresh paint. Add it up."

His cigarette was hanging in midair.

He'd been so upset by the charges and the publicity and the unrelenting persecution that his ability to reason had been impaired. She was right. He hadn't appraised his situation at all. He'd been too busy defending it.

He shifted closer to her, and bent to talk more softly. "If your brother was behind it, would you tell me?"

"I love my brother," she said quietly. "I'd do almost anything for him. He doesn't realize that he's become entangled in this mess, too, but I do. Someone is using the campaign as an excuse to destroy your company and your credibility. I get cold chills just thinking about what could happen. It's cold-blooded and shrewd, and there has to be a very intelligent purpose behind it. I just can't think what. But it has to be more than an underhanded way to help Clayton win the election, don't you see?"

His eyes narrowed as he finished the cigarette and ground it out under his heel. "What good would it do to put me in front of the media as a target?"

"I don't know. But there must be some reason. Kane, I know you weren't responsible for what happened," she said fiercely.

He searched what he could see of her

features. His head turned then and he stared out over the bay, toward the ocean, his eyes unseeing on the moonlight that sparkled in the waves.

"Why don't you think I did it?" he asked.

She sighed as she leaned her head against the tree to study him. "You love the ocean, don't you?" she asked. "You're a naturalist through and through. People like that don't try to destroy the environment."

His head turned toward her. "You're perceptive."

"I suppose so, at times. What will you do?"

"Nothing, except to keep my eyes and ears open."

"Kane, you won't go to jail, will you?" she asked worriedly.

"There's very little chance of that. Why?" he added. "Are you afraid I might drag your name into it for an alibi?"

"I know you wouldn't," she said quietly. "But I'd let you, if it meant a jail sentence otherwise."

His heart jumped. "And throw your brother's political career into the garbage?"

She didn't blink. "Yes."

He felt himself moving, without conscious volition. He reached for her, lifted her, riveted her to his powerful body. Then he kissed her, with the wind blowing in from the bay rippling her hair.

He backed her into the tree and edged himself between her jean-clad legs, shifting her abruptly so that the core of her was suddenly pressed to his raging arousal.

She gasped, but he didn't slow down. If anything, he became more ardent. She felt his hands on her thighs, under her taut bottom, lifting and pulling her into his hips so that only the fabric kept his body from penetrating hers right there.

"The bark would hurt your bare back," he said tightly, his breath moving against her lips as he spoke. "That's the only reason I haven't unzipped your jeans."

Her senses were dimmed, but returning. She shivered. The contact was so intimate that she was glad he couldn't see her face.

He moved sensually against her hips and she heard his breathing deepen. "Feel it?" he whispered. "I'm going to explode any minute."

She did blush, and buried her face in his throat.

Curiosity suddenly overcame his desire. His body stilled. "Nikki . . . what's wrong?"

She made a gesture with her head, and her burning face pressed closer.

He was remembering things. Confessions she'd made, little hints about a man she'd loved. She'd been married, but she'd said that her husband never wanted her. She'd said at one time that the man she loved . . . couldn't.

He felt his chest collapse under a rush of breath. He eased the crushing weight of himself away from her softness and rested gently on her, instead.

"You'd better tell me, Nikki," he said slowly.

She drew her closed eyelids against the furious pulse in his throat. "You know already," she whispered. "You're very experienced, aren't you?"

"Experienced enough to know that I've shocked you. Nikki, I don't think you know what sex is. Am I right?"

"Oh, I'd say I have a pretty good idea of what it is, right now," she managed with black humor.

He lifted his head and moved her so that he could see her flushed face in the moonlight. He eased her up, pressed to the tree, and softly thrust against her. Her expression was unmistakable.

"So many emotions," he remarked while he fought for control. "I see fear and shock and, beyond it, desire. But I don't think I could make you desperate enough to forget the consequences, could I?"

"No," she whispered.

He let her slide down the tree. The bark was rough at the back of her sweatshirt. He held her by the waist, not quite touching him, and studied her.

"You've avoided men since the divorce, they say," he said. "Why? Because he couldn't and you didn't want to end up in the same trap again, wanting a man who couldn't take you? There's no possibility of that happening with me. I'm capable, in every way there is."

"So I noticed," she replied sheepishly.

"Nor do I practice irresponsible sex," he persisted. He was almost shaking with passion. His hands contracted. "My house is empty. Deserted. And it's not bugged. You could scream if you wanted to," he whispered seductively. "I might even make you want to."

She remembered the feel of him against her and the sound she'd made. It was a little embarrassing.

He smoothed back her disheveled hair with hands that had a faint tremor. Then he began to unbutton his shirt, slowly, letting her see his chest come into view. There were beads of sweat clinging to the thick hairs that covered him to the collar-bone, and his bronzed muscles were damp.

"You're sweating," she remarked nervously.

"I want you," he replied simply. "A man's body reacts in various ways to a woman's allure. It becomes damp, it trembles. When he's very much aroused, he swells." He caught her hand and pulled it gently to him, pressing it the length of his arousal.

She tried to jerk her hand away, but he held it securely.

"Relax," he said softly. "Just relax. Don't be embarrassed. It's as natural as the waves rolling onto the beach, as the wind blowing. Touch me, Nikki."

He pulled her cheek to his bare chest and smoothed her hair, kissing her forehead while his free hand curved around hers and helped her learn his body.

"Not so frightening now, is it?" he whispered. He loosened his grasp and lightly stroked the fingers that touched him. He caught his breath and laughed at her expression. "You didn't hurt me."

She drew her hand away just the same and he let her. His big hands slid around her, under the sweatshirt, against her bare back. They unclipped her bra. When she started to protest, he bent and brushed his open lips lightly against her mouth. The action stayed her movement.

"You know what I feel like," he whispered as his hands moved around her. "Now I want to know what you feel like."

She stood very still, barely breathing. His hands moved around her rib cage and tenderly lifted the slight weight of her firm breasts. His thumbs slipped over the hardening tips and stroked them lightly while he kissed her.

"Lean back, Nikki," he whispered. He eased her spine to the trunk of the tree. His hands bunched the fabric of the sweatshirt and slid it up, with her bra, baring her pearly breasts in the moonlight.

She shivered. It was the most erotic sensation she'd ever had, the breeze on her bare breasts and a man's sultry gaze appreciating them.

"Arch your back, little one," he whispered. "Offer them to me."

She must be crazy. She was certain that she was. Her back began to arch slowly, her breath coming rapidly through parted lips. She shivered in the breeze, and then his warm, moist mouth was covering her, his tongue moving softly over the hard nipple, making her body undulate while she moaned with helpless pleasure.

"The poor fool," he whispered hoarsely. His hands fought snaps and a zipper while his mouth made a banquet of her. "God, the poor . . . man!"

He was touching her! She tried to resist, but his mouth on her breasts made her too weak with pleasure. Her legs parted for him and she sobbed as he worked witchcraft on her aching, helpless body. She clutched his mouth to her breast and shivered again and again as he brought jolts of white-hot pleasure that robbed her of breath and strength.

She couldn't bear it. The tension was making her frantic. She lifted to him, her hands clawing at his shoulders as she tried to make it happen, tried to make the tension snap . . .

She cried out, stiffening. His mouth quickly covered hers to silence the sharp little cries. She shuddered again and again and he laughed against her lips with arrogant, wicked delight.

When she softened in his arms, he kissed her hungrily and she heard the sound of another zipper moving. The pressure of his mouth grew suddenly insistent. She was his. There was no thought of resisting now, when she knew what he was going to give her.

The hard thrust shocked her, but the pain was fleeting and as he lifted her, she felt him all the way inside her body.

She made a sound, a gasp, and he felt her tighten.

"Gently," he whispered into her lips. His body was faintly tremulous, like his voice. He was stimulated beyond stopping, beyond reason. He wanted the mindless pleasure he'd given her. He wanted to feel it like silver knives through his powerful body.

His hands cupped her bottom, protecting it from the tree bark. He kissed her and lifted, thrust, with smooth motions of his hips that very quickly made her his conspirator. She shivered with each slow movement, barely able to breathe, her lips touching his as he guided her body back to his again and again.

"I've never done it like this," he whispered huskily. "I've never felt it like this. I can't be tender enough, I can't touch you . . . inside . . . deeply enough," he choked. His hands contracted and he groaned in hoarse anguish, his legs shivering as hers wrapped around his hips. "Nikki, make . . . it . . . happen . . . to . . . me!"

His hands gripped her painfully and he began to shudder, to sob, as his mouth claimed hers. She felt the jolt of fulfillment all the way through her as he went over the edge. The sound he made into her mouth was shocking in its inhibition, and she wondered if she would be riveted to him forever. It felt like that. He was still moving, and what she'd felt at first began to build in her. But there wasn't enough time. He'd let her back to her feet and he was leaning against the tree beside her, shuddering in the aftermath, gasping for breath.

She wanted to cry. He hadn't used any protection and she hadn't tried to stop him. She'd promised herself that this would never happen to her, that she would never allow herself into a situation where she might lose her head and give in to a man's ardor. Now she had. The first wave of terror hit her like acid.

Her hands fumbled with fabric and fasteners. He was quicker than she was. Seconds later, dressed again, he helped right her clothing.

"Don't cry," he whispered gently, brushing at her eyes. "It's all right."

"No, it's not! I let you . . . !"

He picked her up in his arms and began to kiss her, with breathless tenderness. "I lost my little boy," he said at her mouth, his voice unsteady. "Give me a baby, Nikki."

Chapter Fifteen

Nikki couldn't believe she'd heard him right. Her body felt stiff and sore and bruised. He wasn't letting go, though. He moved to the other side of the tree, where its roots stretched toward the beach, and eased her down. Sitting down beside her, he pulled her across his lap and leaned his back on the tree trunk while he held her cradled against him.

"You don't believe in promiscuous sex," he said. "Neither do I. You love the environment. You like politics. There are hundreds of other things we have in common. The baby will be the foremost thing."

"It's happening too fast," she began dizzily.

"I know it is. I wanted you too much. Next time, I'll give you what I had." He looked down at her. "Did it hurt very much, Nikki?"

She flushed. "I wasn't talking about . . . that. I meant talking about marriage and babies . . ."

His big hand pressed down on her belly. "It was your first time," he murmured with unforgivable smugness. "I read somewhere that virgins always get pregnant the first time."

She hit his chest. "I am not going to have a child out of wedlock in Charleston!"

"We'll get married," he said. "The sooner the better, in fact."

She gasped. "My brother would kill you before he'd let me marry you!"

"Not when we tell him you're pregnant," he said smugly.

"I am not!"

His eyebrows lifted. "How do you know?"

"Because I didn't . . . I mean, there wasn't . . . time," she finished, drowning in confusion.

"Because you didn't climax when I took you?" he asked bluntly, chuckling at her expression. "You will next time. I'm sorry to tell you that pleasure isn't a necessary requirement for conception."

"It was only one time," she said stubbornly.

He smiled slowly. He eased her down on the grass-covered soil under the tree. "So far," he murmured.

"You can't!" she said frantically.

He pulled her hand to him and grinned at her surprise. "Yes, I can." His mouth covered hers and he eased between her

336

legs, feeling her tremble. He whispered into her lips, "If it hurts, you'd better tell me now, while I can still stop." He pushed down and she bit her lip.

He sighed, a little sad. "I was afraid that might happen. I was overeager, wasn't I?" He rolled over onto his back and tugged her so that she was resting on his chest. "All this raging masculinity, wasted," he sighed, pressing her hips down to his. "Ah, well, there's always our wedding night. I hope you like short engagements, because we can be married in three days. And we will be," he added when she looked inclined to argue. "I don't know what's going on around here and I don't give a damn, but you're going to live with me until we're finding out."

"I have to go home!"

"Why?"

The feel of his body under hers made her warm and cozy. She lay down and sighed as he absorbed her weight. "Because I can't be underhanded. I'm not ashamed of the way I feel about you."

He was still. His hand smoothed at the nape of her neck. "And how is that?"

"Deeply affectionate. Passionately desirous. I'd think up more adjectives, but I'm sleepy."

"Making love is tiring," he whispered, and his voice smiled. "You won't come home with me?"

"I want to. Oh, I want to! But let's do it properly," she pleaded. "If you're sure you want to marry me, that is."

He lifted an eyebrow. "I'm sure, all right," he said solemnly. "The baby would be a nice consequence, but it's my backbone I'm thinking of mostly."

"Your what?"

"My backbone," he murmured with deep satisfaction. "I like having it melt and blaze up like fireworks. Couldn't you tell how much pleasure you gave me, or is rictus still too new to you?" She looked puzzled and he laughed, whispering in her ear.

"Oh," she gasped.

"You won't be so easily shocked a few weeks from now," he whispered. "In fact, there's every possibility that you'll be shocking me."

"I wouldn't bet on it." Her fingers curled into his chest. She stared out at the movements of the ocean. It was all so sudden. She felt as if she had emotional whiplash.

"Don't brood," he said lazily. "What's wrong?"

"You're still sleeping with your mistress."

"No, I'm not," he said firmly. He rolled her over onto her back so that he could see her face. "I haven't touched her since the day I washed up on your beach. Not even to kiss her, Nikki."

She frowned. "But . . ."

"I took her around with me, yes," he said. "I didn't want it to get back to you that I was mourning because you left."

She smiled. "Oh."

His fingers traced over her face, down to her mouth. "And I was," he added somberly. "Mourning, I mean. I've grieved for you, Nikki, night and day. It knocked me for a loop when I found out who you were, but that didn't stop the longing. Seeing you at the Blairs' party was the most painful thing that's happened to me in recent months."

"You didn't call me," she pointed out.

"How could I? Your brother would like to see me in prison. I have no love for him, either. I didn't want to put you in the middle, put you in the position of having to choose between us."

"I only wanted to warn you," she said. "I really didn't mean to, well, to let this happen."

" 'This' was delicious," he murmured deeply. "Have you any idea what it felt like to have you, to feel you having me, wanting me?"

"A little," she said, her eyes bright.

"I cheated you of fulfillment," he said, "but . . ."

She put her fingers over his mouth and had them soundly kissed. "You didn't," she said. "Before you made love to me, you gave me that."

"It started out to be unselfish," he said ruefully. "I was going to let you see what we could have. But when I watched you at the last, I couldn't control myself. I had to have you."

"There's no need to feel guilty," she said. "I let you."

"Sweetheart, you couldn't have stopped me," he replied quietly. "I honestly didn't mean to let it go that far. I meant for you to have a white wedding, and a proper wedding night."

"I'll have both. Even the puritans allowed intimacy between engaged people," she whispered. She lifted her mouth to his and kissed him softly. Her body sought the length of his and pressed there gently, feeling him wanting her. "You're very big," she whispered daringly, and heard him groan as he answered the kiss. It was a long time before he lifted his head.

"You have to go home," he said harshly.

"You don't want me to go home," she said. She nuzzled close. "I don't want to leave you. But I must."

His hands trembled as they held her head to his chest. He ached from head to toe. "I could have protected you if I hadn't lost my head. I had something in my wallet."

She closed her eyes, thinking about a baby. Her fingers traced the collar button of his shirt and drifted down to tangle in the exciting thickness of hair that covered his chest. "You miss your family, don't you, Kane?" she asked softly.

"I miss my son," he confessed. His hand tightened on her head. "I miss him like hell. God, Nikki, I want another child!"

He rolled over and she opened her arms, cradling him against her. Perhaps grief was making him vulnerable, but she loved him. Given time, he might come to love her, particularly if there was a child.

She reached up and kissed him with slow tenderness. "I'll give you one," she whispered.

He searched her eyes. His hand pressed back the strands of dark hair that clung to her cheeks. She looked beautiful and untamed, and faintly pagan lying there on the grass. He could picture her, nude and wanton, her body undulating slowly.

She heard him gasp. "What is it?" she asked.

"I was thinking about how it would be, to have you here, naked on the grass."

"I don't look as good without my clothes as you do without yours," she said, smiling. "I love to look at you."

He made a rough sound in his throat, and for an instant the chemistry between them almost exploded.

"We were lucky," she whispered. "But someone might come down here looking for me."

He shivered. "And you're not decent."

"And I'm not decent," she agreed. She moved and winced a little, smiling sheepishly. "It felt good."

Color flared along his high cheekbones, but he laughed. "Yes. It felt good."

He got to his feet reluctantly and helped her up. As he held her in front of him, his eyes were watchful. "You look different. Radiant."

She searched his eyes. "You meant it? About wanting to get married, to have a baby with me?"

"I meant every word," he said softly. His expression was breathlessly tender, and he seemed suddenly shocked as he looked at her. "I adore you!" he whispered huskily.

She smiled, her eyes misty with feeling, with delight. "Will you call me tomorrow?"

He nodded. "Like a shot. Come home with me. I'll strip you and myself and we'll lie naked in each other's arms until morning, even if that's all we can do."

"I have to go home." She nuzzled her face against his chest. She wanted to say the words, but he hadn't. It was too soon. But she owned him now. He was hers. She looked up and possession was written on her face. "Leave that slinky brunette alone," she said quietly. "You belong to me now."

"Honey, I couldn't touch another woman now if my life depended on it," he said evenly. "You can't imagine what you did to me."

"I'll get better with practice," she said.

He laughed delightedly. "Could I survive if it did?"

She smiled back. "Good night."

He caught her hand and lifted it, palm up, to his lips. "Dream of what we did."

He walked back toward the beach, where he'd left the small motor launch that he'd piloted over to see Nikki. She watched him go, her body tingling, her heart full. Life was very good, she thought. She couldn't regret what had happened. She was a woman now, and soon she'd be a wife. Kane Lombard's wife. Her feet hardly touched the ground all the way back up to the beach house.

Nobody noticed that she was back. Phoebe and her male companion were dancing to loud music and munching potato chips. Nikki curled up on the sofa and dreamed of the future until it was time to go back into Charleston.

The telephone call early the next morning was so unexpected that at first she simply held on to the receiver and stared blindly at the wall.

"What did you say?" she stammered.

"I said, I got some very racy photos of you and Lombard last night. Hot stuff, lady. Suppose I turn them over to the tabloids?"

"Kane Lombard's father owns a tabloid," she said quickly.

"Not the only one. He doesn't mind slandering other people. But how is he going to like having his own son on the front page of somebody else's tabloid? Sister of congressional candidate makes out with her brother's worst enemy on the beach," he rattled off. "What headlines!"

She slid down the wall to the floor. "What do you want?" she stammered. If the telephone was bugged, she was dead. Her whole life flashed before her eyes.

"I want you to stay away from Lombard," he said. "And I want you to keep your mouth shut about why."

"But . . . !"

"You don't really think he wants to marry you?" he chided. "I've got some juicy photos of him with his mistress, the one he hasn't touched, remember? Taken two days ago. They were on the yacht, naked. Do you want me to send over some prints?"

She felt sick. She wrapped her arms around her legs. "You're perverted."

"Who isn't?" came the mocking reply. "If you go near Lombard, those pix go straight to the papers, with four-column cutlines. And we'll be watching. So be a good girl."

The line went dead. If only she'd had the presence of mind to tape it! She hadn't been followed. She knew she hadn't been followed. So how had they found her?

She buried her face in her hands. This couldn't be happening! Kane wanted to marry her. What would he think when she wouldn't talk to him, or see him? What if he caused a scene and these people were hiding outside with cameras to capture it all on film? Her heart stopped. It would be on all the news shows. Irate lover attacks congressional candidate's sister. Publicity. Bad publicity. Clayton would be knocked out at the polls with such sordid goings-on.

But Kane's character would be even more blackened, wouldn't it? She didn't know what to do now.

Derrie answered the knock on her door wearing a beige and gold and white caftan with her hair trailing down her back. She was ready for an early night, and not expecting company. It did occur to her that it might be Cortez, and because she thought of him as a friend, she opened the door a little eagerly.

When she found Clayton Seymour standing there, her heart skipped wildly. She'd actually thought it was over, that she felt nothing! How silly. Loving him was a bad habit, she thought miserably. If only she could break it!

The sight of her made Clayton stop in his tracks and just stare. He'd rarely ever seen Derrie like this. For some reason, he found it much more affecting than he should have. He smiled lazily. "Well, hello. Have you missed me?"

"Not particularly," she said. Her legs were trembling, but she managed to keep him from seeing.

He sighed. "Ah, well. I suppose Hewett's given you the big head, appointing you executive advisor. Maybe I should have done that myself."

"But you didn't think women were capable of handling that much responsibility."

"Bett is," he said maddeningly. "I didn't think you were. More fool, me." He stopped just inside the door and frowned as he looked at her. "I only asked you to call the television stations. Someone else would have done it anyway, you know."

"I do know. But it wasn't going to be me. What do you want, Clay?"

He shrugged, jamming his hands deep into his pockets. He hadn't realized until now how much he'd missed her. She was different now. More confident. Much less intimidated. He found himself attracted, more than ever. "I thought I might persuade you to come back."

She shook her head. "Not a chance. Especially not as long as you've got Haralson on your staff."

"What's wrong with Haralson?" he asked defensively. "Everybody attacks him lately. First Nikki, now you!"

"We're intuitive. You aren't. He'll drag you right down if you aren't careful," she said slowly. "You have no idea how much trouble you could be in because of him."

"Because he knows how to take advantage of a weakness in my worst enemy?" he laughed. "For heaven's sake, he's a political advisor. He's good at his job. Better at it than you were," he added. "I've never had so much media attention."

"You may get more than you want one day."

"If it's what I said about you, I've already apologized," he said, eyeing her. "You've changed, haven't you?" he asked suddenly. "You're different, somehow."

No doubt, she thought. Having responsibility and praise were new to her. Sam Hewett appreciated her abilities as Clay never had. As Cortez had said, she was only now fully utilizing her brain and her expensive college education.

"We all grow," she said noncommittally.

"You've done some wonderful things for Hewett," he tried again. "I like your promotional ideas. They're solid without being sensational." He hesitated. "You could come back and we could try a few of them."

She smiled at him. He sounded almost boyish. "How's Bett?"

He grimaced, snapping his hands into his pockets. "She wants to get married," he said roughly. "She was the one woman in the world whom I never expected to think of it."

So Cortez had been right. Her heart sank. She would never have gotten Clay, not in a million years. Bett would always have the inside track.

Her face gave her thoughts away. Clayton winced as he looked at her. Derrie had loved him. Why hadn't he realized it in time? Now he was tangled up with Bett and Derrie was lost to him. She wasn't immune, but she was fighting the old attraction. As she grew in power and strength, she would meet other men. She would marry and have a family . . .

"I've been unfair to you in every way there is, haven't I?" he asked quietly. His pale eyes searched hers. "I used you, took you for granted, finally threw you out of the office and my life. And do you know what, Derrie?" He laughed bitterly. "The girl I hired to replace you is afraid to open her mouth. She can type, but she can't spell. She's pretty and sweet. But she isn't you."

"Why don't you let Bett run the office for you?" she asked dully. "She'd be a natural."

"Bett doesn't want to work for me. She wants to remain a lobbyist. She likes the money, you see. Even my salary can't compare to what she makes." He turned away to the window and stared out it. "She's deciding where we're going to live even now. What a girl."

"I'm sorry if you aren't happy," Derrie said. "But it's really none of my business."

He turned, his face solemn. "It was once."

"Those days are gone. I miss working for you, but I'm very challenged with Sam. He's a good boss." She forced a smile. "And we're going to beat your socks off at the polls in November."

His eyebrows levered up. "I'm no lost cause."

"Keep Haralson on and I can guarantee that you will be."

"He's spending the weekend in Washington."

He drew in a long, slow breath, and his

eyes were hungry as they searched over her. "She tells me where she wants to go, what she wants to do. She even tells me what to do in bed." He smiled sadly. "Did you ever wonder how it would feel to sleep with me?"

She wouldn't blush. She wouldn't! "Once or twice," she confessed tautly.

His eyes narrowed and he smiled. "You're blushing. You haven't ever done it, have you?"

She hated that superior attitude, the way he was looking at her. "I dated a college boy in my senior year in high school," she said curtly. "He was handsome and very persuasive, and I was stupid. I slept with him, one time, and that's why I haven't slept with anybody since," she said, shocking him.

He moved closer, scowling. "Why?"

She shifted uneasily. She didn't like remembering. "Because I didn't want to. He parked the car and I thought we were just going to make out a little. But he pushed me down and before I even realized what was happening, he was . . ." She wrapped her arms tightly around her breasts. "I hated it! He was in a hurry and it hurt awfully. Then he said that if I didn't like it, it was my own fault, because I'd led him on.

All the girls did it, he said, so why should he have thought I was any different from them?"

He felt outraged. He'd never even suspected. He'd always thought that Derrie was a prude, that she never dated because she was afraid of being seduced. He hadn't thought it would be a reason like this.

"You should have taken him to court," he said curtly.

"What defense would I have used?" she asked bitterly. "I was in love with him, or so I thought. Everyone knew we were a couple. It would have been my word against his and he was captain of the football team and the eldest son of one of the most influential families in Charleston."

"I begin to see the light."

"I thought you might," she replied. "They talk about equality and justice. Let me tell you, the wealthy people make the laws and decide who pays the penalties. If you don't believe that, look at the inmates in any prison and see how many rich kids you find there."

"Were there consequences?" he asked.

"Luckily, no," she said heavily. "I didn't get pregnant and I had myself tested for HIV twice, months apart. But it scared me to death. I never wanted to take the same chance twice."

"You worked for me for six years," he said. "Why didn't you ever talk to me about it? It must have only just happened when I hired you, the first year I ran for the state legislature."

"It had," she said. "But I couldn't even tell my parents. How could I have told you?"

"He should have been arrested," he said angrily.

"Ironically, he died in an automobile accident the very next year," she said, lifting her eyes to his. "I didn't even cry when I heard. I guess I didn't have any tears left."

"Why should you?" His eyes slid down the caftan, lingering where her breasts thrust against it. Her silky hair flowed like waves of gold around her shoulders. She wasn't a beautiful girl, but she was disturbingly attractive. She was sexy, he decided finally. He'd forced himself not to notice that before. He was involved with Bett, and he'd thought Derrie a virgin. But inside, he was churning, changing. He felt himself growing uncomfortable as the sensuality of her appearance worked on him.

"Derrie, do you know anything about Haralson?" he asked suddenly.

She moved away from him toward the

kitchen. "Nothing that you won't find out eventually," she said, remembering her promise to Cortez to say nothing, even to Clay. Why she should trust a man she'd just met was strange, but she did. She knew somehow that he wasn't going to do anything to hurt the Seymours. He had it in for Haralson, though, and Derrie wasn't going to lift a finger to save that dirty dog.

He paused in the doorway, leaning against it while she put coffee on to brew. His face was troubled. "What you aren't telling me could cost me the election."

She turned. "Would that bother me, when I work for your closest competitor?" she asked mischievously.

He pursed his lips, smiling faintly. She was sexy when she smiled like that.

He shouldered away from the door and moved toward her, intent in his eyes.

"You stop right there," she told him, wielding the scoop she was using to put coffee into the filter basket. "I'm seeing someone else. He's from Washington and he's very handsome . . ."

He didn't even slow down. She kept talking until he took the scoop and tossed it aside and suddenly pushed her back into the counter with the weight of his hips.

"Shut up . . ." he murmured against her mouth.

She stiffened at the unfamiliar contact with his aroused body. She hadn't even known that he got aroused in the six years she'd worked for him, although it was certain that he did with Bett.

Bett. She had to remember Bett. She did try, but his hands were framing her face, his thumbs coaxing her lips apart so that his mouth could press between them. He smelled of spice and soap and he tasted of coffee. She could taste the woody tang of it on her tongue when his mouth began to open and she breathed him.

A sound passed her lips, but he ignored it. His mouth grew slowly more insistent until she stopped fighting the pleasure and gave in to it. He was warm and strong and he smelled good. She relaxed into his aroused body with a little sigh and felt his arms enfolding her.

Not until his long leg began to insinuate itself between hers through the caftan did her drowning mind come swimming back to reality.

"No," she gasped under his mouth.

He lifted his head. His eyes were as turbulent as hers. He frowned slightly. His gaze fell to her mouth and further down.

He eased her back so that he could see the stiff peaks of her breasts and their jerky, quick rise and fall. If he was aroused, so was she. He hadn't lost her. He hadn't!

His eyes lifted to hers. "Derrie," he said huskily, savoring the sound of her name on his tongue.

"I won't . . . sleep with you," she choked.

He moved back, just a little, his eyes curious, puzzled. He smiled. "I know. But you want to," he said, amazed.

"I've wanted to with a lot of men! It isn't just you!"

He knew better. He smiled, a little sadly. "I'm getting married, you know," he said wistfully. "And I've just realized that I don't want to. The thought of a lifetime with Bett makes me want to throw the election and sail to Bermuda."

"Sam Hewett and the rest of us would appreciate it," she managed breathlessly.

He chuckled. He felt better and brighter than he had for a long time. And all because of Derrie!

He let her go with flattering reluctance. "You still taste like a virgin, despite that cowardly so-and-so back in high school," he said quietly. "Suppose I give Bett the heave-ho and come back? What would you do?"

"Nothing until after the election," she said abruptly, although she was bluffing and they both knew it. "I won't fraternize with the enemy."

He lifted an eyebrow. He was still tingling all over and finding it hard to breathe. "How about after the election?"

She folded her arms over her telltale breasts and laughed jerkily. "Well, we'll see."

He smiled wickedly. "That's worth waiting for." He turned toward the door, paused and turned back, surveying her. "I guess I've turned a blind eye to Haralson, just as Mosby has. It's time we did something before it's too late."

"I can't possibly agree with you, because I work for the opposition," she stated.

"So I noticed." He drawled it, his smile sensuous and teasing.

She flushed and glowered all at once.

He laughed at her bridled fury. "Pretty thing," he murmured. "Now I know why the world went dark when you left."

"Why?"

"I'll tell you," he promised, going out the door. He stuck his head back in. "*After* the election!"

Chapter Sixteen

Nikki avoided calling Kane all morning. She also avoided answering the telephone every time it rang. But that night it started and refused to stop. She put on the answering machine. That was worse.

"Answer me, Nikki," Kane growled. "I know you're there. What the hell is wrong with you? Have you had second thoughts? Changed your mind?"

She swallowed. In order to save Clay — and Kane — she was going to have to lie. There was no other way. The thought of those sleazy photographs in the tabloids made her sick. She couldn't bear it.

She picked up the receiver and fought down nausea. "Kane, I have had second thoughts," she said in a dull, defeated tone. "I'm sorry. I really can't do this to Clayton."

"Your brother has his own life to live," he pointed out. "Nikki, we made love!"

"Yes. Th-thank you for the tutoring," she stammered, clutching the receiver. "I'll put it to good use."

There was a shocked pause. The receiver

slammed down in her face. So much, she thought, for victories.

Clayton noticed Nikki's pallor, but he didn't understand what had caused it. She was so secretive lately, so tense. And he had problems of his own. Derrie and Haralson came immediately to mind, although in different ways.

"Are you all right?" he asked.

"Sure. How was Derrie?" she returned.

He smiled with soft pleasure. "Delicious, thank you," he murmured. "Odd that I never noticed her in six long years, isn't it?"

Nikki brightened at the look on his face. "Yes, I always thought so," she confessed.

"She's full of surprises, our Derrie." His smile faded and he began to look worried. "I wish I had time to explore them all. But there's a campaign waiting to be won and a few problems to solve. I'm not going to marry Bett," he said abruptly, facing his sister.

"Will wonders never cease?" Nikki sighed, smiling.

"I know, you never liked her."

"I never trusted her," came the dry reply. "Women can usually see through other women, Clay. She was never quite what she seemed, and it was pretty obvious to me that she liked *what* you were more than she liked *who* you were. As a congressman, you were of great value to her. If you'd lost the election, I'm afraid it would have been another story. She doesn't look at you like a woman in love should look at a man."

He searched her green eyes and realized abruptly what she meant. The way she'd been with Kane Lombard when they danced had been a revelation to him. Not since Mosby had Nikki looked like that. He felt rather sad that he'd been so adamant about keeping her apart from the industrialist. On the other hand, Lombard was a polluter and deserved everything he got. But there was still the problem of Haralson. He owed the man for his help; especially his help unmasking Lombard's polluting of the natural environment. But Haralson was becoming a liability that he couldn't afford. It was just a question of time before the man was going to cross the line and do something illegal.

His eyes narrowed. "I've had time to do some serious thinking about Haralson, especially since Derrie seems to agree with you. I've decided that you're right. I'm going to send him back to Washington and get someone else to run my campaign."

She brightened a little. "Oh, Clay. I'm so glad. You're doing the right thing!"

"I suppose so. But he was a hell of a campaign coordinator. Who's going to replace him?"

"Me."

His eyebrows lifted and then he chuckled. "Yes! Why not? You'd be a natural!"

He wouldn't have thought so even a week ago, but apparently the way he'd misjudged Derrie had turned his attitude around. Nikki knew that she could do a better job than Haralson, and in a less underhanded way.

Nikki watched him move toward the door. "Where are you going?"

"To give Haralson his walking papers, of course," he returned. He grinned at her. "I'll expect you at the office at eight sharp tomorrow morning, Miss Seymour. You are now a working stiff."

"You can count on me," she assured him.

She could only hope that with Haralson out of the picture, the threat of those photographs hanging over her might conveniently disappear.

Kane was half out of his mind over

Nikki's change of heart. He could hardly believe that she cared so little for him. He'd been certain last night that she loved him.

But what if guilt was making her turn away from him? She was a virgin, and he hadn't known. He'd backed her into a corner, all but forced her. Did she hate him? He had to know! But how was he going to find out?

Mrs. Yardley knocked on the door and peeked around it. "It's Mr. Jurkins, sir," she said. "He'd like a word with you, if it's convenient."

"It's convenient," he said dully. "Send him in."

Will Jurkins was wearing a two-year-old suit with scuffed shoes. He looked the least prosperous of any employee Kane had. He stared at the other man for a long moment. If he'd suspected Jurkins of taking kickbacks to change solid waste companies, it was hardly evident.

"Yes, Jurkins? What can I do for you?" he asked with faint impatience.

"I keep hearing gossip," the other man said slowly. He was twisting a paper clip in his nervous fingers. "I just would like to know if they plan to try to put you in jail over this, sir."

"Bob Wilson says that it's unlikely," Kane replied. He perched himself on the edge of his desk. "Probably we'll be fined. But that sewage leak didn't do us any favors with the state and federal environmental people."

"Yes, I know, and that's my fault. That leak was a legitimate accident, Mr. Lombard," Jurkins said earnestly. "I wouldn't do anything illegal. I mean I wouldn't have. I have a little girl, six years old," he stammered. "She has leukemia. I can take her to St. Jude's for treatment, you see, and it's free. But there's the medicine and she has to see doctors locally and the insurance I had at my old job ran out. She isn't covered under the insurance here. It's that preexisting conditions clause," he added apologetically.

"I know about that," Kane replied. "Almost thirty million Americans have no health insurance, you know, and people with preexisting conditions can't get any, period. If we get a new administration in November, perhaps we'll have a chance of changing all that."

"I hope so, sir. But that wasn't why I came."

Kane lifted a questioning eyebrow. Jurkins was almost shaking. "Sit down,

Jurkins," he said, gesturing to a chair.

Jurkins looked oddly thin and frail in the big leather armchair. He was still twisting the paper clip. "I hope you won't get in too much trouble."

"At least they aren't going to shut us down," Kane returned.

Jurkins hesitated. He looked up and opened his mouth. He wanted to speak. But he couldn't make the words come out. He got to his feet again, jerkily, red-faced.

"I'll, uh, get back to work now, sir," he said. His voice was unsteady. So was the smile. "I hope it works out."

"So do I." Kane sat on the edge of the desk when the man left and kept going over the odd conversation. Something was definitely wrong there. Jurkins knew something and he was afraid to tell it. He pushed the intercom button. "Get me Bob Wilson," he said.

"Yes, sir," came the quick reply.

Haralson stared at Clayton Seymour as if he couldn't believe his own ears.

"You're firing me?" he asked the other man. "Are you serious?"

"I'm afraid so. I'm going to give Nikki your job."

Haralson, always so cordial and kind,

suddenly turned nasty. He sat up in the chair, holding his cigar between his cold fingers, and reached into his desk drawer. "No, you aren't. Want to know why?"

"Do tell me," Clayton invited with smiling, cool confidence.

Haralson drew a photograph, an 8 x 10 glossy, out of the drawer and tossed it across the desk to Clayton.

"If you want to see that on the front page of every tabloid in the country, fire me."

Clayton gasped. It wasn't blatant, for a photograph of that sort, but it made innuendoes that were unmistakable. That was Kane Lombard — and his sister!

"I'm sure you'll see things my way," Haralson said pleasantly. "I'm going to get you back in office, of course, that's a byproduct. But my main purpose is to bury Lombard. He cost my father his cabinet position. He found out that my father was having an affair with an intern and he told his family and they spilled it to the whole damned world!

"I was in my last year of school when it happened, but I never forgot. We lived in a small town in Texas, and that sleazy tabloid ran the story week after week after week! My mother killed herself over it, and

I swore I'd make Lombard and his family pay! It's all been a means to an end — my job with Torrance, everything! Torrance had no choice but to hire me, and to send me here to help you when I told him to," he added, laughing. "You see, I have friends who know the ins and outs of the detecting game. And I know all about Mosby Torrance."

"What do you know, exactly?" Clayton asked.

"That he's gay."

Clayton couldn't reply. He didn't dare say a word. The man was unbalanced, and if he wanted to believe that about Mosby for the time being, it might be safer than the truth. He looked down at the photo.

"Take it with you," Haralson invited. "I still have the negatives. And tell your sister she'll have no opportunity to make that monster, Lombard, happy. I told her on the phone that she'd see those pictures published if she took one step toward Lombard. I won't let him have any happiness. He's going to pay and pay and keep on paying until he's as dead as my mother is!"

Clayton wandered back to his office with

his mind in limbo. Haralson was dangerous. How could he have missed the signs? Mosby was afraid of the man because he thought Haralson knew the truth. In fact, he didn't, but that hardly mattered if he had Mosby on the run. Now he had Nikki on the run. Clayton didn't know what to do. If he showed the photo to Nikki in her present state of mind, she might lose it.

The election was less than a month away. Haralson had something else up his sleeve. No doubt he was going to publish those photos anyway. He'd probably wait until the last possible minute and then let fly. The scandal would destroy Nikki socially. It would ruin Lombard in the process. It might even do enough damage to Sam Hewett's campaign — because Kane's brother was his campaign manager — to cost Hewett the election. Clayton wanted to win. But not that way!

He only knew of one possible thing to do, to stop Haralson in time. It was probably the mistake of his life. He got in his car and drove out to Seabrook, to the new Lombard beach house.

If Kane Lombard was shocked to find Clayton Seymour standing on his doorstep, he hid it quickly. He had a glass of scotch and ice in one big hand. His eyebrow jerked as he stood aside to let the shorter man enter.

The beach house was luxurious, Clayton thought, and right on the marina. It must have cost a fortune. Well, Kane had one.

"Is this a social call?" Kane drawled.

"Thank your lucky stars that I'm not homicidal," Clayton returned. He glanced around. "Are you alone?"

Kane nodded. "What is it?"

"I think you'd better have a look at this." He took the photograph from the inside of his suit jacket and tossed it on the coffee table.

Kane's eyes darkened. He cursed violently.

"Who?" he demanded, his eyes promising retribution.

"My reelection campaign manager," Clayton said heavily. "I went in to fire him this morning and he handed me that." He glared at the older man. "I could kill you for doing this to Nikki."

"I made love to Nikki," he returned solemnly. "Please notice the wording. I didn't seduce her, have sex with her, or any number of less discreet euphemisms. I made love to her."

Clayton relaxed a little. Not much. He was still furious. "Did it have to be on the beach?"

"I couldn't make it to the house," came the rueful reply. The smile faded quickly though. "Has Nikki seen this?" he asked suddenly.

"No, Nikki heard about this," he said. "She was warned not to go near you or these pictures would be smeared over the front page of every tabloid he could reach by the next morning."

"So that was all it was. Thank God." Kane relaxed, looking as if he'd just won a state lottery. In another state, of course, South Carolina didn't have one.

"Haven't you talked to her?"

"I've tried to do nothing else," the other man said heavily. "She said it was all a mistake, and I believed she meant it." His head lifted. "But now I'm going to marry her. If you don't like it, that's tough," he added without blinking, his face hard and relentless.

"At least you're honorable enough to stand by her," Clayton said stiffly.

"Stand by her, hell. I love her! Do you think I'd have touched her in the first place if I hadn't had honorable intentions?" he demanded. "She was a virgin, for God's sake!"

Clayton gaped at him. He hadn't expected that answer. "A virgin?"

"You didn't know?"

"It's hardly the sort of thing a man can discuss with his sister." He hesitated. So many things were beginning to become clear. "I thought Nikki knew it all. She doesn't really know anything . . ." He looked up. "You said you loved her."

"I loved her the day I met her," came the grim reply. "I couldn't stop. I tried, though." Kane took a sip of the scotch. His head lifted and he glared at the other man. "You're a damned blackguard of a politician. You planted that waste at the dump site deliberately and led the media to it."

"No, I didn't," Clayton said honestly. "Haralson had one of his cronies find the dump and call in the media. I still don't know all of it. The one thing I'm sure of is why he did it. Your father apparently printed a story about his father that got him kicked off the president's cabinet some years ago and Haralson's mother committed suicide. It's you he's after, not Sam Hewett."

Kane whistled. "I wondered why the name sounded familiar. It's a wonder I didn't recognize it sooner, but I had other things on my mind." He looked up and frowned. "But why are you here?"

Clayton didn't even blink as he replied. "Because I can't let him blackmail Nikki — or myself — for that matter. If I lose the election, I'll do it honestly. I don't need to use underhanded methods."

"Who else is he blackmailing?"

"My ex-brother-in-law."

"Torrance is gay, I take it?" Kane asked quietly.

"It's a little more complicated than that," he replied. "It's his secret, although he did tell me when they got divorced. I thought Nikki knew, but I don't suppose that she does now."

"I won't tell her. But I'm going to know."

Clayton hesitated, but only for a minute. He shrugged and quietly told the other man what he wanted to know.

Kane was silent for a long time. "You read about these things. You never quite believe them." He glanced at Clayton. "Haralson knows, I gather?"

"No. He suspects what you did," Clayton replied, smiling. "What he doesn't realize is that if Mosby were gay, he wouldn't be hiding it in the first place. He's not the sort. In fact, he has any number of gay friends."

"Which is probably where the rumors started."

"No doubt."

Kane stared at the photograph again. He grimaced. "Nikki isn't going to like this, but I only know of one way to stop a blackmailer short of killing him." He picked up the photo with a regretful smile. "I think you know what has to be done."

"That's why I came." He got to his feet. "You'd better marry her soon. She lost her breakfast this morning."

"And this is only the first week." Kane grinned like a Cheshire cat. "My poor Nikki."

Clayton glared at him. "You ought to be ashamed of yourself!"

"For making a baby?" he asked, eyebrows levering up. "I lost mine," he said, his voice deepening. "My son. I thought my life was over, that I'd never have the nerve to try again. But Nikki opened up the world for me. Ashamed? My God. I'm going to strut for the rest of the day, and then I'm going to drag Nikki up in front of the first minister I can find." He reached in a drawer and produced a document. "That is a marriage license. You can come to the wedding, but after that, we will not expect you to be a regular visitor. Especially until after the election, which my candidate is going to win."

Clayton found himself grinning. "You bastard."

Kane grinned back. "It does take one to know one," he pointed out.

"You're going to print that?" he nodded toward the photograph.

"Can you think of another way?"

"Not off the top of my head."

"Then the sooner, the better. Don't tell Nikki. I'll break it to her tonight."

Clayton glanced at him. "You'd better make her happy."

"That's a foregone conclusion. She loves me, you see," he added quietly. "She might not know it — or admit it — just yet, but she does."

"Does she know how you feel?"

Kane stuck his hands in his pockets. "I've been keeping that to myself." He looked up. "We always expect women to read minds. I guess sometimes they need telling."

"I guess." He went out the door. He looked back at Kane. "Like hell your candidate is going to win," he tossed over his shoulder. Deep laughter followed him into the yard.

Bett was lounging on her sofa with the phone to her ear. She started cursing and her face grew redder and redder. She sat up.

"But he can't do that! He can't fire you!"

Haralson laughed. "He isn't going to. I had his sister followed recently when she had a clandestine meeting with Kane Lombard. I got some photos that he isn't going to want to see printed."

Bett relaxed. "Thank God for that. What are we going to do?"

"I thought you were going to marry him."

"Are you out of your mind?" she shot back. "He's useful, but not that useful. I have no intention of living in Charleston, South Carolina."

"Snob."

She twisted the cord around her finger. "Mosby won't like it if you use that photo. He's still protective of Nikki."

"He won't know until it's too late. He won't bother me, either. I know something about him."

Bett smiled. "What?"

"That's for me to know and for you to find out."

"Be secretive. I'll make Clayton tell me."

"You'd better hurry, then, because he had a long tête-à-tête with his ex-secretary the other night and he's having lunch with her today."

"What?!"

"I didn't think you knew. If I were you, sweetie pie," he said sarcastically, "I'd spend a little time protecting my hunting preserve."

"Call Sam Hewett," she said shortly. "Tell him that his exec is out hobnobbing with the enemy camp!"

"I had that in mind," Haralson said.

"What will you do if Clayton comes up with something to use against you?" she asked after a minute.

"Mosby will save me. He'll have to."

"Then it will be all right, I guess."

Haralson laughed. "Of course it will."

Senator Mosby Torrance was fielding questions from reporters after a news conference. He'd supported the president on a vote to assist U.N. troops in the Serbia-Bosnian hostilities. His eyes lit on one particular female reporter for CNN, a beauty if there ever was one.

After the conference he paused to talk to her, his blue eyes appreciative on her exquisite skin. She had to be in her thirties, but she was a heavenly combination of beauty, brains and personality. She made his head spin. . . .

A telephone call was waiting for him when he got back to the Senate Office Building. He motioned his secretary to put it through.

"Great timing!" Haralson laughed curtly when he heard Mosby's voice. "I caught you coming in the door, I guess?"

"I guess." Mosby was bitter and sounded it.

"Did I interrupt something? I hope not. Listen, I'm turning some photos of your ex-wife over to the press."

Mosby went silent. "What sort of photos?"

"Pictures of her with Kane Lombard in a, shall we say, compromising position." He laughed. "I don't expect you to say a word," he added coldly. "I know what you are. Unless you want the media all over you, closet queen, you'd better do as I say."

Mosby's eyes widened. "What did you call me?"

"Stop playing dumb! You've always known that I knew. You're gay."

Mosby's eyes twinkled. He felt liberated. He'd kept this barracuda on the payroll for years because he'd had the threat of exposure hanging over his head. And all along Haralson had thought he was gay?

He started laughing. He started and couldn't stop.

"I'll tell the whole damned world!" Haralson was threatening.

The laughter got worse. Vaguely, Mosby was aware of cursing and the slam of the telephone receiver. This was too good to be true.

But when he got hold of himself, he remembered what Haralson had said about some compromising photos of Nikki. He really couldn't allow her to be hurt by his own blackmailer. He owed her a warning.

He had his secretary dial Nikki. But the number he had wasn't the right one. It had been changed. He'd have to call Clay. He hoped there was enough time to save Nikki from whatever diabolical fate Haralson had planned for her.

The phone rang several times before it was answered. Finally a feminine voice replied, "Hello?"

Mosby recognized the voice. It was Bett. He almost spoke, but then he remembered that she and Haralson were thick as thieves. Had she been selling him down the river all along? He couldn't let her in on what he knew.

Slowly, he put down the receiver. He thought for a minute, then he buzzed his secretary. "Get me on the next flight to Charleston," he said.

"But, Senator, you've got a committee meeting . . ."

"Call and explain that I have an emergency in my district. Tell them," he added, "that it's a family emergency."

"Yes, sir."

He hung up and reached for his attache case. If he hurried, he might be in time to avert a disaster for Nikki — and, inadvertently, one for Clayton.

Chapter Seventeen

A tall, slender man wandered into the executive offices of Lombard International. He was wearing jeans and boots with a long-sleeved red shirt and a denim jacket. His hair was in a ponytail and he wore dark glasses. He flashed his credentials and was immediately allowed into the big boss's office.

Kane Lombard was big and fierce-looking — not a man Cortez would have enjoyed tangling with.

"What can I do for you?" he asked Cortez after motioning him into a chair and offering him coffee.

"I want to talk to a man who works for you — a man named Jurkins."

Kane scowled. "Will Jurkins?"

"That's him." He hesitated. "There's something I'd better tell you up front. I do work for the government, but I have no jurisdiction here and no authority to question anyone in this particular circumstance." He leaned forward. "But if you'll give Jurkins to me for about three minutes, I think I can help you extricate yourself from this damned mess that I helped

Haralson mire you in."

"You . . . ?"

"Sit down," Cortez said wearily, motioning an infuriated Kane back into his executive chair. "I'm a tenth degree black belt. Just take my word for it and don't ask for proof. I didn't know what I was doing. Haralson wanted a favor. I hate polluters. I've prosecuted any number of them over the years. But I'm on my first vacation in a decade and Haralson cost me any rest I might have gotten. Why don't you send for Jurkins and I'll let you in on a few closely guarded secrets about that toxic waste dump?"

Kane only hesitated for a minute. "All right." He hit the intercom button. "Get Jurkins back in here. Don't tell him I've got company."

"I wouldn't dream of it," came the dry reply.

The last person in the world that Nikki expected to find on her doorstep was her ex-husband. Mosby Torrance looked tired, but he smiled as she stood aside to let him into the house.

"Sorry to show up like this, Nikki, but you and Clay changed your telephone number," he explained, when they were seated in the living room.

"We had to," she said. "Too many people had it." She studied his face with quiet affection. He was older, but still devastatingly handsome. Mosby, with his blond hair and blue eyes and perfectly chiseled patrician face. If it hadn't been for Kane, and the feelings he'd ignited in her, she might still be mourning Mosby.

"Haralson called me earlier," he told her. He leaned forward with his arms crossed over his knees. His eyes narrowed. "Nikki, he's got some photographs of you and Kane Lombard."

"Yes, I know," she said tightly. "But I've dealt with Haralson. He won't print them."

"Yes, he will," he said finally, watching her react. "Oh, not now, probably — but closer to the election, yes, he will. He's gone over the edge, Nikki. He wants to hit everybody. If he publishes those photographs, he can hurt a lot of people."

She looked at him with anguish in her face. "I didn't know I was being followed. I was so careful . . ."

"You have no idea what sort of people he conspires with," he told her quietly. "Nikki, they have cameras so tiny they can be fed under doors, through windows. They have cameras and sound equipment

381

that can pick up actions and conversations from great distances. Haralson has connections at the FBI and even the CIA."

"He's angry at Clay because I wanted Clay to fire him. He's angry at me, too. He'll cut us both down . . ."

"I'm not going to let him cut down anybody," he replied. "He thinks he's got me on a meathook. In fact, I know someone who can settle his hash for good."

"Why didn't you do something before?" she asked.

"Because he had something on me. Or thought he did." He searched her eyes sadly. "You never knew why I couldn't consummate our marriage."

"I found out," she said, averting her eyes. "You let me find out."

"I let you find me in bed with a man," he replied. "But I'm not gay."

She turned back toward him, her eyes wide as saucers.

"Ask Clay," he said wearily. "Tell him I said it was all right to tell you. I've come to the conclusion that he was right all along. If I'd admitted the problem in the beginning and had something done, who knows how it might have turned out. As it is, I'm going to have to do something, as distasteful as it seems to me. I can't go on like this, risking blackmail and pretending to be something I'm not just to spare myself embarrassment." He opened the attache case while a puzzled Nikki stared at him. He tossed a packet of papers onto the coffee table. "Think of it as counterblackmail," he said. "Give those to Clay, with my blessing."

"What are they?" she asked, picking up the sealed envelope.

"Things you don't need to know, little one. Tell Clay that I've already set these wheels in motion. The material in there —" he pointed to the envelope "— is just for his information. He won't need to do a thing. Not one single thing. He thought he had an ally, you see." Mosby smiled slowly. "But it was my ally."

He got up and moved closer to Nikki. His fingers lightly stroked down her cheek and his regrets were all in his eyes. "I was trying to save my political neck when I let your father force you into marrying me," he said quietly. "I panicked. Because I did, we both suffered. We couldn't have a normal marriage and I thought too much of you to make a travesty of it, so I pretended to be something I wasn't."

Her eyes searched his. "I wouldn't have

cared what was wrong," she said huskily. "I loved you!"

He drew in a long, hard breath. "I know." He smiled sadly. "That's the cross I have to carry with me. I'm glad you found somebody, Nikki. I hope he can make you happy."

"He could have," she said miserably. "I love him very much. But Haralson has killed it all. He made me lie to Kane, and now Kane will hate me."

"Oh, I doubt that." His fingers loosened and fell away from her face. "You deserve a little happiness."

"What about you, Mosby?"

He shrugged. "I'll go overseas and have some discreet surgery," he said mysteriously. "After that . . . I'll see." He laughed curtly. "I'd rather not, but I seem to have very few choices left. There's always a Haralson around."

"Everybody has skeletons, didn't you know?" she asked.

"Most people are lucky enough not to have them disinterred, though." He smiled. "Don't look so morose, Nikki. Dreams still come true."

"Not in my life, they don't," she said.

He searched her sad eyes one last time and left the house as quickly as he'd entered it.

Nikki studied the envelope in her hand with a curious frown. What in the world could Mosby have in there that would save Clay from Haralson?

Jurkins entered the office for the second time in as many days. He was more nervous this time, though, especially when he saw the dark-haired man sitting across from Mr. Lombard.

He stopped just inside the closed door and stared from one man to the other.

"This is Cortez," Kane introduced. "Will Jurkins," he indicated the other man.

They shook hands. Cortez noticed that Jurkins's palms were sweaty and hot. The man was almost shaking with nerves.

He sat down heavily in the chair adjacent to Cortez's. "Yes, sir, what did you want?" he asked Kane.

Kane leaned back in his chair and crossed one long leg over the other. "I want to know how you managed to pay off your daughter's medical bill at the local clinic."

Jurkins's caught breath was eloquent. He shivered.

"Several thousand dollars in a lump sum," Kane continued. "You paid cash."

Jurkins started to try to bluff it out, but

these men weren't going to fall for any bluff. He was unprepared, caught red-handed. Well, there was one thing he could try. He slumped and put his head in his hands. He let out a heavy, hard breath. "I knew it would come out," he said huskily. "But I couldn't turn him down. I was afraid they'd stop treating my baby if I didn't have the money. It's just me, we haven't got anybody else. I couldn't lose her."

He lifted tired eyes to Kane's. "She's all I got in the world. It didn't sound so bad, when he explained it to me. All he wanted me to do was say that one company wasn't working out and hire another one to take its place. That's all. He never said I was to do something illegal, Mr. Lombard. He just said I was to tell you the other company didn't do its job right. He said I was to do that, and to hire Burke's to replace it. That's all."

"You didn't ask him why?" Kane asked coldly.

"My little girl's got leukemia!" Jurkins said miserably. "I had to get her bills caught up so they wouldn't let her die!"

Kane felt the man's pain, but Cortez showed no such reaction. He leaned toward the man. His dark eyes were steady, intimidating. "Your little girl goes to St. Jude's," he said quietly. "The only expense you have is at the clinic and it isn't several thousand dollars worth. Your daughter does have leukemia. She is also in remission, and has been for six months. However, Mr. Jurkins," he added very quietly, "you are a heroin addict. And the clinic you frequent is the province of one of the most notorious drug lords in the Carolinas. You took the money from Haralson to support a habit — not to secure your daughter's health."

Jurkins had jumped up, but Cortez had him in one lightning-fast motion, whipped around and shoved back down into the chair. Cortez stood over him, powerful and immovable, and Jurkins decided to cut his losses while he could.

"All right, I did it. But I couldn't help it," Jurkins groaned. "I couldn't, I couldn't . . . !"

"Would you telephone the local police, please," Cortez asked Kane. "I think we'd better have the assistant D.A. over here, too, and the Department of Health and Environmental Control field representative."

Kane shook his head as he studied the broken man before him. "Jurkins, didn't you have enough grief already?" he asked sadly.

"I had . . . too much," the man whispered, his head down. "Too much grief, too much pain, too much fear . . . and too little money and hope. It got to me so bad. At first it was just enough to make me sleep, when she was in the hospital, to make me forget how bad it was. But then, it took more and more . . ." He looked up at Kane. "It was just to hire another company to haul off your trash," he said, as if he couldn't understand what all the fuss was about. "What's so bad about that?"

Kane and Cortez exchanged glances. It was just too much trouble to try to explain it to him. He didn't understand at all.

After Jurkins was taken away Kane drank coffee with Cortez, trying to find the right way to thank him.

"It's my job," Cortez said with a lazy smile. "Sometimes, though, I don't enjoy doing it. Jurkins's little girl is the one who'll suffer the most."

"No, she won't," Kane promised tersely. "I'll make sure of that. He'll get treatment and I'll try to have the charges against him reduced. I'll get him a damned good lawyer."

Cortez smiled quizzically. "He nearly closed you down."

"So he did. But a miss is as good as a mile."

Cortez finished his coffee and got to his feet. "I'm glad it worked out for you."

"It hasn't yet. But maybe it will." He shook hands with the other man and scowled curiously. "Listen, how did you get onto Jurkins?"

"Through Haralson. He's been watched for several months," came the surprising reply. "He was supplying the clinic where Jurkins got his stuff — part of his money-making operation."

"I saw him with Clayton Seymour one day. I did wonder how a senate aide was able to afford a BMW," Kane had to admit.

"Through selling drugs," Cortez replied. "I let Haralson think I was here on vacation. I didn't know he was after you, but I was hoping for a link to that clinic. And there it was."

"Luckily for me," Kane said.

"Indeed. Fingering the clinic was only one part. I had to have corroboration from a witness who would testify. Until now, I couldn't get one. Haralson played right into my hands. I traced the dump site back here and found your man Jurkins at the end of it. He tied up all my loose ends at once."

389

"What happens now?"

Cortez lifted an eyebrow. "I have Haralson arrested for drug trafficking and merge back into the woodwork in Washington." He lowered his voice. "I'm not supposed to be working in this area."

"You're government," Kane pointed out.

"I was FBI. At another time I was CIA. But now I'm not so visible, or in quite the same sort of work. A friend of mine died of an overdose earlier in the year," he added surprisingly. "Haralson was involved. I had a score to settle, and the timing was right."

"If you're no longer in law enforcement, what sort of work do you do?" Kane asked, curious.

Cortez chuckled, but he didn't answer the question. He held out his hand. "Good luck with the media. I hope they give you the same coverage now that they gave you when you were supposed to be a bad guy."

"Are you kidding?" Kane asked cynically. "They'll apologize on the classified page. But my family will attack them on the front page." He grinned wistfully. "There are times, mind you, when I don't mind having a father who publishes a tabloid."

"I can understand why."

"Who are you?" Kane asked with an amused smile.

"Can you keep a secret?"

"Sure."

Cortez reached in his pocket and handed him a small battery. "I'm the Energizer Bunny." He grinned and walked out, leaving Kane no wiser than before.

Derrie was sitting in the outer office of Sam Hewett's headquarters when Nikki walked in the door.

"A spy, a spy!" Derrie exclaimed dramatically, pointing a finger at the newcomer.

"Oh, shut up," Nikki said pleasantly. "As one campaign manager to another, let bygones be bygones. The voters will pick the best man."

"Thank you," Sam Hewett said with a grin as he joined Derrie and Nikki, with the other campaign workers chuckling before they went eagerly back to work.

"You haven't won yet, Mr. Hewett," Nikki said, smiling as she shook hands with him. "But you're a nice man to fight. You're a clean hitter. No low blows."

"I wish I could say the same for your brother," Sam replied quietly. "But I haven't forgotten the way he attacked Norman's brother Kane."

"I can tell you truthfully that you've seen the last of the sneak attacks," she said, noticing that Curt Morgan was paying a lot of covert attention to the conversation.

"I do hope so."

"Can you spare Derrie for lunch?" Nikki asked. "I really need to talk to her."

"Certainly. Go ahead."

"Thanks."

The two women left. Curt was frowning, but he made no attempt to follow them.

"Curt is up to something," Nikki said.

"Oh, I know that," Derrie replied. "He's Senator Torrance's man. But he isn't spying on us to hurt Clay. In fact," she added with a grin, "I'm pretty sure that he's found a way to help."

"I know he has. Mosby came to see me. He left me some documents for Clay."

Derrie stopped walking. "Did you give them to Clay?"

"Yes, about ten minutes ago. He looked at them and gave a whoop and took off out the door."

"Good for him. I hope he nails Haralson to the wall."

"What's going on?" Nikki asked pointedly.

"I'm not quite sure," Derrie said, "except that Mr. Haralson has made a lot of people very angry. Fred Lombard went racing out of here early this morning, grinning from ear to ear. Whatever it is, I think most people know except us."

"Mushrooms. We're mushrooms."

"Why?" Derrie asked curiously.

"Because they keep us in the dark and feed us . . ."

". . . don't say it!"

Nikki chuckled. She linked her arm through Derrie's. "Let's have lunch. Then I want to ask you to supper tomorrow night."

"I won't come and eat with Clayton and Bett," Derrie said firmly.

"My dear, Bett is on her way to becoming yesterday's news."

"I don't understand."

"You will, sooner than you think. How about Chez Louie?"

"That's fine," Derrie said. She stared at Nikki, but the other woman wasn't saying another word.

Bett glared at Clayton from across the desk. "What do you mean, I'm fired?"

"Just what I said," he told her. "I fired Haralson. Now I'm firing you."

She smiled coolly. "You can't fire me,

dear man. What Haralson knows, I know. If you try to remove me, I'll tell everybody about Nikki and Kane. I'll tell everybody about Mosby, too."

Clayton moved around the desk and sat down, propping his legs across it. "Do go ahead," he invited. "I'm sure it will make great reading."

"Well, I will," she said, shaken. "I mean, it will damage you. It will certainly damage Nikki. And it will probably destroy Mosby's entire career. He might even commit suicide."

He shook his head. "Mosby's far too fastidious. He wouldn't want to get blood over a suit he paid several hundred dollars for."

"Several thousand," she stated.

"I never said he was cheap."

She hesitated. She wasn't used to having anyone call her bluff. "Clay, you're overwrought. Let's go out to eat and just relax for a while."

"I don't need to relax. And Derrie's coming over for supper. It will be just like old times."

"You promised to marry me," Bett said coldly.

"Did I? When?"

"In bed!"

"No. You said you were going to marry me," he corrected. "I didn't agree that I would."

"You'll be sorry if you go through with this," she said very quietly.

"I'll be sorrier if I don't." He picked up the telephone. "Don't let me keep you, Bett. I'm sure some of the groups you lobby for would love to discuss strategy with you."

Her hands clenched by her sides. "I had to force myself to sleep with you," she said with a cold smile. "I hated every minute of it!"

He smiled. "Yes, I know. I'm sorry you had to sacrifice yourself in such a distasteful way."

She turned, picked up her purse and jacket and walked out without looking back. Clayton watched her, but only for a minute. His mind was on Nikki.

The telephone rang over and over, but there was no answer at the house. He hung up, and his face was troubled. That photograph he'd given Kane was going to be in print and on the stands by early afternoon. He didn't want Nikki to see it before he'd warned her what was coming. The shock might harm her or the child.

The child. He smiled. It was early; probably too early to tell if Kane was right and she really was pregnant. But he thought what a wonderful mother Nikki would make. If she loved Lombard, he supposed he could force himself to be civil to the man. He wouldn't admit for all the world that he saw something in Kane Lombard to admire.

As for Bett, that was a lucky escape. No doubt she'd go running to Haralson and that set of photos he had would be offered to the highest bidder. But timing was everything, and with any luck, Lombard's tabloid would hit the stands this afternoon with enough impact to knock Haralson's eyes out. Clayton hoped with all his heart that he'd done the right thing.

Chapter Eighteen

The front page of the Lombard tabloid was shocking. It showed two people making feverish love against a tree; but only from the waist up. The headline above it was even more shocking. It read, "Romeo And Juliet For The Modern Age; Adversaries Become Lovers."

The young woman staring at it on the shelf had gone a pasty shade of white. Her companion was tugging at her arm, even as one of the women in line belatedly recognized the face on the cover and equated it with the white face leaving the drugstore.

"He printed it!" Nikki gasped. "Haralson printed it, did you see? Oh, my God . . . !"

"Nikki, that was the Lombard tabloid," Derrie pointed out uneasily, helping her friend into the car.

"I hate him," Nikki whispered, sobbing with rage. "I hate him! How could he do that to me, to Clay?"

"Calm down, now," Derrie coaxed. "You'll make yourself sick. I'm going to drive you home, Nikki. It will be all right.

397

You have to stop crying."

"I can't. I want you to drive me to Lombard International. I will not go home in tears. I'm going to break his jaw for him!"

"No, you aren't." Derrie kept driving toward the Battery, ignoring Nikki's outbursts that lasted all the way there.

"Thank God, Clay's home," Derrie mused as she pulled into the driveway.

Clayton came out onto the porch and she motioned furiously for him to come. He ran to help Nikki into the house.

"I'll make some coffee," Derrie said, leaving Clay to watch his sister.

"The animal. The swine. The filthy pig!" Nikki choked. "I'll break his neck. Have you seen it? His family tabloid, and they printed that . . . that disgusting photograph! They're in league with Haralson, I knew they were . . . !"

"Calm down," Clay said, holding her wet face against his chest. "Calm down, now, and listen to me. I tried to fire Haralson and he showed me the photos, Nikki."

"Wh . . . what?"

"That's right. He tried to blackmail me." He grinned. "Nobody blackmails me. I took them to Kane Lombard."

She stared at him, heartbroken. Her own

brother had sold out to his worst enemy.

"We compared notes about Haralson," he told her. "And then I made the comment that I'd like to skewer his liver for what he did to you. That's when he explained things to me. It seems that you're marrying him very soon because you're pregnant."

There was a crash as Derrie dropped two cups of coffee on the spotless lacquered wood floor.

"I hope you enjoy mopping," Clayton told her calmly. "And I'd like mine in a cup, please."

"You know what you can do with the cup," she replied, smiling nicely as she turned to go back into the kitchen.

"I'd like to hear you repeat that flat on your back on the kitchen table!" he shouted.

"Clayton!" Nikki gasped.

He grinned at her. "Don't worry. We're not going to fight. Two things, Nikki. Are you pregnant, and are you going to marry Kane Lombard?"

"I am not pregnant," she said violently.

"You're losing your breakfast."

"I hate breakfast!"

"He loves you, he says," he added.

Her face softened magically. "He does?"

The softening went into eclipse. "That's a lie! He does not, or how could he have let his venomous relatives print that ghastly photograph of us and distribute it all over Charleston? Oh, Clayton, people stared at me as if I were some hussy!" she wept.

"We know you're not a hussy. But if you're pregnant, I don't really think Kane is going to let you remain single for long. He seems pretty intent on dynasty building."

"He lost his son."

"I know. He told me. But that isn't why he wants to marry you, if the way he looks when he talks about you is anything to go on."

"I don't want you to think I was meeting him behind your back deliberately," she began.

"I know that."

"I only wanted to tell him about the waste dump," she continued. "I know he didn't do it. He isn't that kind of man. But Haralson is, and he hates the Lombards."

"So I found out. Derrie and I put our heads together. She has a friend who found out a few things I missed. Now Lombard has the whole picture, and Derrie's friend went to see Kane with enough evidence to get his neck out of the noose. Added to what Mosby sent me, it's more than enough to send Haralson to prison."

"What was in that envelope that Mosby gave me for you?" she asked.

"You're better off not knowing." He searched her green eyes. "You aren't carrying a torch for Mosby?"

She smiled. "I think I'm carrying one for Kane." She touched her stomach with a wry grimace. "Although how he can know before I do . . ."

"Maybe it's like that when you love someone," Clayton said quietly. "I don't know."

"Maybe you will someday," she replied.

He leaned over and kissed her cheek. "Ready to go and buy a trousseau? Kane Lombard doesn't strike me as a waiting sort of man."

"I haven't said I'll marry him," she pointed out.

"And you'd better put the announcement in the paper pretty soon," Clayton added, ignoring her protests. "After what came out in that tabloid today, there'll be a scandal if you don't."

"Say, did you see the afternoon paper?" Derrie asked, scanning it as she came in with a tray of cups and saucers and a pot of coffee. "There's an announcement of

Nikki's engagement to Kane Lombard."

"He didn't! He wouldn't!" Nikki burst out.

Derrie chuckled. "He did."

Nikki glowered at both of them. "Well, I won't marry him."

They both looked at her stomach. She put her hands over it protectively. "I won't," she repeated.

"Have some coffee," Derrie invited, handing a cup of it to Clayton.

"Don't mind if I do."

"I'd like some, too," Nikki began.

Derrie handed her a glass of milk, smiling.

"I hate milk!"

"It makes babies big and strong," Derrie coaxed.

"How did you . . . ?"

"Eavesdropping," Derrie nodded. "I learned from him." She pointed toward Clayton. "He was always standing outside conference room doors with his ear to them."

"I was not." He glowered at her.

"How do you think he knew how to vote while he was in the state legislature?"

"I read the issues and made up my own mind," he reminded her.

"After I explained them to you." She

polished her nails on her skirt and looked at them. "God knows how many mistakes you'd have made without me."

He started to speak, stopped, and shrugged carelessly. "Well, I'm not making any new ones. Why don't you come back and run my campaign for me?"

"Because I'm running it," Nikki replied.

"You're pregnant."

"So?"

"Sam would never forgive me if I left him now," Derrie told him. "But we can be friends. Until after the election."

He lifted one eyebrow and smiled slowly. "Just friends?"

She laughed softly. "Well, anything's possible," she said demurely.

The phone rang and Nikki reached beside her to answer it. It was a well-wisher. She hung up. It rang again. Within ten minutes, it seemed that everyone in Charleston and North Charleston had recognized her in one paper or the other and wanted to comment on the Romeo and Juliet story. Nikki was fuming by the end of the day, and not at all in the sort of mood to answer the phone one last time and find a smug Kane Lombard on the other end of it.

"You!" she exclaimed. "Listen here, you

snake in the grass . . . !"

"What time tomorrow do you want to be married?" he asked. "One o'clock would suit me very well, but if that isn't convenient, we can try another time."

"How about another century? I am not marrying you!"

There was a pause. "My father would love that."

"Excuse me?"

"He's got the next headline set in type already. Want to hear it?" He began to read, "Mother Of Romeo And Juliet Baby Refuses To Marry Heartbroken Father Of Child."

"Oh, my God!"

"Yes, sad, isn't it? I expect people will call and write and accost you on the street, you heartless Jezebel."

"Kane, how could you?"

"Well, you did help, after all," he reminded her. "In fact, you remarked that it felt very good." He paused. "I wonder how that would look in print?"

"You blackmailer!"

"I did the only thing I could, you know," he relented, his voice soft and quiet. "He would have published the photographs."

"I suppose he would have."

"As it is, I've cut the ground from under

him. He now has photos that have no intrinsic value to shock or humiliate. And you and I have some unfinished business."

"This isn't the way it should happen," she pointed out.

"Probably not," he agreed quietly. "All right. We'll do it the right way. By the book, my dear."

"By the what? Kane? Kane!"

But the line was dead. She glared at the receiver. "You're a horrible man and I will not marry you!"

"Oh, I'll bet you will," Clayton said. He held out a glass. "Drink your milk."

John Haralson had finished his third glass of scotch whiskey. He heard his motel room door open but it didn't really register until he saw Cortez and a uniformed man standing in front of him.

"Cortez!" he greeted. "Have a drink!"

"No, thanks. You'll need to come with us."

He blinked. "Why?" he asked with a pleasant smile.

"It's a pretty long list." Cortez read the warrant. "Violation of the controlled substances act, possession with intent to distribute, attempted extortion, bribery . . . you can read the rest for yourself."

Haralson frowned and moved a little unsteadily to his feet. "You're arresting me?"

"No. He is. You're being arrested right now for violation of South Carolina state law. You'll be arraigned on federal charges a bit later."

"You're on vacation."

Cortez smiled coldly. "I haven't been on vacation since I engineered the first meeting with you at FBI headquarters where you were trying to dig information out of one of your cohorts," came the quiet reply. "And by the way, you'd better have this back." He handed the startled man the two-dollar-and-fifty-cent gold piece.

"You bought it."

"Not really. I don't collect coins. But it was helpful to let you think I was obsessed with that particular one, after I saw you buy it."

"Of all the underhanded things!" Haralson roared.

"You wrote the book on that." Cortez slid his sunglasses back on. "He's all yours," he told the police officer. "Take good care of him for us. We'll be in touch."

Haralson yelled after him. "You don't have any jurisdiction down here or in this case! You work for the FBI!"

Cortez lifted an eyebrow. "Do I?" he

asked with amusement, and kept walking.

The same evening, the front door at the Seymour home opened to admit a gift-laden Kane Lombard. He walked past Clayton into the living room, where he dumped his burdens on the sofa next to a startled Nikki.

"Roses," he said, pointing to three large bouquets, one of each color, "chocolates, CDs of romantic music, two books of poetry, and perfume. Chanel, of course," he added with a grin.

Nikki gaped at him. "What is all this?" she asked dully.

"The accoutrements of courtship," he explained. He sat down beside her, ignoring Clayton. "The ring is in my pocket, somewhere. It's only an engagement ring, of course. You have to come with me to pick out the wedding band."

"But I haven't said I'll marry you . . ." she stammered.

"Of course you'll marry me," he said, extricating the ring in its velvet box from his jacket pocket.

"I hate diamonds," she began contrarily as he opened the box.

"So do I," he agreed. "That's why I bought you an emerald."

He had, too. It was faceted like a diamond, with incredible clarity and beauty. Nikki stared at it, entranced. She knew that a flawless emerald commanded the same price as a quality diamond; in fact, some were even more expensive. And this stone had to be two carats.

She looked up, her eyes full of delighted surprise.

He smiled at her. "Never expect the obvious from me, Nikki," he said gently. "I'm not conventional."

She studied his broad, leonine face, reading the sorrows and joys of a lifetime there. Her hand lifted to touch it, to trace its hard contours. She did love him so.

"Marry me, Nikki," he said softly.

"All right."

He smiled, holding her hand to his cheek. "My father will cry, you know," he said.

"He can always find another headline." She nuzzled her face into his chest. "Perhaps Haralson's arrest will make a good one."

"Oh, no," he told her, glancing at Clayton, who was just coming into the room with a tray of coffee and milk. "Haralson's going to be top secret until the Justice Department is through with him. I understand that their chief prosecutor is taking a special interest in the case."

"He could plead insanity and get out of it," Clayton remarked as he set out cups of steaming coffee for Kane and himself and a cold glass of milk for Nikki.

"I told you, I hate milk," she muttered at her brother.

"And I told you, it's good for the baby," he replied with a knowing look.

Kane didn't even look embarrassed. He was beaming.

"You needn't look so smug, either of you," she told them, sitting up to drink her milk. "I haven't had any tests. It's too early to tell, anyway."

Clayton leaned forward. "Nikki, how about some scrambled eggs?"

She paled and began to swallow noticeably.

"She loves them," Clayton told Kane. "But just lately, the mention of them makes her sick. Interesting, isn't it?"

"It was potatoes when my mother was carrying my youngest brother," Kane told Clayton. "She couldn't eat them until he was born."

"How many of you are there?" Clayton asked curiously.

"Four. Three boys and one girl. Our

sister is married and lives in France. My mother is dead now, but my father already thinks there's nobody like Nikki. He knows the Blairs, too," he added, chuckling. "Claude has been singing your praises to my father ever since he realized that we knew each other." He hesitated. "He's also arranging a wedding present."

"A cat," Nikki said without pause.

"How did you guess?" he chuckled.

"She's missed Puff," Clayton remarked. "It will be nice for her to have another cat." He studied Kane. "You knew that Haralson had been arrested. How?"

"Haralson's so-called friend Cortez came to see me," he replied. "That gentleman would make one bad enemy, so I'm glad he's on my side."

"Mosby thought he was helping me by sending Haralson down here," Clayton said heavily. "Neither of us knew that he was playing right into Haralson's hands. And none of us had any inkling that the Justice Department was already watching Haralson for another reason entirely."

"Who is Cortez?" Nikki asked curiously.

They both looked at her. "FBI," Clayton said. At the same time, Kane said, "DEA." They both stared at each other.

"Which?" she persisted.

They laughed sheepishly. "It seems that he has some uncoordinated credentials. Perhaps he's a stray KGB agent looking for work," Clayton replied.

Kane put down his cup. "Whoever he is, he's saved my neck. I'll have to pay a fine to help with the cleanup, but they found toxic waste from a number of other companies in that dump. Burke is in trouble up to his neck and faces a jail sentence, along with my errant employee."

"I won't be getting any more mileage out of your situation, either," Clayton promised the older man. "However," he added meaningfully, "if you were still polluting, and doing it deliberately, the fact that you're going to be my brother-in-law wouldn't help you."

Kane chuckled. "I'm glad to hear it. Integrity is a rare asset these days. Nice to know it runs in the family."

Clayton nodded, acknowledging the compliment, and sipped his coffee.

The small café in downtown Charleston was busy. Phoebe didn't really understand why she'd bothered to go back there every day, sitting and waiting for someone who was surely already back at his job in Washington, D.C., and out of the state. It must be some mental aberration resulting from too much time spent digging up old pieces of pottery, she told herself.

She was halfway through her second cup of coffee and it was time to leave. She had shopping to do. She started to get up, just as a tall man in sunglasses came in the door.

His hair was loose, hanging down his back in clean black strands. He was wearing jeans and boots and a denim shirt with pearl snaps. A couple of people gave him a frankly curious stare. He ignored them, making a beeline for Phoebe. He took off the sunglasses and hooked the earpiece into the pocket of his denim shirt. He held out his hand.

She took it, ignoring the covert looks of other customers, and let him lead her out the door.

He put her into the rental car without a word, climbed in beside her, hooked his sunglasses back on his nose and drove off.

Neither of them spoke. He drove to the coast and parked on a dirt road overlooking the ocean, in a spot lined with live oaks. He got out and so did she. They walked down to the deserted beach.

The wind blew his hair as he looked out over the ocean, and her blue eyes studied the bronzed smoothness of his face, its straight-nosed, high-cheekboned profile adding to the subtle mystery of him.

"You're leaving," she said perceptibly.

He nodded. "I have a backlog of work waiting. Two new cases will be coming up pretty soon, too, from here — a discrimination suit and a drug trafficking charge."

"You'll have to testify, you mean," she said.

He took off the sunglasses and turned. His dark eyes slid over her face quietly. "To try the cases," he said. "I'm a federal prosecutor — an attorney for the U.S. Department of Justice."

She was impressed, and it showed. "You said you were FBI."

"Oh, I was," he agreed readily. "And I worked for the Drug Enforcement Administration and the CIA just briefly, too. But law was always my first love. It still is." He smiled slowly. "I was a fairly decent lawman. But I'm a hell of a prosecutor."

She didn't doubt it for a minute. He had the look of a man who could intimidate anyone on a witness stand.

"You must like your work."

"For now," he agreed. "I was offered a job as a defense attorney for a Native American rights group. I almost took it,

413

too. Maybe someday. The best way to fight for any group is in the courts, Phoebe. Fighting in the streets only gets you arrested."

"I suppose so." She searched his dark face. "I'm sorry I didn't get to know you," she said. "You're not like anyone I've ever met — and not just because you're Comanche."

He smiled sadly. "The years are wrong," he said gently. "You're barely twenty-two. I'll be thirty-six my next birthday. I grew up in rural Oklahoma in a town populated by Comanche people. I practice my native religion, I live according to my cultural heritage. If you've ever heard of cultural pluralism — and being an anthropology student, you should have — I'm a prime example of it."

"I know what it is — living in the mainstream while clinging to one's own ethnic identity."

He nodded. His lean hand touched her soft face and his thumb drew very lightly over her mouth. "But I'd like to keep in touch with you, just the same," he said. "I don't have so many friends that I can turn down the chance of adding one to my life."

She smiled back. "You can come to my graduation in the spring."

414

"Send me an invitation."

She pursed her lips. "Don't come in a loincloth carrying a rattle and a feather," she murmured with a feeble attempt at humor.

He didn't take offense. He smiled quizzically. "Medicine men carry feathers and rattles. Why would you connect them with me, I wonder, instead of a bow and arrow?"

Her pale brows drew together briefly. "Why . . . I don't know," she said with a self-conscious laugh.

"My people have been medicine men for five generations," he said surprisingly. "The old people still go to my father for charms and cures."

Her face brightened. "But, you never mentioned that."

"I know." He smiled. "Uncanny, isn't it?"

She nodded. Her eyes slid over his long hair with curiosity and pleasure. He had wonderful hair, thick and silky and long. She wanted to bury her hands in it.

"Go ahead," he said with a long-suffering sigh. She looked puzzled. He shrugged, answering the question she didn't ask. "You aren't going to rest until you know how it feels, so go ahead. I'll pretend not to notice."

Her eyebrows lifted. "What?"

"You can't stand it, can you?" He caught her hands and lifted them to his hair. The action brought her very close. She felt weak-kneed at the proximity, and tried to disguise the uneasy breathing that he was sure to notice.

His hair was as silky as it looked, cool and thick and very sexy. She was fascinated with it.

He endured her exploring hands with stoic pleasure, enjoying the expressions that passed over her face as she looked at him close-up.

"I feel like a museum exhibit," he remarked.

She looked up into his eyes, thrilling at the expression in them. "Why?"

"I can see the wheels turning in your mind," he replied. "You're equating my bone structure with what you know of Mongolian physiology and you're dying for a look at my dentition to see those shovel-shaped incisors."

"Actually," she corrected, searching his eyes, "I was thinking how sexy your hair is to touch."

"You shouldn't think of me in those terms," he said, his voice deep and very slow.

"Because you're Comanche and I'm white?" she queried breathlessly.

He nodded. "And because I'm more than a decade older than you."

"You said that we could be friends," she reminded him.

"We can. But you can't notice that I'm sexy."

"Oh. All right."

Her hands went to his face, to trace its elegant lines. His eyes closed, so that she could touch the ridge where his thick eyebrows lay, and the long, thick lashes of his closed eyelids.

His nose was broad and straight, and below it, he had a wide, chiseled, very sexy mouth. His teeth were white and straight. She'd read somewhere that Native Americans had very few cavities compared to white people.

While she was exploring him, his body was reacting to the closeness of hers. He moved back a few inches and his eyes opened. His lips were parted, and his breath came too quickly through them.

His lean hands caught her waist and lingered there, without pulling or pushing, while they looked at each other.

"You smell of spring flowers," he said.

"And you of wind and fir and open land."

His dark eyes wandered slowly over her face, capturing expressions, texture of skin, eye color, hair texture. "Take your hair down."

She only hesitated for a minute. "Why?" she asked as her hands went to the bun. "Do you want to compare length?"

"Perhaps."

She took the pins out and shook her head, letting waves of platinum blond hair fall around her shoulders. His hands lifted to it, testing its baby softness, its fine silky texture.

"It isn't quite as long as mine," he remarked.

"Or as thick," she added. Shyly, her hands slid back up and into the cool strands of his own hair, clutching handfuls of it as she moved imperceptibly closer. Dimly aware that she was being provocative, but unable to stop herself, she tilted her face up to his.

His eyes fell to her parted lips and lingered there while he touched and lifted the silky strands of her hair and fought to maintain his reason.

"The only thing I ever really liked about white culture," he said huskily, and his head dipped closer, "is the way you kiss each other."

Her lips parted in breathless anticipation, and she felt his hand contract in her hair. "Careful," she whispered unsteadily. "I may be addictive."

"So may I."

His hand tilted her face at a closer angle and his mouth brushed in tender, brief strokes across her lips. The touch was arousing, especially when it was complicated by the gentle nip of his teeth on her lower lip and the nuzzling contact of his face with hers.

Her nails bit into his upper arm as he tormented her mouth. "That isn't fair," she managed shakily. "You didn't say . . . you were going to do that."

"Now you know." He nudged her lips a little roughly. "Open your mouth for me," he whispered. "And I'll show you how hot a kiss can get."

She felt the sun on her face through the trees as she complied, felt his arms suddenly swallow her up and lift her against the length of his powerful body. Then she felt his mouth grinding down into hers, his tongue penetrating the soft darkness behind her lips. She heard a high-pitched gasp echoing in the madness of the passion he was kindling, and realized with wonder that it had been torn from her own throat.

The slamming of a car door barely registered. Cortez heard it, though, and pulled his head up. He didn't look at Phoebe's face, because he knew the temptation it was going to represent. She was trembling in his arms. He let go of her, steadying her, just as a family of tourists descended on the beach.

"Don't you kids go too close to that water!" the man yelled. "You'll get sucked under!"

"That's right, you wait for us!" the woman called.

The normality of it brought a faint smile to Cortez's face. He did look at Phoebe then and he grimaced. She looked devastated.

"I knew it was a bad idea," he said.

She felt shaky inside. She touched her tongue to her swollen lips and tasted him on them. "So did I."

He caught her hand in his and led her back to the car. He hesitated as he started to open the passenger door for her.

"Look at me."

She lifted her eyes to the storms in his.

He searched them intently, with an unblinking scrutiny that made the shaky feeling much worse. She could barely breathe at all, and it showed. He wanted nothing more in the world at that moment than to invite her back to his motel room and spend the rest of the day making unbridled love to her. But it would mean nothing. It would lead to nothing.

"I'll drive you home," he said, turning away to open the door.

"I would . . . go with you, if you asked me," she said tautly, not looking at him.

"Yes, I know. And I want to ask you to," he returned honestly. "But we've already agreed that addictions are unwise and that this is a relationship without a future. We kissed and it was very good," he added, looking down at her with a wistful smile. "Leave it at that."

Her soft eyes held his. "I'll bet you're the Fourth of July in bed," she said.

"Christmas and New Year's Eve, too," he returned with a smile. "Eat your heart out."

"I probably will," she sighed. "It would have been the high point of my life."

"The world is full of men," he said cynically. "Most of them make love well enough."

"I wouldn't know."

His eyes cut back to hers and searched them. They narrowed with intense feeling.

"I was waiting for someone explosive and mysterious," she explained. She smiled demurely. "If you come to my graduation, who knows what might happen?"

He didn't smile. He wasn't sure he was still breathing. "The years are wrong. You need someone your own age."

She lifted an eyebrow. "If you really thought that, you'd never have kissed me at all."

His jaw clenched. Damn women with logical minds, he thought. He opened the door for her without another word and drove her back to the café where she'd left her vehicle.

"I don't know that I'll be able to get down for your graduation," he said stiffly when he was ready to leave.

She looked in the driver's window at his expressionless face, and knew without words that he was finding it difficult to say goodbye. So was she.

She smiled at him, her blue eyes twinkling. "You'll hate yourself for the rest of your life if you miss it," she told him. "I promise you will."

He grimaced and glowered at her. She couldn't see his eyes through the dark glasses. "Maybe."

She stood up, away from the car. "Drive carefully. I have proprietorial rights now."

"Because of one kiss? Dream on!" he said curtly.

"Cultural appropriation," she told him. "Primary group assimilation. I'm going to assimilate you." She licked her lips slowly. "Just thinking about it should keep you sleepless for the next seven months."

He was going to break out in a cold sweat if he didn't leave. He put the car in gear. "Hold your breath," he invited, and pressed down on the accelerator.

Phoebe chuckled softly to herself, watching him run for it. He'd be back, all right. She smiled all the way home.

Chapter Nineteen

Nikki was knee-deep in invitations for her wedding to Kane, with the phone at her ear while she addressed envelopes, trying to get a stubborn government agency to give her permission to hold a political rally in their building.

"I have certain inalienable rights," she quoted, frowning as she crossed a "t" on an address. "One of them is the right to public assembly at a place of my choosing. You only own the building, not the street in front of it. Is that so?" She chuckled. "All right, have us arrested. That should make a very tidy headline for the morning editions. You wouldn't like that? I didn't think you would. Yes, I thought you might see things my way. I'll look forward to meeting you. Thanks. Goodbye."

She hung up, her mind more on the addresses than her *savoir faire* at manipulation.

Kane, watching her, was laughing to himself. She had a keen brain and she exercised a form of diplomacy that might have come out of his own book. He adored her.

She felt eyes on her downbent head and lifted her own to meet Kane's. She beamed.

"I'm on the last one hundred invitations," she said. "I wish we could coordinate the wedding to coincide with the election, though," she pondered. "It would give us such an advantage at the polls . . ."

"Your candidate, not mine," he chided.

"Your future brother-in-law," she corrected pertly.

He bent over her, his eyes acquisitive and warm. "Did I mention that I loved you this morning?"

"Only five times," she replied. "A few more never hurts."

"Say it back."

"I do, every time I look at you. Kiss me, you mad fool!" She draped her arms around his neck and jerked him down onto the sofa with her in a tangle of arms and legs.

While he was trying to keep them from tumbling onto the coffee table and into her cup of cooling coffee, a throat was loudly cleared at the doorway.

They looked up. Clayton glowered at them. "Can't you stop that?" he muttered. "For God's sake, we haven't even had breakfast yet!"

They looked at each other. "Are you sure he's your brother?" Kane asked.

"He must be adopted," she murmured, smiling against his lips. "Otherwise he wouldn't be such a wet blanket after all I've done for his campaign. Something must have upset him."

Clayton took that as an invitation. He moved right to the huge coffee table, moved the coffee cup and invitations aside, and linked his hands on his knees, ignoring the fact that he was interrupting a very private conversation.

"Derrie's on that soapbox about the owl again," he began with a long sigh. "Now, listen, Nikki, we've got to get this owl off my back. I know we can't . . . Nikki, will you stop nibbling on your fiancé long enough to pay attention to what I'm saying. This is important!"

Nikki sighed. She arranged Kane into a sitting position, curled herself into his lap, and gave her brother her undivided attention in a bit of physical diplomacy that left both men speechless.

Kane lifted an eyebrow at her. "It will be a pity if he loses the election," he said, nodding toward Clayton. "You're a natural at politics!"

"I'm going to be a natural at motherhood, too," Nikki pointed out, smoothing a loving hand over her belly. "Besides, I'm going above and beyond the call of duty on my brother's behalf, already."

"You mean with the campaign?" Clayton asked.

"I mean that I'm producing a new voter for you. The thing is I'm not going to be a lot of help to you after I finish this latest bit of organization. You see," she added with a loving glance at Kane, "I had to go to the doctor this morning for a checkup and he listened to the baby's heartbeat."

"Are you all right?" Kane asked at once. "You didn't tell me you were going to the doctor!"

"I was saving it for a surprise. I'm all right!" she said, exasperated by the terrified looks in two pair of eyes. "It's just that things are a little more complicated than we thought."

"Complicated, how?" Kane asked tautly.

She curled up in his arms with a loving sigh. "The doctor heard two heartbeats."

"Two . . ." Kane began.

". . . heartbeats!" Clayton finished.

The men exchanged complicated looks and Kane's was positively arrogant.

"Twins!" Kane burst out, beaming down

at her as he wrapped her up closer in his arms.

Nikki chuckled. "Yes. How's that for family loyalty, brother mine?" she added, smiling at her brother across Kane's broad chest. "I'm not just producing one brand-new voter for you — I'm producing two!"

About the Author

Diana Palmer is a prolific writer who got her start as a newspaper reporter. As one of the top ten romance writers in America, she has a gift for telling the most sensual tales with charm and humor. Diana lives with her family in Cornelia, Georgia.

The employees of Thorndike Press hope you have enjoyed this Large Print book. All our Thorndike and Wheeler Large Print titles are designed for easy reading, and all our books are made to last. Other Thorndike Press Large Print books are available at your library, through selected bookstores, or directly from us.

For information about titles, please call:

(800) 223-1244

or visit our Web site at:

www.gale.com/thorndike
www.gale.com/wheeler

To share your comments, please write:

Publisher
Thorndike Press
295 Kennedy Memorial Drive
Waterville, ME   04901